THE
Truth Stealer

THE
Truth Stealer

KENDRA MERRITT

Blue Fyre Press

Copyright Page

Cover Art by:

MiblArt

Cover Design by:

Rashed AlAkroka, Sean Olsen, Melissa Gay & Quincy J. Allen

Map Design by:

Sean Stallings

The Truth Stealer / Kendra Merritt — 1st ed.

ISBN: 978-1-951009-50-2

Blue Fyre Press

www.kendramerritt.com

To the liars and the thieves.

What is Eldros Legacy?

The Eldros Legacy is a multi-author, shared-world, mega-epic fantasy project managed by four Founders who share the vision of a new, expansive, epic fantasy world. In the coming years the Founders committed themselves to creating multiple storylines where they and many others will explore and write about a world once ruled by tyrannical giants.

The Founders are working on four different primary storylines on four different continents. Over the coming years, those four storylines will merge into a single meta story where fates of all races on Eldros will be decided.

In addition, a growing list of guest authors, short story writers, and other contributors will delve into virtually every corner of each continent. It's a grand design, and the Founders have high hopes that readers will delight in exploring every nook and cranny of the Eldros Legacy.

So, please join us and explore the world of Eldros and the epic tales that will be told by great story tellers, for Here There Be Giants!

We encourage you to follow us at www.eldroslegacy.com to keep up with everything going on. If you sign up there, you'll get our newsletter and announcements of new book releases. You can also follow up on FaceBook at facebook.com/groups/eldroslegacy.

Sincerely,

Todd, Marie, Mark, and Quincy
  (The Founders)

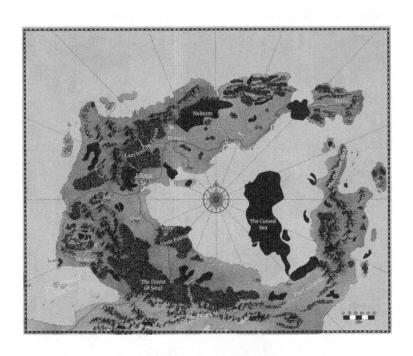

THE SHATTERED WAVES

PALMOLIVAR

ENDLESS BRIDGE

AULI' POLI

EXILES' MANOR

THE ISLE OF TAUR

HALL OF STORIES

Chapter 1
Bex

E ven this deep underground, bits of stone stuck up through the soft dirt like so many rotted teeth through diseased gums. Bex clambered over a ruined wall and stuck her torch into the ground. Its light bounced off the walls and ceiling, sending jagged shadows dancing in an uneven jig through the cavernous ruins.

She whistled through her teeth as she dug the end of her spade into the dirt. A landslide had buried the entire fortress but there were still places clear enough to move. This hallway ended in an entryway that peeked through the rubble. And if she was careful about how she excavated, she'd be able to get inside.

The stronghold, abandoned for more than a hundred years, was supposed to have belonged to a group of mages. Her source had been adamant that they'd kept their failed experiments deep at its heart.

Some of the spells might still be active. All of them would be valuable.

As long as Bex could find them. If she couldn't... well, then it might be time to rethink her life.

Gradually she cleared enough of a hole to slide through, and she tightened the rope around her waist before diving in, thrusting her torch out ahead of her. The rope pulled taut and then went slack as the hands on the other end played out enough to let Bex squeeze through the broken entryway.

She'd done this so often, she could pick her way through an ancient building with one hand tied behind her back. And she usually did. She kept her right hand tucked up against her chest as she slithered and slid over broken masonry, her torch held aloft with her left.

Although to be fair, the last two ruins had given her a lot more trouble than heaps of stone should. Even though they'd both been aboveground and most of her search had been done in the sun, sifting through weather-worn debris, looking for the odd glint and glimmer of something extraordinary.

The little trinkets she'd already found were still in her bags where Conell waited for her to emerge. She hadn't wanted to risk losing them somewhere in this warren.

Of course, right now she was more likely to lose herself. She tugged the rope so it ran over the rough stone behind her as she slid through the small space between the dirt and the archway. It would keep her from getting lost, even if it didn't keep her from getting into serious trouble.

Halfway through, her hips got caught on the rough keystone, and she twisted to dislodge herself.

The edge dug into her skin, and she winced.

Uh oh.

She wriggled and thrashed but remained stuck tight, breath coming harder and faster through her teeth. Her grip went sweaty on the handle of the torch.

Crap, maybe she *should* have brought Conell. He wasn't doing any good above ground, worrying. She'd told him to guard the packs, but they both knew that was just an excuse to keep him out of the way.

Dust clogged her nose, and Bex pushed back the creeping dread that told her she was trapped and she'd never see daylight again. She shifted to push more dirt back toward her feet. There she could kick it out of the way.

More dirt cascaded away from her, and she yanked herself free, rolling down into what used to be a corridor. The rope twanged behind her.

She laughed out loud and stood, brushing herself off.

"There," she said. "Nothing I can't handle." She always worked better alone, anyway.

Bex curled her wrapped hand against her chest and raised the torch. Walls of stone stretched before her, mostly intact. Old mud broke through in only one or two places, dried into a hardened clay that would foil Bex's little spade.

At the end of the corridor, her light bounced off the thick boards of a wooden door.

Her breath hissed through her teeth in triumph. "Yes," she whispered.

She tip-toed lightly down the hall. Dirt and debris half-covered the little etchings in the floor tiles, but she was expecting them and avoided trouble by clambering up and over the mounds of clay.

Mages and their traps. She could have pulled their teeth if she wanted to, but it was easier to just go around rather than tangle with whatever spells the ancient mages had left behind. She shook her head in disgust and slid down the last mound to land lightly in front of the door.

The door stood right where her source had said it would be. This had to be the storeroom. The iron-banded door was thick enough to keep out an army, and little symbols curled around the latch, carved into the metal itself.

Bex's right palm tingled under its wrapping. Her lips compressed in a flat smile, and she wedged her torch into an

3

empty sconce nearby. Then she clipped the spade to her belt and pulled out a steel stiletto knife instead.

She recognized the symbols and the order they were in. An explosive spell. Anyone opening the door without disarming the spell would be blown back at least twenty feet, and they probably wouldn't live to stand back up again.

Of course, if you knew that and carved another notch here and scratched a long mark into the last symbol there...

Bex shifted her grip on the stiletto and dug the tip of the blade between two lines in the last symbol and pressed down.

The blade, reinforced for this very purpose, cut neatly across the lines. She raised her right hand and held it directly over the latch, but the tingle in her palm had faded.

Perfect. All that was left was a normal lock, and she could deal with those easily. She slipped the stiletto back in its sheath and pulled the pry bar from its strap at the back of her belt. Some problems needed a precision stroke with a needle. Others needed a good smack with a hammer.

She shoved the end of the pry bar into the crack of the door and threw her weight against it.

The latch broke with a crack that echoed down the empty hall, and the door groaned open.

Bex caught her breath and peered into the gloom.

The light of her torch bounced off bare walls and surged into empty corners.

Nothing.

Her throat ached as she stared, and her shoulders fell. The anticipation bled from her limbs, leaving them heavy and numb.

The mages who'd lived and worked here had clearly taken their trinkets and experiments with them when they'd abandoned the place. The spells on the building were still active, but there was nothing here she could pack up and take with her.

She closed her eyes and rested her good hand against the door jam, just breathing.

This would be the moment to rethink her life. Time to give up her treasure hunting ways and pick a more stable career with fewer cobwebs and creepy basements.

The thought made her laugh, and she took a deep breath through her nose before opening her eyes again.

She could always move forward. Even if the way was blocked, there was always a path around, over, or through. Sure, she had nothing to bring home from this trip, but there were the trinkets she'd picked up at the last two digs. And whatever happened, she wouldn't let Anera suffer for her failures.

That was what it meant to be a sister. She carried her own burdens and Anera's, too, and she wouldn't let the weight fall on Anera's thin shoulders.

Just to be sure, Bex grabbed the torch from the sconce and stepped into the storeroom, lighting up every square inch, looking for anything that might have been left behind.

As the sole of her boot hit the tile, her right palm tingled and heat flared under its wrapping.

Shit.

Bex threw herself backward as the latent spell pulled the ceiling down and rocks tumbled around her.

The whole ruin rumbled, the stones of the mountain shifting and grinding. Bex scrambled back down the corridor as the roof collapsed behind her.

But the shift had closed the space she'd wriggled through earlier. A massive groan registered in her ears, and she had just enough time to fling herself into an alcove along the wall where a stone archway held up the ceiling.

She flung her arms over her head as bricks and loose mortar rained down. Her torch went skittering across the ground and was instantly buried in the avalanche of stone.

Darkness cascaded around her, and she cried out.

The rumbles faded, leaving only the clatter of loose rock.

Bex dropped her arms from around her head, but the dark didn't dissipate. She blinked, trying to see anything. Even just an outline of rock and stone.

Nothing. Black had swallowed the entire world.

Her breath came in ragged gasps, and her hands shook hard enough that she banged her elbow on an outcropping of stone.

She gulped down the sobs that rose in her throat and fumbled for the shape in her pocket.

Come on, come on. It had to be there. It was always there. She'd double checked before she'd climbed down here, just like always.

She could feel the dark against her skin, even though she knew it was just a trick her mind played on her any time a light was doused. It crept and crawled like tentacles up her arms to circle her throat until she couldn't breathe.

Her fingers closed around two skinny lengths of metal, and she yanked the flint striker out of her pocket. The familiar pieces of it pressed against her palm, nearly calming her panic.

Nearly.

She squeezed the two ends together, working the spring so the flint struck sparks against the block of steel at the end of the gadget.

Once, twice. Sparks flickered in the dark, making her catch her breath.

On the third strike, the sparks caught on the wick built into the end of the striker. The tiny flame grew, fed by the little reservoir of oil.

It wasn't quite a candle or a lamp. More like a long-lasting match. But it was enough.

The flame lit up the tumbled rocks, illuminating the fall that had tried to kill her. With it, her breath slowed as her heart rate returned to a normal rhythm.

The rockfall had cut off her exit. It would have killed her, too, if not for the arch over the alcove standing strong, despite its age.

The mages clearly hadn't put their magic into the walls. Just the ceiling.

Stupid. They took everything with them and then booby-trapped an empty building. She should have guessed; every mage she'd ever known had been a malicious cur.

The rope swung as she moved, its severed end unraveling.

Bex tried to shift the stone, wedging her fingers into the cracks with one hand as she held her light aloft with the other.

It wouldn't budge. Even her pry bar did nothing.

Bex frowned. That didn't seem natural. Her right palm tingled and itched as she waved it over the stone.

Her lips thinned. Magic. Land Magic, probably. It lay over the stone, binding the rubble in place—a secondary piece of the spell keeping her trapped.

This was fine. Everything was all right. She could handle it. As long as her light didn't go out, she could take it one step at a time. She'd been in worse situations. She'd been in places where even flames did nothing against the dark.

She clutched the flintstriker in her teeth. It had been a present from Anera nearly two years ago, after that first time Bex had woken before the sun rose and destroyed her rickety bed in panic.

With both hands free, Bex pulled off her gloves. Under the leather, her right hand had been bound in linen. She unwrapped it, rolling the bandage neatly as she went.

The last of the linen fell away, revealing a shiny burn, long healed into curving lines criss-crossing her palm. Exposed to the air—and the magic nearby—the mark heated, and her fingers curled.

The sight always made her stomach churn, but nowadays it also came with a fierce surge of pride. She could get out of this. The mages who'd burned the mark into her palm hadn't meant

7

to give her an advantage, but she'd molded it into one all the same.

She placed her hand palm down against the rock and stone, and the mark flared, sending out a flash of light.

Bex couldn't see magic, but she could feel it swirling toward her hand and up her arm, lodging somewhere under her breastbone as a ball of warmth.

The stone around her shifted and fell, tumbling loose now that the magic holding it in place had been released.

Bex drained the rest of the spell, leaving it powerless, and the mark on her palm stopped tingling all at once.

This was her one little piece of magic. It wasn't even a spell. Just a way to drain the power out of a mage's working.

Bex rewrapped her hand, carefully tucking the ends of the linen under so they held, and she scrambled out of her hiding place, kicking stone behind her.

Near the archway where she'd squeezed through before, her questing fingers found the rough end of a cut rope. She sighed in relief and settled down to dig herself out.

Chapter 2
Bex

The sun had been down for hours by the time Bex dragged herself out of the ruins. Scratches marred her hands and arms all the way to her elbows, and a little blood trickled down the side of her face where a falling rock had clipped her right at her hairline.

Conell stood at the entrance to the stronghold, next to the pile of dirt and rubble they'd excavated to reveal the old cellar door. He clutched the end of Bex's rope in his hands, the slack coiled nicely at his feet.

The moment Conell saw her, he stepped forward. "Bex, thank Senji. You were gone for ages. Did you find anything?"

Raggedy trees dotted the slope around the tumbled walls of the stronghold, and beyond their bulk, she could just make out the lighter slash of the landslide where it had cut a swathe through the thin forest, burying the back half of the fortress.

A fire crackled behind Conell, and Bex staggered to the circle of light, the tension going out of her shoulders. The dinged cook pot hung over the flames. Her nose itched with the smell of carrots and potatoes that had simmered for too long.

The moment the light hit her, Conell's words dried up, and he went white-lipped and wide-eyed.

She must look worse than she thought. She ran a hand through her hair and grimaced when a shower of dust fell around her. Well, that was the advantage to keeping her black hair short. Easier to clean.

"Trouble?" Conell said as she flipped her head upside down and brushed the debris out.

"Nothing I couldn't handle." She made her voice as light as she could, pushing aside the panic of the last few hours. Besides, it was the truth. She was alive, wasn't she?

He stepped around to the other side of the fire and peered at her intently. "Did you find anything?"

She ran a hand through her hair, tucking the single white lock of her otherwise dark hair behind her ear. Then she sighed. "Just some books and jewelry in an old dormitory," she said, digging them out of her deep pockets. "No magic."

Conell's shoulders slumped. He had bright red hair, curly enough to stand up from his head, and blue eyes that disappeared when he smiled.

He wasn't smiling now.

He was as invested in Anera's well-being as Bex was. Neither of them wanted to head home and tell her they'd found nothing.

"You should have brought me," Conell said.

Bex hid a grimace and crouched by the fire, brushing the last of the dust and grit from her loose clothing. At least she'd chosen a sturdy, linen shirt and canvas pants. Nothing was terribly torn, just stained.

"Maybe I could have helped."

"I work better alone," Bex said.

Conell blew out his breath. "You always say that. And then you come out looking like a Night Ringer after a fight. If I was there, maybe we would have found something."

Bex rolled her eyes. "It was an empty room, Conell. You wouldn't have been able to do anything. It's not like I was careless and missed something."

He shook his head hard enough to make his curls bounce. "That's not what I meant. You're never careless. I just..."

He paced around the fire, boots kicking the dry scrub that remained at the edges of their fire pit. The light flickered against the boughs of a dead tree still clinging to the side of the mountain.

"I just can't sit up here doing nothing while you're trying to save Anera's life. I love her, too, you know."

Bex kept her expression mildly amused. Annoyance served a purpose, but Conell never responded well to it, and she wanted him to agree with her.

"You think I don't know that?" she said. "That's why you need to stay up here where its safe. So you can go back to her. She'd be devastated if anything happened to you."

He stopped his frenetic movement and stared across the fire at her, brows drawn down. "She'd be devastated if anything happened to you too. So would I."

Bex couldn't help the wince and the curled lip that flashed across her face.

"I mean it," Conell said. "I don't want to come with you just because I feel useless up here. You need someone to watch your back."

The words made a lot of sense on the surface, but the sentiment made her skin crawl, and she busied herself packing up the trinkets and the books they'd found so far.

Most treasure hunters worked with a partner, but she'd never liked that feeling of someone breathing down her neck. Conell was great for Anera, but he didn't know nearly as much about the ruins of Usara as Bex did. She would spend all her time holding his hand and making sure he didn't trigger any traps she couldn't dig their way out of. In the end, he'd just get in her way.

"My back is just fine, see?" She cast him a grin and wriggled her shoulders, turning as if to show off her spine.

Conell frowned.

Hmm, maybe her shirt was more stained and blood-spattered than she thought.

"Conell," she said. "I'm fine. This was just a string of bad luck. We have a couple of spells for Anera from the last dig, and I'll find something else soon. The ceiling might have collapsed a bit, but I got out, didn't I?"

He dropped beside her with a huff, but she could tell there was no heat in it. Only exasperation. *That* she could deal with.

"One day you're going to run headlong into a problem you can't solve by yourself," he said.

She laughed. "Maybe when the world ends." She bumped his shoulder with hers. "Come on. I'm very good at what I do."

He didn't meet her eyes. In fact, he propped his elbows on his knees and hung his head as if he'd given up.

She'd won. He wouldn't bug her about coming with her on her next dig. Maybe ever again. That was a good thing.

So why did she feel like she'd knocked a nest out of a tree and found there were eggs inside?

She sighed and stretched out her hand to rest next to his. She didn't touch him. Not quite. She was too careful for that.

"You can come with me next time," she said.

He glanced at her hand, then at her face, his eyebrows rising. Then he snorted. He must have been able to see something there she didn't mean for him to see.

"I promise," she said. It was easy to say the words and not mean them in the slightest. She'd had a lot of practice. But even if they weren't true, they made him feel better, and they might even get him to stop complaining until the next dig.

Besides, he was telling plenty of lies himself.

Conell loved Anera. But the only reason he cared about Bex was as a means to help his beloved. Whatever he said, Bex had no worth outside of that.

At least in this they were in agreement.

Chapter 3
Bex

Maybe one day, Bex could afford a horse so she wouldn't have to walk to every ruin in Usara. But with every spare moment spent looking for magical trinkets and every spare coin going toward their rent, that seemed like an unlikely future.

Bex resigned herself to sore feet and dusty boots as they finally trudged back into the city near dusk on the third day after the cave in. The streets bustled with an energy Bex didn't share after an unsuccessful dig. Shop owners hurried by on their way home, mothers haggled over bread and cheese and onions as their children tugged at their skirts, and several ladies in silk dresses gossiped beside a fountain.

Without a word, Bex and Conell passed the more respectable shops at this end of the city, situated to catch the tourists and travelers in a net of fine clothes and keepsakes that cost the craftsmen of Usara a fraction of what they sold them for. On the next street over, the air hung heavy with the scent of roasted venison and turkey, and bright light spilled from windows lined with etched glass.

Bex's stomach rumbled, but she pressed on toward the

harbor, where the streets grew narrower and the smells were far more pungent and far less pleasant.

A couple of street kids kicked a ball out of an alley and across the street. Bex kicked it back with a grin, aiming for the goal post set up at the end of the alley. She touched the wide brim of her hat when they shrieked with glee.

Along the street, several vendors had set up boards across a couple of crates to make booths to sell used clothing and meat pies.

She jerked her chin at Conell who took the hint and went to buy dinner while Bex stopped in front of a stall with bits of tarnished jewelry and dusty knickknacks scattered across the counter.

"Let me know if you see anything you like," a girl said. She sat with her back against the wall of the house behind her, her nose buried in a tattered book. "Finest secondhand shop in the city." She waved a hand to indicate her wares as if she wasn't that invested in Bex believing her or not.

"Finest my ass," Bex said. "Do you actually make any money when you ignore everyone that passes, Mags?"

The girl looked up, a lopsided grin lighting up her face. "Bex!" She stood up from the crate and plopped the book down. "I do pretty well for myself, as you know."

"Sometimes I think you wait around just for me to come sell you the good stuff." Bex leaned on the makeshift counter with a wink.

Mags pushed her hair behind her ears with a little laugh. Her dress might have been an unflattering color and threadbare enough you could see her elbows through it, but Bex had always thought she had the most beautiful hair, light and shining.

"Maybe I do," Mags said. "What did you bring me this time?"

Bex pulled her bag around and dug inside for the things

she'd found on her last trip. She laid out a stack of books and two necklaces, one with a brass pendant as big as her fist and one with a delicate chain made of interlocking links and tiny jewels set into the joints.

Mags examined them quickly and efficiently. "I'll give you the usual for them. I can sell them uptown just fine. These though..." She set her hand on the stack of books. "These I'll do double."

Bex kept her expression carefully neutral. "That's fine."

Mags gently lifted the cover on the first one. "I know a collector who'd love to get a hold of them. First editions all, and this one is at least a hundred and fifty years old."

Bex knew her treasure, but Mags knew her books.

"Where did you get them?"

"Old library was having a sale." She didn't even know why she lied. Mags wouldn't care if she was raiding abandoned mages' strongholds. "That's all you can get for them?" Bex asked—because it paid to be sure.

Mags raised an eyebrow. "How long have we known each other?"

"Accumulated or total?" Bex said, tilting her head with a grin.

Mags rolled her eyes. "Do you ever give a straight answer?"

"Ten years," Bex said. "Give or take."

Mags slid the necklaces off her table and into the box beneath her booth where she kept the really good stuff. "Minus that time a couple of years ago where you just disappeared off the street. No one knew where you went."

She counted coins carefully into a purse and pulled the drawstring shut.

Bex watched, lips pressed tight to hide her expression.

"Are you ever gonna tell me what happened?" Mags said, handing the money over.

Bex made an effort to loosen up enough to smile. "Nope,"

she said. "I guess you'll just have to keep luring me back in the hopes of finding out."

Mags coughed an incredulous laugh as she tucked the books away, and Bex turned to find Conell finishing up with the meat pie vendor.

He held a pie in each hand as they wove their way down the dingy street to a building that seemed to lean over the cobbles below. It stretched two stories above the ones around it, but that only made it seem like it was going to fall over faster.

The landlady met them at the door, blocking the way with a powerful frown and her arms crossed over her broad chest. Bex dug in the purse Mags had just given her and fished out most of the coins. She stacked them so they glittered in the lamp light and held them in front of the landlady's face.

"That's for this month's rent and the next." Bex tried to hand it to her, but the landlady snorted and didn't extend her hand.

"You're not staying," she said.

Bex's lips thinned.

"What?" Conell said behind her. "Why?"

"I'm not a nursemaid, and I don't let sick people stay in my boarding house."

Bex took an involuntary step back and flicked her gaze to the second window on the left of the third story. But the shutters remained shut tight.

Bex smoothed her expression and gave the landlady her most winning smile.

"That's understandable, and the rest of us appreciate it. But my sister isn't sick."

The landlady's eyes narrowed.

"She's tired. She works long hours and is exhausted by the end of the day. That's why she looks so bad."

"I've never seen her leave to work," the landlady said.

"See?" Bex spread her hands. "She leaves so early and comes in so late you haven't even noticed."

The landlady's eyes flicked between Bex and Conell.

Bex sighed. "She's just so dedicated to the kids at the orphanage. I've tried to get her to take better care of herself, but she tells me 'Bex, who will take care of *them?*' And what am I supposed to say to that?"

There was this thing Bex did when she lied, where she... pushed. Just a little bit. It was stupid. It didn't do anything, obviously, but it made her feel more in control. It relieved the pressure of anticipation, that knot in her throat as she waited for someone to believe her or call her a liar.

The landlady blinked, her face twitching as Bex's words hung in the air between them. Finally, she grunted and shifted back a step.

Bex didn't hesitate to take that tiny capitulation. She pushed forward, crowding the landlady back another few steps into the dark, cramped hallway of the boarding house. She lay the stack of coins on the woman's arm so she had to take them or let them tumble all over the floor.

"Thank you," Bex said with a broad smile. "You're a good woman."

The landlady's mouth softened the barest bit, but Bex was already on the stairs, climbing to the third floor and the second room on the left.

"Why would you say that?" Conell asked behind her, quiet enough not to carry. "Why not just tell her the truth? It's not like Anera's contagious."

"You think she'd really let Anera stay if she knew?" Bex snapped. "We may not spread disease, but there's still danger. No one likes hiding someone who's on the run."

Conell fell silent as Bex pushed the door open.

It wasn't hard to see why the landlady thought Anera was sick. The thin door didn't stop the smell of an unwashed body and an overfull chamber pot. And if she'd peeked in here, she would have seen the half-eaten meal abandoned on the table, the clothes left on the floor where they'd been dropped, and the shutters closed as if the occupant just didn't have the energy to stand and open them.

A young woman lay on the threadbare sheets, wan face turned toward the door. She raised a thin hand and tried to smile as they came in.

Conell caught his breath. "Oh, Nera."

Bex swallowed against the smell and strode forward. "We're here," she said, sinking onto the side of the bed. "We're back."

Anera's dark hair lay lank on the pillow as she turned her head to gaze at Bex. "I'm glad," she whispered.

She was definitely sick, but it wasn't like the landlady thought. This wasn't a plague or a flux. The only way she would hurt someone else was if she managed to touch them exactly the wrong way. And Anera was too careful for that.

Bex reached out to take Anera's hand in her good one, the one that wasn't wrapped. Then she dug in her bag while Conell swept around the room, cleaning up a little of the filth left behind from someone who barely had the energy to live, let alone take care of themselves.

From her bag, Bex pulled out a ring. It looked much simpler than the jewelry she'd sold Mags, but this one made her hand tingle.

She pressed it to Anera's palm.

Anera smiled, pale lips pulling tight, and held the ring to her chest. Below the edge of her shift, Bex could just see a brand, a burn scar with lines that matched the one on her own palm.

The mark flared bright, just as Bex's had done in the ruins.

Anera took a deep breath and tried to sit up, but her thin

arms shook, and she fell back against the bed, shaking her head. "It's not enough."

Bex pulled out a stone that flickered and glowed like a candle reaching the end of its wick. A light stone. Who knew how old it was, but it clearly still had a little bit of magic left in it. She'd found this one and the ring in the first ruin she'd gone through before the cave in.

She'd snagged it as a backup plan to the ring, but she pressed it on Anera anyway. Anera held it to her mark, and the lines flared to life, pulling the light from the stone, leaving it cold and gray in Anera's hand.

Finally Anera sat up, some of the color returning to her face, and Bex heaved an enormous sigh, the ache of worry flowing out of her shoulders as her sister gave her a wide smile.

"You've saved me again," Anera said, lifting her hand to brush back the white lock in Bex's hair.

Bex's throat closed up, and she tried to find a joke, but nothing came to her. Anera had already saved Bex once a long time ago now, and no amount of trinket hunting would ever make up for that.

They weren't really sisters, at least not by birth. But they had been victims of the same experiment.

Bex didn't have real family, not even parents. She'd been one of hundreds, thousands of kids left orphaned after Vamreth's coup and had spent years living on the city streets.

That made her an easy target when the king's mages had rounded up people that no one would miss, hiding them away in cells under the palace.

One by one they'd burned their spells into their victims, looking for a way to extend their magic, creating little store-houses of power for themselves—and a living hell for their victims.

Anera and Bex bore the same mark, but for some reason, Anera's mark was trying to kill her, and Bex's... wasn't.

Over the years she'd figured out how to use it, how to drain the power out of spells and keep the traps of ancient mages from killing her. But she'd never figured out why Anera was dying.

And she wasn't about to find a mage to ask. Even if she trusted any to tell the truth, there weren't any left after the experiments.

When the new queen overthrew Vamreth, the project had been shut down, and Bex had heard it all ended in violence as the mages tried to cover their tracks by killing their victims. She hoped they'd all been executed for it.

Of course, she didn't know firsthand. She and Anera had escaped before that.

Bex stepped back as Conell pushed forward to hold Anera's hands and offer her a meat pie. Anera took the food with a murmur of thanks, and for a moment, her eyes met Conell's and they leaned their heads together. Anera raised her hand to press her palm into his cheek.

She couldn't do more than that. No matter how much they wanted to. If Anera so much as hugged Conell, her mark would drain him. Even though he had no magic. It would find the energy in his body and steal the life out of him.

Bex turned her head and pretended she couldn't hear them murmuring to each other as she picked up where Conell had left off, gathering the laundry into a pile and clearing the debris off the table.

If she'd just been faster, more prepared, stronger, maybe she could have gotten Anera out before the mages marked her. Then none of this would be happening right now.

Bex shook her head to dislodge the familiar guilt as she filled the pot with tepid water from the jug. Then she placed it next to Conell and backed away as they started whispering about a bath.

Bex took the chamber pot out to give them some privacy for a few minutes.

When she returned, Anera sat on the edge of the bed in a clean shift, her hair damp. She licked the last of the meat pie from her fingers, making little noises of appreciation.

Conell took the second pie and raised an eyebrow at Bex. She nodded. It had been a while since she'd seen her sister with any appetite, and everything in her wanted to encourage that.

She'd give Anera her life if she thought their magic would allow it.

The thought always came with one specific memory. A wave of light washing away a wall of black. It was just torchlight, but it had sat behind Anera, making her glow as she held out her hand and pulled Bex from the dark.

Anera tried to stand, wincing as her legs shuddered. Conell slid his arm under her elbow to steady her, careful to stay away from the mark on her chest.

Anera stumbled a few steps and fetched up against the table even with Conell's help. She swore under her breath.

"What's wrong?" Bex said, rushing forward.

Conell glared at her, but Anera just gave her a thin-lipped smile. "Nothing. This is normal."

"No, it's not. You just drained two different spells. You should be fine."

"Bex, please don't tell me how I should and should not feel." Anera cast her an exasperated look between strands of damp hair.

Bex bit her tongue.

Anera blew out her breath and pushed herself up straight. "I'm sorry. It's just infuriating. I want to feel better. I should feel better. But I just... I'm so tired all the time."

Bex choked back the platitudes that crowded to the front. Her worries and problems drove her to do something. To act. When she encountered a problem, she had to fix it. One step forward then another step forward. All the time. How much harder was this for Anera, who wanted to be able to do things and just couldn't?

"That's not everything," Conell said, voicing what Bex was thinking but in a tone that didn't make either of them snap at him. "It's getting worse, isn't it?"

Bex held her breath.

Anera dropped her gaze and then sat at the table, her shift pooling around her and nearly sliding off her thin shoulders. She'd always been slim, but hadn't that shift fit the last time they were here?

"Yes," Anera said quietly. "It's getting worse. The spells you left me last time only lasted a few days."

Bex sucked in a breath. Days? That wasn't possible. That should have been a month's supply of magical energy. If it had only been days, how long had Anera lain here with barely the energy to feed herself?

"Why didn't you say something?"

"You weren't here."

It was a simple fact, but it cut Bex deep enough to bleed.

Anera lifted her gaze. "I'm sorry. I've known for a while. But how do you tell your sister you're dying?"

Chapter 4
Bex

Bex kept her face as smooth as possible. The panic and the futility battered at her insides, but none of that would help Anera. It would only make her feel worse.

Conell and Anera sat at the table, sharing the last meat pie, their heads bent together. Anera had dropped the knowledge that she was dying and then gone back to living her life. Because she'd known. She'd already been living with it this whole time.

Had Conell known? He seemed to treat her the same way he always had. As something special, cherished. With stolen moments here and there where they could bask in each other's words and looks.

Anera chuckled, a low, quiet version of her laugh, and she clasped his fingers on the rough tabletop.

Bex swallowed and excused herself, giving them time and space. And giving herself a moment where she didn't have to mask her expression or lie through her teeth that everything was going to be all right.

She slipped out the door and latched it behind her, stuffing it all down under the thought, *I can fix this. I can still fix this.*

At the end of the hallway, past the spot where some disgruntled neighbor had punched a hole in the wall, there was a staircase just wide enough for Bex's narrow frame.

She trotted up the stairs and pushed open the trapdoor at the top.

Bex surged up into the cool night air, the sky stretching vast and empty above her, pricked with stars that didn't care what her words or face said.

She heaved a deep, shuddering breath, the muscles in her cheeks going slack for the first time in days.

There was no one to convince here. No one to persuade or cajole or threaten or extort. No one but herself. And she didn't have to lie to herself.

Their system wasn't working.

No matter how many spells and trinkets Bex brought home, Anera's mark was still draining her life and energy. Bex's left her alone unless she actively touched something with magic in it or another person. It was always searching, but remained dormant unless it found something.

Anera's mark seemed to always be feasting, taking her sister's life away moment by moment.

Bex had tried to break the magic on Anera many times, but she barely knew how any of it worked. All she knew was what had been done to them. She knew the mages had burned their marks into their skin, so first she'd tried changing Anera's mark, cutting it with a knife so a scar ran through the lines. Then she'd tried a burn of her own, always trying to disrupt the mark of the spell.

But the lines had remained, etched deep enough that nothing disrupted them. The only thing that worked to keep Anera upright and feeling a little like herself was draining the magic out of spells and artifacts. It gave her mark something to feed off of, besides Anera. Like a ravenous monster that demanded sacrifices to keep it from laying waste to the countryside.

But if it took more and more magic to appease it, what would they do next?

Bex stepped to the edge of the roof and plopped down, dangling her feet over the edge.

Buying spells in the market was already too expensive. That's why Bex searched out places where magic might have been abandoned and no one would miss them.

But her last three digs had gone terribly. Either because her information had been bad or because the area had been too dangerous. Or both, like the last one.

Bex was great at hunting down hints and rumors of artifacts, but she was no historian and it showed.

They needed to try something else. Hiring a mage to break the magic would be even more expensive than buying spells in the market. If Bex could even trust a mage. And she couldn't. They would just take Anera and use her up like the mages who had done this in the first place.

What they needed was time. They needed an artifact or spell big enough to last Anera a while. Long enough to find a way to break the mark for good.

Bex leaned back on her hands and stared out across the darkened city. Lanterns and torches lit up the night like mystical pools scattered across the sea of buildings. Clear on the other side of the city, stood the palace, the facade lit so it glowed against the black sky.

But between Bex and the palace, rose the massive walls of the Night Ring, towering over everything around it. Built of black stone blocks, the arena dominated the center of the city. Even from here, Bex could hear the faint sounds of the crowd drifting over the walls. It wasn't nearly as loud as it used to be when Khyven the Unkillable still fought in the arena, but there were some promising new ringers. Even Bex, who never bet, couldn't help hearing about them on the streets.

Her eyes narrowed, picking out the flickering light around the maw of the arena's gates, the archways tall enough for a Giant.

That's what they said. That the Night Ring had been built by Giants back before Humans had been more than a nuisance scuttling in caves. Of course, others said the Giants were fairy-tales, myths to frighten children.

But the treasure hunters of Usara knew there was at least some truth to the stories. They were the ones who marked out different ruins on their maps. Most places were normal with Human-sized doorways and broken furniture and architecture that was recognizable even if it was from a different era.

But there were others.

Some of the older treasure hunters spoke of such places in whispers, describing stairs built just a bit too tall and chairs large enough to curl up and sleep on. Old Brody always said the walls felt like eyes watching, and there was a creeping, crawling feeling down the back of your neck. Their strongholds still stood steeped in magic, he'd said.

Of course, Old Brody loved a bit of drama.

He'd also never lied to Bex.

All the stories said Giants had magic. They'd left artifacts behind, and there was nothing more powerful in this world.

Or more dangerous. Which was why she'd never tried to go after one before. But Anera was worth it.

By now, Bex was an expert in hiding it, but she hated that little room where her sister slept. She hated the way it smelled, the way trash accumulated because Anera didn't even have the energy to toss it away. She hated the shift Anera wore because real clothing had too many buttons and ties and she couldn't manage them without getting winded.

It wasn't fair to hate the things Anera did because she

couldn't live any other way, but that didn't mean anything when the anger rose and simmered under the surface, and she had to keep it hidden to protect her sister.

Bex hopped to her feet, her toes hanging over the edge of the roof as she stared at the Night Ring, her hands clenching at her side.

A Giant's artifact could fix all of that.

But where would she find one? She remembered a little of the maps the treasure hunters used, but that had been a long time ago. Before they'd noticed she wasn't selling all the treasures she found. She'd left before they started asking questions.

Besides, if the Giant's ruins were marked on a map, those areas would probably be cleared out by now. Or so dangerous that whoever had tried to clear them hadn't come back.

So, she'd have to find someone who knew where to find Giant artifacts.

At least she had people for that.

Chapter 5
Bex

Bex's nose wrinkled. She wouldn't have thought she'd miss the trash and Human waste smell of the lower city, but up here, the air flowed clean, and somehow that made her *more* on edge.

Early spring flowers spilled over the edges of marble containers, their bright purple blooms stark against the white stone. Spires rose into the sky behind, stabbing upward like swords raised by an army.

Bex's teeth clenched, and she struggled to relax her jaw.

Conell gulped beside her. He had been born a merchant's son and had more manners than Bex. But he'd spent most of his life in the lower city before Anera insisted he join Bex on her excursions.

This marble-and-greenery-encrusted domain would be just as foreign to him.

"We're going in there?" he said, gaping at the imposing facade.

"The palace? Yes," Bex said. "The front door? No."

The man she was looking for would be found there, but it wasn't like she could just walk in and say "hey, take me to your head mage." He was an important man now, or so the story went down in the city. The guards weren't just there to keep people from hurting the queen. They were there to keep riffraff like her from interrupting those important people.

Carriages passed on their way to the gates, but she ducked off the wide, stone path that led to the front of the palace, taking a dirt track that wound around to the side. Conell followed. There was something soothing about kicking up dust instead of scuffing her boots along smooth cobbles. A few other people in sturdy work clothes traveled to and from the servants' entrance so they blended right in. That was better.

"Who are we looking for?" Conell asked.

"A mage," Bex said. "I asked around this morning and found a few people willing to talk to me."

"Your old treasure hunter friends?"

Bex shrugged, carefully careless. "I didn't have to go that far. The shopkeepers gossip about who's buying what, and someone important is gearing up for an expedition. Apparently the queen's head mage is looking for some fancy artifact. And given the way no one's saying what kind, I'm sure it has to do with Giants."

"Bex, I know you've worked for collectors before, but this is so far above your normal type of client." He craned his neck to stare up at the towers. "What makes you think this mage will even see us?"

Bex grimaced. "Because I know him." The sound of his name when she'd first heard it this morning had made her stomach clench. She touched the white streak in her hair as unpleasant memories tried to surface, but she pushed them back down.

Anera is worth it. Anera is worth anything. Even seeing one of them again.

"His name is Slayter," Bex said. "He... he was around during Vamreth's experiment."

Conell stopped in the middle of the dirt path. "What?"

Several of the servants around them stopped to glare.

Bex hauled on his arm to get him moving again. "Keep walking. Don't draw attention." She sucked in a calming breath. "This wasn't one of the people who ran it," she said. "He was an apprentice of one for a while. So I know him. But he works for the queen now. Rumor is he was working for her the whole time, even while she was in exile."

"You think that's true?"

Bex bit her lip. "I don't know. It's a nice story, but..."

"But what?"

"But I don't know if I believe in happy endings. He's definitely working for the Queen now, so I think it *could* be true."

"You think he'll remember you?"

"I'll make sure he does," she muttered. Not being one of the ones actively hurting people wasn't normally enough to get Bex to trust someone. But she kept reminding herself, she didn't have to trust Slayter in order to use him.

"Slayter knows everything," she said out loud. "Or at least he thinks he knows everything. If I can get him talking, he'll just keep going until he gives us exactly what we want, because he can't help himself."

"People *do* tell you things. Even things they don't want to tell you." But his voice trailed off like he wasn't completely confident in her people skills. Which was silly of him.

Around the side of the palace, the service entrance opened onto the kitchen courtyard. Crates and sacks waited in the corners, and enough brooms to equip an army stood along the wall. Enough people bustled around the area that Bex's shoulders relaxed.

"Here," she whispered to Conell. Then she thrust a crate of apples into his arms.

"What?"

"No one asks questions if you look like you're busy."

She piled up a couple of sacks that smelled of mushrooms and swept them into her arms. Then she led the way into the palace, following a wide woman in a kerchief who had flour up to her elbows.

The woman turned into a big doorway where the sound of pots and pans rang and the smell of burnt fat poured through the opening. But Bex kept going straight.

"How do you know where you're going?" Conell whispered.

Bex shook her hair out of her face and grinned. "I don't."

A guard in boiled leather armor with a surcoat over top eyed her from down the hall, and Bex made straight for him.

Conell hissed behind her. "What are you doing?"

She ignored him and stepped right up to the guard, giving him a winning smile and a glance up and down.

He stood straighter all of a sudden.

"We're delivering the spell supplies Slayter ordered last week," she said. "But he forgot to tell us where to bring them. The silly man just said 'the palace.' I don't suppose you know where his work room is?"

"I sure do," he said, returning her look.

"See? I told you royal guards know everything," Bex said over her shoulder to Conell. She leaned closer to the guard as if to share a joke. "I guess there's a reason Slayter's a mage and not a guard."

She touched his elbow, and he laughed along with her.

"Me? I adore competent people," she said. "If you show me the way, I'd be... very grateful."

The guard couldn't move fast enough. "It's just this way."

He hurried to lead them down two flights of stairs to a long hallway.

"Would your friend mind if I walked you home?" he said.

Bex cocked her head at Conell, who straightened and did his best to look bored. "We're both due back at my master's shop, but you can always find me there later. It's Master Herschel's Alchemical Reagents and Supplies in the upper city."

"Maybe I'll stop by tonight."

"Maybe I'll be there." She gave him a broad wink as he gestured to a door and then left with a slightly dazed smile.

"That was only slightly awkward to watch," Conell muttered under his breath as Bex took his crate and stashed it on the floor against the wall along with her sacks.

"It got us here, didn't it?" Bex knocked on the door and then walked in without waiting for permission.

"—not like I can find it right at this moment—oh. Hello?"

Two men occupied the basement room, clearly arguing about something, but Bex immediately focused on the one to the right.

Slayter wasn't nearly as tall as she remembered, and somewhere in the last two years, he'd lost a leg and gained a metal one.

"Hi," she said flatly as his gaze went mildly confused. He didn't give her the same look as the guard outside. His eyes stayed focused on her face as if trying to recall something trivial yet nagging.

"You're not supposed to be in here," the other man said.

Bex's gaze flicked to him and then back again. Her eyebrows came down with consternation.

Where Slayter was slim and a little jittery with his movements, this man was a brute. He stood tall enough that Bex had to crane her neck to meet his gaze, and he'd earned enough scars to look dangerous.

Who wore armor indoors besides guards? Was he some sort of fighter?

The shape of his scars fell into place, and she finally recognized his face. There'd certainly been enough posters around touting the prowess of Khyven the Unkillable, the ringer who'd finally earned his freedom and put the queen on the throne.

Bex did not like the number of weapons she could see on his person. That meant there had to be a few more she couldn't see.

"I'm serious," Khyven said. "How did you get in here?"

"Oh the guards let me in, so I assumed it was fine." She tried out her smile on him.

He also looked her up and down, but his heavy frown didn't waver.

All right, so the smile didn't work on him.

"I heard you've been looking for certain artifacts," she said, cutting right to the point. "I'm here to offer my services."

"And you are?" Khyven said.

"Bex. One of Usara's finest treasure hunters." She did not meet Conell's incredulous gaze.

"If you're one of the finest, why haven't I heard of you?"

"*He* has." Bex cocked her head at Slayter.

Slayter's brow scrunched like he was working through a problem before it finally smoothed. "You," he said.

Bex placed her hand on her heart. "Me."

"You know this person?" Khyven asked Slayter.

"Yes. Technically. We never really spoke so it's hard to call it 'knowing.' But I saw her, so—"

"Slayter," Khyven said, an exasperated warning in his tone.

"She was part of one of Vamreth's experiments."

"Part?" Bex said with an indignant huff. "That makes it sound like I had a choice."

"Experiments?" Khyven said.

Bex wiggled her fingers at him, but her hand was still wrapped, so he couldn't see the mark. "Nasty ones," she said. "Most of us died. He helped run them." She cocked a thumb at Slayter.

It wasn't exactly true, but if she could drive a wedge into

34

Slayter and pry out some guilt, she absolutely would take advantage of it.

"Slayter?" Khyven said.

Slayter raised a finger, face still smooth and unbothered. "I didn't run them."

"There," Khyven said. "He says he didn't run them."

"Are you his gatekeeper?" Bex asked. The little smirk made the remark playful, but underneath that she seethed. She wasn't going to let some ringer get in the way of saving Anera.

"Halenza, my master. She helped set up many of the experiments," Slayter said.

"And you let it happen," Bex said, driving the wedge deeper.

Slayter tilted his head. "I didn't stop her experiments, if that's what you mean. At that moment in time, I calculated the odds of overthrowing Vamreth at close to zero. To disrupt her plans or his made little sense. I likely wouldn't have saved anyone. I'd have been killed, and Vamreth would have continued such experiments indefinitely."

Nothing lurked behind his eyes. No guilt or shame, just steady acknowledgment.

He really felt like he'd done the right thing. Or he was completely devoid of feeling.

She couldn't work with either of those. Clearly she had to change tactics.

"Fair enough. I'll tell you what," she said. "You tell me where to find a Giant artifact, and I'll forget your involvement in my mutilation and misery."

Khyven shifted, somehow becoming even larger. He opened his mouth, maybe to protest her choice of words, but Slayter interrupted, latching onto the idea she'd seeded for him.

"Giant artifacts?" His face lit up.

Khyven made a noise under his breath that sounded like a muttered "here we go."

35

Bex hid her smile. Guilt wouldn't work on Slayter but maybe curiosity would.

She didn't even glance at Khyven, keeping her gaze on Slayter's face. "I hear you're the expert."

"Well, I mean, yes, I guess," Slayter said. "If anyone can really be an expert. I have the most experience, some of it face-to-face. But that's a very generalized query. Nuraghis are many and varied, like the Giants themselves. And there are hundreds, thousands of things they've left behind. I have some fine books about them. Or if you'd like, I could recite the most interesting aspects. Or—"

"Now you see why he needs a gatekeeper," Khyven muttered.

Bex kept her smile unforced even as her eyes tried to glaze over. This was what she remembered. A cascade of information, like a collapsing dam. You could either drown in it or ride the current.

"One," she said, reigning him in, giving him very specific parameters. "I need one Giant artifact. Preferably something no one knows about already."

"Giant magic is dangerous," Khyven said. "Believe me, I was nearly killed by some."

Bex gave him an arched look. "You look fine to me."

"He's tougher than he has a right to be," Slayter said. "Technically, he should be dead, but there was a confluence of events. A Luminent soul-bond, a few drops of Giant's blood, and perhaps a prophecy about him—"

"The Giants were deadly," Khyven broke in. "And everything they left behind is just as deadly. Most of their things were made of Mavric iron, and unless you know how to handle it, Mavric iron will kill you faster than anything else."

"Although not everything they made is Mavric iron," Slayter said. "There's actually plenty of things they made of ordinary metal. Or enchanted, ordinary metal. Which probably makes it not ordinary anymore, technically. Of course the magic itself might be harmful in that case. But we don't actually know from the bits of lore and legends passed down. Nothing is sure until you actually pick it up."

Khyven crossed his arms. "Not helping, Slayter."

Slayter blinked. "Well, it pays to be accurate."

"I'm not looking to carry it around with me," Bex said. She just needed the magic out of it. If whatever she found turned out to be one of the bad ones, Anera could suck it dry, and then they could stash it in a cupboard or something. She'd figure out the details later.

"Why would you want a Giant artifact in the first place?" Khyven asked. "Most people don't even think the Giants were real."

"I'm smarter than most people," Bex said.

Slayter glanced at Khyven, eyebrows raised in surprise. "Khyven is actually right."

"Thanks," Khyven growled.

"Human error and reaction being the most esoteric component of my calculations, your desires bear the need for scrutiny. Why do you want a Giant artifact?"

Bex didn't even need to think fast; she'd been thinking the entire way here. "It's not why *I* want one. It's why *you* want one. Word is, you're looking. Which means you need a treasure hunter."

"So you want money," Khyven said. "That's what this is about."

She shot him a look. "I want a job. A steady job."

"A *dangerous* job."

"What's wrong with enjoying a little bit of thrill?" She grinned at him.

Khyven snorted, but for the first time since she'd walked in the room, his lips twitched like she'd finally said something he could understand.

"I'm sure there are tons of things you want to see for your-self," Bex said to Slayter. "Things you want to study. Things you're too busy to go after yourself now that you're working for the queen."

Slayter's eyes lit with excitement. "Oh yes. I mean, there's Hauneros's Reliquary. Or the Gates of Panoplin. I'd give my other leg to see the Mavric iron sword Stavos used in the last great Giant battle."

Bex leaned forward. "Which one is the most important to you? Which one are you most excited about?"

"Oh that would have to be one of the Noktum Mirrors."

Bex straightened. "Which mirror?"

"The Noktum Mirrors. I've only found references to their creation. Apparently they were hand mirrors. Though if it was made for a Giant, they probably look like more of a regular mirror to us. Except with a handle. A big handle. But even the references are obscure. If they ever did exist, they've been hidden for millennia. And we're not—"

"I'll get it for you." She said it without thinking. Why waste time when she knew she'd do anything, go anywhere for Anera? And some of the other things he'd mentioned sounded impossible. The Gates of Panoplin? How would she transport a gate home? Let alone get it up the steps to Anera's room. And that Mavric iron sounded like something she didn't want to mess with.

But a mirror, even a Giant mirror, sounded perfect.

Slayter stopped, his mouth still open but his eyes moving like he was thinking.

"I'll find it for you," she pressed. "I'm good at what I do. And you can pay me when I bring it back. I won't even charge you up front."

"How kind..." Khyven said with a snort.

"And I'll give you a discount, because of our previous history," Bex said, casting an annoyed glance at the damned ringer. He was too suspicious by half.

"What does this mirror do?" Conell asked.

Bex closed her eyes with a sigh. He'd been doing so well not drawing attention to himself.

Khyven raised his gaze to the ceiling as if to say "now you've done it."

"Oh, well. That's a scintillating question. The truth is, we barely know." Slayter hopped off his stool and clattered about on his metal leg. "But with the amount of secrecy that went into its making and the effort gone into hiding it, it must be powerful. Clearly, it's connected to the noktum somehow, likely in a profound way. The scribe who wrote down this particular history—well, more of a memoir, really—was all agog about it. This particular scribe, a priest of Senji, speculated that the mirrors were some kind of super weapon the Giants created to finish the war—in the Giant's favor. Clearly the weapon didn't work, but I think that was more because they didn't have the chance to implement it. Or it malfunctioned. It was hard to tell. He had particularly bad handwriting, this priest—"

"Slayter," Khyven said in warning tones.

"I'm just saying. If you're going to chronicle something, the least you can do is make it legi—"

"Slayter!"

"Well, they asked," Slayter said.

Khyven just shook his head.

Bex rested her elbows on the table and folded her hands. "Where should I start looking?"

"You're not going after it," Khyven said.

"Why not?"

"Because, as Slayter was just about to say, we're not looking for a treasure hunter. Your information, wherever you got it, was wrong. We already have someone looking for such things."

Bex's brow drew down.

"Sir Kerrickmore."

"A knight?" Bex said. "A knight is your treasure hunter?"

"A Knight of the Sun. The... finest fighters in the kingdom." A little grimace crossed Khyven's face as if he'd swallowed something particularly bitter. "At any rate, highly competent and unquestionably loyal to the queen." He said the last in a pointed manner, eyes fixed on Bex.

Damn. "You could send me too," Bex said, feeling the chance slip away from her.

"No."

"Why not?" she and Slayter said at the same time.

Khyven glared at Slayter. "Because they'll just get in the way of each other."

Bex decided she really didn't like Khyven the Unkillable.

"Two is more than one," Slayter said.

"There aren't two... Kerrickmore will have six people with him. It's—"

"Eight is more than six," Slayter said brightly.

"It's not about the number of people! It's about *loyalty*. Besides, the queen has allowed one writ for this, and she's already given it to Sir Kerrickmore."

"You don't even like Sir Kerrickmore."

"I think Kerrickmore is... he's a fine... that's not the point!"

A writ, huh? Bex had never worked a job for anyone with a high enough rank to write a writ. It would allow this knight to cross borders without interference and request help and funding from loyal nobles. The queen must really want the mirror. Not just Slayter.

She turned her shoulder on Khyven and leaned over the table toward Slayter. "Send me," she said, just to him. "I promise I'll get it for you. I've been doing this for years. I'm far better at tracking down hidden things than some knight."

Slayter hesitated and Bex pushed, like she'd done with the

landlady. Just a nudge. Like trying to tip over an unbalanced chair.

"You owe me, Slayter." It was the wrong tactic for him, but the words came unbidden, his face bringing too many unpleasant memories to the surface.

Slayter didn't react. He stared at her like she'd handed him a small puzzle.

Khyven, however, sighed.

"We're not sending you after the mirror. But I tell you what, we will enlist your services for something else. There are plenty of other artifacts you can find besides the mirror," he said. "There are nuraghis in Imprevar and Triada that might still have something. We can give you a map."

The conversation was done. Bex dropped her gaze, like she knew she'd lost. But she had enough now. Not much, but enough for the next step.

Chapter 6
Khyven

Khyven watched as the door closed behind the young woman and her mostly silent companion.

"I like it. Two teams. It'll be like a contest," Slayter said.

Khyven glanced at the door, his brow wrinkled, then back at Slayter. "What do you mean two teams? I specifically told her we're not sending her."

Slayter waved a hand at the door. "She's not going to listen to you. She'll go after the mirror and try to get it before Sir Kerrickmore."

"She's not going to get paid."

"Oh, if she shows up with the mirror, she will. I think."

"If you suspected she was just going to ignore us, why would you let them leave?"

Slayter raised his eyebrows, but he didn't raise his head from the papers he'd begun perusing. "It's more likely the mirror will be found now. It could be an important piece, Khyven."

"That woman had ulterior motives, Slayter. You could feel

42

it radiate from her. She's not going to bring it back to us. If she can even find it."

Slayter squared the pages on the table. "She's more competent than you think."

Khyven's eyes narrowed. "Why? What do you know about her?"

"Not enough," Slayter said. "But there was something there. Something more. She... pushed me. She has resources no one else has."

"As a result of that experiment?"

Slayter shook his head. "Maybe. I don't have enough information to know for certain. But if she finds it... *when* she finds it, we'll just find her and make sure the mirror comes to us."

"I think it's stupid to trust her even that far."

"It's funny you should say that. She reminds me of you."

"Of me?"

"Pigheaded and driven. She's not going to stop until she gets what she wants."

"I'm not... That's not..."

"But I've learned to trust pigheaded people with strange magic." He gave Khyven a pointed look.

Khyven rolled his eyes. "I hope you know what you're doing."

"I always know what I'm doing. I'm the one doing it. It's predicting what other people will do that's the tricky part."

Chapter 7
Bex

"Y**ou think one of these other places will have what we need?"** Conell asked, looking at the map Slayter and Khyven had provided as they emerged from the kitchen into the sunlight.

"Nope," Bex said with a glance at the markings. "Most of them are marked on the treasure hunters' maps. So they'll be picked clean by now. But we don't have to worry about that."

She set off down the path away from the palace, merging into the traffic along the cobbled road while she tucked the useless map into her vest.

"We don't?" Conell said with a sharp frown. "Bex, what are you planning?"

"Don't look at me like that." Bex raised her chin. "Do you want to follow the rules, or do you want Anera to live?"

Conell's steps faltered. "Did you really just say that to me?"

Bex winced. "Sorry, but you know what I mean."

Conell followed, staring at his feet. She bore his pouting in silence until he finally spoke again. "You said he was a mage. He worked with the mages that gave you and Anera your marks."

Bex's lips tightened. "I did."

"So he's a Line Mage. Why didn't you just ask him to help Anera?"

Bex spun to face him. A cart driver swore at her and swerved to avoid them. "Because it was a Line Mage who did this to us." She held up her wrapped hand. "To her. Do you really want to trust another one? Someone who was there and didn't do enough to stop it before it hurt her?"

"You trusted him enough to get him to tell you where to look for giant artifacts."

Bex turned and resumed walking, tucking her hand back into the front of her vest like a sling. "That's not trust. That's just using him for information. Besides we're not going to look where he told us to look. We're going to look where he said not to look."

* * *

Some inquiries around town led her to a house in the upper city with a garden full of statuary and a high fence all around. Bex squinted at the coat of arms carved into the stone gateposts.

"Yeah, that's Sir Kerrickmore," she said.

Night had fallen over the city while she'd searched out the knight's home. A couple of servants stepped out of the gate and lit the lanterns over the coat of arms, giving her a suspicious look where she leaned against the wall on the opposite side of the street. She gazed up at Conell and laughed like he'd said something hilarious.

The servants glanced at each other and went back inside.

"What do you think we're going to do?" Conell whispered, his voice cracking. "Go in there and ask nicely, 'hey can I please have your job?' This is insane, Bex."

Bex cared for Conell because he cared for Anera, but she really had no imagination sometimes.

"*We're* not doing anything. You're going to stay right here and keep watch."

"Keep watch," he said, voice going flat. "Just like at the ruins, huh?"

"No, not just like at the ruins. There's no rope here." She gave him a grin. "I need you to whistle if you see anyone coming."

"See anyone...? Bex, it's a street. There's loads of people—where are you going?"

She slipped away, down the alley that ran alongside the manor. The queen must really like this guy if she'd gifted him this place just for being good with a sword.

The stone fence was not as high back there. It was built up to look impressive in the front, but all she had to do was take a run at it and launch herself up the surface to grab the top with her good hand. Then she could haul herself up.

She balanced there for a second, peering into the darkened walkway beside the manor. Only one lamp hung in a window here. Bex jumped across the space and swung from the windowsill. She pulled herself up and jiggled the latch. Sometimes these older ones were loose enough...*there.*

She slipped inside, keeping her movements smooth and quiet.

Unlike at the palace, she kept out of sight. In a house like this, everyone knew everyone else, and it would be impossible to convince someone that she was supposed to be there. But the manor was quiet and still, the only noise coming from the kitchen where the servants gossiped while they cleaned up.

The study wasn't hard to find. What other room would be lined with bookcases full of dusty tomes? An enormous desk made out of dark wood stood in the center.

Bex leaned her back against the wall and craned her neck to peer through the cracked door. No one occupied the study, but another door stood open on the far side of the room, and she couldn't see what lay beyond.

She didn't like that. Open doors meant people coming in or out. But the longer she lurked in the corridor, the more likely it was that she would be caught.

She slipped inside, barely moving the door to slide through the opening, and hurried across to the desk, the obvious place to look for any papers or writs or maps having to do with the mirror. Slayter must have given Sir Kerrickmore something to go on. And she knew these old knights. They were all ancient and nearsighted with memories like a leaky bucket. He would have written everything down.

And anything written down, she could take.

It wasn't even stealing. A good treasure hunter would have made half a dozen copies by now and hidden all of them so any rivals couldn't do what she was about to do.

She reached the desk and grinned. Sir Kerrickmore was the perfect type of rival. He kept everything neat and tidy with a sheaf of parchment neatly labeled "Expedition Notes."

Bex rolled her eyes. *Amateur.*

Something caught her gaze, and goosebumps raised along her arms. A mug steamed on the desk beside the papers. As if someone had been working and left just a moment ago.

And was obviously coming back.

She had maybe a few moments. But there was no way she could pass up an opportunity like this.

She plunged her hand into her vest, looking for the packet she'd picked up earlier that day when a tentative plan had been forming in her head.

The paper envelope crackled a little with the movement as she pulled it out, and she tore the top off with her teeth, carefully keeping her marked hand away from the contents. The Life Mage who'd sold it to her had assured her of its potency.

The magic in the little pellets wouldn't be enough to help Anera, but would be plenty to do this job.

Footsteps creaked in the adjoining room, and her breath caught. No time to be precise. She dumped a few pellets into the mug. And two more for good measure before diving under the desk.

The footsteps paused on the threshold, like they'd heard something.

Bex froze, holding her breath as her heart raced.

The footsteps continued into the room and came around the desk. The edge of a red brocade dressing gown came into view, brushing the tops of a pair of knit slippers.

Bex shrank against the backside of the desk.

Don't sit down. Don't sit down, she pleaded in her head.

The feet leaned forward, like they were peering at the papers.

Bex's lungs burned. She had to breathe eventually. She tried to take tiny sips of air.

In her mind she urged him, *pick up the mug. Take a drink. Come on, come on.*

Papers shuffled. The feet stepped across to a bookshelf to take down one of the tomes.

Bex fought not to clunk her head against the desk in frustration.

The feet came back to the desk and the book thudded the top. Then there was a scrape like a mug against wood.

Yes.

It was probably too much to wish he would slurp so she could tell if he took a sip for sure. But her imagination provided the sound effects.

That's it. Any moment now. The Life Mage had been so confident. And the pellets had cost enough that they should act almost immediately.

An ominous gurgle rang in the room, and Bex smiled to herself.

The owner of the feet made a noise kind of like a mix between a moan and an "oof." And then they raced from the room.

Bex let her breath out finally and sucked in a lungful of air.

That could have gone so much worse. And now she knew her plan had worked. Sir Kerrickmore wouldn't be able to leave the privy for days, giving her plenty of time to get a head start.

She crept out from under the desk and slid the whole expedition folder into her vest, checking only to make sure there was a map along with all the rest of the papers.

With Sir Kerrickmore distressingly distracted, the way out was much easier, but she did have to pause at the corner to wait for a couple of the kitchen staff to pass. It sounded like a few workers were staying in the courtyard out back, camping out before they left on their expedition to find the mirror. Diggers and hostlers, probably. Bex couldn't really imagine who else you would need for something like this. Still it was an opportunity, and she still had a few pellets.

She waited for a clear moment when the last of the cooks finally left the kitchen, and she slipped inside to find the pot that held the tea for the workers. She dumped the rest of the pellets in. The dose wouldn't be exactly right since it was distributed across an entire pot, but it would have an effect, even if it was milder.

No one from the Kerrickmore household would be leaving anytime soon.

Chapter 8
Bex

Conell still waited out on the street. He didn't exactly bite his nails, but Bex could read the tension in his shoulders even so.

"Relax, I'm back," she said, slipping up to him.

He blew out his breath as she took his elbow and steered him away from the manor.

"That took forever. What were you doing?"

Bex snorted. She'd been in and out in twenty minutes tops. Conell just worried about everything.

She stopped at the next corner, far enough away that even if Sir Kerrickmore crawled out of the privy long enough to sound the alarm, they wouldn't look immediately suspicious.

The streetlamp overhead lit the folder as she pulled it out of her vest. Now she could actually sort through the papers and take a look at the map. When she saw where they were going, she raised her eyebrows.

The mirror was on a large island named Taur to the southeast. Presumably. There wasn't an actual location, just a general area. They would have to do a little investigation to find the mirror's true resting place.

"I was getting us a direction," Bex said. "Ooh, look. And an official writ." Sir Kerrickmore, bless his organized soul had kept the queen's writ with the rest of the notes.

Conell's lips thinned. "How did you convince him to part with those?"

Bex rolled her eyes. "I didn't. But he was too busy in the privy to care. He'll be delayed long enough, we can get a good head start."

He drew back like she'd struck him. "You poisoned him?"

Bex sighed. "You don't need to sound like I killed him. I just gave him the runs for a few days."

She tucked the papers back in her vest and started down the street, her mind already running off to think about all the things she had to do. Would she need a ship? Was that something you could rent? And where would she get the money for that? Sir Kerrickmore seemed to think he'd need diggers. Maybe she needed diggers too.

"Bex," Conell said behind her.

"Hmm?"

"Bex, wait."

She huffed and stopped on the next corner. "What?"

"Look, I want to help Anera just as much as you do. And... I think you're right. She needs something big. Either something she can drain for a while or—or someone who can break the mark's magic." The streetlight glinted from his bright curls as he ran a hand through them. "But I don't like how you're doing all this."

"Doing what?" Her brow drew down. "Solving the problem? Did you have a better idea?"

"No." He paced to the edge of the nearest building and back. "But I don't like all the lying and the stealing. This is going to get you into trouble. More trouble than you can get out of."

"I'm not lying or stealing for myself. I'm not even doing it for you. This is for Anera. Anything is worth it if it will save her."

"Even if it hurts other people?"

"It's barely hurting them. Lying to get into a building doesn't hurt anyone. And a couple of stomach cramps are uncomfortable but ultimately not that bad, all right?"

Conell's lips pursed, and he glanced away, unconvinced.

"Look, everyone else in the world is out for themselves," she said. "At least, we're doing this for someone we care about."

Conell glanced up into the sky, but there wasn't much to see standing under the street lights like they were. "Anera wouldn't want this."

The words stabbed at Bex, but it was a familiar pain, and she turned her shoulder like the words would hit her back instead of her heart.

Anera was one of those few people in the world who actually cared about other people more than herself, who saw light in them and tried to do things for the "greater good." She had ideals, and Bex would do almost anything to keep from shattering them.

Because some things just needed to be done. No matter how unpleasant. Which left them to her.

"Anera doesn't need to know. Now there are some things we'll need—"

"Why do you keep saying we?" Conell said, the planes of his face going stark and flat as he frowned. "None of these decisions have been mine, and you don't even let me help you when I want to. We might have the same goal, but we're not a team, Bex. And I don't think I want to be, if this is how you're going to do everything."

Bex blinked at him, too startled to school her expression. Her chest burned, and her fingernails dug into the wrapping across her palm. But she couldn't snap at him.

Because he was right. She didn't let him help. She didn't

want his help mostly, but it wouldn't have been terrible to let him feel needed and useful. To feel like he was actually doing something for the woman he loved.

She pushed down a weird lump in her throat that came out of nowhere and cleared her throat.

"Fine," she said, and it came out much more measured than it could have. "You can stay here with Anera." She turned and started for the rooms where Anera stayed.

"What?" Conell scrambled after her. "Bex, wait. You're still going?"

"Anera is still dying. This artifact is going to take weeks to retrieve. I have to start right away."

"How do you even expect to find it? All your digs have been going wrong recently."

He couldn't see her wince from where he followed her. He was right again, damn it. She'd had a horrible string of luck recently. And she'd never even been outside of Usara. The problems and pitfalls of a dig like this rushed to swamp her thoughts, but she batted them away. One step in front of the other.

"That just means I'm due for some good luck," she said, casting a smile over her shoulder. "Besides, what's to worry about. The Giants are so long dead, no one even believes in them anymore."

* * *

Bex kept her good hand wrapped around the papers hidden in her vest as they walked back through the city. Conell kept his head down, barely looking at her.

She refused to feel bad. She worked better alone. Her methods got results, and that was what counted when it came to saving another person's life. He'd see the necessity when

Anera could finally hold him without worrying that she'd drain the life out of him.

She raised her chin and fought down the urge to make him understand. She didn't need to justify herself.

They reached Anera's room before midnight. She was already asleep, curled up on the far side of the narrow bed. Without a word, Conell slid in beside her, keeping his hands to himself. But even if he didn't touch her, Anera clearly felt him there anyway. Her breathing went softer and deeper, and she uncurled just enough that their shoulders touched.

Bex turned and stretched out on the threadbare sofa, her mind going over all the things she would need to pack for a trip around the world.

In the morning, she woke bleary-eyed to find Anera in the tiny kitchen, while Conell watched her with a small smile from the table.

Bex surged up off the sofa with a huff.

It wasn't like Anera was cooking. Just taking an old loaf and some cheese from the cupboard to lay it out for breakfast, but still. Conell just sat there, not helping.

For once, Anera wore a soft blue dress tucked in at the waist, and her color looked better. But how long would that last?

Bex brushed herself off, trying to de-rumple her clothes, and fluffed her short hair so it wasn't so flat on one side. Then she cast a glare at Conell—which he completely missed since he was so focused on Anera—and stepped up to her sister.

"I'll do that. You should be sitting."

Anera's smile went thin and flat as Bex took the bread and cheese out of her hands. "I feel pretty good this morning."

"That's great. But you should save it for something important."

Anera heaved a sigh. "Bex, you're coddling me." She slid into a chair. "You can maybe let me do one thing for myself."

"You'll have to do plenty for yourself. I'm leaving on another dig today." And apparently Conell was just going to sit and watch Anera wear herself out.

"So soon?" Anera said.

Bex swallowed and set the food on the table. "This one is different. I don't know how long I'll be gone. I should get started right away."

Anera's brows drew down. "Where are you going?"

"South," she said and cast Conell a glare to keep his mouth shut about the particulars. Anera didn't need to know them, and they'd just make her worry. "Pretty far south. I'll have to catch a boat."

"You've never sailed before."

"No, but it will be good to get out of the city, see a bit of the world." She leaned forward to lay her hand beside Anera's where it rested on the tabletop. "It's necessary."

"Is it?" Anera said. "Maybe this isn't a good plan anymore. Maybe we should just accept this is the way I am." She laid her hand on top of Bex's, and Bex fought not to flinch. It was so rare she actually touched another person. Even Anera.

"You want to feel like this for the rest of your life?" she said.

"No, but this endless searching for a solution isn't any better."

Bex looked at Conell. "You're not going to say anything?"

"I love Anera just the way she is," he said quietly. "Whatever she chooses."

Bex jerked back. "And I don't?"

"That's not what we meant," Anera said.

Bex's mouth went tight. *We.* They were a united front. Maybe it wasn't supposed to be against her, but it sure felt that way.

"Bex, I'm worried about what you're doing. What lengths you'll go to for me."

Bex scowled at Conell. What had he been telling her?

"Don't you dare tell me you're not worth it," Bex said.

Anera's shoulders jerked. "I wasn't going to. I was just going to say, please don't lose yourself to this."

Bex hauled back on the anger before she snapped at the woman she'd chosen as her sister.

"That's fine for you," she said quietly. "You get to believe the best in people. You get to keep your ideals. I'm the one who has to be more realistic. For you."

Anera's face crumpled, but Bex turned so she wouldn't have to see it. She gathered up her satchel and packed the rest of the clothes that she owned, slipping the papers she'd stolen from Sir Kerrickmore behind them so they wouldn't get damaged.

Judging by this morning, it seemed like Anera could take care of herself while Bex was gone, but she knew that could change any moment. She could wake up tomorrow and not even be able to get out of bed. And Conell loved her, yes, but could he care for her well enough?

Bex was the best person to take care of everything, but she couldn't be in two places at once. She had to leave. The mirror was the only plan Bex had left. Unless she wanted to turn Anera over to the mercy and whims of a mage like Slayter.

Never.

"Keep the door closed and locked unless you're going in and out," Bex said as she strode to the closet. She turned and kicked the back wall, and a false panel opened. It wasn't so much built-in as it was just a broken piece of the closet that they'd never fixed. It made a perfect hiding spot.

"You can use one of these every couple of days." She pulled out a box that jingled. Little magical trinkets littered the bottom. Rings with one basic spell attached, a couple of vials of potions potent enough to sell for a little gold, a dagger with the remains of an ever-sharp charm in the blade. It was Bex's backup hoard. Just in case she didn't find anything on one of her digs.

"Don't overtire yourself or you might use up the stash before I get back."

"I know how this works, Bex."

"I've paid the landlady through the next month so don't let her kick you out early."

Anera stood, and Bex's frenetic energy bled out of her as Anera gazed at her. "I know you don't trust anyone, but you don't have to worry quite so much you know."

"I trust people," Bex said with a huff.

Anera raised an eyebrow.

"Some people," Bex amended. "Look, I'm trusting Conell, right now. I'm leaving him here to take care of you." Mostly because they'd fought, and she didn't feel right dragging him half a continent away from the love of his life.

Anera's look grew sad. "You tell the best lies to yourself, you know. Sometimes I think you don't even trust me."

All the breath went out of Bex at once until she stood there empty.

Bex needed to feel like she could control things. Sometimes the only way she could get that feeling was to talk. Over and over she spouted words trying to change what was happening. But did those words make Anera feel even worse? Was she just rubbing salt into an already open wound?

She couldn't draw Anera into her arms the way she wanted. All she could do was reach out and take her hand. She squeezed, feeling Anera's warmth and the thin bones of her fingers tight against her own.

"I trust you to be here when I get back," she said. "You're stronger than anyone else I know, so just... hang on until I can see you again."

Anera's expression softened, but the skin around her mouth was still tight. She just nodded.

Bex gave Conell a nod before she scooped up her pack and slipped out the door.

Down the stairs and out into the street, Anera's words rang back and forth in her mind. *You don't even trust me.*

She did trust Anera. She just... also wanted to take care of her and knew that her sister couldn't do everything herself. That was just truth. Wasn't it?

Truth and trust are completely different things. You can't compare them.

It was another block before she identified the feeling trying to crawl up her throat.

It's lonely living in a world where you're the only one you can rely on.

She stopped on the street where Mags usually set up her booth, but the secondhand merchant wasn't there to flirt with today.

Bex did not like this feeling. She stood alone, even though the street bustled with people all sliding by without noticing her or caring who she was.

Anera cared. Maybe Conell cared too. But she'd left them behind.

I had to. They can't come to Taur.

No. But as much as she hated to admit it, Conell was right. Her last few digs hadn't gone well, and she had no idea where to go from here. One step after the next only worked when you knew where to put the next step.

She needed a partner. Someone to watch her back, like she'd never let Conell do. Someone who knew Giant artifacts and how to find them. She needed an expert. An antiquarian.

And since she had high standards, she needed to find the best antiquarian in Usara.

Chapter 9
Rowan

Rowan stood at the edge of the tiny field, her breath coming in little anguished gasps. And she hadn't even started tilling yet.

The peaks surrounding her valley home rose around her, steep walls designed to keep anyone and everyone out. But they were just as good at keeping her in.

She grabbed the hoe from where it was propped by the fence and swung it over her head and down. It struck the hard ground, the force of it going up her arms and jarring her twisted back.

She grimaced, but she was used to a little pain.

She swung again and grit her teeth. All right, she was used to a lot of pain too.

"The ground is still frozen," Gavyn said behind her. "You're going to hurt yourself."

Rowan didn't turn, just braced her feet and swung again. "I know what I'm doing." By that, she meant, *I know how much I can take before I have to stop.*

When Gavyn didn't answer, she glanced back to find the

squat figure of a brass dog sitting beside the fence, its bulky head gazing at her.

Gavyn sat on solid ground where he wouldn't get mud in his delicate joints. He didn't say anything. With a sigh audible through his new voice box, he carefully laid down and propped his chin on his front legs.

"I need something to do," she said and went back to her work. "Otherwise I'll just go back inside and rearrange my books. Again." *Or maybe scream a little.*

The crawling feeling under her skin had only gotten worse in the last few months.

Far inside the sanctuary, a bell rang, its tones carrying through the open door and into the crisp afternoon air.

Rowan straightened and shaded her eyes with her hand. That was one of the perimeter alarms. Had someone breached the wall of mountains to get to her?

No. There on the peak directly ahead, a mountain goat leaped down the steep slope. Nothing more than an animal tripping the delicate spells laid around her prison.

She went back to her tilling, almost wishing it had been an actual threat.

Almost.

Her hands tightened on the hoe's handle even though she knew it would give her blisters.

Usually, when the crawling feeling grew too much or she started wishing for threats to her sanctuary, she just had to pass through the front doors into the main hall. There, the lantern sat on its pedestal, its cold light shining against the stone walls and copper pipes. Safe as always. Or at least as safe as she could make it.

Whenever she got bored or antsy, she just had to see its pale light washing across the room to remember exactly why she was here. The memory of Lord Karaval was never far away.

Sometimes it even felt like he stood beside her, present in the light of the Grief Draw.

His sacrifice still weighed on her, along with every other mistake she'd made. If she'd been faster... If she'd figured out that they couldn't destroy the lantern sooner... If she'd done everything differently, maybe Mellrea would still have her father. Maybe Darryn wouldn't be lying in a coma. Maybe she wouldn't be trapped in this valley for the rest of her life.

She shook her head and stepped down the short row she'd managed to turn over, her uneven gait making lopsided footprints in the dirt.

She'd chosen this. No one had forced her to come. No one had convinced her to give up her life to protect the Grief Draw. It had even been her idea. So why did she chafe so much now?

Sometimes she just stood in the field and stared up at the sky between the peaks for hours. Gavyn would always find her and lay beside her. He didn't have to say anything; his company was usually enough to pull her from the black thoughts that marred the bright days.

And she would remind herself that her prison was far better than his had been.

Chapter 10
Bex

It had been over a year since Bex had set foot in the Unlocked Door, a tavern off a side street in the lower city. Close enough to the docks you could smell the dank, waterlogged wood of the piers.

There was nothing so official as a treasure hunter's guild. Just a tavern where they could gather after their adventures to drink and boast. She'd spent a lot of time here before she'd gone freelance.

She pushed the door open. This early in the day, the common room was deserted, the lamps unlit, but she could tell the place hadn't changed much.

She slid her fingers across the edge of a table as she crossed the room. Their maps were still carved directly into the table-top, hills and valleys following the grain of the wood. Paint marked the locations of ruins. Blue for unexplored, black for plundered. And red for Giants.

There was a lot more black than the last time she'd been here. But there was also a new map on the table at the far end of the room. Someone had carved out the eastern tip of Usara, and a ton of fresh, blue paint marked clean ruins.

Bex itched to study it. But no, she had a different target in mind, and hers was so fresh it wasn't even pictured here.

Along the walls, plaques displayed old tools and replicas of famous and infamous treasures brought back by patrons of the tavern over the years. Across from her hung a replica of Queen Grasina's diadem, the many-times-great-grandmother of their current monarch. The real diadem was displayed in the palace now. Next to the replica hung the hand pick of Maxern "Quick Dig" Pathforge. Although, rumor was the real one had been buried with him.

Her favorite was still Old Brody's Lucky Rope, the one that had snapped when he was "this" close to the Helm of Yorn Hammerthought, plunging him into a twenty-foot hole—and saving his life in the process when the firetrap had gone off.

A man stood behind the bar, lining up glasses for the day.

"Hey, Eckert," Bex said, sliding onto a stool. "Has Brody been down yet today?"

Eckert pursed his lips and shook his head so his bald pate glinted in the little light that came through the high windows. "No, but I heard the door hit the wall a bit ago, so it won't be long. Something while you wait?"

"What is there for breakfast?"

"Salted meat. Jerky. Some bacon, but I'd have to start up the stove for that one."

"What kind of meat?"

"You don't want to know."

"I guess I'll take the mystery meat, then."

"How you been doing, Bex?" Eckert said as he fished a packet of jerky out from under the counter. "Still in the business?"

"Yeah, just not around here as much. Mostly little jobs to keep us fed."

There was a thump from the balcony above, and an old man stepped out of one of the rooms lining the second story.

He thumped to the stairs at the end of the room and stomped down them so he could plop down at the bar.

"Where's my breakfast?"

Eckert rolled his eyes and pulled a bowl out from under the counter. "Same as every day, old man," he said.

The man pulled the bowl closer and dug his spoon into the cold, day-old porridge, smacking his lips. Eckert shook his head and pushed through the door into the back of the tavern.

"Hey, Brody," Bex said.

"Bex." Old Brody kept his eyes on his breakfast.

"I'm sorry I haven't been around as much," she said, turning her mystery meat over and over in her hands.

"I know how it goes, kid," he said. "No hard feelings."

She hadn't expected there to be, but it was nice to hear anyway. He'd been her mentor once. Before she'd decided it was safer on her own.

"Now, what do you want?" He turned his head to fix her with a watery, blue eye.

"What?" She laughed.

"Clearly you came back because you want something."

"I couldn't have just missed you?"

He rolled his eyes. "Your lies don't work on me, kid."

She snorted. "Fine. I need an antiquarian. Someone who knows Giant ruins really well. I figure you have to know the best one in Usara."

He raised an eyebrow. "What have you gotten yourself into?"

"If you don't want me to lie to you, then don't ask questions I can't answer."

He waved a hand as he dug out another spoonful and shoveled it into his mouth. "Fair enough. Antiquarians, eh?"

"Only the best, now."

"Well, there was Jannik Tagersonn. He was the most renowned antiquarian west of the capitol for decades."

Her eyes narrowed. "Was?"

"He was. But word is he's dead now."

She blew out her breath. "That doesn't help me, Brody."

"No, but maybe his apprentice might."

Bex straightened. "Keep going."

Old Brody grinned into his porridge. "Rumor is he was teaching someone his trade. But she bested him by taking the artifact that was his life's work. Some sort of magical weapon. And then she killed him with it."

Brody cackled and slurped his sticky spoon, delighting in the story. But then he'd always loved a juicy bit of gossip, and he was the king of all the stories the treasure hunters brought through. Which was why she'd come here in the first place.

The apprentice sounded like trouble. But if she'd bested Jannik at his own game, clearly she'd be the best of the best now.

"So where can I find his apprentice?" she said.

"No one knows. She disappeared a couple of years ago."

"Well, what's her name?"

Old Brody shrugged. "No idea."

Well, she hadn't expected it to be easy to find a good partner. And at least he hadn't said the apprentice was dead. People left better trails to follow than ancient artifacts. So Bex should be able to find her easily enough.

* * *

Unless the apprentice didn't *want* to be found. Which was looking more and more likely by the day.

Bex had already wasted most of a week traipsing around the area where Jannik had died, a valley past the mountains that bordered the Laochodan Forest. And all she'd learned for certain was the name of the apprentice and the name of the weapon. The Grief Draw. It sounded formidable, but it wasn't like she knew what it did any more than she had when she'd left the crown city.

Rumors were funny things. People remembered different things than their neighbors, and each one was convinced their version was true, even when proven otherwise.

The only thing anyone agreed on was that both Jannik and his apprentice were last seen during the battle for Lord Karaval's Keep a couple of years before. The fight between two rival lords had rocked the little valley hard enough they still talked about it in excited whispers.

"Did you know Lord Hax brought down the wall?"

"Did you know Lord Karaval was a hero?"

"Did you know my cousin lost his leg in the battle?"

No one could agree on whether Jannik's apprentice had killed him or if he'd died in the battle.

But everyone did know that Rowan Norasdatter had fled shortly after that. And what better reason would there be to flee than if you'd done something terrible to your master?

One old man in Monclaren claimed Rowan was seen with magic cascading out of her hands and a strange, brass wolf with backwards legs.

Bex dismissed him as crazy. There was no indication that Rowan had been anything other than an antiquarian. And the brass wolf didn't even make sense.

Bex grumbled to herself as she trudged up the path to a little town in the foothills of the mountains that locked in the north end of the valley. So many of the people she'd talked to hadn't actually been at the keep during the battle. But several knew someone who had and had directed her to a shop in Harkerton where one of the veterans was making a name for herself as a craftsman.

It was an odd place to make a name for yourself, Bex thought. The town was only a few streets lined with houses and shops packed between snowy peaks.

Bex, who had grown up in the city, thought it was misleading to call these "foothills" when they were clearly full-on mountains, worthy of the name.

The rest of the world thought it was spring. Flowers had been blooming in the upper city, and Bex's nose had itched constantly in the valley where the trees were putting out big, ambitious boughs of blooms.

But here, white still streaked the jagged peaks, and piles of grimy snow lurked in the gutters and the corners between buildings where they clearly hadn't gotten any sun since last summer.

Bex's lips pursed. She'd packed an extra change of clothes but nothing warm enough for a lingering winter. She buttoned her collar a little higher and peered at the shop fronts, looking for one in particular.

At the end of the row, almost climbing up the mountain behind the town, she finally found a sign with a hammer, but instead of the usual pair of tongs to indicate a blacksmith, this one was crossed with a streak of lightning.

The big double doors stood open to the weather, and a pair of lanterns lit the gloomy afternoon. Ringing metal sang out from the opening, echoing across the street.

Bex straightened her shirt. She'd worn the green silk one with her vest situated to cover the stains in order to look more respectable. Her normal work clothes would make her look like a vagrant, and she wanted people to actually talk to her, not shoo her away.

She poked her head in the door and blinked. Hammers and tongs and wrenches hung from the rafters like a prickly forest. Some tools she recognized, a lot she didn't. Strange metal shapes interspersed the tools, and Bex didn't understand what she was seeing until she reached up tentatively to touch one and it moved. It was a well-oiled joint, two pieces of metal clasped together so they could bend and fold without breaking.

What in the world would you need something that size and shape for?

Iron and steel glinted among the tools, but most everything was made from brightly polished copper and brass. In the corner, movement caught her eye, and she stepped back a pace when she saw a metal arm attached to the wall, just like the ones hanging from the rafters. Except this one hissed and moved on its own, clicking over an array of objects.

Oh, maybe for that.

Bex's eyes traveled over it all, cataloging everything she could, even the stuff she didn't recognize. It would make sense eventually. Things usually did as you gathered more information.

The clanging, metal-on-metal noise came from the back of the workshop where a figure hunched over a glowing forge, tapping a piece of brass with a delicate hammer. Curly, roan-colored hair, tied into a bushy braid, draped the figure's back.

The figure held up the piece, a finely curved plate with three rounded corners, and the movement made Bex realize that whoever it was, wasn't hunched. They were just short.

Really short. This woman was built stocky and no taller than Bex's elbow.

"Hello? Are you Lynniki?" Bex asked, brushing aside the low-hanging tools to get closer to the forge. The air temperature improved considerably in the workshop.

"I am." The woman turned. A pair of darkened goggles covered her eyes, and she pushed them up her forehead, leaving a clear-cut line of soot on her cheeks. She raised her hand to rub at the marks with metal fingers. Her entire arm was mechanical, from the fingers, all the way up past her short sleeve. Metal plates slid against each other, and the joints clicked as she moved.

Bex had never seen a Delver before, but of course, there were stories of them passed around the Unlocked Door. Treasure hunters occasionally stumbled onto their cities while looking for plunder. Not that anyone had ever gotten inside one. Bex had always hoped to find Delver ruins someday, but that was even less likely than stumbling into a Giant's nuraghi. At least most nuraghis were aboveground.

"You here to buy something? Or did you need some work done?" the Delver asked, eyes going back to her project.

"I was just here to browse, but..." Bex deliberately turned to survey the tools and bits of machinery. She stepped across to the metal arm that hissed and jerked over the bits of springs and scrap metal, sorting them into rough piles.

"How does it work?" she said, tilting her head to see it from another angle.

"Steam mostly," Lynniki said. She tossed the finished piece she'd been working on into a cooling tank beside the forge and stepped around the counter. "And some other stuff."

Bex's palm tingled as she moved closer to the arm. The mechanism didn't seem to notice her or care when she reached out with her other hand to tap the metal with her fingernail.

"Some other stuff being magic?" Bex said, raising her eyebrows.

Lynniki beamed. "Yeah. How'd you guess?"

"I've worked with enough to be familiar. But I thought Delvers couldn't use magic."

Lynniki rolled her eyes. "We're resistant to magic and have none of our own. But that doesn't mean we can't take it off of other things and add it to our workings."

"You can transplant magic?"

Lynniki puffed up her chest. "It's my specialty."

"Oh? Do you have a mage in your back pocket, then?"

"Ha."

The arm finished its sorting and sagged with a hiss of steam. Lynniki pulled out a dirty cloth and ran it down the arm, adding a new streak of grease to the stains.

"I kind of do. But he can't do magic anymore, so mostly I have to find my own. The Giants left a fair amount behind."

She said it so nonchalantly as if collecting Giant magic was as easy as going to the market. Bex hadn't even considered it before Anera had taken a turn for the worse. But then if Delver's were resistant to magic, maybe going after Giant artifacts wasn't as dangerous as it was for Humans.

"Sounds familiar," Bex said, hiding her surprise. "I'm in a similar line of work myself."

"You're a crafter?" Lynniki cocked her head.

Bex took a look at the tools around them and laughed. "No, I'm a treasure hunter. I specialize in finding magical artifacts and selling them to people like you and other collectors."

Lynniki perked up. "Huh. Does that pay well?"

Bex waved a hand. "Well, I've worked with knights and nobles and a few others I really shouldn't name."

Which didn't answer the question and wasn't exactly true, but it served the persona she was developing in her head—and the one she was trying to build in people's minds.

"I love your work," Bex said. "It's nice to meet someone else who appreciates reusing things that have been lost or forgotten."

Lynniki's grin returned. "Exactly. There's no reason to throw something out when there's still a use for it."

"And even if it doesn't have a use, we can always learn from our mistakes," Bex said, taking an educated guess based on the successful projects around them... and the bin of broken pieces that sat beside the forge waiting to be melted down.

"Ha!" Lynniki slapped the wall beside the arm. "Yes." She tilted her head. "It *is* nice to meet someone like-minded. You have any bits or parts you want repaired? I'll even give you a discount."

Bex thought over the tools in her pack, but there wasn't much that was this sophisticated. "Not really," she said. "This is about the only thing I have that might interest you. And I'd rather it didn't have any magic put on it."

She pulled her flintstriker out to show the Delver.

Lynniki took it with a reverence Bex appreciated and turned it over in her broad hands. "Clever use of springs. Nice craftsmanship. You got this in the crown city?" she guessed.

Bex nodded.

"It's nice. Why don't you want magic on it? I could make it waterproof."

Bex wasn't about to explain the mark on her palm or the fact that any magic would be useless if she accidentally touched it. "It's... sentimental," Bex said. "And I prefer to rely on simple tools in ruins where there might be magic traps."

"I can understand that," Lynniki said, handing it back. "Let me know if you see something else that interests you."

Bex glanced at the hanging tools and felt it was time to press forward. "I appreciate your work, but I'm looking more for a person."

"A person?" Lynniki said, moving back behind her counter.

Bex followed and leaned her elbows on the pitted surface. "I heard you were at the battle of Karaval Keep."

Lynniki cocked her head. "I was. What about it?"

"I need to find an antiquarian," Bex said. "Jannik Tager-sonn was supposed to have been there."

Lynniki's eyebrows drew down. Perplexed but hopefully not suspicious. Not yet.

"He died there," she said, her voice going flat. "You wouldn't have wanted to work with him anyway. He was a bit of a rockhead."

Bex fought down a laugh. "A shame," she said instead and carefully traced one of the bigger pits in the counter with her fingertip. "Whatever happened to his apprentice?"

"I have no idea." The Delver turned back to her forge,

picking up a poker and stabbing it into the opening, making the flames spurt higher.

As an accomplished liar, Bex could spot another liar a mile away. And Lynniki wasn't very good at it.

"Well, I'm just looking for an antiquarian. A really, really good one. Do you know who took over Jannik's work after he died?"

Lynniki fixed her with a curious stare. "Why?"

Bex lifted her gaze and met the Delver's eyes. "That information is reserved for the antiquarian."

It wasn't that she didn't trust Lynniki, but the Delver used Giant magic. She might decide she wanted the mirror to incorporate into her workings.

Lynniki raised her eyebrows. "Then it's going to be hard to help you." She went back to her work.

Damn. Bex didn't think she'd burned that bridge too badly —Lynniki had still been polite—but she was clearly hiding something. Did she know Rowan? Did she know where she was? Had the apprentice really killed the master, and had her friends help her go into hiding?

"Thank you, anyway," Bex said since she didn't want to burn any bridges with the Delver. They had enough in common Bex could use that connection another time, perhaps.

She stepped to the open doorway, mind ticking along the next line of reasoning. Where did she go from here?

She'd have to monitor Lynniki to see if she sent any messages to Rowan or contacted her some other way, but how long would that take? She was running out of time to beat Sir Kerrickmore to the island of Taur.

Bright metal glinted in the lantern light, and Bex stopped in her tracks as a strange creature trotted down the street.

It had four limbs and was about the size of a dog, but the comparison ended there. The entire thing was made of brass and had a glowing bit of metal clamped over its hindquarters.

Its jerky movement took it in a zigzag line down the street toward Lynniki's workshop.

As it drew even with Bex in the doorway, the bulbous piece on the front that had to be a head nodded at her. "Good afternoon," it said, its voice tinny and rough.

Bex choked.

The creature chuckled and entered the workshop.

Bex clenched and unclenched her hands, eyes fixed on the creature's hind legs...which bent backwards at the knee.

Like the crazy, old man had said.

Bex had enough presence of mind to duck out of sight and plaster herself against the side of the workshop. Then she crept around to the back door that stood open a few inches.

Was this the brass wolf Rowan had been seen with? It was hardly a wolf. It was barely even a dog, but Lynniki clearly knew something about Rowan, and here was another link to the antiquarian. It didn't take long for Bex to recognize Lynniki's handiwork.

She shoved her ear up against the crack.

"One day you're going to give someone a heart attack, prancing in here like that," Lynniki was saying. "I didn't give you a voice box so you could surprise people to death."

"But Humans are so amusing when they're shocked," the tinny, brass voice said.

Lynniki snorted. "*You're* Human."

"*Was* Human. Now it's more fun to watch them from the outside."

The argument must have been an old favorite, because Lynniki laughed. "There you go. Now get going. I think it's going to snow tonight."

"Meh, weather barely slows me down."

"Yeah, but if your joints freeze, I'll have to make a house call. Then I'll have to take you apart piece by piece, and you'll be stuck without a body for who knows how long—"

There was a clanking sound, like a brass creature shivering. "I get the point. I'm going, all right."

Bex slipped back around to the side of the building to catch a glimpse of the brass creature disappearing up a narrow path into the mountains behind the town. It wore a leather satchel made to fit over its back like a pair of saddlebags.

Bex chewed her lip. Lynniki and the brass dog spoke like they were old friends. And it had walked off with a bag full of... something. Like they'd done this a thousand times.

And Rowan had been seen with a creature of brass with backwards legs.

All of this added up so there was only one way forward.

Bex followed after the dog, leaving Lynniki's workshop behind.

Chapter 11
Bex

Bex shivered, but she'd had no time to find a coat before chasing the brass dog. She hadn't wanted to lose sight of it, so now she suffered as the first few flakes of snow swirled from the sky.

This better be worth it.

The brass dog was clearly going somewhere interesting. It trotted with a single-minded purpose down rocky paths she wouldn't even have noticed were there if someone hadn't pointed them out, pausing only to resettle the pack on its back. According to Bex's map of the valley, there was nothing up here. But *where* was it going?

Bex hoped it was to Rowan.

She kept well back, slinking from the shadow of a rock here to the bend of the path there, keeping the dog in sight, but not getting close enough that it would hear her.

Full night had fallen, and Bex squinted along the darkened trail. Damn, could the creature walk all night without rest? Why hadn't she thought of that? Maybe it wasn't headed anywhere close by, and she'd be stuck making this ill-planned trip over the mountains without any warm clothes or snow gear.

Just as she had that thought, the dog glanced over its shoulder, then disappeared into a crack in the sheer rock of a cliff.

Bex sucked in a breath. If she'd blinked she would have missed it.

She raced forward to the space where the dog had vanished and ran her hands over the stone cliff face.

Nothing. It was like it had been swallowed into the mountain itself. There wasn't a path or an opening or anything as far as Bex could see.

And her hand didn't tingle, so there wasn't magic involved either.

Where had it gone?

Maybe there was a passage that you had to know was there before you could see it, or maybe it was a mechanical doorway with a hidden trigger. Either way, she was stuck.

She stepped back to crane her neck up.

It... wasn't that high. And climbing a mountain couldn't be that different from climbing a building or a ruin, and she'd done that plenty of times before.

She settled her satchel so the strap draped across her front but the weight of it hung against her back, and she started up the cliff, finding places that weren't as steep to scramble up and wedging her hands and feet into every chink and crack she could find.

It would have been way easier with a rope, but burglars couldn't be choosers.

The cold threatened to numb her hands, but she quickened her pace as she went, finding the rock grew rougher and easier to traverse the higher she climbed. Almost like the lower parts had been cut to make them harder to climb, leaving the heights in their original shape.

Bex smirked. Maybe no one had expected trespassers to be this determined.

She reached the top of the cliff. It was only about the equivalent of a three-story building. She hauled herself up over the edge and crouched there to survey her surroundings.

The sky seemed low and gray, spitting little bits of rain mixed with freezing snow, but it hadn't made up its mind yet if it was going to storm or not.

Below was what she was looking for. Bex caught her breath.

A ring of peaks and cliffs surrounded a tiny, cultivated valley. They formed a rough circle around the space, and from here, it was finally clear that someone had definitely cut them into a defensive shape, forming a natural-looking barrier between the valley and the rest of the world.

Inside this wall, there was just enough room for a plot of tilled ground, waiting for the spring planting, a cut stone path and courtyard, and a building lit up with candlelight. It had been built into the side of the mountain, so who knew how big it was on the inside.

Bex grinned, and her breath hissed through her teeth, fogging in the cold air. Clearly she'd found Rowan Norasdatter's hideout.

Why the antiquarian felt the need to barricade herself in the mountains was beyond Bex. Maybe she really *had* killed Jannik for his artifact.

It didn't matter to Bex. And actually a secret like that might make things a little easier. If Rowan didn't want anyone knowing about it...

People with secrets were always so eager to keep them.

Bex crept toward the edge of the barrier peaks, ready to climb down the other side, but her hand tingled, and she froze. There was magic here.

She held up her hand, palm out, and tried to discern the differences in the way it felt as she moved sideways across the top of the cliff.

There was magic all along the edge. Well, that was exciting.

The sky might have been threatening snow, but the ground was still too warm for it to stick.

The bare rock bore signs of working, and Bex crouched to examine it. Here and there, pieces of metal were inlaid into the rock, almost like they'd been melted into place, and Bex recognized Lynniki's handiwork, even if she didn't recognize the individual spells.

Further along, she spied a grid of wire fixed to the clifftop like a mesh welcome mat. This spell she recognized. Plenty of mage strongholds bore something similar. It was a simple alarm spell cast by a Land Mage, set to trip if anyone tried to cross it.

Bex chuckled. She knew just what to do with that one.

She unwrapped her hand and flexed it, the scars stiff in the cold. That was all right. She didn't need any dexterity for this.

She laid her palm against the wire mesh and drew the energy of the spell up through her mark. The mark flared, blinding against the night, but Bex had already closed her eyes. The energy raced through her veins, settling under her breast-bone like a mini sun.

Rubbing at the faintly burning sensation had never worked to ease it, but that didn't keep her from trying it almost every time.

The discomfort would ease over time, but that had been a much bigger spell than she'd been expecting. She'd have to be careful for the next day or two that she didn't draw any more.

Many of the other victims of the experiment had died over the years they'd been captives together, and that was one of the fastest ways to perish. Drawing too much energy, either by accident or because their mage captors had forced them.

Funny how that was completely the opposite of Anera's problem.

Bex rewrapped her hand, to be on the safe side, and stepped across the now-inert spell. No alarm rang, and the building below remained quiet and lit up like no one inside had been alerted to her presence.

The way down was a lot easier than the way up. This side of the mountain hadn't been cut smooth, and it sloped much more gradually toward the little valley's floor. Bex hopped down, keeping a careful watch for more spells.

But there weren't any more here. This looked like a path someone would take every day from the building to the little field and back. A hoe stood against a fence with dirt still caked on the end. Bex followed the path up a set of wide stairs to the porch lined with a stone railing.

The building rose in front of her, its steep-pitched roof ready to shed any snow that would accumulate in the winter months. Light flickered in diamond-paned windows lined with thin leading.

"Well, at least someone's home," Bex said and straightened her shirt and vest, brushing at the dust from travel and climbing. It wasn't perfect, but she was trying to look official here.

Then she knocked on the door.

As the sound rang out, the house immediately went dark, and metal shutters rolled closed over the windows.

"What?" Bex almost laughed. That had to be Lynniki's handiwork, too, but what was with the overkill? The amount of work required to find this Rowan was getting ridiculous.

Bex planted her fists on her hips and glared up at the facade. Everything had gone dark, as if the place had been abandoned, but she knew better than that.

The only sign of life was the curl of smoke rising from the chimney.

"I'm getting in there one way or another, Rowan Norasdatter," Bex muttered. "There's nothing you can do to stop me."

Chapter 12
Rowan

The advantage to a self-imposed exile was that you learned your home really well. After years in her sanctuary, Rowan knew every nook and cranny of it. She knew every pipe and the sound it made as the steam system came to life on cold days. She knew the feel of the rocky dirt between her fingers when she loosened it up in the spring. She knew all the little magics Lynniki had tucked into the corners to make the sanctuary not just a safe haven but a home as well.

So of course, she knew when someone was trying to get inside. What she hadn't expected was the persistence.

When the first bell started ringing, she took the kettle off the stove in the snug kitchen and slid the cover over to smother the flames. Then she carefully poured hot water into the waiting tea pot before reaching up to still the bell without looking.

It was probably just another mountain goat. It always was.

But in the quiet moment between the ringing of the bell and the hiss of the steam from the kettle, a faint tap made her narrow her eyes. Like a stone dropping from one of the cliffs into the courtyard.

Mountain goats weren't nearly so careless.

Her mouth pulled in a frown, and she limped from the kitchen into the study, her uneven gait making the tea slosh before she placed it on the table beside her chair. Lynniki's traps would stop anyone actually trying to get in.

Another bell rang.

Maybe this was a more serious type of goat.

From the main hall, the light of the lantern flashed against brass plates.

"Welcome back," Rowan said, stepping into the hall as Gavyn shook droplets of water from his carapace. "Did you find what you were looking for?"

Gavyn sighed. "No."

He didn't have to say more. His disappointment and frustration weighed down that one word.

Rowan bit her lip but hid the way her shoulders relaxed. She had no idea what she would do when or if Gavyn ever found a way to destroy his nemesis. The lantern had left so much of his life in ruins that it made sense he would fixate on trying to get rid of it, but what would happen if he actually found a way?

A lone candle sat in a sconce on the wall. It lit as she passed, the flame bursting to life on its own.

Rowan's breath caught. That had been a very expensive little addition to the working of the sanctuary. Lynniki was the only one who could make it light from her end.

It flashed in a pattern that they had established. The one that meant, "danger, interest shown."

Someone had been asking about Rowan.

She spun to Gavyn. "Were you followed?"

"What? No, of course not," he said. "I haven't been followed once in the two years we've been here."

A third bell went off. This one linked to one of the spells in the courtyard.

Gavyn tilted his head. Lynniki hadn't built his head with any features, but Rowan was getting better at telling what movement meant which expression. He'd just winced.

"I guess it's possible," he said. "I didn't think so, but I can't see behind me."

Rowan knew each of the defensive spells and traps Lynniki had installed, but she'd never actually had to use them before.

Before she could think which one she could reach first, someone knocked on the door.

Rowan lunged for the lantern and snatched it off the pedestal, gritting her teeth against the burn of the metal. She didn't place her hand on the button that meant "all clear," so the movement triggered a series of events.

Lightstones situated all around the main hall went dark, and metal shutters rolled down over the windows while Rowan's heart hammered in her chest.

She'd seen the sanctuary lock down like this once before. But that had been a test. This was anything but.

"What kind of thief knocks first?" Gavyn hissed through his voice box.

"I don't know." Rowan held the lantern close. "But I'm not going to answer it to find out. Maybe they'll go away once they realize they can't get in."

They stood frozen in silence, ears straining. Rowan couldn't tell if she actually heard the disgruntled murmur right outside the door or if she was just imagining it.

How many were out there? Had an entire army managed to follow Gavyn and scale the walls? Lord Hax was long since dead, but he'd left a young heir behind. Perhaps the boy had taken up his father's grudges.

Nothing broke the silence of the darkened hall except Rowan's ragged breathing.

Then there was a tap above her like a bootheel against a shingle, and the hair along her neck stood on end.

"They're on the roof," she whispered, her eyes tracing their possible path along the ceiling.

"How did they even...?" Gavyn started, then shook his head. "Never mind. They can't get far. It's solid rock past the..."

Rowan's mouth went dry, and she struggled to swallow. "Past the chimney," she whispered.

"Lynniki put traps on that too, right?"

Rowan opened her mouth to respond, but at the moment, she couldn't think of a single spell protecting that narrow opening. It was such a tight space, it shouldn't have needed it.

There was a scuff. It sounded like it came nearly halfway down the wall. The inner wall of the study.

Gavyn sprinted through the door into the room lined with bookshelves. Rowan took an extra moment to secure the lantern to her belt so she had her hands free.

She apologized to Tera in her head for not strapping her sword on every morning. She'd never wanted to carry it through the sanctuary, day in and day out, especially after that first year when absolutely nothing had happened. So instead of forcing herself to wear it, she'd stashed several blades in convenient places around the building and outside in the courtyard.

Now, she grabbed the one set into the wall just inside the study and joined Gavyn beside the hearth.

There were fail-safes in case someone managed to get in. Lynniki's mind worked like a labyrinth with all sorts of twisty turns, and she'd set her full attention to defending this place.

But while Rowan was willing to do anything to protect the lantern, theoretically, that didn't mean that she actually wanted to flood the place with poison or collapse the sanctuary while she and Gavyn escaped with the lantern.

She would absolutely stab someone though.

Today had been one of the warmer days in the valley, and

the fire had remained banked. Without the lights from the hall, the study stood in near darkness.

With a scuffle, the interloper landed on the banked coals, sending up a cascade of sparks that made them curse.

They rolled out of the fireplace, scattering hot coals across the flagstones.

Rowan lunged with a yell, stabbing the point of her blade down.

The figure swore and knocked her blade aside with an arm and leaped to their feet with fluid grace.

Rowan drew in a sharp breath. Their attacker was no more than a moving shadow in the darkened study, lit in strange, angular patches by the lantern swinging from Rowan's waist. But they rose tall and straight, and Rowan caught the flash of hands and the angle of a sharp chin.

Tera's voice rang in her head. *"You only have the advantage for a few seconds. Use them."*

Rowan pressed forward, confident Gavyn would close in on the other side. She kicked a coal back at the attacker, making them flinch, and in that second, she darted forward, moving faster than most people thought she could with her spine twisted and curved. She'd feel it in the morning, but that split second was crucial.

Rowan might be able to use a sword now, but she couldn't fight with strength. So she fought with everything else.

She dropped the point of her blade, which her opponent clearly hadn't been expecting, and her movement brought her directly up against the other person. The lantern threw harsh light at them, and Rowan tracked the attacker's movement in the sudden glow.

Her free hand shot out to grab the attacker's wrist. A point of heat beat under Rowan's thumb, and she let the spark that lived behind her eyes grow, filling her vision with a picture. A memory.

This worked much better on an object than on a person. Even though it was Life Magic, people muddled the memories. They carried too many for her to sort through. But sometimes she could see one clearly. And she'd refined her gift now down to the point where she could narrow it down so that one would be useful. It would show her a weakness or fault. Something she could use to unbalance her attacker and gain an advantage.

Black swept across her vision carrying an image with it. A girl as thin as a rail, with dark, lank hair, knelt in the dark, cradling her right hand. All Rowan could see of it was a palm, raw and bleeding. The girl hunched over it, sobbing hard enough to make her shoulders shake.

The image faded fast enough that only a moment or two could have passed. The visions left her disoriented and dizzy, but she knew how to plant her feet and push through the fog.

Their attacker yanked their right hand from Rowan's grasp and stepped back.

Gavyn darted in from the side. He got kicked across the room with a clank, and Rowan cried out, raising her blade.

"Stop!" the figure cried. "Stop, I'm unarmed. I just want to talk."

The figure held up their hands as if that would stop Rowan and Gavyn from defending themselves.

"Who comes down the chimney just to talk!" Rowan shouted.

"Well, I did knock first. You were the one who didn't answer." The figure kept her hands in the air, not at all worried about the sword Rowan had trained on her throat.

This... this was technically true.

"Usually when someone doesn't answer it's because they aren't home."

The person snorted. "Maybe in polite society. I'm sorry, I'm in too much of a hurry to be that polite."

The lantern finally stopped swinging, and Rowan got a good look at the interloper in its cold light.

The young woman straightened to her full height, which topped Rowan by almost a foot. She had short, black hair, wavy enough to stay out of her face when she brushed it back, and a sharp nose over a pointed chin. She could have doubled as a fox with very little effort.

A single streak of white marred the darkness of her hair, catching the lantern's light.

The woman's arms were well-muscled and built for climbing. That and her height made her look bigger than she actually was because she was also painfully thin. Skinny enough to shimmy down a chimney apparently.

Linen bandages wrapped the woman's right hand, and Rowan's gaze fixed on that tiny detail for longer than she'd meant it to.

The intruder kept her hands raised to show she indeed was unarmed. No weapons in sight at all. Just one little belt knife hung on her hip.

Rowan blinked and lowered the point of her sword, feeling oddly overdressed all of a sudden.

"You shouldn't be here," Rowan said. "The doors are locked for a reason."

The young woman cocked her hip and finally lowered her hands. "I did have to go to great lengths to get in here. But how else was I going to get to meet you?" She grinned, flashing an infectious dimple at Rowan.

Rowan stammered, words failing her. Who grinned when they'd just been threatened with death for trespassing? Who would risk death just to... meet her? To capture the lantern made perfect sense. But Rowan was just the unlucky soul who happened to be carrying it.

There was a splutter of static and a muffled curse from Gavyn's voice box as he staggered to his feet. He twisted his head to check down the rest of his body. "Senji's teeth, if you dented me..."

"Sorry I kicked you," the woman said brightly. "You look a lot like a dog. And once you've been bit, you try to avoid teeth marks in the future." She spread her hands like she was inviting Rowan to see her side of it.

Rowan realized her mouth was still open, and she shut it with a click. This was not a normal thief. This was not a normal *woman*, as far as Rowan could tell.

The woman brushed the soot from the puffy sleeves of her silk shirt, completely ignoring the smudge across the bridge of her perfect nose and the arch of one of her slanted eyebrows. Current beauty standards dictated brows that curved delicately over the eyes, but this woman's arched in two different shapes, giving her a jaunty air even when she was being serious.

That is, if she was ever serious.

"What are you doing here?" Rowan asked, fingers still locked on the hilt of her sword. "Who are you?"

"I'm Bex." The woman did not hold out her hand to shake, and Rowan wasn't sure she would have shaken it if she'd offered. Too much of her mind was still reeling.

"Aren't you going to invite me to sit? Have a cup of tea?" The woman—Bex—gestured to the pot that still steamed on the side table.

Gavyn snorted, and Rowan choked. "What?"

Bex shrugged. "You were the one who was so worried about being polite earlier." She cocked her head to give Rowan a lopsided smile. "Don't you want to know the answers to your questions?"

Rowan realized she'd taken a step back and let her sword fall to her side. But what else was she supposed to do? Attack the woman who wasn't even trying to defend herself right now?

All her defenses, all the ways she could fight and win were based on being prepared or being clever about how she used her limited strengths. This Bex had bypassed them all, slipping into the middle of the sanctuary and standing there with empty hands and a grin that dared Rowan to share some private joke.

She'd been protecting the world from the lantern and protecting the lantern from treasure hunters for years, and now that someone had actually breached her sanctuary it was not at all what Rowan had been expecting. Bex hadn't once looked at the lantern on Rowan's belt. Her eyes were firmly on Rowan's face.

"I'm not a threat," the woman said. Her smile fell away, leaving a solemn expression and earnest eyes. "I didn't even bring a weapon. Didn't think I would need one. I'm here to ask for your help."

Rowan wasn't going to answer. She was going to give Gavyn a signal, and they could attack together, maybe overpower this confident young woman who hadn't even thought to threaten them with violence.

But she hesitated.

Bex stared at her openly. Stared at her face. Not her back, not at the lantern, not at the talking dog that had to be at least a little bit of a novelty.

Her mouth opened and instead of a signal for Gavyn, she said, "Help with what?"

Bex's grin returned, and she gestured to the side table. "Pour the tea, and I'll tell you."

Chapter 13
Bex

Bex made herself comfortable on the only other chair in the room while the owner of the sanctuary, presumably Rowan, went around relighting lightstones so they could actually see. The lantern hanging from her belt was pretty enough, but it had this strange, silvery light that gave Bex a headache and made oddly shaped shadows against the bookcases and stacks of tomes.

Bex shifted in her chair. The upholstery creaked like it was brand new and hadn't been sat on much, while the other one where the steaming teapot sat seemed to have a nice, worn feeling to it. Clearly, the girl didn't get a lot of visitors.

But she must travel enough to collect all these books. Or maybe she sent her brass lap dog. Either way, the room was filled floor to ceiling with her collection. There weren't any windows back here to illuminate them, but Bex was willing to bet they were far enough into the building that they were actually under the mountain now.

While Bex waited, the brass dog sat beside the fireplace, staring. At least she assumed he was staring. He had no eyes but his blocky head was trained on her.

Bex leaned in the chair, trying to look as nonchalant as possible, but her heart rate was only just now returning to normal. It wasn't usually people who threatened her life. She was used to traps and magic and old buildings trying to collapse on top of her, but there weren't usually guards with swords. She stayed alive by being somewhere else when the swords happened.

But she couldn't be somewhere else now. She had one chance at this. If she couldn't convince the antiquarian to come with her, then she was going to have to go after the mirror alone. She couldn't waste any more time.

The young woman came back into the book-lined room. Thankfully she'd left the eerie lantern somewhere else. Bex could finally get a good look at her in the warmer glow of the lightstones.

Bex would have been surprised that no one so far had mentioned Rowan Norasdatter was a cripple, except she hadn't moved like one when she'd been threatening Bex with a sword. One of her shoulders rose higher than the other, her spine twisted so much that it bunched her back up like a rumpled sheet. She walked with a slight limp, her gait a little uneven on one side, but the sword she carried naked in her hand didn't waver as she sat in her worn chair and stared back at Bex.

She pushed a long braid, somewhere between blonde and brown, over her shoulder and rested the blade against her knees. Then she handed Bex a full cup.

"Thank you. It's not often I get to drink with interesting women."

The woman's eyes narrowed. "That is not the word most people use to describe me."

"Then they're paying attention to the wrong things. A scholar who swings a sword? How else am I supposed to see that besides interesting?"

The woman shook her head. "Answer my question," she said. "Help with what?"

Bex tilted her head. "Straight to the point. I like it. But first, are you Rowan Norasdatter? Apprentice to Jannik Tagersonn?"

Something twitched in Rowan's round face. "I was never his apprentice. Only his assistant. I kept his notes and organized his workers."

Bex could read between the lines. "Uh huh," she said. "And by 'kept his notes' you mean you did all the work and then he took credit for it, right?"

Rowan's mouth fell open, and a surge of triumph lit in Bex's belly. It was always nice when she read someone right the first time.

Bex leaned back in her chair and crossed her long legs with deliberate grace. Rowan's gaze caught the movement and then, interestingly, passed to her right hand with the wrapped bandages.

"Let me guess," Bex went on. "He never recognized your talents. Or even gave you a raise."

The brass dog snorted. Rowan gave him a look.

"What?" the dog said. "She's not wrong. He never did give you that bonus."

Bex rested her bandaged hand on her knee. The one Rowan couldn't seem to stop looking at. Most people fixated on her legs or some other asset she didn't mind showing off. Hands were new, but she could work with that.

She tapped her finger against her knee, and Rowan's gaze locked on the movement again.

Time to lock this in.

Bex put both boots flat on the ground and leaned forward. "Did you kill him?"

Shame was such an easy lever. Secrets and blackmail kept people in line, but shame kept them docile as long as you handled it right. Drive the wedge in and sit on it until they did what you wanted. Even Slayter had eventually given her something she could use against him.

Bex expected a reaction somewhere between prevarication and hostility. And could work with anything in that range.

But Rowan's face went stony and blank. Just before she shut down, there was a split second of confusion in her expression.

"Did you come here to accuse me of murder?" the woman said, voice flat.

The brass dog unfolded from his seated position with a whirr of joints that sounded a lot like a dog's growl.

Uh oh. Bex didn't often misread things that badly, but this would be one of those times. That moment of confusion, that split second had been the true reaction. She'd wanted to use Rowan's guilt, but that wouldn't work if she didn't have any.

Bex scrambled to get her thoughts under her. She could backtrack. This wasn't a complete disaster yet.

She put her elbows on her knees and linked her hands, meeting Rowan's eyes earnestly. "No," she said quietly. "I came to ask for your help. I'm in a similar line of work to yours. I'm a treasure hunter."

The brass dog spat a foul word as Rowan stood abruptly, hiding a brief wince. "I think you should leave," she said, each word closing a door between them until Rowan stood shuttered and locked down, staring at Bex.

"What?" This was not going at all how she'd planned. "What did I say?"

The dog lunged forward, and Bex fell over the armrest to avoid the jaw that swung open and revealed a razor's edge instead of teeth.

"Whoa, watch it."

"The lady of the house asked you to leave. I'll escort you out."

"After I tried so hard to get in here? I don't think so."

"It wasn't a request." The jaws snapped, and Bex danced back a step. Behind him, Rowan's grip tightened on her sword.

The dog rushed forward, and Bex darted out the door of the book room, into the long hall. The lantern glowed from a pedestal, washing the walls with a silver light, highlighting the copper pipes climbing the stone surfaces.

The brass dog snapped at her heels, herding Bex toward the front doors which opened of their own accord as she stumbled forward. Snow swirled through the air just beyond the open portal.

All right, *now* it was a disaster. She had not come here to be thrown out into a blizzard before she'd even made her request. So she'd said exactly the wrong thing—and who knew what that was—but she could fix this. She could still get Rowan's help. She could still save Anera.

She had to.

"No." She slipped to the side, letting the dog stumble past her, then lunged for the wall and the copper pipes running up to the ceiling.

She scrambled up the vertical surface, using the pipe as a handhold and clung to the wall just under the ceiling. She tucked her wrapped hand under her arm, just in case. She didn't feel any magic right here, but this whole place was completely different from a ruin. The pipe under her hand steamed and hissed, and she didn't want to absorb anything accident.

"I'm sorry for whatever I said," Bex said. She could backtrack with the best of them. "I didn't mean it, I promise."

Rowan limped to stand directly under her, hands on her hips. "I don't deal with treasure hunters."

Bex turned a growl of frustration into a laugh. "Like what you do is any different."

Rowan gave a wordless cry and dropped her fists from her hips. "I study history. I do not steal it."

Bex rolled her eyes and reminded herself that her goal was not to be right. It was to get Rowan on her side. "Look, I'm not interested in whatever you've got squirreled away up here."

"Squirreled away—?"

"You've hidden yourself well enough that I'm probably the only one who's even gotten close to finding you. But even if you want to keep hiding, the world is still turning without you."

Rowan's mouth went white, her lips tight. "I'm not hiding," she said. "I'm here to protect people."

The dog's head snapped around to look at her, and Rowan sucked in a little breath.

Bex hid a smile. Rowan didn't look happy she'd let that slip, but Bex was used to getting people to talk. At least enough to know how to tug and pull them in the direction she wanted. And now she knew exactly how to tug Rowan.

"That's why I need you," she said, meeting Rowan's dark eyes. "You know about Giant artifacts. You know how dangerous they can be. I'm going after this mirror for... a lot of reasons, and I need your help to find it."

Rowan's brow scrunched. "What mirror?"

Bex gestured to the brass dog. "Will your friend let me down?"

Rowan glanced at him. "He has a name."

"Pardon," Bex said. "We didn't really have a chance to be introduced before he was chasing me up a wall. What is your name, sir?"

"Gavyn," the dog said. "How did you know about the Giant artifacts? Why do you think we have experience with them?"

Bex eased herself down the wall. The pipe was growing hot under her hands, and she jumped the last half, landing lightly in front of Rowan.

"Rowan Norasdatter is an antiquarian. That's supposed to make her an expert," Bex said. She straightened and brushed the hair from her eyes. "And everyone says she's even better than Jannik."

Gavyn snorted. "Who's everyone?"

Bex ignored him, fixing her gaze on Rowan. "I can also make an educated guess. An expert in Giant artifacts holes up in a hidden sanctuary in the mountains in order to protect people? Clearly you're doing important work."

And just as clearly, Rowan must have stashed away a Giant artifact. Something dangerous. Jannik's weapon maybe? Bex wasn't interested in prying whatever it was out of Rowan's hands. She and Gavyn were clearly ready to defend it, and Bex preferred long-dead adversaries to live ones, thank you very much. She only stole *little things* from the living. Things that wouldn't get her skewered or locked up in jail. It would be easier to pry Rowan out of her hiding spot than to pry whatever she was hiding out of her hands.

But all of that meant Rowan was someone like Anera. Someone who believed in the greater good. And if she really had sacrificed herself to this noble cause, then Bex knew just where to nudge.

"I need an expert," Bex said, pulling a sheaf of notes from her satchel. "And you're the best."

She handed them to Rowan. It was a copy, of course. She was good at what she did, and a good treasure hunter didn't rely on paper and parchment that could so easily be damaged, lost, or burnt.

Or stolen, but she wasn't thinking about that right now.

Rowan glanced at Bex with a wary frown before propping her sword against the wall and taking the notes. Her face changed as she flipped through them, her mouth going slack and her eyes widening.

She blinked up at Bex. "Do you know what it is you're looking for?"

Bex shifted her feet. "Only what's in there." She gestured to the notes. "Do you recognize it?"

"No, but you were right. I have experience with things that the Giants worked very hard to hide." Rowan went back to reading.

"Like the mirror?" Bex said, eyeing the notes. "Slayter said it was hidden for a long time."

Rowan flipped the edge of the pages through her fingers. "If the Giants were that afraid of it, then... you should be too."

Rowan tried to hand the notes back.

"Unfortunately, I need to find it," Bex said, tucking her hands behind her.

"Trust me," Rowan said. "You don't want to get involved."

"I'm not going to pretend to know what it is or how it works," Bex said quietly. "But I know it's important enough that the queen and her mage want it. They hired the best treasure hunter in Usara to find it." Bex gave her a little smile. "And I decided to find the best antiquarian to help me. If it's that dangerous, then we were right. We have to keep it safe, Rowan."

She did not reach for Rowan's hands like she had the urge to do. But she stepped forward, just to the edge of Rowan's personal space so Rowan had to look up to meet her eyes.

"I need you to help me," Bex said. "The queen needs you."

"That's very convenient. Do you have proof of that?" Gavyn asked with a tilt of his head.

How could you feel someone's gaze on you when they didn't have eyes?

Bex slipped the writ from the pocket of her vest. It was her most valuable possession right now and something she couldn't copy, so she kept it close to her heart.

Rowan took it and held it with the stack of other papers. Her fingers smoothed over the paper, and her gaze went glassy and distant for a strange second.

The most successful lies were just distortions of the truth. Tell someone something they wanted to hear and you could twist them any way you wanted.

Rowan stared back at her, and Bex could feel her teeter on the brink between believing and throwing her out of here on her ass.

Bex pushed, just a little. Not like she was thrusting someone off a cliff, but like she was nudging someone toward a present they wanted but didn't think they deserved.

Please, Bex thought. *For Anera.*

Rowan blinked and folded the notes and the writ under her arm. "All right," she said quietly. Her round cheeks had gone flushed, and she turned back toward the room lined with books.

Bex swallowed, her throat dry. "All right?" she said.

"I'll help you."

Chapter 14
Rowan

owan packed everything she could think of into a small pack. A change of clothes, notebooks, pens, ink, her old tools from her time with Jannik. She ran her hands over the chisel and one of the brushes, pausing before sliding them into her pack. They reminded her of a time when she'd thought she could be something different.

Well, she wasn't Jannik's assistant anymore, but she also wasn't the godsblighted of Lannasbrook anymore either.

She closed the flap of the pack before she could think too hard about Bex's question the night before.

Did you kill him?

She tightened the strap with a yank, her lips thin.

"What were you thinking?" Gavyn's voice said from the doorway. "I can't believe you agreed to this."

Rowan didn't jump. She was used to him showing up wherever she was in the sanctuary.

"I know it seems crazy to leave after I've spent all this time trying to keep the lantern hidden," she said quietly without turning around. "But I think it's the right thing to do."

"You're right," Gavyn said. He clicked into the room and laid down beside the bed. "I think you're crazy."

She turned to face him, leaning back against the table. This room sat at the very top of the sanctuary, in the peak of the roof above the main hall. She had one window that looked out across her little valley and the field she'd tried to till the week before. Her bed sat against the slanted wall to one side and her table against the other.

"Gavyn, last night I touched the writ and the notes Bex gave me."

Gavyn looked up. "With your gift? What did you see?"

"I saw the queen and some of her friends. Maybe they're bodyguards or advisors. I'm not sure. But they were putting together the notes on the mirror. And they were worried."

"I thought your gift didn't usually come with feelings."

"It doesn't." She gave him a grin. "Only on special occasions. But I didn't need magic to read their faces. They need this mirror, and they need it for something important."

Rowan's gift had always been small. She found touchpoints, little bits of heat on an object or sometimes a person that she used to see moments in time. They were memories from someone who had touched that thing in the past.

Her gift might have been small, but she had honed its use until she could seek out a specific type of memory. When she fought, she tried to see a person's weakness, something she could exploit. When she studied, she found points in time that gave her clues to an object's use or the person who had loved it.

"I don't want to leave," Rowan said. "But I think I have to. Bex needs the help, and there aren't that many antiquarians around... now that Jannik is gone."

Gavyn shook his head. "I don't trust her. She has strange skills for someone who works for royalty. Who would think climbing down the chimney is normal?"

Rowan bit her lip to suppress a smile. "Well, we did lock the door on her. Maybe it just means she's a good treasure hunter, like she says."

Gavyn gave her a look, and she winced.

"I know. I hate the idea too. Too many treasure hunters would look at the Grief Draw and think it's something valuable. Worth stealing. But I don't know. I think Bex might be different."

"What makes you think this isn't some elaborate ploy to get you to leave the sanctuary? The moment you're vulnerable, she can just take the lantern."

Rowan crossed her arms and stared at the floor. "We were vulnerable last night. She got inside. Further than anyone's ever gotten before. If she'd wanted it, she could have fought for it, but she didn't." She raised her chin to meet his gaze. "She didn't even look at it once, Gavyn. I don't think she even knows what it is."

"Are you sure you don't just want to trust her because she spent the whole time flirting with you?"

"Gavyn!" She said it with half a laugh.

"What? You didn't notice?"

She snorted. Of course she'd noticed. That didn't mean she was swayed.

Bex was... fascinating, not just because she was the first stranger Rowan had talked to in years. Her easy smile pulled at something inside Rowan, making her stomach flutter. But then the woman turned around and claimed to be the thing Rowan hated most in the world. Or she twisted Rowan's words so suddenly she was on the losing side of the argument without realizing how she'd gotten there.

Equal parts attractive and infuriating.

And the way she'd casually mentioned Jannik's death...

Rowan rubbed her eyes. No, all of those things led to a

baffling picture of the flirtatious treasure hunter and were not the reason Rowan had decided to trust Bex.

"I read her, Gavyn," Rowan said, lowering her hand. "During the fight."

Gavyn sat up on his haunches. "Looking for weaknesses?"

"And I found one. I would have used it too. If she'd even tried to fight back." Rowan held up her right hand. "She keeps her hand wrapped."

"A new wound?"

Rowan turned her own hand around to stare at the palm. "Or an old one."

The vision she'd seen in that split second she'd touched Bex had definitely shown her the treasure hunter but as a younger more vulnerable version of herself. Rowan had practiced memorizing as much of a vision as she could in the moments when she touched someone. Specifically so she could recall the details later.

The girl had been huddled over her damaged hand, tears streaming down her dirty face. Darkness suffused the room, nearly hiding the moldy straw on the floor and the gutter running against the back wall full of murky water.

Touchpoints allowed Rowan to see memories, but the fact that she could see all of Bex, not just her hands or feet or whatever she was looking at, meant that Rowan was seeing someone else's memory. Someone who had touched Bex recently with that memory in their mind. And it had been strong enough to stick.

Rowan's fingers curled around her palm. She couldn't see enough to know what had happened or how long ago, but Bex still kept her damaged hand wrapped. And she almost never used it. Except for that moment when Rowan had grabbed her, Bex avoided touching anyone or anything with her right hand. As if it hurt her.

"She's a little bit broken," Rowan said quietly. "Just like me."

Gavyn had no face for Rowan to read, but he glanced away as if to hide an expression. "You can't trust everyone just because they might have suffered in the past. It makes you easy to manipulate."

"Maybe," Rowan said, pushing up off the table. "Maybe it makes me vulnerable. But I refuse to harden myself against sympathy for others."

Gavyn sighed heavily and stood.

"That's what I have you for," she said. "You can be the suspicious one."

"Oh good," Gavyn said. "I'm glad I didn't spend all night watching her for nothing."

"You know, you don't have to come," Rowan said. "You can stay here and—"

"And worry the whole time that you'll let your guard down?" Gavyn snorted. "No thanks." He stretched kind of like a real dog, but Rowan knew he was loosening his joints in the cool, morning air. "Besides, I need to expand my horizons."

Rowan raised her eyebrows. "Expand your horizons?"

"I've exhausted all the libraries in Usara. At least the ones Lynniki had access to. And I still haven't found a way to destroy the Grief Draw. Perhaps Taur has some magic that could help."

Rowan chewed her lip. Arguing that destroying the Grief Draw wasn't the answer when it could still be useful had never worked in all the years they'd been here. So she didn't even bother bringing it up.

But Gavyn had spent almost as much time outside the sanctuary as in it, searching for anything that might help. A magic tool or a weapon that would be powerful enough to destroy something that had already proved to be indestructible.

And every time he came back empty-handed, he grew more and more bitter.

"Gavyn..."

"What?" He didn't quite snap, but he jerked his head at her sharply.

"I'm just... not sure this obsession is healthy. I know you're looking for a way to destroy it, but—"

"But what?"

"Maybe you need another hobby?" She winced. "I just don't like the way it's taking over your life."

"Like protecting it took over your life?"

Rowan's mouth snapped shut. "Point taken," she said quietly.

She turned to pick the lantern up off of the table and braced herself for the burning pain that shot through her hand when she touched it. She stared at its panes for a moment. Four lenses remained intact, each with a distinct design. The one on this side depicted endless waves reflecting each other.

Unbidden, an image of a mage lying dead on the floor came into her mind, and she had to close her eyes and take deep breaths before she could banish it.

"I guess we both have an unhealthy obsession." She slipped the lantern into the case on her hip. The one Lynniki had made. The Delver had hammered thin sheets of metal into a vessel that held a pint of salt water. It was heavy with the lantern nestled inside but well worth it for the protection it offered ordinary people against the lantern's toxicity.

She might be leaving the sanctuary behind, but there was no way she was leaving the lantern behind. She still had a duty to keep the world safe from its effects and keep any treasure hunters from taking it for their own purposes. It was safer in her possession than it would be here, no matter how many traps Lynniki set up.

"Are you going to tell her what it does?" Gavyn asked.

No need to clarify who he was talking about.

"No," Rowan said without having to think.

It didn't matter what she saw in Bex's past. She was still a treasure hunter.

And nothing was worth revealing the truth of the Grief Draw.

Chapter 15
Bex

Bex waited in the courtyard as the sky grew pink and orange with the sunrise. It would be a long while yet before it was high enough to shine directly into this pocket valley, but Bex was already wide awake.

She hadn't slept much considering she'd spent most of the night watching the brass dog who had been watching her. He'd stood in the open door of the study, staring at her where she lay on the sofa, not even bothering to hide the fact that he was standing guard.

She'd been right, then. The brass creature must not need any sleep.

Too bad Bex did. She yawned as she hitched her satchel higher up her shoulder, then slipped her hand inside her vest to be sure the notes, the map, and the writ were still safely tucked away. She busied herself by pulling her leather gloves on over the linen bandage and tucking the ends in so they didn't bunch.

This was it. She had everything she needed to save Anera. From here on out, her success would depend on her wits and her ability to use them. And Rowan's skills as an antiquarian.

She jerked her chin up, suppressing the sudden chill that

raised goose bumps along her arms. *Just the air this morning.* The ground still held a dusting of snow from the night before, and Bex was perfectly happy to get out of these mountains.

The doors of the sanctuary swung open, and Rowan appeared with Gavyn at her side.

"Oh great, the dog's coming too," Bex muttered under her breath.

She took a moment to admire the antiquarian as the windows of the sanctuary reflected a little of the morning sky. Rowan wore a pair of sensible pants, but she'd layered a long, leather coat over it, cut around the legs to allow her the freedom to move. The linen shirt she wore underneath was in much better shape than the silk one Bex was wearing, masquerading as the Queen's "official treasure hunter."

Bex was strangely glad to see Rowan wasn't carrying anything that could be Jannik's mysterious weapon. A normal-looking sword swung on her hip. It looked a little odd with Rowan's uneven gait, but the young woman had proven that she could use it effectively despite the hump of her shoulder and the way she winced when she moved too quickly.

Other tools and pouches weighed down her belt like a sleeve for a notebook and spaces for pens and brushes and chisels. And one oddly shaped metal box with a handle sticking out the top.

Bex shrugged. Rowan could bring whatever she felt was necessary. And a little piece of her was glad Rowan hadn't felt like a Giant's weapon was necessary.

It made it that much easier not to be tempted to steal it and take it to Anera.

Bex let a bright smile spread across her face as the sanctuary doors swung shut behind Rowan and the antiquarian joined her on the terrace.

"Ready?" she said.

"As ready as I'll ever be." Rowan glanced back up at the

building, then around at the terrace and the valley. A strange mix of sadness and anticipation pulled at her lips. And maybe... guilt?

"It's good to get going," Bex said, hoping to erase the last one. "We've got a long way to go, and we have to do it quickly." She turned to start down the steps to the path that presumably led out of the valley. "We'll head back to the crown city and catch a ride in port—"

"Wait," Rowan said.

Bex paused, thinking Rowan meant she was walking too fast, but Rowan hopped down the stairs like she'd done it a million times before. "We have a stop to make first. We need a team."

Bex's brow drew down. "What kind of team?"

Rowan raised an eyebrow at her, looking very much like Old Brody when she'd asked a particularly dumb question.

"Diggers, experts, guards. That writ gives you the right to ask for funding from any local nobility, and you should probably take advantage of that. Passage down the continent will be expensive."

Bex flushed. It all sounded so reasonable. But now that she had Rowan, she hadn't thought she would need much else.

And more people meant more lies and more chances for the whole story to come unraveled. Bex could hustle, but could she hustle fast enough to keep Rowan and Gavyn and an unspecified number of other people from guessing the truth?

Rowan saw her hesitation and stopped on the stone path. "This is why you wanted my help," she said. "Right? You wanted an antiquities expert. Someone who can help you find what you need. Well, I'm assuming you and the queen want this done the right way. Without any mistakes."

"Mistakes delay and endanger you and can damage what you're looking for," Bex said, quoting Old Brody.

"Exactly," Rowan said. "I'm glad you understand."

"All right, you don't have to say it like I'm dumb," Bex said. "I'm just—we're kind of in a hurry."

"Well, if you don't want someone who knows what they're doing, I can go back to my sanctuary. I had a book I was going to read today—"

"No, no, you're right," Bex said. "You're the expert." And also not a stranger to manipulation apparently.

Rowan grinned. "Yes, I am. Now the expert says to wait... hmm, five more seconds ought to do it, don't you think?" She glanced down at Gavyn.

He tilted his head. "I'd say three."

Bex opened her mouth to ask what the hell they were talking about, but there was a *click* behind her.

It sounded so much like stepping on a trap in an old ruin that Bex couldn't help spinning with a gasp.

A Delver with a thick, reddish braid and a metal arm knelt on the path just inside the ring of cliffs, disarming the trap she knelt on.

Lynniki adjusted the flagstone and a puff of smoke went up, making her cough.

"Ahem, that one still had some power," she said.

"I still think you should make a safe route through for those of us who are supposed to be here," Rowan said with a little smile.

"If it's safe for me, then it's safe for an intruder," Lynniki said. "This way, there's nowhere to step that won't trip an alarm until you get to the courtyard."

Bex glanced between Lynniki and Rowan, who had clearly been expecting her. "You have a message system."

"One of Lynniki's own designs." Rowan grinned. "All I had to do was mention the words 'Giant magic,' 'travel,' and 'danger,' and I knew she'd be here by morning."

"I know an open invitation when I hear one," Lynniki said.

Bex frowned at the Delver and then down at the flagstones under her feet. "It's... all trapped?"

"Every inch," Lynniki said. "All the way to the courtyard, and that's only safe because Rowan needed to be able to move around freely. Some of it's magic. But most of it's practical gadgetry. Like this one." She kicked the flagstone back into place.

Bex glanced at Rowan who bit her lip, hiding a smile.

"You tripped at least three alarms on your way to the front door," Gavyn said with what had to be a smirk.

Bex's cheeks went hot. And she'd thought she'd been so careful.

Rowan waved to Lynniki. "Meet the first of your team."

Lynniki stood, shifting a huge pack higher up onto her shoulders. She was clearly dressed for travel, and she clanked when she moved.

"I've found having a tinker is essential for any dig," Rowan said. "But if you're going anywhere near Giants, you want my aunt, Lynniki."

"I thought they were all dead," Bex said. "Wait. Your aunt?"

"We get that a lot," Lynniki said. "Yes, I'm older than I look."

"Yes, I'm half Delver," Rowan chimed in.

Gavyn lifted one of his oddly jointed legs and flexed it. "I'm all right with this situation. I think there's something wrong with this leg. You can look at it as we go."

"I told you to get out of the cold last night," Lynniki said.

"Lynniki, this is Bex. Our new patron." Rowan gestured to Bex.

Patron. That sounded very official. Bex liked it.

"We've met," Lynniki said with a weighted look at Bex. "Well, you did say you wanted to talk to Rowan. You must have said something special to pry her out of this place."

Rowan flushed a bright red and cleared her throat. "Do you want to rest first if you've been walking all night?"

Lynniki shrugged. "I hitched a ride and napped most of the way here. So I'm ready." She spun on her heel to head down the path. "I guess I know where we're headed next."

Rowan and Gavyn followed with a laugh.

Bex muttered, "I don't," but she hurried to catch up.

Chapter 16
Bex

I t became clear to Bex very quickly that they were headed to Karaval Keep down in the valley. Once out of the mountains, the air grew warmer again, much more in keeping with springtime where Bex was from, and she didn't have to worry she was going to die in a freak snowstorm anymore.

Snowmelt swelled the river until it ran swift and dangerous past them and spilled into the valley, flooding the plains around Karaval Keep. The area glinted in the sunlight, a whole swathe of water between them and the town that rose on the crest of the hill.

Rowan led them across a narrow land bridge that wound toward the front gate. Wagons full of produce trundled along in front of them, and a shepherd herded his goats in a bleating bundle behind.

This was more like it. Bex felt right at home in the bustle, unlike the rocky slopes of the mountains, which she could still see ringing them to the north and the east and a bit to the south. Far, far to the west, a dark shadow marred the horizon beyond Karaval Keep. Bex shuddered and kept her eyes front so she wouldn't have to look at or even think about the noktum that lurked over there, like an ever-present storm cloud just waiting to suck someone into it.

The steady stream of travelers wound their way through the big front gates which stood wide open with grass growing under the edges. They clearly hadn't been closed in a while. Maybe since the battle. But oil gleamed from the hinges so they must be ready in case someone attacked again.

Who was it the first time? Lord Hass? Harris? Something like that. Bex did not keep track of nobles. As long as they stayed far away from her and Anera, she figured they were fine. Any closer and they'd have a problem.

Big watchtowers stood above the gates and on each corner of the outer walls. Fresh mortar showed through the cracks, and when Rowan asked Lynniki a passing question about the improvements, the Delver went on at length about the lenses she'd installed at the top of each that allowed a watcher to see far into the distance and the messaging system she'd put in place.

Bex, walking behind them, raised her eyebrows. The Delver must have played a much bigger part in the battle than she'd originally realized.

As they passed through the gates, the traffic got a little better as the travelers around them spread out through town. Rowan kept waiting for someone to notice Gavyn and start screaming about magic and brass demons, but instead, he was greeted with friendly waves and respectful nods.

Like he was a familiar sight.

Bex still hadn't gathered the courage to ask what exactly he was. He had the intelligence of a Human but had clearly been constructed. Was he some invention of Lynniki's built to guard Rowan and keep her company? Or was he something else, a mix of Human, brass, and magic?

Bex followed the others up the hill since they obviously

knew where they were going, passing market stalls full of grain and apples and cabbage. On the corner, she had to dance around a hen that had escaped its seller. It was a familiar sort of chaos despite being a completely different town in a completely different part of the country.

Ahead of her, Rowan walked with a bounce in her step. Normally the antiquarian had a hitch in her gait that made her step further with her right leg than with her left, and her whole body swung with the uneven rhythm of it. But suddenly she seemed to move easier, looser, like a tension had unspooled in her spine.

Rowan gazed at everything with a soft, indulgent smile. Even treating the escaped chicken with a ridiculous little wave.

Bex watched with a perplexed grin. The rumors said Rowan had disappeared after the battle. Had she spent every moment since then in that mountain sanctuary? She certainly acted like this was the first time she'd seen the outside world in years.

The keep itself, an ugly, square fortress, sat at the top of the hill, looking out over the town like a fat goose keeping watch over her goslings.

Bex immediately didn't like it.

"Who are we recruiting?" she said. She'd assumed they were heading for some associate Rowan had in town. Not the keep itself.

Rowan turned enough to give her a look with an arched eyebrow. "You have a writ that allows you to ask for help from the local nobility, do you not? I assumed you would want to talk to someone about passage to Taur. Unless you already have a ship booked?"

Bex clamped down hard on the shiver that slithered through her gut. "Oh. No. If you have resources, then..." She didn't even bother finishing. Rowan had thought of everything.

And she was right about the writ even if Bex hadn't really thought about using it for this exact purpose.

She hid her grimace behind a plastered smile and let Rowan lead them through a small door in the side of the keep and up several flights of stairs to a long hallway.

Bex couldn't help noticing that there were plenty of guards, but all of them straightened when they saw Rowan, Lynniki, and Gavyn, and they let them pass without fuss.

Bex raised her chin when they looked curiously at her and reminded herself of the lies she was currently telling the world.

I belong here. I'm an agent of the queen's. I'm on important business.

At the end of the hall, a door stood ajar, and Rowan strode toward it, confidently.

Then stopped short as raised voices carried through the opening.

"If you're upset, just say something," a woman's voice said, smooth and lyrical but with a bit of steel and exasperation underlying it.

"I'm not upset." That was another woman, but this one was gruff, and Bex could well imagine her yelling commands across a battlefield.

"You're something. You hate this, I know you do. If you have a solution, I'd love to hear it."

"You know I don't."

Bex would have sat there and eavesdropped shamelessly to find out what happened next. The second woman sounded stiff and implacable, but the first voice sounded like they couldn't decide if they wanted to take a swing at the other woman or kiss her.

But Rowan cleared her throat and pushed the door open, revealing a study lined with books. Where Rowan's study in the sanctuary had piles of tomes lying around, proving she actually used the space to research, this one was tidy with an air of disuse. Only the desk seemed well loved with papers spilling across it and a comfortable chair pulled up behind. Like the occupant had slipped into someone else's space and was trying to keep their disturbance to a minimum.

Beside the desk stood a woman with sleek, dark hair tied back in a complicated knot behind her head. Her hand rested on a naked sword lying across the desk, but incongruously she wore a brilliant red dress that sat rich against her pale skin. Its square neckline accentuated certain features that had Bex wondering if she was jealous or in love.

Another woman stood directly in front of her, in a stiff parade rest.

Bex had seen traders from Demaijos in the crown city— flirted with a fair number of them too—and this woman would have fit in with them perfectly with her deep brown skin and crinkly, black hair pulled into a sensible bun. Bex couldn't see them from this angle but she'd bet her eyes were mismatched.

The woman wore a guard's uniform with captain's markings on the shoulder and a longsword hung at her belt. Bex was suddenly aware that she'd seen more swords in the last few days than the last three years put together, and she wasn't happy about it.

Neither woman looked up at their entrance, their gazes locked on each other.

"You could at least talk to me," the woman in red said.

The guard stared back at her, face stony. Even Bex could tell talking wasn't her strong suit.

"I'm sorry for the interruption, Mellrea," Rowan said quietly.

The woman in red shook herself, like she really had been so intent on her conversation that she hadn't noticed them walk in on it. She closed her eyes for a brief moment, and in that second when she lost eye contact, the guard captain's face spasmed, a fleeting expression of pain scuttling across it, only to be replaced with stoicism again. The moment was gone by the time the other woman opened her eyes again.

"Nothing to apologize for, Rowan. I think we both would appreciate a distraction." The woman moved around the desk to stand beside the chair.

Wait, Rowan had called her Mellrea. Bex gulped, her mouth suddenly dry. This was Lady Karaval. Her father had died in the battle of Karaval Keep, and she'd been overseeing these lands ever since.

Bex suddenly found her a whole lot less attractive.

Mellrea took a moment to collect herself before finally looking back up at them, Rowan specifically. She blinked. "I... never thought I'd see you outside of the sanctuary again. Is something wrong?"

"No, not wrong. Just important." Rowan turned to gesture toward Bex as if she expected her to step forward and actually speak to a noble. "We've been asked by the queen's representative to help find an important artifact made by the Giants."

Mellrea's eyes landed on Bex, and she stiffened.

"Bex," Rowan said. "This is Lady Mellrea Karaval and her captain of the guard, Tera. Mellrea, Tera, this is Bex. The queen's representative."

Oh gods, they were all friends. How cute. Being friends with a noble might have worked just fine for Rowan, but Bex couldn't suppress the flashes of another life far before this one. Memories of darkness, moldy straw, and hard flagstones crept through her. Her palm pulsed with remembered pain, and a voice rang in her ears.

"Any progress?" it said.

"Yes, King Vamreth. This one does not seem to be dying."

Dead eyes stared at her out from under a coronet that glinted in the harsh light of a torch. "I suppose that's something. And what of the experiment with the noktum."

"We'll proceed with this one first thing in the morning. As long as we still have your permission."

"Do it."

Bex's hand curled, and she held it close to her chest, breathing hard.

She wasn't back there anymore. She hadn't lived in that dank sewer in years. She and Anera were free. And Lady Karaval's eyes didn't study her like they were trying to find every way to pry her open and scoop out her insides.

Not every noble is like Vamreth, she tried to tell herself. *Speak, Bex. You're going to lose them.*

Rowan glanced at her, brow furrowed. "Are you all right?"

Bex cleared her throat. "Fine," she grated.

Tera's eyes narrowed.

She had to do better than that. She pasted a bright smile on her face. "Sorry. Just... It's fine."

Rowan's gaze dropped to Bex's hand. The glove covered the bandages, but Bex let it fall to her side and hid it behind her hip, out of sight.

She gave Mellrea a slight bow, keeping all the mocking irony out of the movement. "Thank you for seeing us," she said, channeling all the manners she had.

"You're welcome. Whatever you are after must be important if Rowan agreed to help you."

"It is, my lady. The queen herself is very interested in the artifact, and her mage Slayter sent me after it."

Mellrea tilted her head.

Senji's spit, did she know the queen personally? Did all nobles talk amongst themselves? No, that was completely ridiculous, right? Mellrea had been busy here, rebuilding her father's town. And the queen was busy in the capital, doing... whatever it was that queens did.

"What is this artifact?" Mellrea said. "And why is it so important to the queen?"

Bex clasped her hands behind her back. "I'm sorry, I can't say. I'm sure you understand the value of secrecy when it comes to certain matters of state. There's a reason I was sent alone."

"So there'd be less of a path back to her if things don't go well?" Tera said with a snort.

Bex gave her a wink. "And because I'm discreet and good at what I do. So there's less of a chance of that happening."

Mellrea gestured to Rowan. "But you know what you're after?"

Rowan nodded. "Yes. And I can guess enough of the rest to know this is important, Mellrea."

"Important enough...?" She made a vague gesture like she was holding something up and swinging it to and fro.

Rowan seemed to know what she meant. "Yes," she said simply.

Bex would have given an arm to be in on the secret. But she made do with looking lofty and official, like someone who could command the country's best antiquarian to come out of hiding to help her.

"All right," Mellrea finally said. "What do you need?"

Bex started to pull the writ out, but before she could even wave it around, Rowan said, "Passage to Taur would help immensely. And I thought you both should come along. We still need a guard and someone with political clout would help in foreign territory."

Bex's stomach clenched, but before she could protest, Mellrea shook her head. "I can help with the passage. I have plenty of contacts in port who owe me a favor or three. But I will have to stay here. I'm brokering an alliance, and it means I'll be planning my wedding soon."

From the slight grimace that pulled at her lips, this was not a happy announcement.

And from the way the others all sucked in a breath and

glanced at Tera, it was the guard captain who would be the most affected by it.

Hmm, jilted lover? Bex stored that away for safekeeping. That must have been what their argument was about.

Tera's expression didn't change, at least not while the others watched her. But Bex was good at people. She knew to glance at Tera whenever Mellrea wasn't looking, and that's when she caught the most honest expressions on Tera's face. There was anger there, yes. But buried so deep under it that it was easy to miss was a long-standing pain and the type of sadness that built over years of watching something you knew you couldn't have. Not fully.

"Congratulations," Rowan said quietly like a mourner at a funeral.

"Thank you." Mellrea's hand stroked the sword on her desk before she pulled back and straightened her spine. "I can't come with you, but Tera should go. You will need her expertise."

"My duty is here," Tera started.

Mellrea turned to the wide window behind her where they could look out over the town. "Your guards are well trained. They'll protect me in your absence. And don't forget, you taught me yourself. I've kept myself alive before. I can do it indefinitely."

Tera twitched, like she was caught between strangling Mellrea and drawing her close. She did neither. She clasped her hands behind her and raised her chin. "Very well... my lady."

Later that night, when the others were all asleep in their fancy guest rooms and Bex was restless with the memories Mellrea had stirred up, she caught the murmur of voices down the hall from their rooms.

Slipping out such well-maintained doors was much nicer than in her part of the city where the floors creaked and the hinges squealed. She pressed her back against the corner of the wall and listened.

"It will all turn out all right," Mellrea was whispering. "I promise."

"How? How will it be all right?" Tera's voice was low and raw. "All right for you while I have to spend the rest of my life watching you with someone else? I've already spent years knowing this was coming. It did nothing to make me accept it like you apparently have."

"Tera, you know what this is doing to me."

Tera didn't answer.

"Please, trust me," Mellrea pleaded. "I have to do this, but it's not the end for us. I know it's not."

Tera said something low and growly that Bex couldn't catch.

"Then maybe it's better if you're not here to watch," Mellrea said, a bit of steel threading through the resignation.

Footsteps came toward her, and Bex slipped back to her room, her throat unexpectedly tight.

Chapter 17
Bex

Mellrea loaned them horses to get to the port. Bex had only been on a horse once or twice before, and she did her best to not do anything to fall off or spook the thing.

The noblewoman watched them ride away from the top of the outer wall, and Bex caught Tera looking back once and only once when they crossed the land bridge.

Bex tried to meet the guard captain's eyes as she turned back to face their road, but the other woman lifted her chin and glared at the horse in front of her. Bex rubbed the back of her head and gave up.

Their port lay just south of the crown city, a small town in a natural harbor with one dock. Obviously it didn't bustle the way the crown city did, but Mellrea's contact gave them no trouble and they were aboard and under way after a day spent provisioning.

As they cast off, Bex scanned her crew. Rowan spoke with the ship's captain, laughing as they planned their journey down the coast. Gavyn sat at her heels. Lynniki perched on the main hatch, turning a screw in something bright and shining in her hands. And Tera stood at the railing opposite Bex, staring across the water, her expression shuttered. Their team was now complete.

Bex had managed to collect a lead researcher, the researcher's guardian, a tinker, and a guard.

So what did that make Bex? Their manager? Or just the reason all of these people had left home?

She squared her shoulders. All she'd done was ask Rowan to join her. She hadn't forced anyone else to come. If Rowan said they needed them, then they needed them. She was just antsy because more people meant more chances for her secrets to slip out.

But if it saved Anera, it would all be worth it.

Bex spent the first few hours of their week-long journey standing at the rail, watching Usara pass beside them. She didn't need to dig out the map to know they would have to sail the whole way through the bay of Usara and out through the narrow opening past the Cliffs of Qhor before they could even begin to head south along the coast to Taur.

Her hands twitched on the railing, urging the ship to go faster. This was going to take forever. And she had very little room on the deck to pace.

A familiar clicking noise sounded on her right, and Gavyn came to stand beside her. He jumped his front legs up onto the railing so he could see over and stare at the passing landscape.

"Have you ever been outside of Usara?" Bex asked him. She'd thought he was just a construct made by Lynniki for Rowan, but the way he'd been greeted by the people in Karaval Keep proved he was more of a traveler than Bex had thought.

"I have not. I grew up in the crown city actually, and I've really only traveled the valley with Rowan and Lynniki."

Bex was startled enough to forget the antsy squirm in her gut. "You're from the city?"

He cocked his head at her, and she wondered if she was

just imagining the smirk in his voice. "Why is that so surprising?"

She narrowed her eyes. "Because I've spent most of my life there. How have I never heard of you? A brass dog would have turned the city upside down. Everyone would have know about it."

He snorted. "Well, I was born Human. And that was well over a hundred years ago."

Bex blinked trying to think of something to say to that. "You're looking good for your age?"

Gavyn barked a laugh.

Bex leaned her elbows on the railing and gave him her full attention. "All right. What's the rest? What are you exactly?"

"I am an unfortunate series of accidents," Gavyn said with a laugh that tasted bitter.

Bex waited, eyebrow raised. "I assume you're going to elaborate."

"I was a Land Mage," Gavyn said.

Bex immediately stiffened, but her mind caught on the word he'd used. *Was.* She'd never heard of a mage who'd stopped being a mage. But she'd also never heard of a brass dog.

"Land mages work with materials, right? Rock and metal but also fire and glass."

"You know a little about magic, then." Gavyn said.

Bex knew some, if only so she could avoid it. But she wasn't about to tell a mage that.

"I was kidnapped," he said. "Forced to work for someone who wanted some magic done."

Bex's jaw tightened. "A non-mage?"

"Yes."

Bex turned to hide her expression. She knew all about mages trapping and experimenting on non-mages. But she'd never heard of the opposite.

123

"I didn't know non-mages were powerful enough to do something like that to someone with magic."

"I was young. Inexperienced. And it just goes to show you the powerful will always exploit the weak."

She agreed, but she'd never thought of mages as weak before.

"When I tried to escape, I was trapped in a spell. A hundred years later, Rowan finally freed me."

Gavyn turned to face Rowan who was poring over Slayter's notes and had a book open on her knee.

"But by then my body had died, leaving my mind behind. So Lynniki built me a new one."

"And you're no longer a mage," Bex said.

"No." Gavyn hopped down from the railing. "Now I'm a brass dog." The words were clearly supposed to be a joke, but there was a pain under them she could hear in the tone of his voice even through the voice box.

Rowan called to him, and Gavyn trotted away without looking back, leaving Bex by the rail.

She could tell he'd left out tons of the story, but she didn't chase him down asking for the rest. Even if she really wanted to. She liked to know everything. It made steering people that much easier, and mysteries left holes she had to jump over.

But maybe if she pretended to believe their lies, they would be more willing to believe hers.

Bex tried not to chafe the entire time they were at sea. Some of the others spent a couple of days seasick, but Bex didn't even have that as a distraction.

Instead she spent the time learning her new companions.

Gavyn was hard to read, considering he had no face, but he'd willingly told her some of his story, and she was getting better at parsing his thoughts from the tone of his words.

Lynniki was the easiest to talk to. All you had to do to wind her up was ask a leading question, and she would happily ramble about her tools and trinkets and gadgets for hours. Bex even managed to learn a few things from her about magical traps and the spells Lynniki transplanted onto her contraptions.

Of the four of them, Bex figured Lynniki was the least likely to keep a secret, though she had managed to keep Rowan's whereabouts behind her teeth, so clearly she was capable.

On the other hand, Tera was monosyllabic.

Bex attempted to approach her exactly once in the entire trip.

The captain spent most mornings on deck, drilling in sword work as if she was still back in the keep protecting her mistress. The thought made bile fill Bex's mouth, but she swallowed it down. Maybe the captain would be more approachable now that they weren't near the noblewoman who held her strings.

Bex found a nice spot to lean against the railing to watch as the captain went through her drills, sweat soaking her linen shirt and shining along the muscles of her arms.

Bex tilted her head with a slight smile.

Tera stopped in the middle of one of her forms and dropped her arms to face Bex.

"What?" she snapped.

Bex tried to blink innocently. "Nothing. I was just watching."

"Why?"

"Because it's nice to see something pretty for a change." She gestured to the scenery which was mostly water and more water with the occasional spit of boring land in the distance.

Tera scowled.

Bex leaned her elbows on the railing behind her. "I adore competence, Captain. And you're clearly very good at what you do."

Tera's brows came down. She stalked toward Bex and Bex gulped.

Oh gods, did it work that well?

The captain leaned in, sword still naked in her hand. "You might have Rowan fooled. And you might have Lynniki fooled. But I know what you are."

Oh no. It worked that badly.

She gave Tera a tight smile. "And what is that?"

"Somehow you wormed your way to the top, enough to work for the queen," Tera said, eyes intent on Bex's face. "But once a thief, always a thief."

How the hell...?

Bex cocked her head, keeping the panic shut tight behind a quizzical smile. "That's a lot of name-calling. What did I ever do to you, Captain?"

Tera jerked her chin at Bex's hand. She'd left the gloves off today, but bandages still wrapped the right one.

"They brand thieves in the crown city. You should keep those gloves on next time you try to hide it."

Bex almost laughed in her face. This conversation had taken a turn for the ridiculous. The captain had no idea how right she was, but in all the wrong ways.

She schooled her expression to one of mild amusement. "Of course I was a thief," she said. "Almost everyone was where I grew up. You had to become a thief just to steal your stuff back on a daily basis. Does that make me less than you? No. It makes us equals. We both learned certain skills to survive. I may... acquire things. But you wormed your way to the top too. By sucking up to nobles."

Bex slid out from between Tera and the railing and straightened her vest with a tug. "And you're not nearly as perceptive as you think you are if you can't see that my true calling is people. I love seeing how they work."

She took her life in her hands and winked at the captain. "Thanks for the insight."

Tera stood frozen. There was always that telltale twitch of

the eyes when someone was caught between rage and incredulity.

Tera shook herself. "Flirt with me again and I toss you in the sea and forget to yell 'man overboard.'"

"Noted," Bex said as Tera stalked back belowdecks.

Rowan stepped up next to her and Bex let out a shaky laugh.

"Don't let her bother you," the antiquarian said. "She'll come around."

"Do I want her to?" Bex asked, wondering how much Rowan had heard.

Rowan turned her face into the wind, letting it blow dark blond curls out of her eyes. "She is a fierce friend once you get past that first wall."

Bex ran a hand through her hair. "I'll take your word for it."

Rowan fixed her with a look. "You should. She called me 'godsblighted' for days before she finally warmed up to me."

Bex winced. "Gods, I didn't know anyone still believed in that rebirth crap."

Rowan's smile went pained. "My village did. They believed I had done something to anger the gods, and that's why I'm like this." She gestured vaguely to her high shoulder and twisted spine.

"That's just dumb." Bex turned to face the sea alongside Rowan. "I don't think the gods care enough to smite anyone nowadays."

Rowan laughed like it had been surprised out of her.

"Of course, if they do, that means I'm probably gonna get it first."

Rowan widened her eyes. "Well, thank you for taking that on for the rest of us."

Without meaning to, Bex found herself flushing.

Rowan's gaze flicked away to the horizon, then back to Bex's hands lying lightly on the railing.

"Does it hurt?"

Bex drew her hands back to her sides. She couldn't help the instinctive movement.

"What?"

"Your hand. You keep it bandaged. Does it still hurt?"

Bex opened her mouth to say "no," then thought about the way it felt when she drained the magic out of some spell. The heat, the sting, and the unpleasant feeling of fullness in her chest.

"Sometimes," she said instead. "But it's an old kind of hurt."

"Hmm. I'm familiar with old pain." Rowan didn't meet her eyes again, staring out at the waves.

Bex stole a look at her profile, from her round face with its strong nose, down the curve of her neck to the crooked line of her spine. She could imagine all those bones and muscles twisted up inside didn't play nice together.

When her gaze returned to Rowan's face, she found Rowan's eyes on her again. Bex flushed again.

"It's all right," Rowan said. "You can't say anything I haven't heard before."

"Why did you become an antiquarian?"

Rowan blinked. She might have heard it before, but she hadn't been expecting it right then, clearly. The moment of surprise gave Bex a chance to get her gloves back on. And if someone was talking about themself, they were way less likely to pry into anything about her.

"Jannik believed in me when no one else did." Rowan's lips twisted in a self-deprecating smile.

Bex did not make the mistake of asking if she'd killed him again. Now that she knew the woman a little better, she couldn't figure out where that rumor had come from. Rowan would never have flat out killed a man to take an artifact. But if she hadn't, what had happened to Jannik? Why was Rowan keeping his weapon safe?

"You were right. He didn't appreciate me the way I thought he did, but that doesn't change the fact that he gave me the chance to learn and do something useful that didn't require physical strength. That was... incredibly important to me."

Bex snorted. "You can stop pretending to be an invalid. It's not working on me."

Rowan's face went slack. "What?"

Bex leveled a look at her. "When I came down your chimney, you attacked me. And you would have won, too, if I hadn't gotten you to stop swinging a sword. You were fully prepared to kill me, and I would have been dead. You're plenty strong."

Rowan's mouth worked for a moment before she burst out laughing. "I guess I made a good impression. It turns out some strength is learned, and you never know how far you can go until you absolutely have to."

"I'm just glad you're on my side now. I get a fighter and an antiquarian in one package."

Rowan tilted her head. "I'm still a better antiquarian. Speaking of, I've been looking over our notes and trying to figure out where to make our landing." She took out the sheaf of notes she constantly carried with her.

"I did notice there wasn't an actual location marked," Bex said, turning to look over her shoulder. "Just a general area."

"That's normal. Often we have to do a lot of research and investigation to find the best place to dig. The locals might be able to tell us more. There is supposed to be a port here." Rowan pointed on the map to the north side of the big island. "And if we go inland from there we should be in the right area at least."

"I'm mostly familiar with Human ruins. Places that haven't been buried as long. Places you can get into from the surface. Do you think we'll have to dig very far?"

"I won't know for sure until we see the site. I'm more worried about this." She pulled out the notes. "Your friend Slayter has made some notes here on something we might need to get in. Something he called a 'key of gathering.'"

"What does that mean?"

"I don't know. I've been looking into it with the books I've brought, but so far nothing has come up."

"Slayter might be smart, but he goes about a mile a minute and has a tendency to leave the rest of us behind. Maybe he missed something when he wrote it all down."

"Or maybe we don't have all the pieces of the riddle yet. We'll know more—"

"When we get there, yes. I get it." Bex heaved a sigh. "I've always hated waiting."

Chapter 18
Bex

Bex stood at the rail of the ship, watching the massive wall of inky blackness slide past them on their left. She wrapped her arms around herself, eyes locked on the noktum that floated there in the middle of the ocean like a smudge of ink smeared across the water.

"We... we won't get sucked in or anything, will we?" she asked the captain who stood beside her.

"Nah," he said, glancing up at the rigging and back again to the edge of the noktum. "We're well clear of it, and the wind's fair today. Unless it changes to the southwest, it won't blow us in."

It certainly didn't look like they were well clear of it to Bex. It was right there. And she couldn't take her eyes off of it.

She tried to tell herself she stared at it to show it she wasn't afraid, but her fingernails left marks on her elbows even through her sturdy linen shirt.

"Does it flow with the sea?" Rowan asked, tilting her head like she was really interested. Not like Bex, who hid a lifetime's worth of fear behind her words. "Or does it stay in one place like it's anchored."

"Stays in one place," the captain said. He sniffed and dragged his sleeve across his nose. "The water flows through it. I haven't been this far south, so I haven't seen this one personally. But I've skirted the edges of the Cursed Sea in Usara plenty of times. Got swept into it once too. Thought I was a goner when that black swallowed my ship. But we got lucky. The current carried us out again before anything could get us."

Rowan's glanced at him. "Are the monsters there as bad as the ones on land?"

The captain spit over the side with a grim look. "Worse."

Bex wanted to yell at them to stop talking. She wanted to clap her hands over her ears to block out their words. But that would only lead to questions she was absolutely not answering.

She strode to the other railing and fixed her gaze on the fuzzy bit of land that grew clearer and clearer as they drew closer.

"Look," Rowan said, and Bex could imagine her pointing. "There's a bridge. Between the land and the noktum."

Bex couldn't hide her shudder.

That was the worst part. Someone had wanted to get inside that place. Or maybe the bridge had been there when the noktum formed. Which was even worse. That meant someone had been trapped in there.

She could feel it. The ink,y black tentacles sliding over her skin and mouth, muffling her screams as it pulled her inside its impenetrable darkness. A pair of bells rang in her ears, incongruous and ethereal inside the memory.

She leaned over the side of the ship, gagging.

"Are you all right?" Rowan's hand settled on her back.

Bex shivered. She swallowed down the bile, closing her eyes and taking deep breaths, just like Anera had taught her. *In and out, focus on the things around you, like the smell of brine and seaweed and the feel of the smooth rail under your hands.*

"Fine," Bex finally said, and her voice only quavered a little.

She turned and the movement pulled her away from Rowan's touch. "Just a little seasick."

Rowan's brow bunched. "We've been at sea for over a week, and you haven't been sick once."

Damn it. Rowan was too observant and liked questions a little too much.

"Maybe it was something I ate, then," she said. "I already feel better." She straightened. She did feel a little better as the noktum slid behind them and the little port of Palmolivar came into view.

Rowan eyed Bex's clammy face, but Bex gave her a brave smile and turned to survey the docks. Their path lay inland. They didn't have to go anywhere near the noktum.

The thought finally let her unclench her hands from the railing.

By the time the ship docked, her team was ready to disembark. Gavyn carried nothing, of course, Tera wore a set of well-made leather armor all dyed black and had one rucksack with weapons strapped to it thrown over her shoulder. Lynniki wore a pack bigger than her hung all over with hammers and tools Bex didn't even have a name for.

Rowan tucked the notes into her satchel after one last look at them and gave Bex a broad smile.

"Welcome to Taur," Bex said and headed down the gangplank.

A mix of smells hit her nose. Brine and dried fish and a pungent array of spices she'd never encountered before. Something like cinnamon and cloves but earthier.

Big, white bricks made up the sea wall where the docks thrust into the water. Beyond, on dry land, stalls with brightly colored canopies sold fruits and vegetables and fish and who knew what else. There were so many lined up along the wharf between them and the rest of the town, Bex couldn't even count them all.

The similarities to home hit her first. It felt just like walking through the harbor district of the crown city.

But home had never included a seven-foot-tall muscled man with the broad head of a bull walking down the street.

The Taur-El lifted a stack of crates, three at once, and turned to catch her eye. "Greetings," he said, the voice coming from his enormous muzzle. A pair of gently curved horns rose from the coarse hair tufted between his ears.

"Hi," Bex said back, doing her best to hide the tremor that went through her when she realized this thing could snap her in half by sneezing.

He smiled and took his crates down the dock toward the town.

Bex blew out her breath. There, herds of Taur-Els mingled, merchants and shoppers alike. Only a few Humans walked among them and no Delvers at all.

"Wow," Lynniki said behind them as Bex led the way off the dock. The ground shifted under her feet, like the heaving deck of a ship, and she staggered before finding her balance.

All along the docks, smaller vessels waited, their triangular sails bound to their masts.

Beside a stall selling some sort of fish skewer that smelled amazing, a group of Humans stood. Demaijos traders, Bex gathered, from their dark skin and the brightly colored sacks they carried across their backs. They wore darkened glasses as they surveyed the scene.

"What first?" Tera asked, her gaze caught on the Demaijos traders. One of them, a tall, handsome woman with hair going gray at the temples looked her up and down in return.

"We need to find the ruins," Bex said. "The ones where the mirror is supposed to be."

"A local guide would be able to help with that," Rowan said, pulling out her notes. "And perhaps a better map."

Bex drew in a sharp breath as her gaze swept down the next

dock. Another ship had already drifted in beside theirs with the same round lines and square sails as Usaran vessels. A man stepped off the gangplank, directing the crew to place his things along the wharf. Even here on the docks he wore an expensive set of plate armor complete with a shiny breastplate, and his bright red hair glinted in the sunlight.

Bex hadn't gotten a look at more than his feet and the edge of his dressing gown before, but there was no mistaking the crest etched into the metal on his chest.

Sir Kerrickmore.

Bex swore under her breath.

"What is it?" Rowan said, and the others all glanced at her.

"Nothing," Bex said.

Rowan narrowed her eyes.

"All right. We have a slight problem," Bex conceded. "Can you guys find us a local guide? Maybe find out where to get provisions. Food, tents, shovels. That sort of thing. I'm going to handle this."

Bex moved to step away, but Rowan stopped her, reaching out as if to put a hand on her arm.

Bex sidestepped the hand but stopped anyway. "What?"

"Is everything all right?"

Bex opened her mouth to lie again and then blew out her breath. "It's fine. I promise. I'll take care of it. It's just..." Her mind whirred. "There's a fellow treasure hunter who wanted the job for the queen. I didn't want him to get it because I think he has ulterior motives."

Rowan's mouth went thin. "Oh. One of those."

"Yeah. Kind of like you thought I was." Bex flashed her a grin. "It looks like he's followed me here."

Rowan's eyes widened. "Oh no."

"It's fine," Bex said again. "I'm just going to make sure he can't keep following us."

"Bex..."

She sounded so much like Conell in that moment, her voice tinged with uncertainty and a little bit of judgment, that Bex had to suppress a stab of remembered guilt. Which was ridiculous.

"Look, this is part of the job," she said. A little harsher than she'd intended. "It's not just finding the thing. It's also protecting the thing from people who might want it for bad reasons."

She'd literally just made that up, but it sounded really good. Especially for someone like Rowan.

But Rowan bit her lip and looked aside. "Who decides which reasons are bad?"

"Right now?" Bex said, firming her mouth. "The queen, who asked me to do this."

She pushed, just a little bit. And finally Rowan nodded.

"Be careful," she said.

Bex cast a grin over her shoulder. "He won't even know I'm there."

She did have to be a little more careful than usual. In this land, she stood out more than at home. She was tall for a woman, but the Taur-Els all stood at least seven feet tall, if not more. She stuck out just by being a Human.

But so did Sir Kerrickmore, and she could follow his bright head and shiny armor through the streets of Palmolivar.

How to deflect him? Could she steal his map? Again. How many copies did he have now? Maybe she could just change the map so he headed in the wrong direction. But that would require stealing it, altering it, and then getting it back into his possession. And she had no idea how much time she had.

Sir Kerrickmore finally stopped at the opening of a building. The ceiling stood at least nine feet high, to accommodate the owner of the business, a huge Taur-El with a row of earrings along his left ear. Further back in the soft darkness of the building, Bex smelled straw and heard the quiet shuffling of horses.

She slinked closer, pressing her back against the wall as Sir Kerrickmore conversed with the Taur-El.

"How much for a week?" he asked.

"One beast for a week," the Taur-El responded. "Twenty gold."

She heard Sir Kerrickmore choke. "So much?"

The Taur-El chuckled. "My prices are reasonable."

Sir Kerrickmore sighed. "The captain said this was the only stable in Palmolivar."

"This is the only stable until you get to the capital. We don't have much use for horses here. They aren't big enough for us, and anything we need hauled we haul just as far and fast ourselves."

"Right," Sir Kerrickmore said. "I suppose that makes sense."

"Suppose away; it's the truth."

Bex could practically hear him wince. "Sorry," he muttered. "Can I reserve your beasts for the week, possibly for longer if it turns out my stay is extended?"

"All of them?"

"I will need six of the creatures and you appear to have five. So I will have to make do."

"Payment up front."

"Of course."

Money clinked as it changed hands.

"I'll send someone to collect them soon. I must return to the ship to make the rest of my preparations."

Bex scrambled to hide, but the alley beside the stable was filled with bales of hay and barrels that smelled of apples. She threw herself on one of the hay bales and deliberately picked her teeth as Sir Kerrickmore exited the building and turned onto the street.

He glanced her way, and she gave him a jaunty little wave. "Care to buy some apples, sir? Five for twenty gold!"

Sir Kerrickmore shook his head with a mutter. "Is everything so expensive here?" And he headed off toward the docks again.

Bex let herself chuckle out loud. This was perfect. He couldn't have set her up better if he'd been trying.

She waited just as long as seemed reasonable and then slipped into the stable.

The Taur-El was tossing hay into the horse stalls. He straightened when he saw her. "I'm sorry, I'm all out of beasts."

"Oh, I'm here for Sir Kerrickmore's horses," she said. "He sent me to fetch them for him. Five for the week, right?"

"Yes. I didn't expect you so soon. I thought it would be later."

Bex shrugged. "I met him on the way back."

"Efficient."

The horses came with saddles and bridles, and since leading five horses through the streets of Palmolivar would be awkward, she tied them in two strings and led one from each hand. All the way back to the docks.

She checked before stepping out onto the wharf but didn't see Sir Kerrickmore anywhere.

Rowan and the others stood with the traders from Demaijos and another Taur-El. This one wore earrings in both ears and a bright blue cloth the color of the sky draped around his torso and belted to form a wrapped covering around his waist. So far none of the Taur-Els she'd seen had worn boots or sandals, but this one's massive hooves were shod in a set of bright, metal horseshoes. Or were they Taur-El shoes?

"Bex," Rowan said. "You're back. This is Brightstrike. He is going to lead us to his home where we can speak with his elders."

Bex checked over her shoulder toward Sir Kerrickmore's ship. "Great. I got us some horses."

Tera was still talking with the Demaijos traders, but Gavyn cocked his head at their new mounts. "Why five?"

Bex grinned at him. "I didn't want you to feel left out."

Chapter 19
Rowan

Their new Taur-El guide led them through the streets and out a pair of gates flanked by two enormous, bronze statues of bull-headed men. Beyond the gates stretched a sea of grass, waves of gold and green undulating in the breeze. Far, far on the horizon, Rowan could make out mountains and a darker green smudge that could have been forest, but here there was nothing but low hills marching away from them.

Rowan still couldn't get over the fact that this wasn't Usara. It wasn't even the main continent of Noksonon. She'd never thought she would leave the sanctuary again, let alone travel so far. She did her best to sit as straight as her crooked spine would allow and not look like a tourist, but she had the sneaking suspicion that her wide-eyed expression gave her away.

She was glad Bex had found some horses. The Taur-El strode with purpose, his long legs moving in ground-eating strides, leaving the rest of them to hurry to keep up. The traders from Demaijos traveled with them, but they'd brought their own mounts.

Tera had introduced the older woman as Hunaa, and she'd told them that Demaijos traded with Taur often, bringing their goods to the towns and people here.

Tera seemed fascinated. Rowan kept an anxious eye on the captain who had been quiet ever since leaving Mellrea. Rowan had tried to talk to her about what had happened back at the keep, but Tera had made it clear she was not going to comment on Mellrea's upcoming nuptials or how she felt about them.

Rowan's heart ached for the captain. She and Tera had taken a while to come to an understanding, but the other woman had been the first one to give Rowan a sword and teach her how to use it. Not because anyone had made her, but because she'd seen Rowan's determination and figured she'd earned it. People didn't earn respect from the captain easily, and it was a friendship Rowan cherished all the more for its difficult beginning.

Now Tera rode with the traders. She was quiet as usual, but anytime Hunaa posed a question, Tera answered it without her normal grumbling.

Rowan bit her lip and nudged her horse faster to catch up with Bex and the Taur-El, Brightstrike.

"Wait," Bex was saying. "What do you mean you've never seen so many females traveling together? Do you lock yours up or something?"

Rowan glanced at her. "Bex, that is extremely insensitive."

Brightstrike lifted his head. Sitting on her horse, Rowan was nearly tall enough to look him in the eyes.

"We do not lock them up," Brightstrike said. "We simply do not have them."

Rowan blinked. "What?"

"We do not have male and female the way Humans do. We have only Taur-El." His voice rumbled from a deep chest.

"You mean only one gender?" Rowan thought back to the Taur-Els in Palmolivar, trying to remember any that didn't have horns or had a different body type than the burly build and muscled arms and legs. Only now did it become obvious that she hadn't seen any variation at all besides clothes and jewelry.

"Huh," Bex said, her gaze distant as if going through the same process in her head.

"But you still prefer we use the word 'he' when we talk about you?" Rowan asked. The Taur-El hadn't corrected her yet so it seemed a safe bet.

"Yes. It is the most accurate because it is the closest parallel to the bodies the Giants gave us. But it does not have the same distinction between individuals in our society as it does in yours. It is simply a word."

Bex's mouth screwed up in a rueful smile. "That must be nice. Not having to fight over things because your society is divided down the middle. Sounds sophisticated."

Brightstrike snorted through his nostrils. "I did not say we are not divided. Only that the division is not based on what is between our legs."

Rowan kept her gaze locked on the road ahead of them. *I'm not asking. I'm definitely not asking.*

"So how do you make little baby Taur-Els?" Bex said.

"Bex!" Rowan cast her a scandalized look.

"What? You can't tell me you don't want to know."

Brightstrike met Bex's eyes. He had a clear gaze with thick, curved horns rising from his head, and suddenly Bex gulped. Maybe she realized it wasn't a great idea to poke fun at someone who could squash you with one hoof if you annoyed them.

"We procreate the same way Humans do," he said.

Bex raised her eyebrows.

"Privately." Brightstrike's wide muzzle twitched in what was probably mirth.

Bex broke out in a wide grin. "Point taken."

"How did this come to be?" Rowan asked, trying to keep

her attention on Brightstrike while rolling her eyes at Bex at the same time.

"Why can it not just be?" Brightstrike asked.

"I suppose it can," Rowan said with a thoughtful look. "But while I know very little about Taur-Els, I do know they are a created race like the Delvers." She gestured to Lynniki and herself.

"And the Giants always had a reason for the things they made," Lynniki said, still trying to arrange her shorter legs on the horse so they fell comfortably. "We don't always agree with their reasons or understand them. But they're there. Delvers were supposed to mine Mavric iron. They built us to be immune to its toxicity."

That alone had saved Rowan's life over and over again. Her elbow brushed the lantern's case in a habitual gesture that reassured her that it was still there.

The Taur-El lifted his gaze to the sky, letting the sun fall across his face. "Perhaps then you understand what it's like to be created for a purpose that is no longer needed."

Lynniki exchanged a rueful glance with Rowan. "Intimately."

"The Taur-Els were created as warriors. We were the vanguards for their armies. Our battle frenzy knew no equal. But they did not need anything other than that. Once they created the perfect warrior, there was no need for variation. Only the same thing copied over and over. And since they controlled our creation, there was no need for male or female."

"Ouch," Bex said. "That's brutal."

Brightstrike fixed her with a look again. "Indeed."

"The more I learn about the Giants, the more I realize they were just really big bastards," Bex muttered to herself.

In the distance, a white haze grew into the square walls of a sprawling town built with the same light-colored brick as the wharf had been.

"Welcome to Auli'poli," Brightstrike rumbled.

There were no walls or gates here. Just a city on the open plain with buildings spilling across the grasslands and the fields where Taur-Els worked between hills of waving grain and tall, green stalks of some vegetable Rowan couldn't name.

Near the outer buildings where the colorful awnings turned into solid, white stone buildings, a figure waited, its hand raised to shield its eyes.

This was not a Taur-El. For one thing, she stood only four feet high, and her skin was a bright white gold. Stark, black horns rose elegantly from her forehead.

"A Brightling," Rowan breathed.

"A what?" Bex said.

There was a time when Rowan had thought *Luminents* were no more than a myth. But here was something even more rare.

Sure Brightlings had to be as prevalent as Shadowvar in their homeland near the Luxe. But Rowan had never thought to meet one. Ever.

"There you are," the Brightling called. "I thought you were never ever getting back."

Brightstrike didn't slow, but he inclined his head to the other creature, and the Brightling spun and skipped alongside him.

"Who are these?" she asked. "Where did you find them?"

"Travelers," Brightstrike answered with a grunt.

Rowan gave the Brightling a little wave. "Hello."

The Brightling's eyes went round. "Wow, Humans."

"You've seen Humans before," Brightstrike said.

"And they're just as exciting every time."

Brightstrike suppressed a smile. "This is Suncall," he said to the rest of them.

"It's nice to meet you," Rowan said. "You're the first Brightling we've ever met."

"We don't get out much," Suncall said.

"Do you live here on Taur?"

The Brightling's face fell for just a moment. "I do now." She shook off the mood and spun so she could walk backward through the streets. "The Taur-Els sort of adopted me. They even gave me a name. I like it better than the old one so I'm keeping it. And Brightstrike lets me stay with him. It's much better than home."

As they passed the fields and into the town itself, it became clear that nearly a third of the outer city was all workshops. Blacksmiths, dyers, and tanners all worked in the open fronts of their shops. Further in, painters and sculptors and jewelers dominated rows of artisans. Hardly any building stood more than a story tall, but each was built to comfortably fit the greater height and bulk of the Taur-Els.

Suncall skipped along next to Brightstrike, barely coming up to his waist, but she didn't seem to mind as she grinned up at the Taur-El. And he smiled indulgently down at her.

Lynniki gasped and pulled her horse to a stop in the middle of the street. Through the open door of a nearby shop, a Taur-El hunched over a workbench, molding tiny bits of bronze and copper and iron into delicate flowers. He held one up to admire his handiwork then tucked it into a bouquet of others, each one unique and exquisite.

"Can we stop?" Lynniki said. "Just for a second?"

Rowan glanced between the Delver and Brightstrike's receding form. "We can come back, Lynniki."

"There's just so much to look at. Everyone's making something, and it's all different."

In the middle of the city's center, they came to a wide square. Gleaming, marble statues lined the space, making an open promenade through the center.

Rowan craned her neck as they passed under the nearest, trying to see the face of the Taur-El. This one depicted a creature with a wise expression wearing a wrap of fabric long enough to drape over the stone at his feet.

The one beside it held a gemstone up to the light and wore a pair of spectacles across his wide nose.

The next held nothing, but his head was bent and his eyes closed as if taking a deep breath before speaking.

"Who are they?" Rowan asked. Each one had been carved lovingly and bore impressive details.

Brightstrike glanced up as they passed the statues. "They are the Revered. Great artisans and thinkers who shaped Taur-El history with their innovations. There's Luminthread." He gestured to the one in the wrapped garment. "A great weaver. Jadecaller, who fashioned a new way to set jewels. And Loreweaver the historian. Among others." He turned his hand to indicate the rest.

"You seem to value creators," Rowan said as Bex pulled her horse up to study the gemstone one was holding. "People who make things and discover."

"We value individuality," Brightstrike said, continuing on under the stares of the Revered.

"They like to find the differences in people," Suncall said over her shoulder. "What makes them unique." She said in a stage whisper, "Even their names are a reference to their individual talents. And sometimes they'll give you one if they like you enough."

She grinned up at Brightstrike. Brightstrike reached out and pushed her shoulder. The blow, which had seemed light for a Taur-El, staggered the Brightling, and she stumbled away across the street before laughing and trotting back.

Tera narrowed her eyes at the line of statues. "None of your Revered are warriors."

Brightstrike glanced back at her, mouth going thin and flat. "No," he said and didn't elaborate.

A building rose at the end of the square, long and low to the ground with great pillars supporting the roof on all sides. It didn't appear that big until they rode up to it and realized the front door was tall enough Rowan could stand on Tera's shoulders and not hit her head.

"You may leave the horses here," Brightstrike said.

The Demaijos traders said goodbye, heading for their own destination, and Tera watched them go with a frown creasing the skin between her eyebrows.

Rowan climbed down from her horse with a wince.

From the exterior of the building, Rowan expected grand halls and a soaring throne room. But the interior was modest, with warm wood paneling and colorful rugs softening the floors. The room Brightstrike led them to was a large council chamber made cozy with wall hangings and enormous chairs upholstered in green brocade.

Two Taur-Els conversed, one in a loose tunic with wide open sleeves that was belted at the waist and another in a garment that draped his shoulders like an open robe. He wore nothing underneath as if there was nothing to hide. And after a quick glance, Rowan decided there actually wasn't. The Taur-El's broad chest was bare, but below that was only a thick pelt of fur.

The one in the tunic looked up as they entered. His brows came down as he noticed the Humans trailing into the room.

"Heif Brightstrike," the Taur-El said.

Rowan wasn't an expert on Taur-El expressions, especially since their faces were so different from Humans, but she thought this Taur-El greeted Brightstrike with a hint of wariness. Or maybe it was something more complicated. Regret or worry tied together.

Brightstrike inclined his head and gestured to Bex and Rowan and the others. "Apologies for the interruption, Koa Lightway. I've brought you visitors from Usara."

He beckoned them forward. Rowan let Bex step ahead of

her; she was the one who'd gathered them and led them, even if Rowan had more expertise as an antiquarian.

"This is one of our Guides," Brightstrike said. "Wise Taur-Els who lead us. Koa Lightway serves on the council in the capital when not here in Auli'poli."

"Koa?" Bex said carefully.

Lightway, the one in the tunic, stepped forward and rested his hands on the back of one of the chairs. "It is merely a title. A term of respect," he said, then he cocked his head with a small smile. "It means I have children. 'Heif' is the title for one without."

Rowan cast a quick glance at Brightstrike wondering if this was the division between Taur-Els that he'd mentioned earlier.

Bex inclined her head. "Well met, Koa. I'm Bex, and this is my team. We've come from Usara."

"You are not just Humans," Lightway said, casting a glance at Brightstrike who lifted his head. "You are Delvers as well."

Bex turned slightly to indicate Rowan and Lynniki. "Yes?"

Rowan gave her a bright smile then turned it on Lightway. "I'm Rowan. I'm half Delver. And this is my aunt Lynniki."

"Welcome, siblings." Lightway bowed deeply. "We acknowledge you as fellow creations of the Giants. And welcome to the rest of you as well." He cast a mildly curious look at Gavyn but nothing as startled as the looks the group had gotten in port just before they'd left.

"Why have you traveled to Taur?" Lightway's companion said. "We get some Humans coming through Palmolivar and Yammen on the other side of the island, but not many."

"This is Heif Mythspeak," Lightway said. "One of our most respected historians."

Bex nodded to the Taur-El in the robe. "Nice to meet you. Rowan serves as our historian. You two would get along great."

Rowan blinked as Bex gave her a wide grin.

"We've come looking for something," Bex continued.

"According to our studies, there is a place of great importance to our history nearby, and we would love to study it."

Rowan bit her lip. That wasn't exactly right. She could see why Bex would... obscure the truth if she thought the Taur-Els wouldn't like them poking around in their lands. But lying about it outright made Rowan's gut squirm.

"What is this place you are looking for?" Lightway said.

Bex glanced at Rowan, and she stepped forward. "We're not certain of its exact location. Only a general area. But we're sure it would be a nuraghi. A ruin of the Giants. Possibly a large one. Are there any ruins nearby?"

Lightway tilted his head to fix them with a calculating look. "Mythspeak?" he said.

Mythspeak gave the group a grave nod. "You are looking for the Shattered Waves."

"Shattered Waves?" Bex said.

"It is a bay to the west of Auli'poli," Lightway said. "The shallow waters are littered with nuraghis, almost as far as the eye can see. If yours is anywhere nearby, it would be there. But..."

"It is forbidden," Brightstrike said.

"Of course it is," Lynniki muttered.

Lightway held up a broad hand, forestalling Rowan's disappointment.

"It is a place forbidden to Taur-Els," Lightway said. "But outsiders are free to go. You plan to enter this place?" He spoke to Bex and the others, but his gaze rested on Brightstrike for a moment.

"This is why I brought them to you," Brightstrike said.

Bex glanced between them before answering. "I guess that depends. Why are outsiders allowed but Taur-Els are forbidden?"

A very good question.

Rowan expected some secret or prevarication, but

Lightway lifted his chin and met Rowan's eyes. "The area renders us incapable of having children."

Rowan's mouth fell open. "Oh."

"How?" Bex asked.

"It is specific to the magic that helped create the Taur-Els," Lightway said. "Therefore it would have no effect on other races. We would have no problem with you going into the nuraghis there. But you will not find any Taur-El willing to sacrifice future children for an excursion into the ruins."

This wasn't terrible. They could still reach their goal and find the mirror. Rowan tried to suppress the itchy feeling of Bex's lie, but it scratched at her, like a spot between her shoulder blades she couldn't reach.

"If we find what we're looking for," she said. "A specific artifact left by the Giants. We would likely take it with us. Is that all right?"

Bex hissed between her teeth and cast her a glare that Rowan easily interpreted as "what did you tell them that for?"

She understood. Now that she'd asked, the answer could be "no." But Rowan couldn't come into someone else's home and steal the first important find she came across. And if the Taur-Els were anything like the Delvers, it would be a moot point.

Lightway fixed her with a glance. Maybe he was impressed by her honesty? "We do not revere our creators. We do not hold their objects as sacred. In fact, many of them are dangerous, and we don't like our people exposed to them."

Rowan inclined her head. They were just like the Delvers, then. That would make things easier.

"However," Lightway said, eyes narrowing. "Everything has value. Even if it is only knowledge of what to avoid."

"That's surprisingly sensible," Lynniki said, who saw the Delver's stance on Giants as more of an irritation than a stricture.

"Perhaps you would be willing to exchange services. Value for value."

"What did you have in mind?" Bex said warily. Her hand crept to the purse hanging from her belt, and Rowan assumed she was worried about the dwindling funds Mellrea had sent with them.

"I believe this is why Heif Brightstrike brought you," Lightway said. "He might be a smith by trade, but he has the mind of some of our great generals."

Brightstrike did not look like he had received a compliment. His mouth went hard, and his gaze locked somewhere on the opposite wall.

"Why?" Bex asked.

Lightway stepped back and gestured Mythspeak forward.

"Will you listen to a tale? I hope it will inform your choices," the Taur-El said.

The words had the feeling of ritual. Bex and Rowan both nodded. Suncall let out a happy little squeal and hopped into one of the massive chairs to listen.

"As with our siblings, the Delvers, Taur-Els are created beings. Except we were not created to multiply. We were created to fight the wars of our masters. They did not need individuals, only masses. Therefore they made us without the ability to create more of ourselves, so we could not rise against them. If we did, we would dwindle and die out without the secret of the magic that created us.

"When the Giants fell, the Taur-Els had to learn how to procreate on our own without the control of our former masters. The first of us were all but extinct by the time we finally learned the secret of creating our own children."

Lynniki tilted her head. "How is it done? The Delvers are a created race, too, but we faced... other problems."

Lightway's mouth twitched. "You'll forgive us for keeping

that to ourselves. It is a Taur-El secret now. No one will be able to take it from us again."

Lynniki shrugged. "That's fair."

Mythspeak gave her a knowing smile. "What you may know is that it takes a group of Taur-Els willing to take on the strength and patience required of parents. Two Taur-Els, sometimes more, sometimes only one if they're determined, gather in a place of power and perform our ancient rites. The place lends power to their will, and a new Taur-El is created to be reared by those who chose to become their parents."

"The place lends power to their will," Lynniki repeated. "Excuse me, I'm not trying to guess your secret, but that sounds like you're still using Giant magic. And Giant magic requires a lot of energy. Especially to create new beings. The power requirements would be astronomical."

Instead of looking annoyed, Lightway extended a hand as if agreeing. "You've sliced right to the heart of our problem." He cocked his head. "Tell me, do you have the resistance that the Delvers are famed for? Either of you?"

Rowan spread her hands. "We do. Even half-Delvers can handle Giant artifacts and Giant magic without danger."

Bex looked at her, then glanced down at Rowan's hands.

Lightway lowered his chin. "You are sure?"

Gavyn chuckled softly through his voice box as Lynniki and Tera both glanced at Rowan with suppressed smiles.

"I'm sure," Rowan said without needing to elaborate. She dug her elbow into the lantern's case on her hip.

Lightway pressed both hands onto the back of the chair, gripping until his knuckles went white even through the dark hair that covered his hands.

"You said that was the heart of your problem. The power requirements," Lynniki said. "Your place of power is dying, isn't it?"

"Yes. After two thousand years, the source is failing. We

have never been a prolific species after everything the Giants did to keep us suppressed. But our numbers are dwindling even more. Our ritual fails more often than it succeeds. You will notice very few calves in our streets and fewer and fewer koas."

"I'm sorry," Bex said.

"Shh." Lynniki held a finger to her lips. "They're getting to the part where we can help."

Bex frowned at her, but Lightway chuckled. "Indeed. We know the Giants made more of these power sources. We believe one of them is in the Shattered Waves. In one of the nuraghis you wish to enter. That is why the Giants barred us from it. But we do not have the resistance to Giant magic that the Delvers were made with. Even if a brave soul sacrificed their right to a family and went to fetch it, the power source would kill them."

"Probably even before they made it back," Lynniki said, tapping her lips. "It can happen very quickly."

Rowan could see the moment it dawned on Bex what the Taur-Els were asking for. Her eyes widened a little.

"If you were willing to enter the ruins and collect this power source for us," Lightway said. "We would let you take any other artifacts with you and help you in any way we could. Apart from actually entering the nuraghi."

Chapter 20
Bex

When the Taur-Els first mentioned a trade, Bex had thought it was a really bad idea. She was not prepared to pay or bribe their way to the nuraghi. But trading an artifact for a power source? That seemed like a pretty fair deal. And Bex didn't need both. The Taur-Els could keep their power source, as long as she could take the mirror back to Anera.

I guess it's a good thing I brought along so many Delvers. She glanced at Rowan. She wasn't sure if the antiquarian knew that she'd been beaming since they'd gotten off the boat. Clearly, Rowan was in her element, taking in everything, from the intricate carvings on the armrests of the chairs, to the pattern of the rug at their feet.

To be fair, I had nothing to do with it. It's a good thing Rowan *brought everyone along.*

Bex cocked her head at Lynniki and Rowan. "This affects you two most of all," she said quietly. "What are you thinking?"

Lynniki answered first. "I should be able to recognize what they're looking for easily enough. I call it a power well. I'd love to see one firsthand," she said. "And we have a couple of things

154

we can do to make it safe for other people to be around." There was another subtle glance at Rowan.

What exactly had they been working on in that sanctuary? A way for someone else to wield Jannik's weapon?

Rowan saw Bex's puzzled glance, and she gave her a brief, dazzling smile. "I'm fine with it. More than fine. We have the means to help these people, and we must."

Must they? They knew where they were going now. They could just go without permission. Grab the mirror, and sneak away back to Usara. But...

Rowan was looking at her, eyes big and expectant. An odd urge in Bex's gut made her want to do anything Rowan said as long as she turned that smile on her again.

Bex shook her head to snap out of it. Like she'd thought before, it wouldn't hurt them to help these people. They had the means, and it wasn't out of their way, and if it meant the Taur-Els would help them in return, then it would make their journey easier in the long run.

She turned back to Lightway and Mythspeak. "We'll try to find your power source," she said. "And if we can, we'll bring it back for you."

Lightway inclined his head, placing his hand over his heart. "Thank you," he said. "And we will provide anything you need in terms of tools, provisions, and guidance. If you can think of anything we can help with, you have only to ask."

Rowan tapped her lip. "I was hoping to hire diggers to accompany us, but I suppose that's out of the question. Wait, I know." She gave Mythspeak a bow. "Do any of your stories tell of a... a thing called a 'gathering key'?"

Mythspeak's gaze went distant as if tracing the patterns on the wall hangings behind them. "No. I do not believe I've ever heard of such a thing. At least not in our local stories. There is however a story that speaks of the resting place of the 'gathering.'"

Rowan's brow furrowed. "Like a name? Something or someone named 'the gathering?'"

"We always assumed it was a tomb for a group of people. But perhaps it is referring to the same thing as your key."

"Where is it?"

Mythspeak smirked. "Do you believe in coincidence? It refers to a nuraghi in the Shattered Waves."

Bex snorted. "Coincidence or a trail of clues?"

Mythspeak laid a thick finger along his nose.

"Which nuraghi is this?" Rowan asked. "Will we be able to find it?"

"I will lead you there," Brightstrike rumbled from the side where he'd been waiting with Suncall.

Lightway sucked in a breath, and Mythspeak's chin jerked up. "Brightstrike."

Brightstrike met Lightway's gaze. "I will travel with our new friends. I will act as their digger, enter the Shattered Waves, and ensure their search is successful."

"You cannot," Lightway said. "Brightstrike, it will be the death of your future."

"Is not the future of Taur more important than mine alone?"

"You will be sacrificing the ability to have any children of your own."

Brightstrike straightened, face an implacable mask. "You know I will never choose children now." His words rang out, each its own death knell. "My fertility is already forsaken. It is not a sacrifice."

"Think about this, Brightstrike," Mythspeak said. "It is not a choice you can undo."

"The choice has already been made," Brightstrike said.

Lightway lowered his sad gaze. "You are a pillar of stone that has already withstood so much pain. I worry that you are isolating yourself. I know why, but be careful that you do not cut yourself off so much that your pillar topples."

Brightstrike did not speak. He only stood, eyes fixed over Lightway's shoulder.

Lightway sighed and raised his gaze again. "Very well. May your sacrifice be honored among our people. You may go. I wish you the best of luck."

* * *

Collecting supplies and gearing up for an extended dig took the rest of the day, and they had to stay overnight in Auli'poli. Lightway allowed them to sleep in the guesthouse across the square from the meeting rooms where they'd spoken.

The delay chafed at Bex. She had no idea how far behind Sir Kerrickmore was and how long it would take him to find his way to Auli'poli and the Shattered Waves. But it only made sense to prepare before heading into danger. Even at her most reckless, Bex had always taken the time to provision herself before jumping into a ruin.

Brightstrike remained with them, and Bex wondered if he had a home to go back to. He didn't seem anxious to say his goodbyes to anyone.

In the morning, Suncall woke them with knock on the carved, wooden door. She greeted Bex with a bright smile when she opened it.

"Hello," she sang. "Are you ready to invade the forbidden zone?"

Bex rubbed her eyes. She'd been so anxious to leave Auli'poli that she hadn't slept well in the huge bed. "I suppose." She squinted at the Brightling, who had a light pack slung over her back. "Are... are you coming too?"

Suncall tilted her head and gave Bex a look that made her

wonder if that had been a ridiculous question or not. "Of course."

And without another explanation, Suncall pushed inside and perched on one of the Taur-El sized chairs until they were ready to depart.

"I think she's attached to Brightstrike," Rowan said as they loaded up the horses. Suncall chattered about nothing, circling the big Taur-El as he stood still and stoic at the corner of the guest house.

Bex snorted. "Ya think?" She climbed aboard her horse and double-checked her packs. "We have everything? Food, bedrolls, tents, tools. What about maps? Do we have an updated map of the area?"

Brightstrike led the way out of the guest house stables and into the bright square of Auli'poli. He wore a large hammer across his back. "I am the map," he said.

Rowan grinned. "Thank you, Brightstrike."

Bex rolled her eyes. "Sure, yeah," she muttered. "I'd still like something I can hold in my hand."

The square remained as it had been the day before except for one thing. Workers surrounded one of the statues at the end of the row. They were eerily silent as they wrapped ropes around the figure resting its large hand on a pickax. With a heave, they hauled it off its pedestal.

"What are they doing?" Rowan asked.

Brightstrike turned away from the scene, leading them down a street away from the workers. "They are removing Revered Stonesinger."

They all glanced over their shoulders at the statue as it swayed.

"Why?" Tera asked.

"He gave in to the frenzy," Brightstrike said. "He has been exiled."

Behind them, a loud crash rang out across the square.

Suncall flinched. Brightstrike remained staring straight ahead.

Bex glanced back to see pieces of the white statue scattered across the ground.

She turned back to find Rowan had been looking as well. They exchanged a look full of raised eyebrows.

Brightstrike said nothing more about it as he led them out of the city and across the wide plains to the northwest. Here, Taur-Els labored in the fields, passing between cramped rows of waving stalks, checking the tasseled heads of their crops. But around midmorning the cultivated fields fell behind them, leaving only rolling hills of golden grass.

They stopped for lunch beside the only break in the scenery for miles. An outcropping of rough stone jutted up from the waving sea of grass, like a dock at the edge of the sea.

"How far is it?" Bex said, standing on top of the rock on her tiptoes, shielding her eyes with her hand. "I can't see anything."

"The Shattered Waves lie there, in a bay on the edge of Taur," Brightstrike said, pointing more west than north. "We will be there before nightfall."

"Thank you for guiding us, Brightstrike," Rowan said as Bex pursed her lips and grumbled inwardly at the distance. She hopped down and scarfed the rest of her cheese.

"It is no trouble." Brightstrike gave the rest of his bread to Suncall and stood, picking up the hammer that was almost as long as Bex was tall.

"Apparently it's a lot of trouble," Bex said. "At least for people worried about following the rules." She cocked her head at Brightstrike.

Brightstrike returned her look with a mild one. "It depends on the consequences for breaking the rules," he said. "Some are there for a good reason. Like exile after indulging in the frenzy."

"And losing your fertility by exploring a Giant's ruin?"

"Yes."

"But you came anyway."

"Because the consequence no longer applies to me. I choose not to reproduce. Therefore I have nothing to lose."

"Why?" Bex asked.

His chest rumbled, and for a second, Bex worried he was growling at her. Then she realized the big Taur-El was chuckling. "Shall I ask why you have no children?"

Bex grinned and shrugged. "I haven't found anyone who can keep up with me yet. Or anyone I want to slow down for." She extended a hand toward Brightstrike. "There. Now you."

He inclined his head. "I did find someone," he said. "And he is no longer here."

"Oh." Bex deflated. "I'm sorry."

"I could choose another, as Lightway hopes. But I will not."

"You could do it alone," Bex said. "Isn't that what Mythspeak said. One Taur-El can go through the ritual if they're determined enough."

"Would *you* make that choice... alone?"

It wasn't the same thing at all, but her mind went to Anera. She could easily imagine what it would be like to walk into that little, rented room and find her sister gone, finally and forever. What would she do next? Would there even be a next?

Brightstrike didn't seem to expect a response. He slung the hammer over his back and started across the open grasslands.

The rest scrambled to mount their horses, but Bex stood for a moment, chest aching.

"What happened to him?" she asked Suncall before the Brightling could catch up to the Taur-El. "Brightstrike's someone?"

Suncall looked at Brightstrike's retreating back and bit her lip. "He was killed on the way between the capital and Auli'poli. It should have been an easy trip. But exiles threaten the route now where there were none before."

She skipped to catch up, leaving Bex behind.

Chapter 21
Bex

By midafternoon, Brightstrike led them to the Shattered Waves. Bex heard them before she saw them, a roaring, rushing sound like the wind across the rooftops of the crown city during a storm.

They came over the hill and looked down where the land sloped to the sea. On their right, the island stretched around to a point off to the north, and to their left, it curved gently, leaving a great cove in the middle. A bay big enough to fit Usara's entire crown city inside.

Throughout the shallow water of the bay rose pinnacles of rock.

Bex squinted. No. Those were ruins.

Her heartbeat sped up. Tumbled towers stood in the surf, and half-fallen walls seemed to lead to nowhere. The waves crashed around them, rushing over the stones on their broken way to the shore, then sucking past them on their way out again.

Bex could see at least three different nuraghis spaced across the entire bay, and she could only imagine there were more she couldn't see out in deeper parts of the water. Even here on the closest part of the beach, a maze of stone lines broke up the sand, and Bex finally realized she was looking at the walls of a building half in the water, half on the beach.

Bex laughed out loud, and the wind sweeping up the hill whipped the sound away over her shoulder.

Rowan glanced at her with a grin. "What?"

"I have a new favorite ruin." Bex threw her hand out to indicate the bay.

"Which one?" Lynniki said, pulling her horse up on the crest of the hill. "There have to be at least five I can count."

"They didn't normally build their dwellings so close to each other," Rowan said. "I always figured the Giants preferred space from each other. I wonder why these are so close."

"Perhaps this place was special to them somehow," Lynniki said. "Maybe it had more power, or it was defensible."

"Then it would make sense they would hide the mirror here." Bex raised a hand to shield her eyes, trying to guess which nuraghi housed their prize.

"There." Brightstrike pointed. "In the center. Our warnings and our stories all point to that area as the source of our suffering. If there is anything important hidden, it will be there."

The nuraghi he pointed to was nearly obscured by the spray of the waves. Clouds had rolled over the sky in the last couple of hours, giving the whole scene a gray cast with the dark rocks of the nuraghis slashing through the white foam of the waves.

But out in the center, a pinnacle of black rock rose out of the water, square and squat, and if she squinted, Bex was sure she could see an archway.

She snorted. "We should have hired divers. Not diggers."

"Yeah, the Shattered *Waves* part should have been a clue." Tera scowled down at the half-submerged ruins.

Bex frowned at her, but the guard captain didn't even notice.

They'd actually been doing well. They'd found the place within a day of landing on the island. And they had a local guide to help. That should be enough to cheer anyone up.

Tera didn't seem to care about any of that. She swung a leg over her horse and hopped to the ground. "Where are we heading?" she said. "Where is this key thing?"

Brightstrike lowered his hand to point at the closest nuraghi. "There. That is the Gathering Tomb."

Bex's mouth twisted. "Tomb?"

"Mythspeak did say resting place," Rowan said, but her brows had come down, shadowing her eyes with concern.

"Great," Tera muttered.

Bex cracked her fingers. "Don't worry, Captain. Tombs are my specialty."

"Only because you were a grave robber in another life."

Bex snorted. "Or maybe *this* life."

She skipped down the hill as Tera sputtered behind her. Who cared where she'd gotten her expertise? It would serve them well now. A Giant's tomb couldn't be that different from a Human's.

Tera set up a picket line for the horses as the rest of them waded into the surf to check out the nuraghi for the first time. The first bit of rain pattered across the bay, and the wind whipped the surface to a froth further out.

Water soaked Bex's boots, seeping through the seams and the cracks she hadn't gotten patched yet. Her feet would be wet for ages, but that hardly mattered when they were so close.

She tripped over a square block, lurking just under the surface, and resolved to move her feet more carefully.

A small building stood in knee-deep water. It took Bex a moment to realize why it set her teeth on edge. The corners weren't square, and the walls stretched away on either side at uneven angles and lengths. Some of the walls tumbled into the waves, leaving jagged blocks of stone to cut through the waves.

But here, facing the shore, was a big, black door made from the same dark stone as the rest of the ruin.

The smooth surface showed no sign of a handle or knob. No way to open it except for an oblong keyhole in the direct center.

"So, we need a key to find the key?" Lynniki said.

"The Giants didn't want anyone getting in," Rowan said. "That's about right. The last locked door I encountered I had to blast open with a fire charge."

"That wasn't the last one," Lynniki said. "There was the tonal lock in Blackfall."

Rowan's face brightened. "Oh right. That one was clever."

"Can we hurry it up?" Gavyn asked as Tera joined them in the shallows. He stared down at the water foaming around his legs. "I'm getting wet in my joints. They're going to squeak."

"Any ideas?" Tera asked.

Bex strode forward. Rowan might have gotten them here, but this was where Bex excelled. Finally, she felt like she was back in her element.

She pulled a set of tools from her belt.

Tera snorted. "Of course you have those."

Bex looked down at the lockpicks and let out an exasperated sigh. "Yes, of course. I'm a treasure hunter. Remember? Lots of locked doors where I work."

Tera stared over her shoulder, a tight little smirk on her lips.

Brightstrike stepped up to the door. "There will be no need for those."

"What? Why?" Bex stared up at him.

The Taur-El ran his hands over the hinges and the joints in the door. "I am a smith by trade." He touched the hammer on his shoulder briefly before going back to his examination of the door. "I make a lot of hinges and fastenings. Sometimes locks. I hang doors so they swing perfectly, balanced so that a small calf can open a stone door twenty feet high. I know them."

He took a step back, eyed the door up and down, then raised his hoof and slammed it into the solid stone.

Cracks spiderwebbed away from his hoof, and the door groaned for one moment before it swayed backward and fell into the water with a splash.

"I have always wanted to do that."

Bex peered around Brightstrike, then up at his shaggy head. "All right my way might not be as impressive, but it still would've gotten the job done."

Suncall splashed up beside them and stared down at the cracked door, then up at her friend, her normally bright smile subdued. "Careful with that."

"That was not the frenzy," Brightstrike said. "Just a release of frustration."

Suncall's lips twisted. "Mmhmm."

"Can someone hand me a torch?" Bex said, extending her left hand.

Tera had brought one of the packs from the horses, and she pulled out one of the torches they'd picked up in Auli'poli.

"I'll have to get the flint and tinder," Tera said with a frown. "That'll be delightful to use in this wet."

Bex rolled her eyes. "Just give it to me, would you?"

Tera scowled and tossed the torch. Maybe she wanted Bex to fumble it and drop it in the water so they couldn't light the thing. But Bex snatched it out of the air and took out the flintstriker Anera had given her. The spark caught the oil-soaked rag wrapped around the end of the torch, sending a flare of light into the dark opening.

"Very handy," Lynniki said. "But I still think it would be better with a little magic."

"Not bad for a grave robber." Bex wiggled the fingers of her right hand. The one wrapped under her gloves.

"Hmph," Tera said. "Probably stole it."

Bex's grin soured, and she turned away to step through the opening into what they'd already guessed was a tomb.

Behind her Rowan whispered. "Why would you say that?"

Maybe it had seemed particularly harsh to naive Rowan, but Bex could just imagine Tera staring at her bandaged hand, imagining the worst.

It didn't matter. Bex knew what she was, and she knew the truth about Anera's gift. How Tera looked at her didn't matter.

Bex stepped into the tiny building, holding out the torch to light her way.

From the outside, one could expect the tomb to be a mere twenty feet across. Of course, Bex hadn't been born yesterday, so the reality didn't startle her at all.

Instead of a room, the interior stretched downward in a series of steep steps. Just like all the stories the treasure hunters told, they were too tall to be comfortable for Humans.

Water rushed around her feet, spilling down the stairs now that the door was open.

Bex set her teeth and started downward, placing each foot carefully and focusing on her mark in case it tingled, informing her of any magic nearby. Considering the way it had reacted to Lynniki's traps in the mountains, Bex was fairly certain it would react to Giant magic in the same way it did to normal magic.

The torch lit the black walls, but the flicker of light didn't travel much farther than a few steps down. Maybe if the walls had been wet they would have reflected more of the light, but they were dry when Bex ran her fingertips along the stone. The only water was the inch or two that cascaded down the steps from the open door.

It didn't create enough of an undertow to worry Bex, but she did make sure her boots didn't slip on the suddenly slick surface.

They'd come down about twenty stairs—with who-knew-how-many to go—when Bex felt a click under her heel.

In Human ruins she knew exactly what that meant.

She threw herself backwards, expecting a pit to open under the trick step. But instead, the stairs under her feet abruptly slanted down, dumping her on her butt on a smooth slope.

"Whoa!" She slid, the water carrying her down the ramp. The others shouted from above.

She tried to get her feet under her, but she had too much momentum, and the stone under the water was too smooth. She only kept hold of the torch because her hand had clenched around the shaft in fear.

Bex bit down on a scream. Any second now this was going to dump her into a pit full of spikes or poison or other unpleasantness. She knew because that was exactly what she would do.

Sure enough, a black opening yawned ahead of her, water spilling over the edge in a dark waterfall. Bex extended both legs, bracing her boots against the walls. She slammed her other hand and the fist still holding the torch into the stone blocks and managed to wedge herself to an abrupt halt just above the pit.

Miraculously, she still clutched the torch in her hand. It reflected in the water and on the damp stone on the other side of the pit.

From here, she could not see into the opening, but it was obviously designed for one thing. To kill trespassers.

"Bex!" Rowan's voice echoed from above. "Bex!"

"I'm all right," she grated. She had to clear her throat before she could call back loud enough for them to hear. "I'm here."

"Where is 'here?'" Brightstrike rumbled.

The others hadn't followed, thankfully. The hinge for the stairs must have been directly under her.

"The stairs all went out and turned into a ramp," Rowan said.

"No shit," Bex muttered under her breath. She hadn't felt any magic, but there had been that click. Trick steps were one of the oldest tricks in the book. Old enough even the Giants used them apparently.

"I think it was mechanical," Bex called back. "I'm—" She gulped. "I'm not dead yet, but I don't know how much longer I can hold myself. Tell Lynniki she's looking for a switch or a lever. The people who used this place would have needed a way to bypass the trap for themselves."

"I'm already on it," Lynniki called down, and there was a rustling from above as they clearly had to shuffle themselves to let Lynniki through.

"And whatever you do, don't slip," Bex called. "If even one of you comes down this ramp, we'll all go into the pit."

"Pit?" Rowan called, but there was an "Aha!" from Lynniki and the stairs under Bex's back flipped back into place, digging into her spine.

She winced and pulled herself to her feet, examining the stretch of stairs where the pit had been just a moment ago.

"Good work, Lynniki," Rowan said above.

"Yeah, good work," Bex muttered. "I only told you exactly what to look for." Bex took a moment before the others got to her to breathe and rest her head against the wall. She'd almost died after all. She needed a second to get her heart rate under control.

The others came into view in the flickering light of the torch.

Tera cocked her head. "You're still here."

Bex bared her teeth in a reckless grin. "Scared you lost me, Captain? I knew you cared."

Tera made an exasperated noise in the back of her throat.

"Oh, I like it when you growl at me."

The guard captain rested her hand on her sword hilt. "What did I say about flirting?"

Bex sighed. "You'd throw me overboard. Sorry. Almost dying makes me reckless."

Rowan saw Bex and bit her lip. "Are you all right?"

Bex transferred the torch to her other hand and shook out the one that was now bruised from slamming it into the wall.

"A few scratches," she said.

"You held onto the torch," Tera said.

Bex raised her eyebrows. "This isn't my first ruin. I've met trick steps before."

"Hmm," Tera said, lips pressed tight. "Maybe I should go first anyway from now on." She drew her sword and stepped past Bex.

Bex straightened with a scowl. "You think there's going to be something you can actually fight?" Her voice rose to ring around the walls as they continued downward. "It's a tomb. It's supposed to house dead things not live ones." She reached out to touch the wall. "Nothing's wet above the stairs, which means it was sealed really well. Nothing bigger than a bat will have gotten in here. It's going to be traps and locks from here on out. Nothing for someone like you, Captain."

"Is that why you don't carry a weapon?" Tera glanced back at her. "I thought you were just unprepared."

"Everything in my line of work is already dead," Bex said. "And if it's not, I can talk to it. I don't have to stab it."

Tera snorted. "I'm sure talking does loads of good." Her gaze flicked to Brightstrike just behind them. "That's all right. It looks like Brightstrike is good in a fight."

Bex ground her teeth.

Behind her, Brightstrike rumbled his dark laugh again.

"You would be disappointed," he said. "My people are proscribed from all violence."

Tera stared at him, pausing for a moment on the steps. "I'm not talking about violence. I'm talking about defending yourself and your team."

"All fighting is frowned upon."

Tera's head jerked. "What? Why?"

"The Giants created the Taur-Els with the battle frenzy. Their greatest gift to us and their greatest curse. Every Taur-El has the frenzy inside, waiting. It is not a thing one has to reach for. It is a thing one has to suppress. Always. Any violence at all could awaken it."

Tera frowned back at the Taur-El. Bex wanted to tell her to watch her feet instead, but honestly, it would serve Tera right if she ended up sliding into a pit.

"What happens then?" Rowan asked quietly from the back of the group. She didn't seem to be having much trouble with the stairs. She limped, but she still managed to keep up, even with her uneven gait.

"Once our reason is lost to the frenzy, we can never be trusted again," Brightstrike said. "The consequence is exile."

Tera's mouth pulled down, deepening the creases at the corners. "It's possible to fight without losing your head."

"But is it worth the risk?"

"If someone is in danger and you can do something to stop it, yes."

Brightstrike ducked his head, staring at the steps as they passed over them.

Tera opened her mouth as if to keep arguing, but Bex jerked her chin at the captain.

"Would you stop," she hissed. "Stop pushing. Maybe he's not like you. Not everyone has to be a brute."

Tera's mouth tightened, and she stomped down the next few steps. Bex hurried after her to tell her to be more careful, or she'd trigger another trap, but she nearly ran into the captain's back as she stopped abruptly.

"What?" Then Bex realized they stood on level ground, the stairs ending in a long corridor.

Black openings yawned on either side, some carrying on

into the darkness, and a couple plunging down more stairs. Water lapped at the edge of the corridor where those stairs ended.

Bex leaned over to eye the black water of the nearest staircase.

"What was it you were saying about this place being sealed?" Tera said.

Bex wiped the consternation from her face and shrugged. "Well, I can't be right every time. Otherwise what use would the rest of you be?"

"Where are we going?" Lynniki asked, craning around Suncall and Brightstrike.

"Um..." Bex said. There were three dry passages to choose from. If the key was down one of the flooded ones, then they'd have to grow gills or come back with some kind of water-breathing spell. She kicked herself. With a name like the Shattered Waves she should have thought of this possibility. In another second, Tera would point that out.

Rowan pushed past the others gently. "Well, if this is a tomb..." she said slowly, studying the walls. "Then it's likely this way."

She stepped past Bex and Tera and held out her hand for the torch. Bex handed it over without argument and followed Rowan to the end of the corridor where it branched both left and right.

Without hesitation, Rowan chose the right.

"How do you know where you're going?" Bex whispered.

Rowan gave her a conspiratorial grin. "Magic?" she said.

Bex gave her a look. "You're not a mage. Try again." If she had been, Bex would have run in the opposite direction.

Rowan chuckled. Then she pointed to the carvings around the opening of the new corridor. "Those tell us."

Bex squinted. They looked exactly the same as the ones around the other opening as well.

"The others don't have that little five-pointed peak in the middle," Rowan said. "In Giant architecture, that means this is the main passage and the others are for auxiliary use. In a tomb, they probably lead to chambers for the lesser dead or rooms that contain burial goods."

"Here," Bex said, moving up to walk beside Rowan. "Let me check for traps. That way you can concentrate on the reliefs."

"That's the part I like the best anyway," Rowan said with another grin.

Behind them, Tera snorted, and Rowan flushed. Bex glared at the guard captain.

Bex guided Rowan around two more traps laid into the floor, one mechanical that she could see a mile away, and the other magical that her mark warned her about.

The end of the corridor opened into a wide chamber lined with long, stone boxes, each at least fifteen feet long. Intricate carvings of eclipsed suns banded each box. Four of them marched up the sides of the room, and at the end, the torch light flickered against a fifth.

Bex and Rowan stood in the entryway for a moment, staring. Bex could feel the way Rowan held her breath, and it made Bex reluctant to inhale, as if she'd break some sort of spell.

Then Rowan stepped forward and ran her fingertips lightly across the top of the nearest box.

"Caskets," she said, hushed tones echoing around the room.

Bex stepped forward, eyes searching for more traps, alert to more spells. Nothing on the caskets themselves.

"Look," Gavyn said, coming into the room behind Lynniki and Suncall. He clanked to the other side of the casket, between the box and the wall. Simple stone cases sat in recessed pockets along the walls.

"More tombs?" Bex said.

"These appear to be less important," Lynniki said.

Rowan nodded. "Servants perhaps or distant family members buried with their masters."

"It does seem like a gathering," Bex said, softly.

"Hopefully that means the key is here," Tera said.

"Maybe with one of these fellows." Lynniki bent to blow the dust from the nearest casket.

"Are there really dead Giants inside?" Bex said. She tilted her head to squint at the casket. It felt... creepy. And that was coming from someone who had been around plenty of Human graveyards and mage burial sites.

Lynniki's eyes went big. "Oh I hope so. Think of what they might have been buried with."

Normally that would make Bex dream about heaps of gold. But they really needed to get that key. Magic would keep Anera safe. Not wealth.

"Concentrate on that one," Rowan said, pointing to the casket at the far end of the room. "It's clearly in a place of prominence. And the number five is significant. It's the fifth casket. That's likely where we'll find our key."

Bex almost jumped to beat Lynniki to the casket, but something stopped her.

So far, Rowan had been doing the heavy lifting. She'd gotten them here, and Brightstrike had gotten them in the door. All Bex had done was slide down some stairs and almost disappear into a hole. She itched to solve this one herself. She was good at this sort of thing. Despite all evidence to the contrary recently.

She wanted to rush forward, but there was something about the room that scratched at the back of her mind.

Tera and the others pulled out three more torches and lit them while Bex stood there, waiting for that niggling idea to become clear.

The walls weren't square.

Like the tomb entrance above, they stretched at an odd

angle, and she realized the room had five sides. They'd entered at the bottom of the pentagon, and she faced the point now. It seemed to point to the fifth and final casket.

Or it could be pointing to the medallion hung on the wall above it.

Set into the corner, where two walls met, hung a gem the size of Bex's palm. She knew her precious stones but had never seen one quite like this before. It was a deep, red, almost black and was set into a mounting of gold.

She stepped toward it as the others crowded around the casket, trying to wedge it open.

"It's sealed," Lynniki said. "Or maybe locked."

"Hey, isn't this what you're supposed to be good at?" Tera said as Bex passed. "Don't you have a set of picks? Or a pry bar?"

Bex ignored her, staring up at the gem. Her palm itched.

The setting at first looked like a sun, with squared rays coming out of it. At the end of five of them, horizontal pieces came off, making them look like a strange, squared-off key.

Bex glanced at the other corners of the room. There were four more gems set into each, but they had fewer and fewer rays with the two flanking the door having only three rays each.

Like this one had gathered more.

And Bex's eyes, trained by years of exploring ruins, noticed that those were set flush with the wall, while this one... This one had the slightest gap, no broader than the point of a knife. As if it was designed to come free.

"I don't think the key was buried," she said.

She hadn't spoken loudly, but the others all halted and turned as if she'd shouted.

Rowan followed her gaze. "Oh," she said with a sigh.

"That doesn't look like a key to me," Tera said.

"Bex is right. The room was built as if for that piece," Rowan said. Then she glanced at Tera. "And we already know the Giants built entire buildings for one artifact sometimes. This could be the same thing."

Tera frowned, then glanced at Rowan's waist and away.

Bex's eyes narrowed. What was that? Some shared memory?

"How do we get it out then?" Lynniki said. "Just yank it?"

"Don't," Bex said, stepping forward. "It's got some sort of magic on it. I don't know if it's the key itself or some sort of trap, but just grabbing it is the worst way to find out."

"How could you possibly know that?" Tera said. "You're not a mage."

Bex rolled her eyes at her. "I told you this isn't my first ruin. *This* is what I do. Picking locks is just for fun."

The gathering key. They needed that to get to the mirror.

She stepped lightly around the room, using her superior height to reach up and twist one of the other medallions. It gave her a moment of panic when it didn't seem to want to move, and she wondered if maybe she was wrong.

But then it ground into motion, and she twisted it so two of its rays pointed at the key.

She did the same to the opposite medallion. The two beside the door turned until one ray of each pointed along the walls to the key.

There was a satisfying click, and Bex walked back to lift the key from its place on the wall, using her left hand of course. Even with the other wrapped, she didn't want to take any chances.

Rowan stared at the key in her hand, then up at Bex's face. "How did you know to do that?"

Bex shrugged. "I don't know. It's a gathering key. It was gathering rays. It seemed obvious. And then you said the thing about the room being built for it."

Bex stared back at Rowan, her grin going soft around the edges as the antiquarian's astonishment turned to fascination.

For that moment, everything was perfect. They had the key, Rowan was gazing at her with rapt eyes, and Bex could believe for just one second that finding the mirror would actually be this easy.

And then something groaned above them.

And the stone slab of the door slammed shut.

"What—?" Gavyn said.

The ceiling dropped about half a foot with an echoing thud.

Bex's mouth fell open. The ceiling dropped again, getting lower and lower.

"Oh, well done," Tera said. "You've set it off."

"Me?" Bex cried as Brightstrike and Lynniki rushed to the door. "At least I wasn't prying away at a useless casket."

"Not now," Rowan snapped. "We need a way out of here."

But the room was a dead end. The culmination of the tomb.

Gavyn hopped up on one of the tombs. "Not to alarm anyone, but the water is rising."

So even if the lowering ceiling caught on the raised caskets, it would still trap them and drown them.

Bex splashed forward.

"If it's a spell, we have to find a way to disrupt it," Lynniki was saying. "Even Giant magic follows rules."

But Bex's hand wasn't tingling. At least no more than it had been. She shoved the key into her satchel, and the slight buzz faded to nothing.

"It's not a spell," she said. "It's mechanical. A trap. There's got to be pulleys, levers, a counterweight somewhere."

"And that could all be unreachable behind stone," Lynniki said.

Brightstrike's horns scraped the ceiling as it fell another half a foot.

Gavyn splashed back into the water. "Squeaky joints it is."

The ceiling crunched into the first of the burial niches,

The Truth Stealer

collapsing the stone. Brightstrike had to stoop or be knocked unconscious.

Rowan cried out as stone rained around her.

"Hurry it up," Tera called.

"Everyone shut up a second," Bex said. "Lynniki, the walls."

"What?"

"You were right. The mechanism has to live inside the walls. Listen for it."

She splashed to the left wall and laid her ear against it as Lynniki did the same opposite her.

At least the others finally got the hint and tried to still their breathing and not splash as much.

Finally, a few feet from the door, Bex caught a faint grinding and clanking.

"Here!" she called.

Brightstrike was beside her in an instant, and though he had to stoop, he swung his hammer around in a mighty arc. The stone of the wall cracked.

He swung again, and the blocks shattered, revealing a complicated mechanism of ancient wire and gears.

Lynniki splashed over to them, still standing tall, though Bex could feel the ceiling beginning to brush the top of her head.

The Delver muttered under her breath and then reached into the wall to yank at the wires.

The ceiling stuttered to a halt and hung there for a moment. Then the door shuddered open.

"What are you waiting for?" Lynniki yelled as they all stared at it. "Go. Before it decides gravity is better than some old wires and a cog."

Chapter 22
Bex

The sun was just going down as they spilled into the open air of the bay, dripping wet and gasping.

Bex did a quick count as they all came into view. Rowan, Lynniki, Gavyn, Tera, Brightstrike, and Suncall. All accounted for.

She kicked the fallen door of the tomb with a breathless laugh. "Hah," she said. "That wasn't so bad."

The others waded to shore with a variety of grumbles, but Lynniki stood beside Bex staring at the door. "Think of all the things we missed though. We didn't even get one of the caskets open."

"No, but we got what we came for." Bex pulled the key out of her satchel and tilted it to show off the gem as she and Lynniki splashed back to the others.

"True. But do you know how to use it?"

Bex squinted at the key. Night was falling, but it was still brighter out here than it had been in the tomb. And Brightstrike was already working on a fire while the others set up camp on the beach, high enough above the high-water line that the tide wouldn't catch them off guard.

"No, but that's tomorrow's problem. A lot of times the solution is obvious once you see the lock."

Lynniki grinned up at her. "Good point. And there might be something even better wherever we're going next."

"Congratulations, Lynniki," Gavyn said, spitting some driftwood at Brightstrike's feet. "You have found someone as eternally optimistic as yourself."

"I don't mind optimism," Tera grumbled, pulling the tent from the packhorse. "It's stupidity I don't like."

Bex stiffened. "Excuse me?"

"Maybe tomorrow we can find what we're looking for without someone getting us all killed."

She should just laugh it off, find a joke that would make Tera flush and give up the sourness. But the words stung worse because according to Bex's experiences, that had gone really well. If she hadn't gotten the key, they all would have been stumped down there and they still might have triggered the trap.

Bex planted her hands on her hips. "Every reward requires a little risk. You'd think you'd know that, or do you swing that sword around completely oblivious to its edge? Maybe working for a noble has made you soft. You don't remember how to get your hands dirty or how to take a hit."

Tera's face darkened, and she dumped the tent in the sand. "You want to try hitting me and find out?"

Bex laughed. "Senji's teeth, no. I know what risks are worth taking. And you're not worth it."

She stalked to the packhorse and pulled one of the bedrolls off, then trudged as far away from the campsite as she could get and still see in the flickering firelight. It wasn't raining anymore, but the sand was damp as if it had stopped recently.

She spread the bedding out with a snap and sat with a huff while Tera turned her back.

Bex ground her teeth. She might have gotten the last word

in but since she'd stalked away, Tera was the one who got to stay in the nice, cozy firelight while Bex would be contending with the encroaching dark.

She hated the dark.

She pretended to ignore Rowan and Gavyn tiptoeing through the sand toward her.

"Don't bother," she said to her boots. "Go on back to your group. I know you wanted her along for a reason."

"You chose me to head your expedition. And presumably you trust my judgment."

Bex glared in Tera's direction. "Maybe that was a mistake."

"Why do you hate her so much?" Gavyn said, plopping his brass butt in the sand. That had to be worse for his joints than the water.

"She hated me first," Bex squawked.

"Yeah but Tera hates everyone at first. You seem like someone who wouldn't normally take that personally. What do you have against her?"

Bex kicked at the sand as if to make it more comfortable to sleep on. "She works for a noble."

"So do a lot of us."

She cast him a glare. "All right, she's in love with a noble. She chose that."

"What's wrong with that?" Rowan asked.

"Nobles are bad. All of them."

Rowan gave her the most disappointed look Bex had ever seen in her life. "That is a blanket statement with no nuance. And I know you're more intelligent than that."

Bex clenched her teeth on an expletive. She knew she didn't want to swear at Rowan. It was just the way the other woman was forcing her to actually think about that squirmy feeling that made her want to run. Or punch something.

"Fine," she said. "*I* don't trust them. All right?"

"Why? You don't even know Mellrea."

"I know plenty of others. You ever heard of Vamreth's experiments?"

Rowan exchanged a glance with Gavyn. "We... heard lots of stories about Vamreth," she said. "But he was the king. We never had much to do with him in Lannasbrook or at Karaval Keep. The closest we saw anything relating to him was Lord Hax. Vamreth usurped the throne, so Lord Hax thought he could do the same with his neighbors."

Bex's lips tightened. "It was way worse in the capital. No one trusted anyone and for good reason. Vamreth's pet mages took people off the streets. People no one else would miss."

Rowan's eyes went wide. "Were you—"

"Vamreth and some of their noble patrons would come check on their progress." Bex turned her face away. "I've never trusted anyone richer than me after that."

"What did they—"

"Don't ask for details you don't want to hear, Rowan. It was bad enough that every moment we spent in Karaval Keep made me nauseous. Made me remember people who looked at me like a bug who'd just managed to escape squashing."

"Mellrea's not like that. Tera's not like that. There are terrible people in this world, but you can't assume everyone around you is going to hurt you."

"Maybe *you* can't." She turned around and lay down. "But it's kept me alive so far."

"Bex—"

"I'm not going to send her back home, all right? I'm sure she's useful. But don't ask me to make friends with her."

After a while, she heard someone moving through the sand back toward the warmth of the fire, and Bex let out all her breath at once.

Someone else moved closer, and she recognized the sound of Gavyn's joints lying next to her.

"Are you going to lecture me about trust too?" she said into the dark.

"No." Something clanked, and Bex could imagine Gavyn's bulky head resting on his forelegs. "Unlike Rowan, I know what it's like to be held against your will. To see someone every day who holds all the power while you sit there helpless in the dark."

She remembered his story on the ship. About the man who'd taken mages captive.

Bex's lips went tight and thin, and she waited a full minute before she asked, "What did you do to yours?"

"I killed him."

She knew she wasn't imagining the bit of grim satisfaction in his voice.

She snorted, still facing the darkness. "I knew I liked you."

Chapter 23
Bex

In the morning, they set out to find a way to the central nuraghi of the Shattered Waves and learned almost immediately that there was no easy way through the bay.

Bex had imagined a boat could take them, but there were areas too shallow for any kind of vessel. She followed one of these out far past the entrance to the tomb, wondering if she could walk the whole way to the center.

Then her boot slipped, and she nearly splashed into water deep enough to drown in.

"Careful," Rowan called, hanging back with the others as Bex scouted ahead.

Bex didn't bother snapping back. She reached under the water to brush at the slippery surface of the walkway. Chunks of algae fell away, revealing rough stone.

"They're walls," she called. "It's all submerged walls."

From here she could see places where the walls stood tall enough to start drying in the sun and places where time had weathered them down beneath the surface.

Rowan picked her way out to Bex, the others strung along behind her.

"It's like a maze," she said. "Even with a boat we wouldn't be able to make it straight across because there are too many shallow parts."

"So we have to find our way across," Gavyn said.

"And quickly," Brightstrike said. "There is a reason this area is called the Shattered Waves. In the afternoon, squalls roll in, and this area will no longer be safe to traverse."

Bex scowled down at her boots, half-submerged on the narrow walkway. The foaming sea sucked at the leather even now when it was fairly gentle.

"Great." With no way to see it from above they would have to test each pathway for dead ends.

"We'll do it methodically. Take it in sections, just like a dig," Rowan said. "If we try to rush, we'll make mistakes, and then we'll be stuck out here with no way back by the time it gets dangerous."

Bex growled under her breath and heard a similar noise behind her. She turned to find Tera staring at her boots with a vicious frown. She looked up at Bex.

Bex turned her chin, refusing to find anything in common with the captain. So far they hadn't needed a fighter. She wished she'd overruled Rowan back at the keep and left Tera behind.

They made their way across the narrow pathways, single file as Rowan jotted a crude map in her notebook, dividing the ruins by some arcane formula and trying each option methodically, crossing them off as she came to dead ends or crossroads where she had to choose one direction or another.

Bex followed her closely. Today, they carried most of their belongs, having left little with the horses on the shore.

Behind her there was a splash and a yelp.

Bex turned to find Lynniki half in and half out of the bay. The walls they used as roads weren't even or smooth. She must have slipped, or a stone block must have gone out from under her.

The Delver kicked and splashed, trying to climb back up onto the path under the weight of her pack.

Something broke the water out in a deeper bit of the bay. A fin sliced through the surface between two shallow walkways.

Bex had no idea what it was, but something in her gut told her they didn't want to find out with one of them in the water.

Brightstrike had already reached to help Lynniki, and Bex hurried to lend a hand.

"Quick," Brightstrike said, his words making Bex's heart thump.

Lynniki's feet kicked free of the water as they dragged her back onto the path. Brightstrike let go abruptly, and Bex scrambled to help Lynniki stand as the great Taur-El pulled his hammer from his back.

The water thrashed, a flurry of teeth and scales and foam. Suddenly the dark shape leaped from the water, and Bex got the impression of an enormous fish with teeth as long as her hand and a snout stretched wide.

Brightstrike stood frozen on the wall, knuckles clenched white on the shaft of the hammer.

Tera stepped forward and swung her sword, catching the thing in midair with a wet *thunk*. It went flying across the surface and splashed back into the water. Bex caught the flash of a tail before it disappeared again.

"Hey," Tera snapped at Brightstrike. "If you're not going to help, then get out of the way."

Brightstrike shook himself and took a shaky step backward.

"What the hell *was* that?" Bex said.

Tera stood beside her, scowling at the water.

"A depthlurker," Brightstrike said. "They live in the waterways, traveling between fresh water and salt, preying on anything that comes too close."

"Oh," Bex said. "So getting knocked into the water by waves or wind or whatever isn't deadly just because we could drown. But also because we could be eaten. Wonderful."

There was another splash, and they whirled but all they could see was Suncall standing on the edge of the wall and the dark shape of a depthlurker slithering back underwater like a dog with its tail between its legs.

Bex thought she caught the glint of a blade in Suncall's palm, but it was gone the next moment. The Brightling glanced at Bex, mouth twisted in a grimace.

Bex jerked her chin at Rowan. "Let's get going. I want to be off these paths by noon."

Rowan's gaze flicked to the open water where another fin circled. "Yes. Me too."

She turned and led them along at a faster pace, her limp growing more pronounced.

"I didn't mean to trip," Lynniki muttered. "The stone broke away and went out from under me."

Suncall waited to one side as they passed so she could fall in beside Brightstrike, who walked with his head down and his hammer limp in his hands.

"I'm sorry," he rumbled, and Bex wasn't sure who he was apologizing to. Lynniki was already ahead of them out of earshot, and Tera stalked along behind them.

Suncall laid a hand along his forearm. "Never apologize for thinking before acting," she said quietly. "I know a much younger Suncall who would have killed for that kind of patience."

Bex hurried to catch up to Rowan.

As the sun grew higher, Bex stared out across the water. Not just to keep an eye on the fins flashing through the deeper waters.

"How much farther do you think?" she whispered to Rowan. The distance to the broken tower jutting out of the water was hard to judge as they made their way across the winding, submerged walls. The two nuraghis nearest the shore had grown to tiny dots just visible against the sand. There were at least two others much further into the bay, but only one ruin rose here in the middle. If this wasn't what they were looking for, they had a long walk to check the others.

Rowan glanced at her. "I don't know. Why?"

"We need to leave time to check the others."

Rowan frowned. "It'll have to be after high tide."

"What?"

Rowan pointed toward the central nuraghi. A tall wall topped with crumbling towers that had been growing as they approached. "You can see the hightide mark. We won't be able to walk the shallow paths when the water is up to our necks."

Bex glanced out at the fins that paced them across the surface and shuddered. The water was already lapping closer to their knees now.

"It's all right," Rowan said with a smile. "We're almost there, and we can rest and regroup at the central nuraghi while we wait for the tide to go out again."

Bex muttered, "How long will that take?" But Rowan had already splashed ahead, making her way to the nuraghi where Bex's hopes waited.

They reached the wall as the sun crept to its highest point and the water started rising to their waists. Brightstrike carried Gavyn and Suncall across his back while Lynniki pushed through water up to her chest.

Depthlurkers splashed just beyond the shallows, circling, their long, slick bodies flashing in the sunlight.

"Can we hurry this up?" Lynniki said.

Rowan stared up at the steep wall. This wasn't made out of the same black rock as the tomb had been. This was a brighter yellow stone cut into enormous blocks, the edges crumbling after centuries withstanding the tide.

"I don't know how..." Rowan started.

Bex waded up next to her. Rowan was almost a full head shorter than her, and the water came up much higher on her waist.

"Take this," Bex said and thrust her satchel into Rowan's hands. Then she pulled a length of thin, sturdy rope from inside. She looped it around her torso and reached for the wall, wedging her fingers into the cracks.

Rowan might stare at this and see an impassable wall. Bex just saw handholds.

She hauled herself up, climbing the wall like a ladder.

She paused to squint upward, the sun making her eyes water.

"Are you all right?" Rowan called.

Bex grinned back at her. "I'm great. This is much easier than your sanctuary."

Even from here, Bex caught Rowan roll her eyes.

But from here, Bex could see silent shadows beneath the calm surface of the water and fins that left menacing wakes behind them as they converged on the party trapped on the disappearing pathway.

Bex redoubled her efforts, scrambling up the wall that was nearly three stories tall.

At the top, she clambered over the edge and caught her breath.

The nuraghi stretched out, a circular platform at least two hundred feet across. But it was empty. There was no building. No door like into the tomb. One pedestal stood atop a dais in the middle, and five crumbling towers rose around the edges of the platform.

This couldn't be right.

"Bex!" Rowan called from below, voice desperate. There was a thud and a splash.

"Shit." Bex hauled the rope over her head and wrapped one

end around the broken tower nearest her, then dropped the other end down to the rest of her group.

"Climb up," she called.

Rowan set her hands to the rope, but it was clear she wasn't going to be able to haul herself up. Her twisted spine made the movement nearly impossible.

Bex heaved, but Rowan only rose partway out of the water.

"Stop," Tera called. "Wrong order. Brightstrike, keep them safe." She pulled Rowan off the rope and surged up out of the water, scrambling up the wall with the help of the rope.

Bex held it steady from above, her eyes on Rowan and the rest, her lip between her teeth.

"There," Tera said, as she scrambled over the top of the wall. "Now, together."

Bex wrapped her hands around the rope once more, grateful for her gloves, and this time when Rowan tried to climb, both she and Tera heaved. Brightstrike gave her a boost with one hand and kept the other on his hammer.

Rowan pulled herself up, hand over hand, and Bex and Tera hauled from above. When Rowan was within a foot of the top, Bex threw herself flat and reached over the edge with her good hand, bracing with the other.

She grabbed hold of Rowan's arm, and Tera joined her to haul Rowan to the top.

"Now Lynniki," Tera called down. "Quick."

Brightstrike boosted the Delver. As soon as Lynniki had a hold of the rope, Suncall cried out, "Behind you!"

Brightstrike spun, and his hammer caught a depthlurker.

He watched as it splashed back into the water and then stared down at his hammer. He squared his shoulders and faced the threat, hammer at the ready.

Lynniki scrambled up the rope. Not as gracefully as Tera, but clearly swinging her own hammer had given her some muscle. She clanked and clattered to the top and hauled herself over the edge with a little help from Bex.

Brightstrike stepped forward to catch a depthlurker's charge, holding it back so he could toss Suncall up the wall. She caught the rope and surged up.

Tera helped her up as Bex leaned over to cry, "Now Brightstrike!"

Brightstrike bashed another depthlurker, sending it skipping over the water. Then he turned and trotted back a few steps, Gavyn still clinging to his back. Brightstrike turned again and sprinted for the wall.

Depthlurkers surged around them, but the big Taur-El plowed through the waves like a ship at full sail, parting the water around him. He planted a hoof against the bottom of the wall and leaped upward, catching the rope one-handed.

"Now," Tera called the others.

At the top of the wall, they all braced the rope as Brightstrike stashed his weapon and pulled himself up hand over hand.

As he reached the top, Bex and Tera both held out a hand to help him up. Gavyn hopped off the Taur-El's broad back and shook himself, brass gleaming in the sun.

Bex leaned over the side to laugh at the retreating depthlurkers.

"Stop that cackling," Tera said. "We're trapped here until after high tide."

Bex sighed. "Live in the moment, sometimes, Captain. We're here and we're alive."

"Hopefully 'here' is where we need to be," Rowan said, planting her hands on her hips and looking out over the wide platform that was completely open to the sun.

"It doesn't look like much, does it," Lynniki said.

"We won't be alone much longer," Suncall said from the edge of the platform. "Maybe this person can help us."

"What?" Bex stepped to her side and shaded her eyes.

Sure enough, someone was making their way across the shallow pathways of the bay. The figure was still a long way off but had already made it about halfway to the central platform.

"How..." Bex started.

"They do not appear to be having any trouble with the high tide," Brightstrike said.

Bex's lips tightened. Was it Sir Kerrickmore? It made sense that he'd caught up, but how was he navigating the deepening water?

Bex blew out her breath and strode across the wide space, keeping an eye out for traps. It was odd. The place felt like a square in the middle of a city. If you ignored the water all around and the fact that it was the only structure for at least half a mile in any direction.

"This is the only thing here," Bex said, approaching the pedestal that was central to the platform. It was just a pillar of yellow stone about as tall as Bex's chest.

With a recessed spot in the middle.

Despite years of weathering, Bex could still make out the grooves arranged around the depression. Like rays of the sun.

She gasped. "It's the keyhole. We're in the right place!"

She ran to Rowan, who still held her satchel and pulled out the key they'd found in the tomb.

"Now wait a second," Tera said. "Maybe this time we should be careful with that."

"I wasn't not careful the first time," Bex snapped. "We won't find out what we need to do unless we try something. Or maybe you'd like to wait until our mystery guest joins us." She gestured toward the figure rapidly approaching.

"It's all right," Rowan said. "Go ahead."

Bex lined up the key and set it into the recess.

Nothing happened.

She glanced over her shoulder, but the figure hadn't slowed.

"All right, maybe we need to turn it?" She tried lifting it and setting it down in a different orientation. Then she tried turning the key on the pedestal.

"Why isn't it working?" she asked Rowan quietly.

Rowan chewed her lip and pulled out Slayter's notes. "I don't know. It just says the 'gathering key.' This is the gathering key. And there's a scribble here about 'noon.'"

Bex looked up at the sky. "We're about as close to noon as you can get without being on the other side of it."

"Yes, but noon of what day?" Lynniki asked, coming toward them. Tera waited at the edge, but Brightstrike, Suncall, and Gavyn joined them as well.

"What do you mean?"

"Well, the sun is at different places in the sky on different days of the year. Even if it's noon on all of them."

Bex swore. "So we could be here on the wrong day of the year?"

Rowan frowned. "It's all right. Don't panic."

"How can I not panic? We could have to wait months!"

"Why is that a problem?" Lynniki said. "Are we in some sort of hurry?"

Yes. Anera could be dead by then. Bex had already taken all this time to get here and who knew how long it would take to get back. Anera didn't have months.

But she couldn't say that.

Bex opened her mouth and stopped. "The queen..." she tried but the lie didn't feel right. Didn't match up with everything else she'd said so far. If the queen needed the mirror so soon why hadn't she mentioned it before?

"Is there something you're not telling us?" Rowan asked, the frown lines deepening in her forehead.

"No."

"Then why are you in such a hurry?"

"I just... I really need this to work." She picked the key up and tried a different orientation again.

"Why?"

"Because—"

A blast of fire swept across the platform, and Bex ducked. The others dove out of the way.

Bex rolled to her feet, Tera's curses ringing in her ears.

"—went straight up and over. Didn't even have a chance to stop them."

Bex rubbed her eyes, clearing away the smoke. Did Sir Kerrickmore have a mage with him? Bex hadn't noticed that back in Palmolivar. How could she have missed something so important?

She shook her head as the smoke cleared and the flames died down. A figure stood opposite her, beyond the pedestal. They must have surged right up the side of the wall and onto the platform.

It was not a knight.

This was a woman in a set of red robes that wrapped around the front and ended at the knee, giving her freedom of movement. Her long, dark hair was bound in a braid that hung over her shoulder, a pair of bells tied to the end.

They swung in the breeze, dinging slightly.

Bex's mouth went dry at the sound. Her palm tingled until it went numb.

"You," she said.

The mage who'd created her mark smiled.

Chapter 24
Bex

The sleeves of the mage's robe were cut short, revealing markings all up and down her arms. These weren't burns like Bex's mark. They were intricate tattoos, incomplete if you looked at them closely enough. And Bex had seen them close up, every day of her life for years. Each one was only as big as a thumbnail so she could fit dozens all up and down her arms where she could reach them.

"I'm sorry," Rowan said. "Who are you? And why are you throwing fire at us?"

"Lystra," Bex spat.

"I'm glad you remember my name," Lystra said with a toothy smile. "At least I made some sort of impression on you. You were supposed to be dead. I cannot believe you dragged me all the way to the other side of the continent when you were supposed to be a corpse."

"How did you find me?" Bex said, fighting the urge to clear the fear out of her throat. Had she tracked down Anera and Conell? Were they all right? Had she taken Anera to use again?

"We'll always be connected," Lystra said, raising her hand and wiggling her fingers.

Bex's fists clenched, and her nails dug into the mark on her palm, even through her gloves. Lystra had placed her mark in the first place. Years ago in that damp dark basement. And now she could track Bex through it? Had she been able to do that all along? Why hadn't she come for Bex before?

Rowan put her hands on her hips. "What has she done that has you chasing her down with fire?"

"She exists," Lystra said with a sneer.

"Well, we are here to do something important, and we're running out of time. If you could refrain from killing her for that long, that would be wonderful."

"Stop talking," Bex hissed under her breath.

Lystra's smile stretched until it seemed like she was baring her teeth at Bex. She extended her pinky finger where she'd filed the nail to a sharp point and carved the razor edge down one of the tattoos, opening the scar tissue that was already there.

The line of blood joined the marking, completing the circle tattooed on her skin.

"No!" Bex cried.

Lystra threw out her hand, and Rowan flew backward into Lynniki.

Bex screamed.

"It would have been better for your friends here, if you'd actually died," Lystra said, cocking her arms so she could cast another spell. "No one should survive the—"

Tera struck her from behind, wrapping her arms around the mage and taking her to the ground. The captain sat up and punched the mage full on in the face.

But Lystra wasn't like any kind of mage the captain had likely met before. She took the hit and smiled through the blood pouring from her nose.

The spell she'd started before Tera hit her, lashed out, sending the captain flying across the stone platform.

Bex lunged and caught Tera's arm before she went tumbling over the side to the water below.

Tera swore. "She's wearing armor under that robe. What mage wears armor?" She climbed to her feet, but Lystra was already ahead of her and carving another spell into her arm.

"One of Vamreth's battle mages," Bex told her. "She's pulling her punches right now, but don't let your guard down."

Rowan and Lynniki had made it to their feet, and Gavyn hit the mage from the side, making her spell flash off into the air and giving Rowan a chance to draw her weapon.

"I'm assuming this is your fault," Tera said.

Bex's jaw clenched as she watched Rowan and Lynniki converge on Lystra. "They don't stand a chance."

"Then help us."

"I can't," Bex cried. *For so many reasons.* First and foremost she didn't have a weapon. Nothing more than a belt knife.

Tera gave her one hard look, then spat to the side and rushed into the fray.

She moved to draw her sword, but Lystra completed another spell, and the blade stuck in its scabbard.

Luckily the captain had no problem using her fists.

But Bex had seen Lystra fight. She'd been hardened in Vamreth's service and moved smoothly from one spell to the next, sending a wave of fire across the stones of the platform, trying to force them over the edge.

All except Bex. Lystra did her best to separate Bex from the rest, forcing Rowan and Tera back. Lynniki and Gavyn tried to flank from the other side, but Lystra treated them like an enemy troop and cut them off with a line of fire.

Bex was torn. Everything in her urged her to flee. Years of nightmares surfaced with just the sound of Lystra's bells.

But running would mean sacrificing the others.

Rowan fought as hard as Tera, even with her twisted spine and uneven gait. She darted in close to Lystra, which seemed like a strange tactic for someone with less physical strength. But it was the same thing she'd done while fighting Bex in the sanctuary. Like she was trying to touch Lystra.

Bex didn't dare get that close.

Lystra's eyes remained on Bex, and step by step she pushed the others back, trying to get to her, fingers reaching to close the distance.

So she could use the energy Bex had stored up. That was the entire point of the experiment. Bex was supposed to be her vessel. A never-ending font of energy. If she got close to Bex and used that energy, there would be no end to her spells.

Bex's fingers flexed. She could try draining Lystra. She could steal all the energy right out of her.

But Lystra was the one who'd placed her mark. It already hummed unpleasantly. What would happen if they tried to drain each other at the same time? Something catastrophic probably. Or nothing. Both would be a problem.

She had to stay out of the way.

Brightstrike watched the mage trying to advance on Bex as the others swarmed around her, doing their best to distract and divert.

"What happens if she gets to you?" Brightstrike said, his eyes following the mage's movements as she tried to get the others out of the way.

Bex's lips thinned. "She gets more powerful. Or we all blow up."

He snorted. "Those are not ideal."

The Taur-El drew the hammer from his back. "We will keep her off of you."

Suncall darted in front of him, holding out her hands as if she could actually keep him from racing forward.

"Brightstrike, no."

"I will be fine. This is important."

"And what if you're not? Would you forsake your people?

The only family that remains to you? Trust me when I say, it's not worth it."

Brightstrike stared down at the tiny Brightling.

Bex's mind raced. The others had avoided Lystra's more serious spells so far, but that was only because the mage was so intent on getting to Bex, not killing the rest of them. She would tire eventually, but would it be before she turned the full force of her wrath on the others?

Bex grabbed for Brightstrike's hand. "We have to get the nuraghi open. If we can retreat inside, maybe they'll all be safe there."

"Help Bex," Suncall said, stepping back from Brightstrike. "I'll help the rest."

"You are not a fighter," Brightstrike said.

Suncall tilted her head. "There is a lot you don't know about me." She stepped back, and her bright skin seemed to disappear into the sunlight, making her nothing more than a blurry pair of horns and eyes.

Then she dissolved entirely. Like a shaft of sunlight when the clouds parted.

"Did you know she could do that?" Bex asked.

Brightstrike snorted a huge breath from his nostrils. "No. But let's not waste it."

Bex raced for the pedestal, the boom of a spell following her footsteps.

The key still sat in its place, but nothing had changed. The lock remained closed.

"What do we do?" Brightstrike said.

"I don't know." Bex gripped the sides of her head. "I've tried everything I can think of. Noon. Gathering key. What's it supposed to be gathering? Sunlight?" She looked up. "There's nothing blocking it, and it's plenty sunny. Why isn't it working?"

"Perhaps the towers..." Brightstrike gestured to the five towers crumbling at the edges of the platform.

"It's worth a shot. There's literally nothing else here." They raced for the one on the south side of the platform. A streak of fire arced toward them, and they dove for cover behind the wall of the tower.

There was no door or opening. Just the solid stretch of stone blocks above them.

"I can climb it," Bex said. "Just give me a second."

Brightstrike didn't give her a second. He grabbed the bottom of her boot and launched her clear to the top of the tower. It was only twice his height.

Bex let out a startled squeak and rolled across the broken roof. "Thanks," she called down.

Below, the others fought. Lystra had finally turned her attention on them, giving them the full force of her focus. Tera yanked and finally managed to get her sword free.

Suncall appeared directly behind Lystra and yanked her foot out from under her, tripping the mage before she disappeared back into the sunlight.

Gavyn limped along one side, and Rowan and Lynniki flanked her other. Rowan carried a lantern in her off hand. Which seemed like a strange thing to use in broad daylight.

Bex squinted. She had an amazing attention to detail when it came to treasure, and this lantern was the same one Rowan had had in the sanctuary. Why would she use it here?

"Do you see anything?" Brightstrike called.

Bex shook her head and surveyed the crumbling debris on top of the tower. It had once had pillars and maybe arches or a roof, but those had tumbled long ago, leaving a mess of stones and moss.

Something glinted among the squared corners and broken edges.

Bex tore through the pile of stone, glad for her gloves. She tossed aside broken bricks and uncovered a large, round sheet of metal crusted with a thick layer of dust and dirt.

A mirror.

This couldn't be the mirror they were looking for? One of the Noktum mirrors?

No, it was a cheap piece of metal, bent into a curve that would reflect the sun's light if she cleaned it off first. But the surface was dinged from the collapsed pillars. It wasn't nearly a good enough quality to be their artifact.

And now that she was at this height, she could see other glints from the rest of the towers. They all held mirrors.

Bex sucked in a breath. "The gathering key. It gathers sunlight."

She swept her arm across the mirror's surface, clearing away as much of the dirt and debris as she could. Then she propped it up, wedging it against the stones until she'd angled the beam of sunlight exactly, and it fell across the pedestal.

"Coming down," she called, then swung her legs over the edge of the tower and dropped, trusting Brightstrike to catch her.

His thick arms cushioned her fall, and he set her on her feet.

"They're mirrors," she gasped. "There are five mirrors that can all face the pedestal. Come on."

They raced to the next tower which was a little more intact. Its pillars were still in place, surrounding the top where the mirror would be. Brightstrike launched her, and she scrambled onto the tower roof to position the mirror.

"Gods, this better work," she muttered as she dropped from the tower, and they raced to the next.

It had to be past noon by now. If the sun had crept from its highest position, would the key still work?

Brightstrike threw her to the top of the next tower. Bex cast a glance at the others fighting below and gasped. Gavyn lay on his side. Lynniki crouched beside him, her hands moving over his surface. That left Rowan, Tera, and Suncall alone against Lystra.

They had to go faster.

"Brightstrike, around to the other side," Bex called. She swiped the ancient dirt from the mirror and positioned it against a pillar so it would stand.

She jumped even as Brightstrike ran to his position, and he turned to catch her.

He didn't even bother putting her down but carried her with huge strides to the next tower to position the mirror. This one was still in its setting and spun easily, the frame on a delicate gimbal.

The last tower was the one closest to the fighting.

Bex clung to Brightstrike's back as he roared and pushed through a wall of fire, raising his arms to protect them from the heat.

He ran at the tower wall and jumped. Bex bent her legs, and at the apex of his leap, she launched herself up the tower wall, scrambling up the cracks to the top.

Brightstrike landed with a *thump* that shook the base of the tower and made the mirror wobble. Bex hauled it into position, kicking aside the bricks that were in the way.

Below them, Suncall appeared behind Lystra again and ducked under her arm, grabbing it to throw her off balance.

But Suncall had used the technique enough now that the battle-hardened mage anticipated it. She planted her feet and brought her bloody hand around to cast a spell directly in Suncall's face.

Brightstrike roared. He tore his hammer from his back and rushed the mage. He brought his hammer around and smashed it down against Lystra's outstretched arm.

The mage screamed and released Suncall, staggering back a few steps. Closer to the base of Bex's tower.

Bex swore. She yanked the mirror into what she hoped was the right position, and she hung over the side of the tower. She winced at the height. This was going to hurt. But it wasn't that much worse than dropping from a roof back in the city, and she'd done that plenty of times.

She aimed and then let go...

And fell directly on Lystra's head.

The mage slammed to the ground, and Bex rolled free of her.

Lystra screamed with rage and pushed to her feet, blood streaming from her arms and her nose.

Bex crawled away, her legs still aching from the fall.

Beneath her palms, the platform rumbled.

Lystra looked down, eyes wide. "What?"

Rowan gasped. "The pedestal."

In the center of the platform the key glowed, five streams of light hitting it simultaneously.

The dais in the middle rose to reveal pillars and a doorway with two great stone doors.

The whole platform continued to rumble even after the doorway appeared, and Bex stared out at the Shattered Waves.

They were rising. The central nuraghi and the other ruins all across the bay, including the walls where they'd walked, lifted out of the sea, shedding water as they went.

Cascades of water came pouring down as entire buildings rose out of the bay.

This place wasn't several disconnected nuraghis scattered across the waves.

It was a city hidden under the water.

Lystra staggered as the platform moved under her, and Bex saw her chance.

She lunged, arms outstretched and pushed Lystra off the edge of the platform.

The mage screamed as she went over and then her cry cut off abruptly.

Bex crawled to the edge to glance down.

Lystra lay on the roof of a newly surfaced building over twenty feet below.

A shadow fell over her, and she looked up and up at Brightstrike, who held Suncall cradled in his arms.

"Are you all right?" Bex said.

Suncall waved a limp hand. "I'm fine."

"I meant you." Bex hauled herself to her feet. "You hit her."

The Taur-El blinked at her. "Yes."

"And you're all right with that?'

"If felt... good."

Suncall winced, but she didn't say anything.

"Was it the frenzy?" Bex asked.

Brightstrike held her gaze, steady. "Am I speaking with you coherently?"

Bex raised an eyebrow. "Yes."

"Then it was not the frenzy."

Tera stepped up beside them, naked blade in her hand.

Below, Lystra cursed and struggled to rise. Suddenly twenty feet didn't seem like all that much.

"Damn," Bex muttered. "Of course it wouldn't be that easy."

Lystra glared up at Bex. She only swayed a little. She raised her arm and the sharpened nail on her pinky.

"Oh now I've really pissed her off. Get inside," Bex cried to the others.

Rowan and Lynniki were trying to right Gavyn.

"Go!" Tera called.

Brightstrike ran for the big double doors with Suncall still in his arms. Tera scooped Gavyn up as she ran past, and Rowan and Lynniki sprinted after her.

Bex was the last to reach the door. It had already swung

open as if it sensed their presence, and the others crowded inside.

"Do you really think she'll follow? She has to be running out of power," Rowan said. "Right? She can't throw spells at us forever."

Bex didn't have the breath to answer her.

There was a whooshing sound behind them, like wind racing up the side of the platform, and Bex's neck crawled. Whatever that spell was, it had to be pushing Lystra to the top, ready for round two.

Bex dove through the door, and Tera pushed it shut behind her.

That wouldn't be enough. Lystra would get it open in a second.

Bex rolled to her feet, her mark tingling. The door had so much magic in it that it nearly made her palm go numb. That made sense. The magic key had opened the magic door without knobs or handles.

"Back up," Bex said, stripping off her gloves and the linen wrapping her right hand.

Tera opened her mouth to protest but took one look at Bex's face and backed up a step.

Bex slapped her bare hand against the door and let the mark work. Brilliant light flashed between her palm and the door's surface, and her skin heated till it burned. Breath hissed between her teeth, but she held herself still as the power flowed up her hand and settled under her breastbone, filling her up from the inside.

It pressed against her ribs, making her heart pound in her chest.

Too much. It was too much.

But if she stopped, if she left any behind, the doors might still open and let Lystra inside.

Bex dropped her head to pant but kept her hand in place, draining every last drop of magic out of the doors.

The flare dissipated, and her palm stopped burning.

She dropped to her knees and rested her head against the doors which were now sealed from the inside.

Chapter 25
Bex

Bex cradled her hand against her chest as she focused on breathing. The burning in her hand had stopped, but the power inside her felt like a small sun, searing its way through her skin. Gods, she'd never taken so much before. She'd have to be careful the next couple of days until it bled off and went away like it always did. Eventually.

They stood at the top of a flight of stairs that led down into the dark.

"Do you think she'll be able to get in?" Rowan whispered behind her.

Her lantern lit the interior of the nuraghi so at least they weren't in pitch black. But they'd left at least one of the packs lying on the stones outside. Hopefully they had enough food to last until they found the mirror and another way out.

Bex shook her head, forcing her eyes open. "She can't get in," she said. "The door is sealed now. She can push all she wants and won't get through. Unless she has a battering ram."

Rowan knelt to help her, but Bex shook her head and winced away. Her hand was completely unwrapped. Nothing between her mark and any of them. She cradled it against her chest to keep from accidentally touching any of them.

Rowan's lips pinched, like she wanted to say something, but she kept quiet.

"So, we're locked in?" Gavyn struggled in Tera's arms until she put him down.

"It's a city," Bex said, bracing her good hand against the door. "An entire city we just un-submerged. There's got to be more exits somewhere."

"Are you all right?" Rowan asked Gavyn.

Gavyn shook himself. "One of her spells disrupted the magic on my joints for a second. I'm fine now. I think."

"I'll tweak it when I get a chance," Lynniki said.

"But first," Rowan said then turned to Bex. "What just happened?"

Bex had to take a deep breath before levering herself to her feet. Damn Lystra. This was going to raise all sorts of questions Bex wasn't prepared to answer. "Which part?"

"All of it," Rowan said, her round face set into an implacable expression. "Who was that? Why did she want you dead? What did you do to the door?"

"Maybe one thing at a time," Lynniki said. "Though I'm also curious, so if you could hurry it up, please."

Bex leaned against the door, head tilted back. "That was one of Vamreth's mages. Lystra," she said.

"But what did she want?" Rowan said. "Why is she after you?"

"Did you steal something from her?" Tera asked.

Bex tried to straighten, but her chest still burned, so she staggered instead. "She stole something from me."

"What?" Rowan said.

"My life." Bex glared at all of them. "Vamreth's experiments? The ones I told you about? She was the one who took

207

me. Kept me. Experimented on me." Bex rubbed her head with her good hand. It was starting to ache.

"That was years ago," she said. "I'd hoped she was dead."

"Why would she be after you now?" Rowan said. She handed over a waterskin, and Bex took it gratefully. "After you've been free all this time?"

"Maybe she didn't want news of her work traveling?" Gavyn said. "She needs to kill you to cover it up."

Bex shook her head. "But how did she find out I was alive?" Bex took a long drink from the skin. "I could have told loads of people what they did by now."

"What did they do?" Tera asked.

Bex gave her a look. "Experiments."

"You said that. What kind?"

"Bad ones." Bex corked the waterskin viciously. "I don't know. I'm not a mage."

Rowan held up her hands. She'd hung the lantern from her belt so it illuminated their room. "If we know, maybe we can help. There must be something going on if she wants to kill you for it. Even now."

Bex gritted her teeth until they ached. Gods, she hated giving up secrets. But it wasn't like she had much of a choice. Lystra had left her with few ways forward.

She blew out her breath. "Fine." She uncurled her hand from her chest and slowly held it out.

"They marked us," she said. "They burned their magic into us. It's some kind of spell."

Tera's eyes locked on the glistening scars criss-crossing her palm. Circles and lines all connecting across the creases of her palm. It very clearly wasn't a thief's brand.

She raised her chin when Tera finally met her eyes.

Tera grunted, and Bex figured that was as close to an apology as she was going to get.

Rowan leaned closer, and Bex fought the urge to pull away. Already her hand shook.

"You used it on the door," she said. "What does it do?"

"It sucks the magic out of spells. They wanted a way to gather and store power for later so mages would have an endless supply. They made us into their vessels."

Lynniki tilted her head, frowning between Bex's palm and the door.

"Who is 'us?'" Gavyn asked.

Bex hid her reaction and shrugged. "Others like me. People no one would miss. They didn't survive. Their marks killed them. But there's something different about mine. The mages considered it a failure, but whatever it is, allows me to live."

Rowan reached for her hand, but Bex yanked it back.

"No!" she and Tera said at the same time.

Bex smiled grimly at the guard captain. "She's figured it out. Whatever you do, don't touch it. It's... always going. Always sucking. It takes the power out of anything. Even people."

Rowan's eyes went wide. "That's why she's chasing you."

"What?" Bex shook her head.

"That's Line Magic," Gavyn said. "Line Magic isn't like the others. One spell and then done. If the lines still meet, then the spell is still active. And any active spell requires power. It must be drawing power from the mage that made it."

"That's..." Bex started. How much could she say before they started to fill in blanks she didn't want filled? "That's what happened to the others. Their marks all drained them."

"And yours drains your mage."

"She's not mine," Bex snapped.

"Of course not," Rowan said. "I didn't mean..."

"It's probably only a small amount normally," Gavyn said, clearing his throat. "Small enough that it would just fade into all her other spells, and she wouldn't even notice."

"But when you use your mark to drain something," Rowan said. "It would... maybe 'flare' is a good word. It would flare and draw more power. Enough that she would notice."

"Enough to track you down and get rid of the nuisance," Tera said.

Gavyn snorted. "Depending on how much you drained, it could be considerably more than a nuisance."

Bex looked between her hand and the door. "I just drained a lot. As much as I can hold."

"Perhaps that is why she is not trying to break down the door," Brightstrike said.

Bex could imagine Lystra lying on the stone platform, knocked out cold by the power drain of Bex's spell. And she could imagine how livid she would be when she came to.

"She's never going to let me go," she said. Her jaw clenched. "I already had to live with this for the rest of my life." She waved her marked hand in the air. "Now I'm going to have to live with her hunting me?"

"Until she kills you or you kill her," Tera said.

Bex swore.

"Maybe we can find a less drastic solution," Rowan said.

"Who's 'we?'" Bex said. "This is my problem. No one else's."

Rowan planted her hands on her hips. "Well, she did just try to kill us too. So it sounds like it's 'our' problem."

"I'm not going to let it interfere with my work," Bex said. She yanked her gloves back on with a wince. Her palm was still a little sore, but she wanted to get it out of sight as quickly as possible. As soon as it was covered, she resettled her satchel on her shoulder and thrust her hand under her other arm to keep it out of the way.

Something clinked, and Bex stiffened, hearing for a moment the jingle of a pair of bells. But it was only one of the tools on Lynniki's pack swaying as she shifted her feet.

"Let's get going," Bex said. "We have to find the mirror and find a way to get out of here. If we go fast enough, maybe we can leave Lystra behind, and you all will never have to worry about her again."

"Leaving you to worry about her on your own?" Rowan asked as Bex passed her and headed down the dark stairs.

Bex pretended she hadn't heard.

Chapter 26
Rowan

The steps plunged downward, a lot like the ones in the tomb, but here they curved around, and Rowan could imagine they traveled along the inside of the circular nuraghi, following the spiraling staircase along its rim. Light fixtures hung on the walls, sconces for candles or some other light source, with mirrors behind to throw the light onto the stairs, but the holders stood empty. Not even burnt candle ends waited there. So Rowan kept the Grief Draw in her hand to light their way. It might have been a bringer of pain and trouble, but it still made a pretty good light source.

And as long as she didn't draw attention to it, there was nothing to indicate to Bex that it was anything other than a normal lantern.

She hurried her steps to catch up with Bex, wincing as the movement jarred her spine. She'd twisted wrong during the fight, and now it hurt to lift the lantern. But at least they hadn't died. The end of Rowan's coat was singed, and she could see Tera trying to hide at least one bad burn under the edge of her cuirass.

But Rowan's heart rate was only just returning to normal. That mage—Lystra—had had a look in her eye that made her stomach clench. A single-minded focus that burned worse than her fire.

Bex stalked down the stairs, eyes on each one as she tested it with her toe before putting her weight on it. Rowan remained far enough back not to interfere, but she held up the lantern to light the way.

The other woman kept her right hand tucked under her arm as if to keep from accidentally touching anything. Or maybe it was to protect the spot where she felt most vulnerable.

"You told me on the ship that it hurts," Rowan said quietly.

Bex glanced back at her, the angry line between her brow shifting to one of confusion. "What?"

"Your hand," Rowan said. "Does it bother you when you drain something?"

Bex shook her head. Not in a negative but like she didn't want to talk about it.

Rowan thought that was going to be it. Bex was so easygoing and charming that it was easy to miss that she never spoke about herself unless pressed. She kept her words light and funny, and that alone kept anyone from getting close to her.

"It stings," she said abruptly, and Rowan had to keep herself from jumping. "Or burns depending on how much I'm doing. And my chest hurts. Like smothering something deep inside. But right now, it's just sore."

She pulled her hand out and flexed it. "The scar is tight most of the time, and it pulls really badly when I try to grip something."

"Oh," Rowan said. "I just noticed you don't use it much."

Bex's lips twitched, but Rowan couldn't tell if it was a smile or a grimace in the swinging light of the lantern.

"No. It's... stiff. It doesn't move very well."

Rowan nodded. "Ah. I'm familiar with that one."

Bex glanced at her, startled, but her gaze remained on Rowan's face without drifting to her rounded shoulder.

She didn't say anything, but now Rowan could definitely tell she smiled. A real smile, not the easy grin she threw around like it meant nothing.

Rowan smiled back.

Brightstrike had let Suncall down to walk on her own two feet finally. She limped a little but seemed to manage the stairs just fine.

"Do you feel any different?" Suncall asked the Taur-El. "Since you're now actually inside the forbidden area?"

Brightstrike held out his hands as if examining them for changes. "No. I do not. But I'm also not trying to procreate right now."

"Thank you for not doing that," Tera said.

Bex snorted.

"That's not how it works." Rowan glanced up and realized Bex, Tera, and Brightstrike were all grinning as if sharing the joke. She rolled her eyes and ducked her head to hide her own smile. At least Bex and Tera weren't fighting anymore.

Bex's step faltered. "Is that... daylight?"

The light along the wall had turned golden, overpowering the sickly, silver glow of the lantern, and Bex hurried forward. As the stairs curved, they saw the steps ended in an open archway. Daylight illuminated the yellow stone.

They stepped out onto a wide bridge spanning the gap between the stairs and another building across the way. Below them, waves slapped the base of the central tower that had risen when the key unlocked the city.

Rowan couldn't help gazing in awe at the buildings and towers all connected with walkways and bridges.

Bex gave it one glance and then peered over the edge of the

bridge and up the side of the tower. Maybe she was looking for traces of Lystra.

"Senji's teeth," Gavyn said as he stepped out into the light. "This place is enormous."

"And kind of a maze." Lynniki lifted her hand to shield her eyes. The sun was beginning to creep down into afternoon, and it struck sparks from the water that still ran down the taller buildings.

"How are we going to find anything?" Tera asked. "Do we have some sort of map?"

Bex looked back at her with a frown. "Of the inside? Of course not?"

Rowan bit her lip. She knew what Tera was actually asking. So did Lynniki and Gavyn. They each glanced at her still holding the lantern.

She gave them the barest nod.

Lynniki and Gavyn moved up beside Bex and Brightstrike and Suncall.

"Look there," Lynniki said. "What's on that tower?"

"Where?" Bex said, raising her hand to shield her eyes from the sun.

"It's glinting."

Tera stepped between Rowan and the others, casually keeping herself in their line of sight and blocking their view of Rowan.

Rowan took that moment to touch the top of the lantern, turning it in a practiced gesture so the white light inside shone through the lens that depicted stylized mountain peaks and trees.

Shadows and light swirled and mixed until Rowan could make out walls and corridors and a stretching bridge superimposed over the ground in front of her. And six blue dots standing where the group had stopped to look at the city.

This was the first use for the Grief Draw that she'd discovered. Jannik had been looking for a weapon, and the Grief Draw certainly could be that in the right hands. But first and foremost, it was a source of knowledge, providing intelligence on enemy strongholds and movement.

It showed her the surroundings in incredible detail and warned of any life forms nearby. Though for some reason, the map never showed Gavyn now that he was a being of brass and magic.

Rowan knew from experience that she was the only one who could see the map, but she still needed to be careful about how she held it and talked about it or Bex and the others would know something was odd. She'd managed it in the tomb just fine, glancing at the map while Bex wasn't paying attention and memorizing the route before putting it away again. The things she'd told Bex about Giant architecture were true, she just hadn't mentioned the fact that she had an advantage when it came to finding her way in dark, underground spaces. Or anywhere else for that matter.

She'd also used the starburst lens during the fight with Lystra. That one could be seen by everyone, but the colors highlighting an enemy's strengths and weaknesses were much more muted and subtle in the sunlight. In a life-and-death situation, Rowan had decided it was worth the risk to use it. Her team knew to look for the colors, and Bex and Brightstrike hadn't been around to see them. She had no idea if Suncall had noticed, and she wasn't about to ask.

The lie made Rowan's gut squirm, and she couldn't quite meet Bex's eyes anytime her hand brushed the lantern. But she would not reveal its true nature. Ever.

It wasn't that she didn't trust Bex. She'd followed the woman across the continent and plunged into ruins with her. But there was something that held her back.

Rowan kept telling herself it was the lantern itself. It was dangerous. It was a secret that people had exploited before. People she'd trusted.

The lantern twisted those relationships, put them at risk. So it was the Grief Draw that she didn't quite trust. Wasn't it?

"It's just glass," Bex said, lowering her hand. "Probably windows." She gave Lynniki a confused look.

"Lynniki, do we know what we're looking for?" Rowan asked. "For the power source that the Taur-Els need?"

Lynniki turned and leaned against the railing of the bridge. It was nearly as tall as her. "Um, I'll definitely know it when I see it."

"That's not as helpful as you think it is," Gavyn said.

Lynniki cast him a look. "Careful or I'll fuse your joints next time you want a checkup."

"I'm just saying..." Gavyn grumbled.

"We're looking for a room set aside where they would have made and kept their power," Lynniki said, ignoring him. "For a city this size, there could have been several. It'll be smaller, unassuming, away from the living areas of the city."

"All right." That wasn't a lot to go on, but she could make it work. Rowan's eyes scanned the map, trying not to look like she was actually scanning the map. She'd had lots of practice with the lantern now, and she'd been reading maps for years. She had a pretty good idea which were living areas and which were public areas based on the size and where they were situated.

There was a room that matched Lynniki's description not too far from them. Smaller, unassuming. Situated near enough to supply power to a good portion of the city but far enough from the living areas to not be in the way.

"The mirror is likely to be lower," Rowan said, mostly to herself. "At the heart of the city."

She couldn't see anything that looked promising yet, but the map would move and expand as they traveled, and she'd keep an eye out.

"We can probably find Brightstrike's power source on the way," Rowan said. She let her arm drop a bit. It hurt her back to hold it up for so long. And it looked conspicuous out here in the light.

"Then let's go," Bex said. She pushed off the railing and gave Rowan a little bow and held out her hand to indicate she should go first.

Bex's grin came too often for it to mean anything significant. She handed them out to anyone and everyone.

But that didn't prevent the flutter in Rowan's chest when Bex flashed her dimple at her.

Rowan swallowed her reaction and went on ahead, keeping one eye on the map and the other on the architecture.

She'd never been in a Giant city before. She'd been to a Delver city, but they built very differently, and their city had been full of brass and gears and steam.

This was full of stone and towers and pillars. They crossed the bridge and plunged into the next building. This one had corridors as wide as a city street, and light filtered down through skylights far above.

Rowan wished she could take notes and carry the map at the same time, but Lynniki had already pulled out her notebook and was sketching away. Rowan tried to take in every detail to remember for later when she could draw the architecture too.

The halls where they walked still dripped, and sometimes little rivers ran alongside them, traveling downhill and out through openings in the walls. Algae grew on the pillars and made the floor slick beneath their feet. In several places, they found fish flapping and gasping in the corners, stranded when the city rose from the bay.

Tera snatched up a couple of big, shiny ones. Rowan had no idea what kind they were.

When Bex gave her a look, Tera said, "What? This will be dinner."

An hour after the bridge, they came out of a dark tunnel that had led mostly down into a vast chamber. According to the map, this room was sunk mostly underwater with only the windows high above letting out into open air. Something magical or mechanical had pumped the water out, but it was still wet. And waves splashed against the windows above them, sending rivulets of sea water down the enormous walls.

Pillars filled the room, holding up the ceiling at least eight stories above them. There was enough space inside to fit Karaval Keep and have plenty of room left over.

Brilliant corals covered the floor, from the door to the far wall visible in the distance. Pink and purple and blue hills and hummocks blocked their way. Limp seagrass spread between them, and Rowan could just imagine what it looked like underwater.

She held her breath at the beauty.

"It's too bad this will all die unless it's submerged again," Bex said softly. "It kinda makes you wish you had gills, doesn't it?" She cast a strange, regretful look at Rowan.

Rowan reached down to pick up a shell that glinted brown and purple in the lantern's light. She ran a finger over its smooth surface.

"It does," she said quietly.

"It feels a little like home," Lynniki said.

"Really?" Rowan couldn't see the resemblance. The Delver city had felt very closed-in to her. Lots of buildings crammed under the dome of the mountain.

"It's a hidden city," Lynniki said, staring up at the waves that sent little spouts of water over the windowsills. "Only this one was covered by water instead of rock."

Rowan glanced around to ask Gavyn if it reminded him of the lab where she'd found him, but he wasn't there behind Tera where she'd thought he'd been.

She opened her mouth to cry out an alarm when she caught

the glint of brass, and he slunk out from around a mound of coral.

Rowan intercepted him as the others spread out through the chamber.

"Where were you?" she whispered.

"Not far. Just looking."

"Gavyn. You need to stay with us. This place could be dangerous."

"I'm being careful."

"What are you even looking for?"

He cocked his head at her. "What do you think?"

She glanced at the lantern and sighed. "Still?"

"Rowan, it's a Giant city. There could be hundreds of solutions to our problem just lying around."

"How would we even know?" She realized her voice was rising and forced herself calm. "I know what you want. And you know I will help. But this is more important right now. We have to get out of here alive. Promise me you'll stay close and not get into trouble."

"Sure, sure," Gavyn said in a voice that gave her no confidence whatsoever.

Rowan winced, but she adjusted the map and rejoined the others. Gavyn was his own person. She could not make his choices for him, but sometimes she wished Lynniki had installed a leash on him.

They found what they were looking for just beyond the coral chamber, down a long hallway much smaller and less grand than everything else had been so far.

Other rooms they'd passed had held broken furniture. Anything wood had rotted away ages ago, but stone tables and a few chairs had remained, cracked and shattered with the passage of time.

Bedrooms, living spaces, dining halls. The coral chamber,

Rowan was willing to bet, had been some sort of ballroom. Maybe a throne room. Hard to tell without a throne.

But this new passage was simple stone with doorways leading to smaller rooms left dark.

"Maintenance," Lynniki said. "I think this is the right place."

At the end of the hall stood the room Rowan had pinpointed on the map. The one that looked like it had been set apart for a purpose.

They stepped inside. The room itself was big, though not as massive as the coral chamber or a lot of the other buildings they'd moved through today. And it was mostly dark, though a subtle glow suffused the air.

Tera stepped forward but stopped abruptly. The light of the lantern lit up the edge of a large pool. Water filled the room, leaving only a narrow walkway just inside the door.

"This is all still full of water," she said. "Where is the power source?"

"Up there." Bex stood at the edge of the water, head tipped back to stare at the ceiling.

They all followed her gaze. Above, on the high ceiling, hung a cylinder. If Rowan didn't know any better, she would have said it was made of glass filled with opaque, blue liquid that gave off the distinct glow that glinted in the water. But if it was anything like the Grief Draw, which was also Giant-made, then it wasn't glass at all but something far harder that couldn't be broken by any normal means.

"Brightstrike?" Rowan said.

"It looks just like the one we use for our ritual," he said, staring at the cylinder. "Only ours has been cold and dead for decades."

"That's a power well all right," Lynniki said.

"What exactly is it?" Tera asked.

"It's a vessel that holds magical energy."

"Like a bucket?" Gavyn said.

"Or a jar?" Suncall added.

Lynniki sighed. "For lack of a better analogy, yes. Sure. But a bucket or a jar couldn't hold magical energy, and this can. It collects it and holds it for later use. Kind of like Bex."

Rowan glanced at Bex, worried about how she'd react to the jibe.

Bex's eyes widened for a split second before she laughed, a bright, astonished sound.

"At least I don't glow." She tapped her lips and looked thoughtful. "Though maybe if I did, I could get Lynniki to examine me too."

She slid a suggestive gaze to the Delver.

Rowan choked.

"Oh my gods," Tera muttered, rubbing her temples.

"You can't tell me not to flirt with you and then complain when I flirt with other people," Bex told her.

Lynniki just raised an eyebrow at Bex. "Little digger, I'm three times your age. At least."

Bex tipped her head and said, "You say that like it's a bad thing."

"I say it like you couldn't handle me." Lynniki gave her a little headshake and stepped to the edge of the water and stared up at the well.

Bex cast a look at Rowan. "It was worth a shot."

"Is this customary Human behavior?" Brightstrike asked. "I'll admit I'm not familiar with your mating rituals."

"No," Bex said. "It's just a perk of being around me."

"I'm starting to wonder what would happen if someone actually said yes to you." Rowan crossed her arms.

Bex just winked at her, sending another unexpected flutter through Rowan's chest.

"I wish the well was connected," Lynniki said, dragging

them back to the task at hand. "It could be powering all sorts of spells if the city was still functioning."

"This was a thing that had to be maintained and serviced, right?" Bex said. "So there has to be a way to reach it."

"Here," Gavyn said from further down the walkway. "While you were busy flirting, I was using my eyes."

"You don't have eyes," Bex said, moving to join him.

Rowan brought the lantern closer. A pedestal of curved metal stood on the edge of the pathway. It held up a pad of smooth stone big enough for a large hand.

"It looks just like the one that locked and unlocked the door in the..." He might not have eyes, but Rowan could tell he glanced at Bex. "In the lab where I was kept."

The same lab where they'd found the lantern. That facility had also been Giant-built.

"I take it you're supposed to touch it?" Bex said. She glanced at her hand. Then she pulled off her left glove and laid her unmarked palm against the smooth, stone surface.

Above them, the glowing well hissed, and arcs of lightning spat out, crackling across the water.

"Oh, shit," Bex said and jumped back.

"It's sending power to different parts of the city," Lynniki called as she pressed herself against the wall beside the door.

"Well, make it stop," Tera said. "Before we're all fried. Turn it off." She glared at Bex.

"No," Rowan cried. "Look."

All around the pool of water, pieces of the wall slid out—big, flat sections forming platforms. Arcs of lightning jumped the empty space to strike them. Then they'd slide back into the wall again as the next one slid out. From the ceiling, a catwalk dropped down, leading from the wall to the well in the center.

"We can use those to get up to it," Bex said, already moving toward the lowest one that slid out and back in just beyond the edge of the walkway. "Lynniki, is there a way to detach it once I'm up there?"

"Yes, but—"

"You can't touch it," Rowan said.

Bex winced, coming up short. "I'll use my other hand."

"That's not what I meant. It will kill you the same way it kills the Taur-Els," Rowan said. "The same way most Giant artifacts kill anyone but Delvers."

"Not right away," Tera said, glancing at Rowan. "And your sister recovered after handling one for a few hours."

"What happened to your sister?" Bex asked sharply.

Rowan sighed, not willing to get into the whole story here. Especially since it involved the Grief Draw.

"She got sick. She recovered, eventually, but it took a long time. Others didn't."

Bex's lips tightened. "All right, how does it kill you? And how fast?"

"Boils and sores," Lynniki said.

"Nausea and vomiting," Gavyn added. "And eventually your skin comes off while you puke up your insides," Gavyn said.

"It's a really unpleasant way to go," Rowan said when Bex blanched.

"Our device only killed those who had been exposed for more than an hour," Brightstrike said. "And even then, they had to have been holding the well directly."

"Delvers are immune?" Bex said, staring up at the well with a wince. "You're sure?"

"Positive," Lynniki said. But she stared between the moving platforms and the others. "I can't get up there by myself," she said quietly.

Rowan winced. She doubted *she'd* be able to get up there at all. Even with help.

Bex blew out her breath. "All right." She strode to the edge of the path.

"All right?" Rowan said, following her. "What—"

"I'll help Lynniki up. I'll be fine as long as I don't stay in contact with it for more than an hour, right? We'll be done in less than that, and then one of you can carry it so the rest of us don't die."

"How do we get up that first step?" Lynniki asked.

The first platform slid out to absorb an arc from the well before sliding back in, but it was as high as Lynniki's head and at least a couple of feet out from the walkway. Bex wasn't sure she would be able to lift Lynniki from that far away.

"Brightstrike?" Bex asked. "You up for more launching?"

"As long as you think you can land the jump," Brightstrike rumbled.

Bex just snorted.

"Wait," Rowan said as Bex leaned forward.

"What?" Bex turned back, but Rowan was left with her mouth opening and closing because she had nothing left to say. Except "*don't do this*" and that wasn't really an option.

"Be careful." That was all that was left—and what a stupid thing to say.

But Bex's gaze softened for a moment in the glow of the lantern. Rowan half expected her to crack a joke about Rowan caring about her after all, but instead she said. "Of course."

Bex hesitated, then added quietly, "I'll get her down safely. Don't worry."

Lynniki dumped her pack on the ground and slid several of her tools into her belt.

Brightstrike knelt, and Bex stepped into his hands like they'd practiced this before. Maybe they had on the platform. Rowan hadn't really been paying attention to how Bex had climbed the towers.

Brightstrike waited, then with an impressive heave, he launched Bex into the air as the first platform slid out. She arched up and over and landed lightly in the middle of the flat surface.

"Quick," Bex said. "Before it slides in again."

Lynniki stepped up to Brightstrike, and before she could stammer something about being ready, he'd thrown her into the air.

Chapter 27
Bex

B ex landed lightly on the flat surface of the platform. It was made of a dark stone, the same as the walls and floor, and it slid out of its slot in the wall so smoothly it must have been on rollers.

Bex caught her balance and spun to see Lynniki flying toward her.

She planted her feet and grabbed the Delver in a bear hug, keeping them both from going over the edge. She figured the water probably wasn't safe with all the energy flickering over the surface.

Lynniki got her feet under her and said in Bex's ear, "Duck."

Bex jerked back. "What?"

Lynniki grabbed the back of her neck and shoved her head down. An arc of lightning streaked just over her and struck the platform.

"Oh."

Lynniki rolled her eyes. "When your tinker says 'duck,' you say—"

"How low. Got it."

Lynniki pointed down. "See that groove. That's where the energy is going. We need to stay out of its way."

"What happens if it hits us?"

"Bad things."

Bex winced as the platform started rolling in toward the wall. "Point taken. Time to jump."

She spun to face the next platform. It rolled out as this one rolled in, and Bex hopped up almost like a big stair step. She grabbed Lynniki's arm to help her haul herself up.

"Great. Only a few more to go." Bex said. "And up again."

They climbed the platforms, avoiding the arcs of energy and trying to get closer to the glowing cylinder in the middle of the ceiling.

It wasn't exactly like climbing stairs; sometimes they had to backtrack in order to get higher. Sometimes they had to climb nearly vertically.

Halfway up, Lynniki slipped, and Bex lunged to catch her as the Delver tipped over the edge. She seemed to hang in the air before Bex grabbed her hand.

The Delver swung, and Bex strained, trying to keep from dropping her in the water far below.

"Lynniki," Bex grated out, and the Delver stared up at her, eyes wide. "I'm going to drop you."

"What?"

"The next platform down. Swing your feet, and on the count of three, I'm going to drop you."

Lynniki tipped her head to look between her dangling feet. "All right."

"One. Two. Three."

Lynniki rolled as she landed, fetching up against the wall. But now Bex had to drop down with her, so they had to backtrack back up the platforms. They were both sweaty and gasping by the time they made it to the catwalk around the top of the walls.

Bex boosted Lynniki up under the railing, then jumped to catch the edge as the platform rolled back into the wall.

A hand grabbed the back of her shirt, and Lynniki helped her haul herself up.

Bex lay there gasping for a second before rolling to face the well. From here they could see it was nearly as long as Bex's arm and crackled with energy.

"This had better be worth it," Bex muttered.

"Saving an entire race's chance at reproduction and survival?" Lynniki grinned. "Of course it's worth it. And I get to see one up close so... bonus!"

She waved to the others down below. "All right, turn it off!"

Below them, Tera stepped to the pad and placed her hand on it. The well immediately stopped sending out sparks, and all the platforms slid back into the wall. With less lightning sizzling around, it also got darker, but since they were right up next to the thing that glowed, they could at least still make out their path.

"How will we get back down?"

"I'm hoping taking it off will activate a failsafe."

Bex blinked, not sure if she wanted to ask what that meant.

"And if worse comes to worst, we can toss the well to Brightstrike and jump into the water." Lynniki edged out to the end of the catwalk, leaning to peer at the well.

"It's a good thing I'm not scared of heights," Bex said to herself, following Lynniki. "Can you get it off?"

"Oh sure. It's just clamped on."

Lynniki pulled a screwdriver from her belt but another tool came loose at the same time and fell, taking a long time before splashing into the water below.

"Oops."

"Here." Bex pulled her satchel around to her front and yanked out the length of rope. "Tie this on. Just in case."

Lynniki nodded and then tied the rope to the top of the well.

"I meant you!" Bex cried.

"Yes, but I can swim," Lynniki said, wedging her screwdriver into the crack of the clamp. "This would just sink."

Bex groaned. "All right, if you're going to be all logical about it, I'll just hang onto your belt."

Bex wrapped the end of the rope around the catwalk and then wedged her hand between Lynniki's back and her belt.

Lynniki dug around at the clamps and swore.

"What's wrong?"

"It's stuck. All the salt water buildup has it wedged."

"How breakable is this thing?"

"Um..."

"What will happen if I kick it?"

"What?" Lynniki cried.

"Move over."

Lynniki crawled backward over Bex, and Bex lined up her boot. She kicked at the well, her heel striking what looked like glass but felt like granite.

She gave it another kick, and something crunched at the top of the cylinder.

"It's coming free," Lynniki called.

"Hold onto that rope." Bex really leaned into it this time, and the well broke free.

It dropped.

Lynniki hauled on the rope, and Bex lunged to help her.

Below them, the water bubbled and gurgled, and Bex stared at the well swinging over the dark fountain. "What's that?"

A pillar rose from the surface of the water, climbing toward them.

"Our way down," Lynniki said with a grin.

They lowered the well as the pillar came toward them and

let the cylinder rest on top. Then they both dropped down onto it.

Lynniki hit the surface with an "oof." Bex couldn't roll with so little space, so she landed hard and let her legs fold under her with a grimace.

"Ouch."

Bex glanced at the bottom of her foot as the pillar halted and then slowly reversed its course, lowering back the way it came. "So am I going to have sores on my feet now?"

"Maybe." Lynniki said. "Probably not. That was pretty minimal exposure, all things considered. We'll check them later when it's safe to take your boots off."

"Are you trying to get me undressed?" She said it by rote. Lynniki had given her the opening, so of course she had to take it. But she was having more fun peering over the side of the pillar at the others.

Rowan stood at the edge of the stone walkway, beaming up at her.

Then she felt eyes on the back of her neck. She turned to see Lynniki staring at her, lips pulled thin.

"What is it?" she said. At the base of the pillar, another platform was rolling out across the water, creating a bridge between their pillar and the walkway.

"I have about thirty seconds to say this so I'm going to say it fast."

"What?"

Lynniki looked over at the others as they raced across the bridge toward the pillar. "Don't hurt any of them. All right?"

Bex reared back. What? Where had that come from? "It wasn't my intention to hurt anyone."

"No. But you might accidentally. It doesn't matter if you didn't mean to; they'd still be hurt." Lynniki was quiet for a moment. "They're my family. Especially Rowan. Her dad wandered off and got himself labeled as 'missing' so I'm looking out for her."

Bex remembered a sword swung directly at her head in the darkened sanctuary. "I think she's perfectly capable of looking out for herself."

"Maybe. But she's not used to as many pretty words as you fling around. You can mess with me all you want. I've got a thick skin. But if you wound my niece, we'll have a problem. I know how to take limbs off, you know." She wiggled her metal fingers.

Bex gulped. "I understand," she said.

"Good." Lynniki stood and brushed a hand down the surface of the well, gaze already distant as she considered the artifact.

"Lynniki," Bex said, standing with a wince. "I didn't mean to hurt you either."

Lynniki snorted. "Thanks for that, little digger. But you didn't. You're not really my type."

Chapter 28
Bex

Rowan led them down through the bowels of the city, using her expertise to figure out where they were going next.

Bex didn't understand what exactly she was looking at, but also she didn't want to make Rowan explain it at every corner. Bex trusted her.

Which was a weird thing to say, even alone in her mind.

She shook her head.

I trust her expertise, she clarified. *That's all it is. Nothing special about that.*

Lynniki had emptied a bunch of scrap metal and springs from her pack in order to fit the well inside, and now they all carried torches as well as Rowan's lantern.

As they got deeper, the corridors got more and more slippery, covered in a layer of black sludge tinted green on top. There were no more pretty, coral forests. They didn't see any more wells glowing blue. Nothing but the expanse of hallways that had lived so deep underwater that no light had touched them in eons.

All along the way, Bex kept a careful eye on the others to

233

keep them from blundering into any traps. That's how she noticed one of their party kept going missing. Over and over.

The third time Gavyn slipped back into line with them, Bex nudged Rowan.

"He's going to get himself killed if he gets caught somewhere without us," she murmured.

Rowan's lips tightened as she glanced back at her companion. "I've mentioned that. I can't keep him in check, short of tying him up."

"Might be worth it," Bex said. "What's he looking for that's so important he'll risk his life?"

"Who says he's looking for something?"

Bex raised an eyebrow. "Please, I know another treasure hunter when I see one."

"He's not—" Rowan stopped herself and blew out her breath. "I guess he might as well be right now."

"Mmhmm. The difference is that I know to be careful."

Rowan sighed. "He's very driven. He was... hurt. By a Giant artifact long ago. Now he would like to find a way to destroy it, so it won't hurt anyone else. He thinks there might be something here on Taur that could help."

Bex grunted as Rowan took the lead again. The antiquarian might use generic language to hide the full truth, but Bex could read at least some of the story between the lines.

Gavyn had been hurt by a Giant artifact. Rowan was protecting a Giant artifact back in that sanctuary of hers. Gavyn was inexplicably bound to Rowan.

Clearly he had ties to Jannik's weapon. And now he wanted to destroy it?

Just as clearly, there was some tension there. Maybe Rowan wouldn't let him or... or... something.

She rolled her shoulders and forced herself to let it go. As much as she'd like to know the whole story, that wasn't what was important.

Using that knowledge of Giant architecture she had, Rowan led them to a long, dark corridor as tall as four Taur-Els standing on each other's shoulders.

"I think we're directly below the central tower now," Rowan said, staring straight up.

Bex glanced up, but she couldn't see anything. The corridor ahead was lined with square tiles buried under thick layers of sea mud.

"We're getting close," Bex said.

Rowan gave her a surprised look. "How can you tell?"

Bex picked up a rock that had been washed into the corner and skipped it down the hallway.

One of the tiles depressed with a click, and a flash of light lit up the dark hallway. An ancient spell waiting to take them by surprise.

Rowan blinked. "Good call."

"Walk in my footsteps," she told the others. "Don't step on anything that looks loose."

Bex tiptoed forward, testing each dirty tile with a toe before putting her weight on it.

It took long enough, Bex's headache came back. The pain pressed behind her eyes, reminding her of every moment that passed.

Anera was waiting back in Usara, possibly dying, and Bex was tiptoeing around a ruin an entire continent away.

They'd taken so long to get here, and days more to find the ruin, find the key, and make their way down here. Bex knew in the back of her head that it was a minor miracle they'd found it so quickly, but that didn't help ease the knot in her gut that told her they were taking too long. Anera would be dead by the time she got back.

She should have picked an easier target, an artifact that was closer. She should have stayed nearer to Anera.

She should have—

There was a click under her boot heel, and she threw herself back into Rowan.

A flash of light lit up the corridor, and Bex squeezed her eyes shut as it amplified over and over, so bright it could blind her.

Blind her? What was the point of that, unless you also...

Bex gasped and pulled Rowan to the ground. "Get down!" she called to the others.

Even with her eyes shut, she heard their muffled thuds as they each hit the floor.

A whirring noise made the hair on the back of Bex's neck rise, and a breath of wind on her cheek warned her to duck even lower. She kept her hand pressed to Rowan's shoulder to keep her flat and held her breath as the whirring whizzed by overhead.

It finally faded, and she could blink the spots from her vision.

"What was that?" Rowan asked.

"I'm not sure, but if a trap is designed to blind you, you can bet it will throw something nasty right after you're stunned."

Rowan's mouth pinched. "Healer's Ghost," she muttered.

"Everyone all right?" Bex called.

She counted five grumbles and let out a breath.

Bex realized she was draped across the other woman, knee across her legs and hand on her shoulder.

She snatched her hand back with a gasp and rolled clear of Rowan. She cleared her throat and stood, giving the antiquarian a hand as well.

"Sorry I pushed you down."

Rowan rubbed at the mud caking the back of her coat. "I think I should be thanking you."

Bex's hands itched to help Rowan brush herself off, and she thrust them behind her. "Well, we're definitely in the right place."

"How can you tell?"

"The traps are light based. And look at those." She pointed to the wall sconces. There were more mirrors to reflect candles that just weren't there anymore.

And at the end of the hall, past two more tiles that seemed looser than the others, stood two wide doors carved with a scene Bex couldn't make out yet. She raised her torch and saw a circular dais before the door. It stood one step above the rest of the floor.

"This looks promising," Gavyn said. He leaped over the last two rows of tiles and sniffed the edge of the dais. Did he even have a sense of smell?

Rowan had made it across the tiles and stood looking at the door, so Bex turned to give Lynniki a hand across the dangerous ground. The well glowed through the crack between the flap and the side of her pack.

When it was her turn, Tera looked at the outstretched hand Bex offered and rolled her eyes before hopping to the safe ground. Brightstrike moved, surprisingly graceful, over to the area around the dais, Suncall clinging to his back.

"You guys have been friends for a while, haven't you?" Bex said with a grin.

"A few years," Suncall said, seemingly comfortable. "Why?"

"No reason."

Tera stepped up beside Rowan to stare at the relief carved into the door. With the lantern lighting up the surface, they could finally see it was a carving of a woman. A Giant with hair down to her waist and a sweeping dress that flowed all the way to the base of the door. She had a horn raised to her lips as if she was calling someone for aid. The image was mirrored on the other side of the door.

Tera put her hands on the door and shoved before Bex could warn her to look for more traps. But the door didn't move.

Bex sighed. "It's not going to be that easy," she said.

"Were we supposed to bring the key?" Lynniki said. "I don't see another keyhole."

Rowan turned. "No. But this dais seems significant."

She stepped to the edge, and Bex joined her.

Rowan glanced up at her face. "Do you think it's another trap?"

Bex knelt to examine the edge. There was enough of a crack here that the platform could move if weight was put on it.

"Maybe," she said. "But I don't see any other way in."

She stepped up onto the dais.

Nothing shifted until she reached the middle of the circle, and then it did sink a little under her weight.

Bex braced herself, but there was no blinding light. No whirring.

There was a cascade of clicks, and little pieces of the dais flipped over along the edge, lining the entire platform with red gems that winked in the torch light.

"Oh," Rowan said, kneeling with a wince. "They're the same color as the gathering key."

"This must be the lock to the door," Gavyn said.

"The opposite of the one above." Bex looked up, but the dark ceiling couldn't tell her if she was directly underneath the pedestal of the central tower.

Her eyes widened. "The opposite."

"What?" Lynniki said.

"It works the opposite. That lock held one key in the middle, gathering all the light. This is a bunch of keys around the edge and we—"

"Have to provide the light!" Rowan said.

They grinned at each other.

Tera cleared her throat, and Bex flushed. She was just standing there, smiling like an idiot.

She held out her torch and spun in a circle making sure the

light struck each gem at least once.

Nothing happened.

Her heart sank. She'd been so sure that was it.

"Maybe it has to be in a certain order," Gavyn said. "Like a combination lock."

Bex stared down at the gems in horror. "There's at least twenty of them. We'll be here for months trying out different combinations."

Rowan held out her free hand as if to calm her down. Bex hadn't even realized she'd raised her voice.

"Don't panic," Rowan said. "Maybe the light just needs to be closer."

Bex stepped closer to the gems to hold the torch over them, but the moment she stepped out of the center of the circle, the platform clicked, and the gems all flipped back into their hidden position.

"No," she said, stepping back. "My weight has to be balanced in the middle."

"And I don't think it's a combination," Lynniki said, tapping her lips. "How would you keep the light on only one gem at once?"

Rowan glanced at the others. "Any ideas?"

Tera leaned against the door examining her fingernails. "I'm the brawn in this operation," she said. "I'll let you guys figure this out."

"Gee, thanks," Bex said.

Brightstrike knelt beside the platform, and Suncall leaned over their shoulder to see the gems. "If it is opposite the one above," Brightstrike said. "Then where are the mirrors?"

Bex looked at her feet. He was right. The key had sat in the middle and gathered the sunlight, but it hadn't worked until the last mirror had been placed in the right position.

"There are twenty-five gems," Rowan said, almost to herself. "Five times five. Five is always significant to Giants—"

"They all need to be activated at once," Bex said, the pieces from the central tower and the gathering key clicking into place. "The light has to hit all of them at once."

She glanced at the flickering torch in her hand. "And it would probably help to have a clearer light. Like sunlight. Rowan, can I borrow your lantern?"

Rowan looked pale as the silvery light of her lantern warred with the light of the torches. "What?"

"Your lantern," Bex said, holding out her hand. "It's the clearest light. Can I borrow it?"

Rowan looked between Bex and the lantern and swallowed. Gavyn and Lynniki glanced at each other and then at Rowan. Tera's eyes glittered from the door.

What's wrong? Rowan is usually a lot quicker than this.

"Why don't I try it?" Rowan said quietly.

Oh, Bex thought. *She doesn't trust me.*

What did that thing do that Rowan wouldn't even let her hold it? Was it so valuable Rowan worried she'd run off with it?

Heat beat in her cheeks, and she swallowed down a bitter taste that filled her mouth. It made sense, right? It wasn't like she trusted Rowan all that much. It just meant the feeling was mutual.

"Sure," Bex said after a moment too long, and she hopped down off the platform, forcing a nonchalant smile.

Rowan stepped up with the lantern which must be special enough to her that she wouldn't even let Bex touch it.

Bex rolled her shoulders like she needed to stretch, but mostly it was a chance to reset herself and clear that strange feeling of disappointment and shame out of her throat. So what if she wasn't someone a person like Rowan would trust? It wasn't like she didn't know who and what she was.

Liar. Thief. Someone who got things done.

She raised her chin as Rowan settled herself in the center of the platform and all the gems flipped to twinkle in the light.

"No good," Lynniki said. "Your shadow covers this side."

"Hold it over your head," Gavyn said.

Rowan took the lantern in both hands and lifted it high, wincing. The movement probably cost her a lot more with her spine all twisted and bunched.

The light wobbled for a second before she steadied herself. The silvery glow of the lantern fell all around Rowan in a perfect circle.

The gems lit and flashed once, twice, and then the platform slowly sank until it was level with the floor. Behind them, there was a crunch.

Bex spun and saw Tera stumble away from the big, carved doors. Dust showered down as the crack between the two doors split right between the two horns. The doors swung inward.

The disappointment that had settled over her at Rowan's hesitation lifted, and Bex skipped forward a couple of steps, trying to get her torch to light up the inside of the room that had been revealed.

The others crowded behind her. Rowan slipped her lantern into the case at her hip as if there were enough torches now that she didn't need it. But Bex knew better. She caught the furtive look Rowan cast her before closing it away. As if Bex were going to leap across the space and snatch it from her.

It didn't matter. They were finally here, and she was about to get what she'd come for. They could all go home after that, and Bex could just forget that look and that moment's pause.

Bex grit her teeth and stepped forward, checking the floor for traps first.

The chamber beyond opened before her, lit with a soft glow that looked like a sunset but came from sconces along the walls.

It was enough to illuminate an enormous room as big as the coral chamber above. Pillars lined the walls between the sconces and the ceiling was lost in the darkness above.

All along the floor sat piles of objects. Some coins and a few gems but also things like piles of armor and weapons. There was a group of watches all laid out in rows. And a whole forest of statues.

Bex stepped inside and moved between the stacks, her heart beating fast.

Something felt off.

This whole place was completely dry. Sludge and unearthed marine life had filled the rest of the city, but here the floor remained dry, and nothing marred the piles.

On her left, she passed a pile of armor. One thing sat on top prominently as if on display—a pristine set of pauldrons from the Galiton era. A sword similar to one she'd seen in the Unlocked Door sat propped against a pillar so the light from a sconce made it glow.

"How is there light?" Suncall said, voice hushed.

Lynniki stepped across to one of the sconces and craned her neck to peer up at it. "Tubes," she said. "Tubes and mirrors. This is actual sunlight reflected down from the surface a hundred times with mirrors."

Mirrors and light again. If Bex had any doubt they were in the right place, that just dissolved it.

"What is all this stuff?" Gavyn asked.

"Treasure," Tera said. "It's a treasure room. Obviously."

Bex kept walking, eyes scanning the piles. Here was a whole group of belt knives, just like the one she carried, but some of these were old enough for their hilts to have worn away and their blades to tarnish.

Treasure room wasn't quite right. Bex knew her treasure, and this was... something else.

"It looks like a dragon's hoard," Lynniki said.

"There's no such thing as dragons," Tera scoffed.

"Maybe not on Noksonon."

Bex reached out to brush a statue of Grina, one of the

Pentathic gods twisted in a flirtatious pose, the beautifully carved folds of her dress pooling at her feet.

Behind her sat a figure Bex recognized from Triada and another from the tribes in the Eternal Desert.

Not a treasure room. Not a hoard. This was too carefully curated.

"It's a collection," she muttered under her breath.

Someone's careful display after a lifetime of acquisition. More than a lifetime if the sheer volume was any indication.

But where was the collector?

At the far end of the chamber sat another dais and a chest.

It set Bex's teeth on edge.

Hundreds of ruins she'd explored in her lifetime, and nothing good ever came from prominently displayed wealth.

She stepped up next to the dais and tilted her head to examine the chest.

Her palm hummed.

"Careful, there's a trap on that," Lynniki said. "Some sort of spell."

Bex snorted. "Of course there's a trap on it."

She glanced around the rest of the room. She didn't see a mirror. Nothing but a blank wall at the end of the chamber. But it had to be here somewhere.

"Sometimes you have to trigger the trap to see what happens."

She stepped onto the dais, but nothing clicked or whirred, and the tingle in her hand remained the same. The magic must be on the box itself.

Her left hand crept to her chest. She had a little bit of space left. The energy she'd pulled out of the door earlier had started to dissipate. Very slowly. It would take days to feel normal again, but for now, she could absorb a little more.

She pulled her right glove off and placed her palm against

the chest. Her mark flashed, and the energy of the spell flowed into her, making her feel full and bloated again.

"You know that's not a solution for everything," Lynniki said, rolling her eyes. The shadows of her face deepened. If the light was coming from above, then the sun must be setting.

Bex pulled the last of the magic out of the chest and reached for the lid. It wasn't locked.

She opened it and stared.

It was empty. The bottom stared back at Bex mockingly.

Rowan's uneven gait rang against the stones behind them. "What is it?" she said quietly.

Bex fought the roaring in her ears.

"It's nothing," Lynniki said, staring over her shoulder. "There's nothing in there."

Bex took a deep breath and then another, trying to calm the panic that clawed up her throat. If the mirror wasn't here, then where was it?

A rustle sounded above them and echoed in the silence between the pillars, making the back of Bex's neck prickle.

She gulped and tipped her head back to stare up into the shadows.

Something moved in the darkness. A shape crawled along the ceiling and down one of the pillars. As it moved into the glow of the mirrored sconces, light flickered across sleek, black fur and feathers.

Claws clicked, the only sound as the creature stepped from the pillar to the floor and unfurled enormous, black wings.

Tera swore under her breath as she and Brightstrike and Suncall backed up, huddling together with Rowan and Gavyn around the dais.

The last of the reflected sunset illuminated a body like a black panther three times the size of a draft horse. Wings as deep as the night rose from its shoulders to block out the other end of the room and the door they'd come through. Its neck was longer than a cat's, and its feline face had been stretched and molded to look more Human, though its nose was still flat like a cat's and slitted golden eyes stared at them through the dark.

Tera drew her sword, and Brightstrike pulled the hammer from his back. Suncall glanced at him but didn't chastise him for it this time.

Bex took a moment to wish she'd learned to wield any sort of weapon.

That Human-but-not mouth parted, revealing sharp, narrow teeth, and the creature spoke.

"The thing you seek isn't here." Its voice was a rumble even deeper than Brightstrike's, and it rolled across the room like approaching thunder.

Bex stood, slowly, working some spit back into her dry mouth.

"How do you know what we're looking for?" she said.

Tera gave her an exasperated look like *"you're talking to this thing?"*

"This place has one purpose," the creature said. "Every step you've taken to unlock this room was guided. The only reason to get this far was to find the mirror. The Voice of Paralos. I am its guardian."

"Slayter failed to mention that little detail," Bex muttered.

"If you are its guardian," Rowan said. "Then shouldn't it be here? Where is the mirror?"

The guardian chuckled. "It is safe. In a place that has no door, has no key. In a place never marked on a map. All of those things are weaknesses. Cracks in the armor to keep the mirror away from Humans."

"Then what is the point of all of this?" Suncall asked, gesturing to the chamber and the city beyond.

"It's a trap," Bex said before the guardian could answer, the truth of it sinking into her bones. "A decoy." Just like the empty chest. Maybe the city had been built before, and they used it to hide the mirror. Or maybe it had been built especially for it, but the result was still the same. It was a big, empty city housing nothing.

The guardian inclined its head to stare at Bex. "The point," it said. "Was to lead you to me."

It lowered its body, like a cat about to pounce, and Tera and Brightstrike lifted their weapons. But the guardian fixed its eyes on Rowan.

"It seems Humans have come further than I'd thought. Wielding the light of Pyranon without consequence."

"What?" Bex said, but the guardian was still staring at Rowan, who gulped.

"The mirror is no longer safe if ones such as you are here," the guardian said. "My master will need it soon. War is coming, and you will be its first casualties." It stretched its wings, and its shoulders bunched. It opened its mouth as if to roar.

"Wait," Bex said. She didn't even know what she was going to say. Could words keep it from pouncing? Maybe. Maybe not. But when backed into a corner, Bex did the thing she was best at. She talked.

"What's your name?"

Tera looked at her like she was crazy.

But the guardian paused. "My name is of no consequence." Its feathers ruffled for a moment.

"How long have you been down here?"

Its face wasn't quite Human, but the look of bafflement certainly was. "Why would this matter?"

"You've had a long time to build your collection," Bex said. "It's impressive. The pauldrons down there. Those are at least three hundred years old, and they're immaculate. Where did they come from?"

The guardian glanced over its shoulder as if it couldn't help itself. "A Triadan warrior made it down here once. I took it off his body."

246

Gavyn made a noise like *"heurgh."*

Bex smiled brightly at the guardian. "And you've kept it nice this whole time? That couldn't have been easy in the damp. And I like your statues. Grina's my favorite. But was that one from the secret sect of the Sandrunners back there? I didn't even know they did graven images. I thought that was against their creed."

"The image of Yakoda is an exception," the guardian said. "The secret sect pray for guidance, and his image is the only one allowed under sect law." The guardian tipped its head. "Do you collect history as well?"

"In a way," she said, feeling like she was running down a steep slope. If she slowed down, she'd fall and die. If she tripped, she'd fall and die. The only way to live was to keep moving forward. "I work with a lot of collectors. I'd love to see more—"

"There," someone called from the end of the room.

The guardian spun, and Bex craned to see who the hell would interrupt this exchange.

A knight stood framed in the doors, surrounded by men carrying torches. Their light flickered in the metal of his armor and against his bright red hair.

Sir Kerrickmore. He must have found another way in. Bex was willing to bet the entire city was interconnected.

"For the mirror," he yelled, and his men rushed forward.

Bex's breath caught between outrage and incredulity. "You've got to be kidding me."

The guardian spun on her with an inhuman hiss. "You tricked me. You showed interest to keep me occupied until your reinforcements arrived."

"No!" Bex said. "They're not with us. I—"

"Humans." The guardian shook its head. "All of you must die now without the secrets of the mirror."

As the first of Sir Kerrickmore's men reached it, the

guardian flapped its wings and lifted into the air with a *whoosh*. The man's blade slashed through nothing, but the guardian landed on him, claws out, and he died with a scream and a crunch.

It spun and fixed on Bex with a cold look.

Oh gods. They were going to die here. All of them. Rowan and Lynniki. Brightstrike and Suncall and Gavyn. Even Tera. And Bex was the one who'd brought them all here just to perish, forgotten at the bottom of the bay.

"Interesting fact," Bex said, trying to keep her voice from squeaking. "That knight's armor comes from Usara and is only given to the first rank of the Order of the Sun. Very rare."

She pushed harder than she ever had for any lie in her life.

The guardian blinked. Then its head whipped around to fix Sir Kerrickmore with a look.

"Go!" Bex whispered to the others. "Go now."

They ran, ducking behind the nearest pillar as the guardian swept through Sir Kerrickmore's men. They were clearly trapped here in the dead-end room, and it could deal with them at its leisure as long as it blocked the doorway.

Rowan had pulled out her lantern again now that the sun had set, and she stepped confidently to the wall. "Here, Brightstrike."

The Taur-El gave her one look before swinging his hammer up and over his shoulder, smashing into the stone.

"Again," Rowan said as Tera peered around the pillar.

Brightstrike raised the hammer, and this time it went straight through the wall.

A big crack opened onto a hallway behind the wall. Brightstrike knocked enough stone out of the way that he could fit his shoulders through.

"That's it," Bex said, watching the carnage with Tera. She grimaced. "Get through, now."

Chapter 29
Bex

They burst out into the hallway, and the group raced back along the wall, looking for a way out.

As they passed an open corridor, Bex caught a glimpse of stairs. "Wait," she shouted. "This way!" She led them toward the staircase.

"How do you know the way out?" Rowan said.

"I don't. I just figure we need to keep going up."

The whole city rumbled beneath their feet, and there was a sudden whooshing noise, like an oncoming waterfall.

The roar grew louder, and as Bex's foot hit the bottom stair, she turned to see a wave of seawater rushing down the passageway toward them.

"Up it is," Tera said. "Go faster."

"Brightstrike," Bex called as she scooped Gavyn up.

"Hey," he said, then yelped when she tossed him to the Taur-El.

Suncall had already climbed to Brightstrike's shoulder, and the Taur-El tucked Gavyn under one arm and hauled Lynniki under the other.

They sprinted up the stairs, Tera right behind them.

"The whole city is sinking," Rowan said, puffing up the steps.

Bex felt the air change and grabbed hold of the railing as the water crashed into the base of the staircase.

"Bex!" Rowan extended a hand to her.

Bex shook her head, brushing the water from her eyes. "I'm fine. It's only up to my waist. As long as we keep going up, we'll come out on top eventually."

She hauled herself out of the foaming water, and Rowan turned to climb with her.

But they'd only climbed about two stories when Tera called back, "What were you saying about coming out on top eventually?"

Bex looked up to see the staircase ended in a broken edge, only continuing on above them after a gap of at least six feet. The shaft of the staircase was dark except for the light from their torches flickering in the window. Seawater rushed past the window, and below, the water swirled up the stairs.

"Brightstrike, can you toss me?" Suncall said.

"I can toss all of you." Brightstrike had already dropped Gavyn and Lynniki so he could tuck Suncall under one arm.

"But how will we get you up?" Rowan said as Brightstrike launched Suncall to the upper portion of the staircase.

"Here." Bex handed Lynniki the rope before Brightstrike tossed the Delver. "Tie it to the railing. We'll haul him up together."

Lynniki did as Bex said even as Brightstrike lifted and threw Gavyn, then Tera.

"Rowan," Tera called down. "You next."

There was a resounding *crack*, loud enough they could hear it above the roar of the water, and Bex instinctively flinched. When she looked up, she found a wide crack running across the window, and little streams of water shot through the openings.

"Shit, it's—"

She didn't get to finish. The window shattered, and seawater poured down the staircase in a powerful waterfall, sweeping Bex and Rowan off their feet.

She had one glimpse of Brightstrike reaching out to her, his other hand wound in the rope, before her head went under.

She tumbled and struck a wall with her shoulder. She tried to kick out, but the current carried her into blackness.

* * *

Bex woke on a rocky ledge, her mouth tasting like salt. Her chest felt bruised and sore, and she coughed and gagged and finally threw up at least a gallon of water.

The darkness pressed in on all sides. Bells jingled in her ears as the blackness reached inky fingers into her eyes and mouth and—

"No!"

It wasn't the noktum. This was just normal darkness. A cave, from the feel of the rough stone under her fingertips.

She drew in a ragged breath and coughed again, willing her heart to stop pounding.

She reached into her pockets with shaky hands. Her flintstriker. Where was it? Her fingers closed over the metal spring, and she drew it out of her pocket. She trembled so hard she nearly dropped it.

The dark was closing in again. It didn't matter how many times she told herself she was being stupid, it still felt like it was reaching for her.

Her breath sobbed in her throat, and she worked the flintstriker, tying to get the flint to light a spark.

But it was wet. Too wet for the wick to catch. The oil might be gone too. She should have let Lynniki make it waterproof.

"Bex?" Rowan's voice echoed from the rock walls, and Bex choked out a sound.

"Bex!" The light of the lantern reflected from wet stone, and Rowan limped into view.

"Healer's Ghost, I thought you were dead." Rowan collapsed on the ground beside Bex, setting the lantern beside them.

The silvery light had always made Bex feel a little sick to her stomach, but not now. Now she curled up beside it, dragging in one ragged breath after another.

"Are you all right?"

Her head pounded, and her throat still ached from throwing up so much salt water, but she nodded, trying to control the shaking. She couldn't let Rowan know how deeply the dark affected her. She had too many weaknesses, too many secrets. Everything crowded forward to swamp her.

She pushed up to her elbows, then her hands. Her wet clothes stuck in awkward places, making her movements jerky. Rowan still dripped as well.

"What happened?" Bex croaked out. "Where are we?"

"We were washed away," Rowan said. "Through another corridor, away from the window. The current carried us here. I think this cave system must be connected underground to the city. Do you remember anything?"

"Just the window breaking. I think I hit my head."

"You're bleeding," Rowan lifted a hand to touch Bex's temple where she felt a trickle of warm liquid.

Bex jerked away out of habit, and Rowan dropped her hand, biting her lip.

"What about the others?" Bex said.

"They were above the deluge and should be safe. And I don't think Brightstrike was swept away. Just us."

An unexpected knot released in Bex's chest. They might be all right, then. Not that it should matter that much to Bex. She and Rowan were still stuck in this cave. Who knew if there was even a way out?

She tried to push to her feet, but everything shook.

"You should take a moment," Rowan said. "You're still shaking."

Bex shook her head. She wanted out of this cave. She wanted to see the sky and the stars. To see light that wasn't Rowan's lantern or a torch. She needed to not feel like the dark was lurking just beyond the circle of light, waiting to grab her.

"I guess you'll just have to steady me," Bex said with a grin that felt forced even to her. "I like having someone I can lean into."

Rowan's mouth went flat and thin, and Bex knew she'd taken it too far. Pushed Rowan so far from the truth that she'd stumbled.

"Don't do that," Rowan said quietly. "I'm already here helping you. You don't have to keep complimenting me like you're afraid I'll decide to pack up and go."

Bex blinked. Oh. Oh shit. She'd done exactly what Lynniki had said not to do. She'd hurt Rowan without meaning to.

"That's not..." Her shoulders drooped.

Would it hurt Bex to be just a little bit truthful? To let out one tiny secret that might get Rowan to trust her again? At least a little. One piece of truth in exchange for one piece of trust.

"I'm sorry," she said. She drew up her knees to wrap her arms around them. "I don't say those things because I'm trying to convince you to stay."

"No?" Rowan said. "Because you say them to everyone. And I think it's a way to manipulate them."

Bex winced. That was... really close to the truth. "Or maybe it's to keep someone from asking anything deeper."

"You don't want people to know you?"

Bex's lips went tight. "No. Especially not deep like that. And my system works too. Try it. Ask me something."

"Bex, why are you still trembling?"

"Because you make my knees weak."

Rowan snorted.

"See? Now you roll your eyes in disgust and forget you ever asked me anything."

Rowan sighed. "Your powers of deflection are amazing."

The other woman stood, picking up her lantern.

"Rowan," Bex said, gazing up at her, wondering how much to say. There was still a crease between Rowan's brows. "I use words to protect myself. But it doesn't mean those words aren't at least a little bit true."

Rowan flushed in the pale light of the lantern. Bex stood and flapped her wet clothes to give them both a chance to compose themselves.

"We need to find a way out and get back to the others," Rowan said. "Why don't you wait here, and I'll see if I can find an entrance."

"No!" Bex grabbed for Rowan's hand. Then realized what she'd done and snatched it back. "Sorry."

Rowan looked at her, and she swallowed.

"Don't..." Bex tried to say. "Don't leave."

Rowan glanced toward the opening of the cave where she'd come in, then down at the lantern. "I... I might be able to find the way out. But..."

Bex's brows drew down. What was this? Rowan was hiding something?

"But you don't want me to see you do it," Bex interpreted. The startled glance Rowan sent her was enough to tell her she'd guessed right.

"Why? What could you possibly have to hide? How do you..." Bex's jaw went slack. Rowan had been leading them through the ruins all day. Bex had assumed it was her knowledge of Giants and their architecture that had led them unerringly to the chamber where the mirror should have been, but there was no architecture here. Nothing to give Rowan clues.

Unless she had something more.

"You have magic." Bex took an involuntary step back. "You're a mage. You've been a mage this whole time."

Again, surprise made Rowan's eyes go wide. "What? No. I mean, yes? But not like that."

"Like what? Like Lystra? Like the ones who imprisoned me? Marked me? Killed my friends and everyone else in the experiment?"

Rowan held up her hands. "No, not like that at all. It's this, Bex." She put the lantern down again to sit between them.

The lantern. The lantern was magic. Bex's brows drew down.

"Why wouldn't you just say that. I'd already guessed as much."

"You're not the only one with secrets you want to keep," Rowan said, gaze steady on her face.

It was Bex's turn to flush. And she'd sort of forced Rowan to tell her this one. How many other magic artifacts had she carried with them to Taur? How many more had she left behind in that sanctuary along with Jannik's weapon?

"It helps you find the way," Bex said.

"Yes."

"And it can help us get out of here?"

"I think so."

"All right." Bex blew out her breath. "Then I won't ask any more questions."

She followed Rowan as the other woman took up the lantern again and led her through the damp, cramped tunnels.

The silence grew between them, and Bex noticed Rowan kept glancing at her.

"What is it?"

Rowan opened her mouth. Then hesitated before saying, "I understand why you wouldn't like mages."

Bex rubbed her forehead. "Are you about to tell me you are one after all?"

"I have a very small amount of magic."

"And you're telling me so that I can hate you?" Bex said with a tight glance.

"I'm telling you because I don't want you to think I was keeping it from you on purpose."

"I don't know, Rowan. We've been traveling together for a while now, and you've just thought to tell me?"

"I didn't know it was an issue. I'm telling you now. Is it going to be a problem?"

"A problem?" Bex cried. "The problem is that mages make my skin crawl."

"And do I make your skin crawl?"

Bex paused. Did she? Now that she knew, was it going to ruin everything? Fester in the space between them until they both rotted?

"No," she said softly.

"I can tell you what I can do if that will make you feel better."

"No," Bex said. "I'd rather not know, thank you."

They continued on until the air changed, and Bex could feel a breeze flowing past her. Her steps quickened, and she came out of the cave mouth on the shore of the bay.

"They're here," a tinny voice called, and Bex turned to find moonlight glinting from Gavyn's brass panels.

"Gavyn!" Rowan called.

"Senji's spit, you're alive," Gavyn called. "We thought you'd drowned. I was looking for your bodies."

"Morbid," Bex muttered, but the others clambered across the beach and crowded around as Rowan stammered out their story.

Suncall, Brightstrike, Lynniki, Tera, and Gavyn. They were all here. They'd all made it out.

"We waited for the water to rise enough to swim down and out the window," Gavyn said. "I thought we would drown before we made it to the surface."

"Can you drown?" Bex asked.

Gavyn stopped and cocked his head. "All right, maybe *I* would have lived, but I would have been alone."

"The city has stopped sinking," Brightstrike rumbled.

They all fell silent and faced the bay. The water still gurgled and swept foam toward them, but out on the water, there was only the tip of the central platform still visible.

A huge, dark shape unfurled itself from the pedestal, wings a blot against the night sky.

The guardian launched itself into the air and climbed until it was a bare speck against the stars.

Bex held her breath, ready to herd them all back into the cave if the guardian decided to go after them. But it wheeled once then winged off over the island and disappeared from view.

Chapter 30
Bex

The others built a fire on the shore behind her as Bex stood in the surf, staring at the sky where the guardian had disappeared.

Lynniki, Brightstrike, and Suncall had gone down the beach to find the horses they'd left that morning. It felt like a lifetime ago now.

Somehow in everything that had happened, Tera still had the fish she'd collected from the interior of the city, and she roasted them over the fire.

The burning in Bex's chest was only a little bit related to the energy she'd absorbed that day. The rest was all in the name etched in her heart.

Anera.

She'd failed. There was no mirror. Even after all of this, the city had been as empty as her hands were now.

Eventually the smell of cooking fish drew her back to the fire, and she left the empty sky to sit with the others in the mouth of the cave.

"Your head is still bleeding," Rowan said as she sat.

Bex lifted a hand to test the area with a wince. "It's dried."

A hand held out a length of bandage and a clean cloth doused in fresh water from one of their skins. Bex turned to find Tera offering her the supplies.

"Thanks," she said, giving Tera a side-eyed look. As far as she could remember, that was the first time the guard captain had offered her anything besides a scowl or sharp words.

"Don't look at me like that," Tera said as she took the cloth and dabbed at the gash on Bex's head.

"I fully expected you to be yelling at me," Bex said. She pulled the cloth from Tera to glance at the blood before pressing it to her temple again. "I risked all our lives, and we still don't have the mirror."

"You also got us out of there," Tera said.

"By throwing the guardian at that other guy," Gavyn said.

Lynniki winced as she sat on the other side of the fire. "Effective but brutal. Who was he anyway?"

Rowan wrapped her arms around her knees. "That was the other treasure hunter, wasn't it? The one who wants to find the mirror for himself."

Bex's lips tightened.

"Do you think he survived?" Rowan asked.

"Doesn't matter," Tera said. "It got us out of there alive." She gave Bex a respectful nod. "Smart move."

Bex couldn't bring herself to say thank you. She'd never killed anyone before. Sure she'd stolen things, sent others on wild goose chases, lied. But she'd never killed anyone.

If Sir Kerrickmore had died in that room, then she might as well have plunged the dagger into his back.

"What do we do now?" Lynniki said.

"Go home," Tera said.

"No!" The word burst from Bex like water crashing through a shattered window.

Tera glanced at her and held out her hands. "The mirror wasn't there," she said. "If you want it, we'll have to follow the guardian and pry it out of its claws, wherever it is. And it said it was supposed to kill any Humans that tried to take it. Is this mirror really worth all our lives?"

Bex swallowed.

"How much does the queen really want this?" Rowan asked quietly, her hazel eyes steady in the firelight.

The lie burned in Bex's chest, making the little bit of fish she'd eaten threaten to come back up.

She could come clean right now. She could tell them the truth. *I lied to you. I don't know how much the queen wants the mirror. I never talked to her. I want it for Anera.*

Then what? Tera would kill her for sure. Lynniki would start taking limbs off. And Rowan... Rowan would look at her with that wounded expression. She'd see the truth, and no one ever looked at Bex the same after they knew the truth of her.

And after that, after she lost them all, she'd still have to go home to Anera. And she'd have to tell her sister that she'd given up.

I'm sorry your life wasn't worth as much as mine.

The worst part was that Anera wouldn't blame her for it. She'd tell Bex "of course it wasn't worth it" and then she'd die slowly, believing that. And only Bex would know the truth of it. That Anera was worth a hundred deaths.

Bex's fingers curled into fists, her nails biting into the mark on her right hand and making it ache. How much more did Anera's mark hurt when it was over her heart? And she couldn't even embrace Conell when the pain grew to be too much.

"Usara needs this mirror," Bex said, pushing the lie with a practiced hand. "The queen wanted it badly enough to send us all the way across the world to get it."

"She didn't warn us about a guardian," Gavyn said.

"She knew there would be dangers even if she didn't know exactly what kind," Bex snapped.

"There's more than that," Rowan said, and Bex's throat ached with tension, waiting for the rest of what she had realized.

"What more?" Gavyn said.

"The guardian is going to retrieve the mirror, but not just because we showed up," Rowan said. "It indicated that people have found that room before, but normally it just kills them and then stays there, guarding the baited trap. This time was different."

"It said 'war is coming.'" Bex let the cloth drop from her head. The bleeding had stopped, so she probably wouldn't need the bandages.

"And it was going to take the mirror to its master because Humans had come further than it thought."

"War with who?" Gavyn said. "The Giants?"

Lynniki blew out her breath. "Oh that's bad."

Rowan nodded.

Bex glanced between them. "How bad?"

"Like world ending bad," Lynniki said.

"I'm going with Bex," Rowan said, then went red. "That is, if you're still going after the mirror. Usara will need it if the Giants are returning. Humanity will need it."

"We don't even know what it does," Tera said.

"No," Lynniki said. "But I think we know enough that it would be a very, very bad thing if the Giants got it instead."

Bex gripped the cloth. This was getting wildly out of hand. She wanted the mirror for Anera. To save one life. Not to save the world.

"You're coming?" Rowan asked Lynniki, but they could tell it wasn't really a question.

Lynniki snorted. "Of course."

"And I'm not going to leave Rowan," Gavyn said.

Bex had the strangest urge to yell, *"No, go home, all of you, before I get you killed."* She clamped down hard on it.

Tera sighed. "I guess that's it, then. Three against one."

"You could always go home," Rowan said. "I know you have... things waiting."

Tera's lips went thin. "That's sort of the point. I don't."

Rowan's face went stricken.

"We must take the well back to my people," Brightstrike said. "But I will help you as far as I can. You should talk with the elders and to Mythspeak. They will give you an idea of where the guardian might be headed."

Chapter 31
Rowan

"Do you ever get the impression that Bex is lying to us?" Gavyn whispered late that night after the others were asleep.

Bex lay on her side, her face to the fire. A piece of her dinner lay forgotten in her clenched hand, and her eyes were closed.

"I think that's a strong word for what she's doing," Rowan said.

"Then you feel it too. She's not being truthful."

"Not entirely, no. But I think... I think she has good reason."

"What reason could possibly justify it?"

"She doesn't feel safe."

Gavyn snorted. "You mean she doesn't trust us."

"Have we trusted her?" Rowan gave the lantern a significant look.

"That's different."

"I don't think it is. She manipulates people to feel in control. She flirts and cajoles and misdirects to keep the people around her from looking any harder at what's underneath."

"Well, I'm looking," Gavyn said.

Rowan sighed. "Leave her alone, Gavyn. Maybe it's none of your business what she's hiding. You don't have to know everything about a person to know you're doing the right thing by following them."

"Maybe she's making you feel that way. With magic."

Rowan rolled over to stare at him. "What?"

"It's more than just little half-truths, Rowan. There's something there in her words that... makes people believe her."

She shook her head. "That's ridiculous, Gavyn. You sound paranoid."

The firelight glinted from his carapace as he stared at the sleeping treasure hunter. "Maybe I am, because I seem to be the only one who can see it. Or feel it."

"Feel what? There's nothing there. Just words."

He turned his head to look at Rowan. "She convinced you to leave the sanctuary when you had dedicated the rest of your life to staying."

Heat beat in Rowan's cheeks. "That might not have been as hard to do as you're thinking."

"I know you were struggling with it," Gavyn said gently. "But I also know *you*. You're loyal and faithful, and you would have done the right thing even if it killed you. You would not have left that mission so lightly if it weren't for her words."

"You're right," Rowan said. "But that doesn't make them magic."

"Just promise me you'll think about it. I'd like to think that my words work on you too."

"Of course they do, Gavyn."

Chapter 32
Bex

Smoke rose from Auli'poli. When Brightstrike saw it in the distance, his footsteps sped up, and soon he was running down the road toward his home.

Bex exchanged a worried glance with Rowan, then kicked her horse into a canter.

At the edge of town, fields burned. Workshops tumbled in broken bricks and splintered beams, and Taur-Els stood in the streets, bellowing their grief.

"What happened here?" Bex whispered. It looked like an invading army had torn through the place with siege engines and unmatched ferocity.

Rowan shook her head, brow creased and deep lines etched at the corners of her mouth.

Suncall rode with Lynniki, but after they passed the first few streets crowded with Taur-Els trying to cope with the destruction, she hopped down and ran through the crowd.

"Wait!" Rowan cried. "Where are you going?"

"To find Brightstrike, most likely," Bex said.

"We should do the same," Tera said.

It was a lot harder for them to lead the horses through the frantic city, but finally they came to the central plaza where they'd spoken with Lightway and Mythspeak.

The plinth that had held the statue of the exiled Taur-El still stood empty, but now it was joined by several other toppled statues bearing scorch marks, and the council building behind them had collapsed to rubble.

Lightway stood in the middle of it, his face matted with soot and sweat. Workers carrying ropes and digging equipment moved through the city, stopping to receive brisk orders from their leader. Runners trotted to and from the plaza, laying lists of names and numbers on a makeshift table beside Lightway.

They found Brightstrike there with his head bowed, a city's worth of grief weighing down his shoulders. Suncall held tight to his hand, but it didn't seem like he'd even registered her presence.

Tera dismounted. The group of Demaijos traders had erected a tent along one wall of the collapsed building and were ushering wounded Taur-Els inside. Tera strode to speak with their leader, Hunaa.

Bex and Rowan dismounted beside Lightway.

"Koa Lightway, what happened?" Rowan asked the Taur-El.

Lightway ran a big hand over his face. His torn tunic had fallen down over one shoulder, and he hadn't bothered to fix it.

"An attacker came in the night," he said, voice ragged. "A huge creature with wings and claws and magic. I've never seen anything like it, but it flew like it knew our skies, and it attacked as if it had a grudge against us."

Bex's stomach dropped, and Rowan glanced at her.

"The guardian," she said. "It came here after it left the Shattered Waves."

"But why?" Gavyn said. "If it's on its way to find the

mirror, why would it stop here? Why would it terrorize these people?"

Bex swallowed.

It had spoken to her, mostly, but the guardian had seen Brightstrike. It had seen a Taur-El working with them. Obviously it had made the connection that they were working with the people of the island and had taken its vengeance.

But Gavyn was right. Why would it bother?

"You said it had magic," Lynniki said, still on her horse.

"Yes. It wielded fire and tore down buildings," Lightway said. "It seemed to crave chaos only. Once we were in disarray, it left."

"That sounds like Land Magic," Gavyn said. "It's a mage as well as a monster."

"We should help," Rowan said. "I know we have to go after it to find the mirror but..."

Bex just nodded. Lynniki hopped from her horse. "I will see what I can do to help stabilize the structures."

Bex stepped to Brightstrike. "I'm sorry," she said, not even sure what she was apologizing for exactly. For dragging them into this mess? For not being able to fix it?

Brightstrike raised his head and met her eyes, and she realized she'd been very, very wrong. It wasn't grief that weighed the Taur-El down.

It was rage.

He trembled, the skin around his golden eyes going red, veins standing out in his neck. The muscles in his arms seemed to grow before her eyes, bunching beneath the edge of his tunic.

"Oh," Bex breathed, resisting the urge to run. Instinct told her that would be a very bad idea.

Suncall tugged on his hand. "Brightstrike," she said under her breath. "Brightstrike, hear me."

Bex remained still, trying not to trigger whatever fighting instinct had risen in the Taur-El.

Suncall climbed a piece of rubble to look him directly in the eyes. "Brightstrike. Not here. Not now. There is nowhere to direct it, and Lightway is right there. If you lose control, this will be the last time you see your people. Ever." She placed her hand on the side of his face, her thumb stroking his cheek. "You can still choose, Brightstrike."

Suncall's words finally seemed to penetrate, and the fury drained out of the Taur-El's eyes. His shoulders slumped, and he leaned against an empty plinth, taking deep gulps of air.

Bex exchanged a wordless glance with Suncall and swallowed.

"Are you all right?" Suncall finally whispered.

"I... am tired." Brightstrike closed his eyes.

Suncall rested her forehead against his.

Rowan came up next to them with Gavyn. "I don't know what else to do. We have to stay and help. But we have to go after the mirror. We cannot let the guardian take it back to its master."

Brightstrike shook his head. "No. You are right. The Giants cannot be trusted with it. Even the guardian cannot be trusted with it."

"Then we have to figure out where it is going," Gavyn said.

"What of Mythspeak?" Brightstrike said. "Have you spoken with him?"

Very gently Rowan laid her hand on his arm. "He was lost when the building fell."

Brightstrike let out a long slow breath, and Bex prepared for another wave of fury, but Brightstrike held on to the thread of coherency. "I see," he said.

"I was hoping to find a healer to look at your head," Rowan said, reaching to touch Bex's temple.

"I doubt there're any that aren't swamped already," Bex said. She didn't flinch away from Rowan's touch, but it was a near thing. And something in her face must have given her away. Rowan bit her lip and stepped back.

"I can help with that," a low, clear voice said.

Tera led Hunaa across the rubble. The older Demaijos woman wore her graying hair in thick braids piled high on her head, and she carried a healing kit with her.

"May I?" she said.

Bex tucked her right hand under her arm and nodded. "Thank you."

"I thought you were traders. But the rest of your party is all in there working as if they've been infirmary trained," Tera said. "Are all Demaijos traders healers, as well?'

"No. We merely serve where we are needed and learn to fill in the gaps." Hunaa spread a salve on Bex's temple. It cooled the skin and tingled a little as it soaked in. "You did not learn this from your family?"

"I grew up in Usara," Tera said. "I have never been to Demaijos."

"That is a great shame."

Tera shrugged. "It's not like I can miss a home I've never been to."

"You can. We call it untethered pain. That hurt that longs for something it doesn't even recognize."

A Taur-El youth, only about as tall as Brightstrike's shoulder came running through the plaza. "Koa!" they cried. "Koa Lightway!"

"What is it, calf?" Lightway said.

"Another attack. A village burned and a great black creature winging away."

Lightway's ears went flat against his head.

Brightstrike straightened. "Why is the guardian set against my people?" he said. "This does not aid it in any way."

"Unless it's trying to delay us," Bex said, the sudden surety sinking into her gut.

"What?" Rowan said.

"It's delaying us on purpose. Attacking Brightstrike's people. It knows we're working together. It knows we won't stand by and let them suffer. It's giving us plenty to do besides chase us."

She knew because it was exactly what she would do. She'd done the same thing on a smaller scale plenty of times before.

"Well, it's right," Rowan cried. "What else can we do?"

"Not play the game."

Rowan dropped her hands and stared at Bex. "What do you mean? What game?"

Bex raised her gaze to pass over each of them. "We don't stop and help everyone along the way. We go around. We get to the mirror first."

Rowan, Lynniki, and Suncall spoke over each other in their haste to protest.

Tera and Gavyn stayed silent watching her.

Bex shifted her feet. "It's logical," she said, arguing to herself as much as to the others. "It's smart. It might be horrible, but it will stop the attacks faster than anything else. The guardian only cares about keeping us from the mirror. If we get there first, then it will have to concentrate on us. Not helpless towns and cities."

The others all exchanged bleak looks. Rowan bit her lip and looked like she was fighting down tears. But Tera nodded.

"It's efficient," the captain said.

"It's... admirable," Rowan said.

Bex blinked. That's not what she'd thought the antiquarian was about to say.

"To put yourself in harm's way so others can remain safe." Rowan gave her a wavering smile.

Bex made a noise in the back of her throat.

Tera raised an eyebrow at her, but Bex looked at her feet to hide her expression.

Was she actually being selfless? She wanted the mirror. But she also didn't want anymore people to die. Could she want both of those things and still be a good person? Or at least not a terrible person?

"We'd still have to outpace a great big, winged creature that already knows where it's going," Gavyn said. "So the question remains, how do we get ahead of it?"

"It's not going in one direction if it's so busy trying to lay waste to the countryside. That's good news," Bex said. "It's distracted and not concentrating on racing us."

She turned to Rowan. "So how would you normally track down an artifact? You know it exists, but you don't have much else to go on. What do you do first?"

"Research," Rowan said without having to think about it. "We find documentation and maps and references, no matter how obscure."

"But the guardian specifically said it wasn't marked on any maps," Lynniki said.

"There can't be nothing," Bex said, trying to channel frustration into action. "Even the absence of something leaves a void."

Rowan straightened with a gasp. Bex instantly locked eyes with her.

"What have you thought of?"

"You're right. If the Giants wanted this thing to remain hidden, there will be stories and legends warning people away from a place. The Giants will have gone to great lengths to keep Humans and Taur-Els from stumbling upon it."

"And we can cross-reference that list with places that the Giants did mark well and look for the gaps," Bex said.

"You can compare stories with Taur-El records and find the most likely place the mirror would have been hidden." Brightstrike nodded to them. "I am not a historian. But we keep our history in the Hall of Stories. We can look there."

"Meanwhile Lynniki and I can help the traders who are helping the towns," Tera said, nodding to Hunaa who was packing up her kit. "Make it look like the guardian's tactic is working, while we get ahead of it."

Chapter 33
Bex

The Hall of Stories sat nestled in the mountains southeast of Auli'poli. Bex would never have seen the entrance if she hadn't been led right to it. It sat between an overhang of rock and a shoulder of the mountain, making a long gorge they had to traverse before they found the opening.

Brightstrike led them inside, lighting a torch at the braziers that stood just inside the entrance.

Bex, Rowan, and Gavyn followed him, gazing at the walls lit by the flickering light.

Carvings crawled across the stone. Taur-Els and men and beasts all marched along, parting only at the openings to individual rooms.

Bex liked this place. Each cave was lit by a pair of braziers which chased the shadows from every corner.

"These are all the stories of your people?" Rowan said, reaching out a reverent hand to touch a carved Taur-El's head.

"Yes," Brightstrike said. "Our historians pass the stories to our calves when they are young, but the originals are kept here, preserved so we never forget."

"Will you interpret them for us?" Rowan said.

Brightstrike frowned at the walls. "I know some of them, but I am not a historian. I do not keep the stories. You will have to interpret most for yourself."

Bex expected Rowan to protest. But instead she gazed at the carvings, the flames from the braziers reflecting in her eyes. "Well, at least that's something I'm good at."

Rowan limped along the broad corridors carved out of the side of the mountain, murmuring to herself.

"I'll try to find things talking about the Giants and their buildings," Gavyn said.

That left Bex staring at the first walls with Brightstrike. He reached out with a broad hand and traced the outline of a Taur-El who wore a thick chest guard and pauldrons that made his shoulders spiked and bulky. Horns rose from a segmented helmet, and he carried a war hammer twice as big as Brightstrike's.

"They're impressive," Bex said.

"They were the vanguard. The elite," Brightstrike said.

Looking at the massive creature taking up most of the room beside her, she could well imagine them as warriors created for a specific purpose.

"It's funny that your people put their pictures here, when they don't seem to like remembering their origins at all."

Brightstrike's mouth moved like he clenched his jaw. "It is not a thing to be revered," he said. "We were created to lose our minds in battle. For a race that saw us only as pawns to be thrown against other pawns."

"Is the battle frenzy that easy to fall into? And that awful?"

Brightstrike dropped his hand.

"It is far easier than I thought. And not nearly as terrible as we have all been told."

Bex remembered the reddened eyes and the bunching

muscles Brightstrike had fought off in the square and wondered just how close to the frenzy he'd actually been.

The Taur-El turned away from the wall. "Our creation is not a thing to be revered," he said. "But I do not believe it is a thing to be forgotten either. Isn't the point of freedom the ability to choose? I can choose who I would fight for. Who I would lose myself to protect."

Bex raised her eyebrows. "If Suncall were here, she'd say these were dangerous thoughts."

"Suncall has lost her home already. She does not wish for me to lose mine by accident. She is not here though. So what do *you* say?"

Bex chewed her lip. "I'm not a warrior. And I'm not all that wise. I'm not sure I'm the one to say anything. But..."

"But...?"

"You can only choose what's right for you. Your people might not like to fight, but that doesn't make them safe from the rest of the world. If they don't fight for themselves, who will? Someone has to choose the abhorrent path if only to protect them."

"That is a sacrifice," Brightstrike said. "Losing my people in order to protect them."

"Yeah, it is." Bex clenched her right hand, thinking of Anera and all the lies that had gone into keeping her safe.

"I would lose my people through choice instead of through accident. I do not know if that is much better."

Bex remained silent.

Brightstrike stepped away from the wall toward the cave opening. "Are you and Heif Rowan all right here by yourselves?"

Bex glanced into the empty cave. "Probably, why?"

"I am going back to help with the rebuilding process. I do not like how these carvings make me feel."

"And how do they make you feel?"

"Strong."

Bex let him go, wondering if she'd just made things worse.

Rowan puttered around one of the inner chambers, making notes and double-checking them with the carvings. Gavyn stalked not too far away, muttering to himself.

"Any luck?" Bex asked.

"So much luck," Rowan cried. "There are stories here from every era. I could spend a lifetime in this cave alone, learning about Taur-El history. Do you know they were a nomadic culture before the Giant war. Their masters had such tight control over their movements and their reproduction that the Taur-Els who managed to escape and live on their own had to travel from place to place to keep from being found. It was only after the Giants died that the Taur-els developed such a deep appreciation for artistry and craftsmanship. They settled into cities so they could pursue the things that made them unique."

The light from the braziers outlined her round cheeks with gold, and Bex blinked. She rubbed her chest with her left hand, trying to sooth the fluttery, breathless feeling that had taken her by surprise.

"What's wrong?" Rowan asked. "You have a funny look on your face."

"Nothing," Bex said quickly. "It's... it's probably just all the magic I absorbed in the ruins. I'll let you get back to work."

Rowan's smile went flat. "I hope I can find something. This is going to be hard."

Bex dropped her gaze. "No it won't. You're too smart for this problem. It won't stand up for long against you."

Rowan rolled her eyes. "You're doing it again. The unearned compliments thing."

Bex bit down on her tongue hard and gave Rowan the straightest look she could manage. "No. I promise I'm not."

She backed out of the cave, leaving Rowan gaping behind her.

Gavyn gave her a look as she passed him.

"What?" she snapped.

"Nothing at all." He went back to his perusal.

Bex continued on into the caves, barely glancing at the carvings. There was a scuffle and a scrape that made her whirl around, but there was nothing there.

This place is too small for the guardian, she thought to herself. *There's no way it could sneak up on us in here. Even if it wasn't busy rampaging around the countryside.*

With that thought at the surface of her mind, one of the carvings caught her eye. A huge cat with wings stood poised in the middle of a stand of trees.

"Do the Taur-Els have stories about it?" Bex murmured, stepping closer to squint at the wall.

She ran her fingers along the raised edges of its wings. It looked like the guardian, but its face was more cat-like and less Human.

The creature sat beneath the leaves, its face tilted up and eyes closed as if it basked in the silence and the sunlight.

In another panel, the cat creature faced a man as tall as it was. Flames flickered around them, but the man didn't seem to be reacting in fear even though he was clearly outmatched.

Further down the wall, the winged cat lay on a slab of stone, its wings draped over the edges, feathers falling to the ground. The man stood over it, and Bex wondered what had happened between those two moments.

She moved on quickly, the sight of the vulnerable creature making her gut squirm.

Finally the cat creature flew toward a city with waves lapping the base. Here its face had the flatter features of a Human but still with the nose and the eyes of a cat and its ears on the top of its head.

Bex stood staring at the last panel with her teeth clenched. The guardian had mentioned that it was made for the specific purpose of guarding the mirror. Just like the Taur-Els. But if this was its story, then it had been made from a natural creature. The Giants had taken it and molded it into something they could use.

Bex had that uncomfortable feeling in her gut again as she thought about that big room and all the treasures it had collected. How many thousands of years had it been there? How long had it been trapped there, living underwater, dreaming of the open skies and the cool forest?

Or was she making it all up in her head? It had left and immediately started destroying things. Maybe it didn't deserve any sympathy.

Bex curled her palm around her mark. What had she done immediately after escaping from the experiments with Anera? She'd spent a lot of time hiding in shadows, but then, she'd been truly free. Her captors hadn't come for her until much, much later.

There were markings under the images that looked like a name.

"Imyuran," she sounded out. "Wings in the night."

The Taur-Els had carved stories about the guardian into their history here. They must have known of it long ago. Had it predated the war? Had it lived alongside them as they were trying to break free of the Giants?

Bex let her hand fall back to her side.

"Bex," Rowan called. The other woman hurried down the corridor towards her. "I think I found—"

There was a tremendous crack. Rowan stopped in her tracks and looked down at her feet.

Bex gasped as she watched the floor go out from under Rowan, and the antiquarian fell into a dark pit.

Chapter 34
Bex

Bex stared at the hole in the ground, horror rising up to choke her.

"Rowan!" Gavyn cried. He skidded to a stop beside the hole. "Rowan!"

Bex fell to her knees at the edge, and as her hand hit the ground, she felt it tingle. The feeling lasted for a second and then was gone, but she knew what she'd felt.

The telltale sign of magic dissipating into the air.

Bex could hear the faint tinkle of bells, but was that her imagination? Or was Lystra here?

Gavyn's legs bunched, and he leaped into the hole after Rowan.

"Wait!" Bex called. But he was already gone.

Bex's teeth clenched, and she glanced down the empty halls in front and behind her. If Lystra was there, she hadn't shown herself. And Rowan was at the bottom of the pit, possibly hurt or dying.

She didn't stop to examine the way her chest tightened, cutting off her air. She tied her rope around a rocky outcropping, then swung her legs around and followed Gavyn into the hole.

She clutched at the jagged edges of the rock to slow her fall, and the rope burned her arm where she'd wrapped it.

Her feet hit the bottom less than twenty feet later. The pit was shallow enough that light from the braziers reached the ground, and the flickering glow lit up the bumpy walls of a second level of the caves.

Gavyn stood at the bottom of the hole, clawing at a pillar of stone that looked far too smooth and regular to be natural.

Bex pulled out her flintstriker and lit the wick so she could see at least a little better.

Enough rock dust floated in the air to make her cough.

"Rowan?" she called, voice hoarse and dry.

"Here." She heard Rowan's voice faintly. Like it came from behind a wall of rock.

Bex stepped up beside the stone pillar. "What happened?"

"Are you all right?" Gavyn called.

"I'm fine. I think. The floor collapsed, and as soon as I hit the ground, this cage sprang up."

"We'll get you out," Gavyn called.

Bex's palm tingled, and her shoulders tensed as she raised her hand to feel the spell holding the pillar in place. At her feet, lines had been painstakingly etched into the stone.

She recognized the spell. From the inside, it would be smooth stone. There would be no access to the spell like there was out here.

This trap had been designed for Bex.

Bells tinkled, and now she knew she wasn't hearing things.

She whirled around, Gavyn following her lead.

"You were supposed to be in the cage," Lystra said. She stood in the shadows where Bex's light didn't quite reach, her red robe the color of old, black blood in the dark. The flame in Bex's hand reflected in her eyes.

"It's much easier to kill cornered rats than the ones who can still scurry."

"I have a name, you know," Bex said, thoughts racing furiously. She could get Rowan out of the trap, but then where would they go? They were trapped down here with the murderous mage, and Bex didn't like her chances in closed quarters without Tera to distract the battle hardened woman. "In all the years you held me against my will, you never bothered to learn it."

"I didn't need to know your real name when I gave you a pet name," Lystra said. "I'm hurt you don't remember it, Subject Thirteen."

Bex gritted her teeth. There was nothing in her satchel that would help. The rope hung behind Lystra, unreachable for now.

"Unlucky number. Unlucky results," Lystra said. "It would have been much better if you'd turned out like your little friend. Having the spell draw on you would have made you much more docile. More manageable."

Oh gods, she remembered Anera. Had she found her before tracking Bex here?

Wait, Anera's mark drew on her, but Bex's drew on Lystra. Rowan had said that would be a huge problem for the mage. If that were true, she'd made a mistake leaving the spell on the outside of Rowan's cage. Where Bex could reach it.

"You want someone more manageable, you're going to have to sweet talk me," Bex said and shifted her feet, working the glove off her right hand.

Lystra's eyes narrowed. "I'd rather just get rid of the problem."

She raked her nail down her arm, opening up barely healed cuts. Fire poured from her, sweeping across the cave.

Bex knelt and slapped her palm across the spell keeping Rowan captive. Light flashed, and Bex dragged the magic out of the spell, too fast to be comfortable, but she needed it as hard and fast as it could be.

The stone pillar dropped back into the floor, leaving Rowan staggering. She threw her arms up to protect against the sudden flare of the fire.

But in that same moment, Lystra cried out and fell to the floor, her spell dissolving around her.

"Let's go," Bex called. She had no idea how long Lystra would be incapacitated, and they had to get all three of them up the rope to the cave above.

"Wait," Rowan said and stepped toward Lystra.

"What are you doing?"

Rowan knelt beside the prone mage, who groaned, her face white and drawn. Rowan reached out to clamp her hand around Lystra's wrist, and her face went slack for a moment.

"What—?" Was this Rowan's magic?

She did not like how close Rowan was to the mage. She didn't like the way Lystra's eyes still managed to find her face. The little twitches of her hand made Bex think the mage wanted to cast another spell at Rowan.

This was Bex's chance. Lystra was prone and vulnerable. One smash to the head and Bex would be free for the rest of her life. She'd never have to worry about Lystra sneaking up on her or trying to kill her friends again.

She snatched up a rock that had fallen from the cave-in and stepped closer to Lystra.

Gavyn watched her do it. He looked between the rock and Lystra. Then he deliberately stepped out of the way.

Rowan came out of whatever trance she'd been caught in and glanced up. "What are you doing?"

"Get out of the way."

Rowan's gaze caught on the rock in her hand. "Oh," she said on a breath. "Bex..."

Bex hated the way her name sounded in Rowan's voice

right then. That tremor of horror and a little bit of resignation. Like she didn't agree, but she would let Bex do it anyway.

What would it cost? What change would that make to Rowan who was like Anera and saw the good in everyone?

She'd see Bex for who she actually was finally. She'd see a thief and a liar and a murderer where there had never been a murderer before.

It would cost Bex something too. She'd lose Rowan.

Rowan stood, either to step out of the way or put herself between them. But Lystra's jaw clenched, and she rolled toward Rowan.

Bex hissed, dropping the rock to drag Rowan back.

Lystra's flailing hand caught on Bex's boot.

A mage hadn't sucked energy back out of her in years. Not since those first few weeks after she'd gotten her mark. But she remembered the feeling well enough. That sickly, sliding sensation, like someone pulled something dark and slimy out of its hole.

It made Bex gag.

The color came back into Lystra's face, and she pushed up on her elbows.

Gavyn yelled and surged forward to bite Lystra's hand.

Bex stumbled back, holding her caving chest. Oh gods, it felt disgusting. A violation and a theft all in one. She coughed, trying to get air into her lungs.

Rowan grabbed her arm and hauled her further into the cave. "Go," she said. "We have to run."

"Where?" Gavyn danced back as Lystra staggered to her feet.

"I saw where she came in. I can get us there."

"Saw?" Bex said blearily as Rowan hauled her back through the caves, but neither of them answered.

She still carried her flintstriker in one hand, and it sent a tiny bit of light dancing ahead of them.

Gavyn loped ahead as Rowan called directions.

"Right," she cried. "Now left."

Bex had enough presence of mind to realize Rowan still had her hand wrapped around Bex's right arm. And the mark was still unwrapped.

She pulled away and ran under own power.

"Gavyn, wait," Rowan called.

Gavyn slid to a stop, but something on the wall glowed and then started blinking.

"Get down!"

The brass dog glanced at the blinking spell and yelped.

An explosion rang out, and Bex ducked, covering her head.

"Gavyn?" Rowan called.

Gavyn cleared his voice box and staggered to his feet. Three plates along his left side had gone concave in the blast, but he shook himself and still seemed to have all his movement. "I'm all right."

"Watch out. She's placed fire charges."

Bex groaned. She had to get her brain working. It didn't matter if everything felt fuzzy after the energy drain. They would die if Lystra caught up.

"I thought they used fire charges for mining."

"Yes," Rowan said, leading them around the blasted wall. "But that doesn't mean they won't blow up whatever you want."

"Including pesky experiments," Gavyn said.

Bex couldn't even muster the energy to glare at him. She hauled in deep breaths, trying to get the world to stop fuzzing around her.

"How do you know where they are?" Bex said as Rowan towed her toward a rocky corner. As they tiptoed around it, Bex could just make out the lines of the fire charge etched into a little, clay disc. This must be how Lystra left spells where she couldn't bleed all over everything.

"When I touched her," Rowan said. "I saw her coming into the cave and setting her traps."

Her chest tightened again, but it had nothing to do with the energy drain. "Your magic," she said.

Rowan glanced at her. "I see memories. Little things that usually don't make any sense out of context. But I've learned to direct it so I can see things that are useful to me right then."

A blast of fire behind them made the hair on the back of Bex's neck curl, and they both flinched.

"Run," Gavyn said.

Rowan picked up speed, though her uneven gait kept her from a flat out sprint, and she tried to lead them through a passage to the right.

A wall of fire cut them off.

They had to take the left, and the wave of heat chased them further and faster through the caves.

"She's herding us into the fire charges," Rowan said. "I can't—"

Another explosion sent bits of broken stone clattering around them. Bex felt one slice her cheek, and she tried to place herself between Rowan and the worst of the falling debris.

They had to get out of here. This was just a death trap unless they could find the exit.

Or unless they could neutralize the one chasing them.

"Can we get ahead of the fire charges?" Bex asked. "Is there a way around? I have an idea."

Rowan opened her mouth, then cocked her head. "If we hurry so she can't cut us off. This way."

Rowan raced ahead, and Bex and Gavyn followed. A dark entrance opened on their left, and Rowan loped toward it.

Heat built, and Bex knew Lystra was sending a spell to cut them off.

She put on a last burst of speed and dragged Rowan with

her. Gavyn leaped into the opening as flames sprang up. But they'd made it.

"Now," Rowan gasped. "This way."

She led them through the cave, using whatever memory she had of Lystra setting her traps, and into a chamber full of pillars worn down by damp and time.

"There's one," Rowan said, pointing to the base of a pillar where a little, clay disc had been attached. "Don't get too close or it will trigger. She'll come out of that tunnel. What did you want to do?"

It wouldn't be long. Bex could already hear the jingle of bells.

"I want..." Bex said and frantically searched the floor for the perfect tool. She wanted a stick or a club. But there was nothing except rock, and she couldn't break any of the stone off. Not with just her hands.

"Here," she said to Rowan and handed her the flintstriker. "Hold this." She felt a pang as she handed over her link to Anera. But she needed her hands free.

A pile of stone lay on the other side of the cave and she snatched up a chunk of rock the size of her fist. Hopefully that would work.

Footsteps and bells came down the tunnel.

"Be careful," Rowan hissed.

Bex didn't have time to roll her eyes. Careful would get them killed. This was a risk that might save their lives.

She sprinted for the pillar with the fire charge on it, then slid to get low enough. As she came into reach, it began to glow, then blink.

She smashed at the pillar with her rock, putting her momentum behind the blow, and a chunk broke free. The chunk with the fire charge.

Bex leaped to her feet and kicked it toward the tunnel

opening. It sailed straight and true, right at Lystra's head as she emerged.

The mage's eyes widened as the blinking fire charge came at her.

She dove back into the tunnel, and the fire charge erupted in an explosion.

Bex threw her hands over her head and fell backward. The rumble went on and on, and the ground shook beneath her feet. Bits of the ceiling rained down on her head.

"Oh shit."

Bex scrambled to her feet and lunged for Rowan and Gavyn, but the cave collapsed around her, leaving her in pitch black.

Chapter 35
Rowan

R ock and stone tumbled down, and the last thing
Rowan saw was Bex's white face disappearing
behind a wall of darkness.

She cried out and tried to push forward to Bex, but debris
still fell, and a large rock hit her hand. She hissed and pulled
back.

Gavyn crowded into her. "Get down."

They ducked down beside one of the pillars, and she
covered her head with her hands as Gavyn tried to make
himself as small as possible.

Rowan waited, heart in her throat, certain she was about to
be crushed to death.

But finally the rumbling stopped, and the world lay still
again.

She shook the dust from her hair and shoulders and took
stock of herself and her surroundings.

"Gavyn, are you all right?" she said with a cough.

"Definitely dented," he grumbled. A layer of rock shifted as
he stood and cautiously extracted himself from the pile of
debris. "Don't let Lynniki yell at me, please."

Rowan still had Bex's flintstriker in her hand. The flame had gone out, but she clicked it again until it lit and she could see where she was.

She wasn't pinned under any debris, but that was about as good as it got. She sat in a pocket of calm amidst the destruction. The pillar she'd sheltered against held up the ceiling above her, but rubble obscured the tunnel ahead where she'd been sure they'd reach the surface. And a wall of rock cut her off from the cave where they'd come from.

"Bex?" Rowan called. She had to clear the dust and fear out of her throat. "Bex, can you hear me?"

Rowan pressed herself close to the tumbled rock, straining her ears. There might have been something there. A whisper? The shift of rock?

Gavyn clambered over to the blockage that kept them from the exit. He scratched at it with his front paw. "Some of this might be loose enough to shift," he said.

Rowan tried standing. Nothing was broken. Her back ached fiercely, but that wasn't anything new.

"You work in that direction," she said. "I'm going to try to get to Bex."

She expected some sort of protest. Gavyn wasn't normally the optimist, so she could just imagine him saying that she was going to bring the ceiling down on them, or that Bex was likely already dead, but he just nodded and started scrabbling at the pile of rock with his brass feet.

They worked for a long time. Rowan couldn't tell how much time passed in the endless dark, but her arms ached as badly as her back now and sweat soaked her shirt.

Finally Gavyn said, "I think I see light."

Rowan paused.

"The cave-in must have created a path to the surface. If I can just get past this stone."

Rowan started toward him to help, but finally she heard

something besides herself and Gavyn. A faint, breathless noise coming from the other side of the rock where she worked. It sounded like sobbing.

"Can you get through?" Rowan asked Gavyn as she went back to pulling rock from the pile of rubble. One piece at a time. Shift this so the ceiling didn't collapse. Take another from the top.

"I think..." Gavyn scrabbled. "Almost."

She pulled away another rock and uncovered an opening. She could hear ragged breathing in between sobs. A bloody hand scraped at the rock where she could see.

"Bex!" she cried. She tried reaching through the opening, but the hand yanked back.

It was Bex all right. She'd never let Rowan touch her. Not voluntarily anyway.

"Bex, are you hurt?"

Bex didn't answer. Incoherent weeping came through the opening, and the sound of someone furiously digging against stone that wouldn't move.

"Rowan," Gavyn called. "I see the opening."

Rowan bit her lip. "Hang on, Bex," she called.

She climbed across the rubble to Gavyn, and he fell back so she could peer through the gap he'd made.

"Sunlight," she said. A thin shaft of light lit the rock at the very end of a narrow crack.

She looked down at the dusty, brass dog. "I can't get through there," she said. "Can you fit?"

"If I wiggle maybe." He glanced back at the wall that hid Bex.

"Go," Rowan said softly. "Go get help. I'll free Bex."

He nodded and climbed up into the gap, flattening himself as much as he could. Rowan gave him a boost, and he wriggled and scrabbled his way forward like a terrier in a rat hole.

When she couldn't reach him to push anymore, she went back to the wall where Bex was trapped.

She wasn't sobbing anymore, but Rowan could hear her breathing in great gulps. Something was really wrong in there.

"Bex, talk to me," Rowan said. Her throat ached. That could just be from the dust, but she hated the way Bex had gone quiet. The treasure hunter always had something to say. Except now.

The barest whisper came from the other side of the rock.

"What?"

"'S dark," Bex's voice barely made it through the opening.

Rowan's chest tightened. She'd never heard Bex sound that small or wounded before.

She pulled the lantern from her belt and set it on a rock while she worked, yanking loose rocks and stone from the opening, trying to make it bigger. "I'm coming," she said. A litany over and over again as she dug.

Finally, she could fit nearly her whole upper body through the hole.

"Here," she said. "Give me your hands, and I'll pull you through."

Rowan couldn't tell if Bex was even comprehending what she was saying. She reached her hands through the opening, but no one reached back.

"I have light," Rowan said.

At last, a thin hand took hers, and she heaved. Her muscles screamed, but she managed to haul Bex through the opening. A few rocks tumbled with her, and Rowan held her breath waiting for the ceiling to come down on them.

But it held.

Bex rolled to the floor and curled into a ball. She made no more noise, either from relief or because she'd worn herself out already.

Nothing looked broken. Bex's clothes were dusty and

stained but not with an excessive amount of blood. The worst injury seemed to be her hands. The skin and nails were torn as if she'd been scrabbling at the rock, frantic enough she hadn't realized she was damaging herself.

She still didn't speak only curling closer and closer to the lantern's light.

Rowan's teeth clenched. Bex couldn't touch the Grief Draw. Even sitting that close might cause problems, but she couldn't bear to take away the only thing Bex seemed to take comfort in at the moment.

She drew in a breath as she remembered and pulled Bex's flintstriker from her pocket.

"Here." She pressed it into Bex's hands.

Bex's fingers closed around the thin metal, and eventually she took a deep, shuddering breath, and her shoulders relaxed.

It wasn't a lot, but it made Rowan release a tense breath too.

Bex pushed to a sitting position. She kept her knees curled to her chest, and she sat as close to the lantern as Rowan felt comfortable letting her get, but at least she was upright now.

Rowan still had a good amount of her tools and notebooks attached to her belt. She pulled out the waterskin and tore a piece from the bottom of her tunic.

"I'm just going to clean your hands." She held out her hand, and Bex blinked at her, eyes wide. Rowan had spoken slowly, thinking Bex needed time to understand, but her gaze held plenty of understanding. And also fear.

Both of Bex's hands were bare. She must have stripped her gloves off and tucked them away before their flight through the caves.

Slowly, Bex extended her hands for Rowan to hold. "Don't touch the mark," Bex grated.

"I won't."

Rowan sat in front of her and gently cleaned the dirt and

dust from the lacerations that marred the other woman's skin.

Bex sat quiet. She didn't joke or try to flirt. She didn't even give Rowan suggestive looks like she usually did.

She sat and stared at her hands. Every now and then she shivered.

Was this Bex with no masks? Nothing between her and the world except her skin?

Or was this Bex with everything stripped away until there was nothing left that made her Bex. The humor was gone. The self-confidence was gone. The carefully projected nonchalance.

Rowan didn't like it.

"Gavyn went for help," Rowan said quietly. She finished with Bex's hands but found she was reluctant to let them go—to let Bex go back to that curled up position.

"Are you all right?" she asked.

Bex stared at her palms. She also seemed reluctant to take her hands back.

"Lots of bruises," she said. Her voice was hoarse, and Rowan's throat pinched. How long had she been screaming before Rowan had heard her? "Nothing's broken."

That wasn't what Rowan had meant. "You're still shaking."

Bex finally pulled her hands back and fumbled for her gloves.

Rowan grabbed Bex's left hand before she could tug the glove back on. She traced the line of a laceration, and Bex winced.

"People don't tear their hands to ribbons when nothing is wrong," she said.

"I tried to dig my way out, Rowan," she snapped. "Same as you."

She didn't yank her hand away, but Rowan could tell she wanted to.

Rowan let go and sat back to stare at Bex in the silvery light

293

of the lantern.

Bex fidgeted, checking the fit of her gloves, brushing the last of the debris from her hair. Avoiding Rowan's gaze.

Rowan couldn't curl her knees to her chest like Bex. It stretched her spine painfully. But she settled herself against the rock pile and waited.

Bex blew out her breath. "I don't like the dark, all right?" she said quietly.

Rowan wanted to laugh. That felt like the biggest understatement of the era. But laughing would be a very bad idea right now.

"All right," she said. If Bex wanted to leave it at that, she could.

Bex swallowed and glanced at her. Rowan tried to keep her face neutral.

"The mages... they kept us in the dark. The only time we saw light was when they came to do horrible things." She flexed her right hand. The one with the mark. "When they thought I was a failure, when they thought they'd gotten everything out of me that they could, they threw me in..."

She stopped to swallow convulsively.

Rowan shifted so she sat next to Bex, not quite close enough for their shoulders to touch.

"They left me to die in the dark," Bex said. Her hand strayed to the lock of pure white hair that hung low across her cheek.

Is that where it came from? Was she so frightened her hair went white?

Rowan's heart ached. Being frightened of the dark, that was something every child could relate to. Except Bex hadn't grown out of it. The mages who'd used her and discarded her had compounded it into a terror that left a normally confident young woman gibbering in panic.

She wanted to put her arm around Bex, but she was pretty

sure that would only push the treasure hunter away.

"Well, light is one thing I never run out of," she said and gestured to the lantern. It was funny, considering how much she loathed the thing and what it had done to her life. But she couldn't deny it had its uses. "You don't have to worry. It never goes out."

Bex looked up at her, blue eyes reflecting the deathless flame of the Grief Draw, but she wasn't looking at the lantern. She stared at Rowan as if *she* was the light.

Rowan's cheeks went hot, and she fought the urge to drop her gaze.

Bex's throat bobbed as she swallowed. She was the one to finally look away. She traced the edge of a rock with her fingertip. "Your magic..."

"Ah," Rowan said. She'd known Bex would come around to asking about it, eventually. It made perfect sense that the other woman hated mages, after what they'd done to her. But the look in her eyes when she'd realized Rowan had magic... it had made Rowan feel like the villain in Bex's story.

"I have a tiny bit of Life Magic," Rowan said. "It shows me memories. Glimpses of the past." She dusted off the toe of her boot.

"It wasn't even enough to train. The mages told my mother it was useless. Just like everything else in my life. I couldn't help my family plant. I couldn't help my mother with her patients. Magic was my only chance to do anything with my life. But it wasn't enough. Then Jannik asked me to be his assistant."

Bex cleared her throat. "I can imagine that seeing the past would be useful to an antiquarian."

Rowan gave her a rueful smile. "You'd think. But I couldn't control it very well. It mostly showed me stupid things. An object sitting on the shelf for a thousand years. Things like that. It turned out Jannik wanted me for other things."

Bex's jaw went tight. "Like what?"

"He knew I was half Delver before I did. He knew I had their resistance to Giant magic and wanted to use it."

"You trusted him, and he betrayed you."

Rowan looked up in surprise.

"It's not hard to see when you talk about him," Bex said.

"He didn't see it that way," Rowan said. "But... that's what it felt like. He was like a father to me. But in the end, we had very different ideas of what it meant to care about someone."

"I'm sorry," Bex said.

Rowan shook her head. "I've spent the last few years learning most people were wrong about me, including Jannik. I'm not useless. I've trained myself and my gift to be strong. Or at least stronger. I can direct it now. I can use it to see someone's weakness while we're fighting."

Bex stared at the lantern. "Have you ever used it on me?" she finally said.

It would be easy enough to say no. But she couldn't, not with Bex sitting there with no jokes, no mask hiding her.

"Once," Rowan said. "At the very beginning in the sanctuary. I saw you in the dark holding your hand. It must have been right after you got your mark."

Bex flinched.

"It made me trust you," Rowan said before realizing she was going to. "You were a little bit broken. Like me."

For the first time since the cave-in, Bex smiled. "I'm glad you find shattered people attractive."

She could have accused Bex of flirting needlessly again, but there was something different in the way she said it. Stripped of its normal assurance, her tone held only vulnerability.

Rowan coughed and cleared her throat. "The funny thing was," she said, thinking back to that image she had burned into her mind. "It was someone else's memory. It wasn't you looking down at your hands. It was someone looking at you. Someone who must have touched you with that in their mind not long before I met you."

Bex's expression shuttered. "That's not right."

"What's not right?"

"There was no one else."

A fierce battle raged in Rowan's head for that one moment. Something deep and constrictive in her gut made her want to believe Bex. The words throbbed in her mind, and she wanted to leave it at that. Bex was alone. Bex had always been alone.

But Rowan had seen the memory, and she knew how her magic worked. She'd seen Bex through someone else's eyes. Someone who cared enough about her that they were still in her life even now, years after the incident.

But Bex didn't want her to know that.

Was Gavyn right? Rowan could understand little white lies Bex might tell to protect herself or protect her feelings. But this had felt like... something else. Something stronger.

Like magic.

It was gone now. But for that one moment it had felt strong. Pushing her to think something she normally would have second-guessed.

Bex hated mages. Did she even know she had magic?

And why would she lie about someone being there in the dark with her.

Unless she was trying to protect them.

There had to be a good reason.

Rowan glanced at Bex, but the other woman's eyes had drifted closed. Bex swayed where she sat, exhausted from the chase with Lystra and from the emotional carnage of spending so long in the dark.

Rowan very gently slid closer until Bex's nodding head rested on her shoulder. Then she leaned her own head back and closed her eyes, keeping her breathing slow and even so as not to disturb the other woman.

Chapter 36
Bex

B ex woke feeling safe. Which was odd. She never felt safe unless she was in the rented room with Anera and she could hear her sister breathing.

There was a shoulder under her cheek, and someone was definitely breathing. But it wasn't Anera's shallow breaths.

She opened her eyes, and the first thing she saw was Rowan's lantern.

Right. The cave-in.

She should move. Take her head off Rowan's shoulder. Put just enough distance between them.

She didn't want to. And that was the oddest part of all.

Rowan knew too many of her secrets. She knew about the mages. She knew about the mark. She knew about the dark.

But for some reason, Bex wasn't worried about her using those things against her. She wasn't worried about Rowan somehow getting to Anera through her.

She turned her head to stare at the broken wall where Rowan had pulled her through. Bex wasn't sure what had happened. The ceiling had collapsed, and she hadn't died. But the rock pressing in around her had felt like the noktum. Pressure all around and dust filling her nostrils had felt like the dark creeping inside her, keeping her from breathing—

She gulped and pushed the thought away before it could overwhelm her again. Rowan had already seen her as a sniveling mess of panic. She didn't need a repeat.

Rowan stirred under her, and Bex sat up fast enough to make her head ache.

The antiquarian stretched and rubbed her eyes, leaving a streak of dirt across her already-dusty face.

"How do you feel?" she asked.

"Fine." Bex meant it to sound strong, but it came out as a whisper.

Rowan's brows twitched like she was trying to suppress worry.

"Let me see your hands. I don't want them to get infected."

Bex's fingers curled inside her gloves, but that made them twinge. "How do you even know what to look for?" she said.

"My mother was a healer."

Bex stood and walked over to the rubble that cut them off from the surface.

"You don't have to take care of me," she said quietly.

"Maybe I want to."

The words made Bex catch her breath. The idea made her feel warm and soft around the edges.

But that was the problem. She couldn't afford soft edges. Not here and not now. "I'm fine. I'm not the one who needs to be taken care of."

"And I am?" Rowan asked with a raised eyebrow.

Bex winced. She'd been thinking of Anera, and she wasn't willing to explore any parallels between Rowan and Anera right that second.

"That's not what I meant. I just mean you don't have to sacrifice anything for me."

"What?" Rowan's face screwed up. "Is that what you think caring is?"

"Of course. When you take care of someone, it means you're doing the things they can't do for themselves so they can feel strong and safe."

"That doesn't mean you have to give anything up."

"It does. If they're not strong enough to do the hard things for themselves, then you have to be the one to do those things."

"Bex. That's not... that's not what's happening here." Rowan's face made Bex think that's not what was supposed to happen anywhere. But that's what it had always been like with Anera. Her sister didn't want to lie and cheat and steal to survive. So that had always fallen to Bex.

"Then, what's happening?"

"I saw you needed help, and I wanted to help you."

"Why?"

Rowan's shoulders drooped. "Because—"

There was a crash, and they both flinched. The little opening where Gavyn had wriggled out had gone dark with night long ago, but now a bit of fresh air trickled through.

"It's Brightstrike with his hammer," Bex murmured.

Rowan bit her lip. "Yes."

Bex dropped her gaze. "We should stand back."

The next blow sent a cascade of rubble down the pile, and suddenly they could hear voices flooding the space beyond the wall.

"It's there," Gavyn cried. "Rowan! Can you hear me?"

"We're here," Rowan said, climbing to the opening and pulling away rock to make it bigger.

Bex tried to help, but her hands didn't want to grip.

It took another half an hour before Bex and Rowan spilled into the night, Brightstrike and Gavyn and Lynniki and Tera and Suncall crowding around to be certain they were all right.

Lynniki drew them to the fire that crackled on the side of

300

the mountain and made them sit. Brightstrike fed them while Suncall checked for any broken bones.

Bex sat, trying to take deep breaths and trying to think of something witty to say that would keep them from looking at her the way they already were. Like she was made of glass that would shatter if they spoke too loud.

What had Gavyn told them? What had he heard while Rowan was trying to get her out?

None of them said anything specific. But Lynniki made her take her gloves off so they could check her hands. Brightstrike pressed dried fruit and a handful of nuts on her.

Tera sat close. "Gavyn told us what you did with the fire charge," she said. "Clever."

"It brought the whole place down around our ears," Bex said.

Tera shrugged. "You do what you have to do."

She'd been wrong. They didn't treat her like she was fragile. They treated her like she was one of them. Like they trusted her.

That was good, right? She could get more out of people who trusted her. She kept her head ducked so she could hide the way the thought made her grimace.

Why did she care so much? She wanted to go back to the time before when she didn't care what they thought. When she didn't feel like she was hurting them by lying to them.

"Is the plan working?" Rowan said quietly, and the others hushed immediately. "Is the guardian still... delayed?"

"It is," Brightstrike said. He bowed his head. "It hit Herontor and Ullellethon today. Please tell me we have what we need to get ahead of it."

Rowan smiled. "We do."

"You found where the mirror is?" Bex said, lifting her head.

"That's what I was coming to tell you when some mage dropped the floor out from under me. I found stories of a quarry. It was abandoned about the right time period that the mirror was brought to Taur. And the Giants spread the rumor that it was haunted."

"That seems like it could be it," Lynniki said. "If that's a place they wanted people to stay away from, then the mirror could be there."

"Where is this quarry?" Brightstrike asked.

"South of here, I believe," Rowan said. "In the mountains."

"That's the direction the guardian is headed," Lynniki added.

Brightstrike raised his head. "Is this a marble quarry?"

"Yes," Rowan said. "Do you know of it? It was supposed to be buried in some sort of accident."

Brightstrike heaved a sigh. "It was. It was dug up. If the mirror was there then we might have an advantage over the guardian. Because it likely is not there anymore."

"What do you mean it isn't there anymore? How would you know?"

"Our historians were unearthing the site. It was an incredible find. It was a quarry once, but when they excavated to see if it could be used again, they found other treasures buried in an ancient complex unmarked on any map. The treasures made it a target for the exiles."

Bex's heart sank. "The rogue Taur-Els your people kicked out?"

"They raided the place months ago. If the mirror was there, they took it along with the other treasures."

"Why are you grinning?" Suncall asked Tera.

"Because, the guardian couldn't possibly know that," the guard captain said. "Brightstrike is right. We can confront the exiles while the guardian is busy digging up the quarry."

Chapter 37
Bex

It was a risk. If the mirror was still at the bottom of the quarry, then the guardian would get there before them and all hope was lost.

If it wasn't, then they had the chance to get ahead of the guardian.

Since Bex didn't see them getting to the quarry before the guardian, even if they started now, it seemed like a good risk to take.

The others had brought the horses, those five beasts Bex had stolen from Sir Kerrickmore days ago. The sight of them gave her a pang, and she wondered if he had made it out of the ruins before the guardian killed him.

The exiles were holed up in a manor along the eastern coast of Taur. They raced the horses out of the mountains and through the forest that separated them from the shoreline.

They saw the place long before they reached it.

"Who built it?" Bex asked. The manor had been built of white stone overlooking the thundering waves of the coast. The ocean stretched behind it, off into the horizon.

Steps led from the road to a beautiful, stone porch and the building rose behind it with great wings stretching on either side.

It wasn't quite a palace, but very nearly. Bex couldn't imagine how many Taur-Els you could squeeze into the place.

"A family built this place almost seventy-five years ago, but it's been abandoned for the last fifty," Brightstrike said.

"And the exiles took it over?" Tera said.

"Yes. They use it as a base from which to attack Taur-Els who travel the roads."

Bex glanced up at him. His eyes were bright and narrowed as he stared at the building on the hill. Hadn't he said that his partner had been killed—

"How many are in there?" Tera asked.

"I do not know for sure. But it is rumored that Revered Stonesinger has gathered the entire population of Taur-El exiles. The ones who have succumbed to the frenzy. We do not keep track when they pass on, but it could be anywhere from twenty to maybe seventy exiles."

Bex choked.

"Just seventy, huh?" Tera said, then swore. "What else can you tell us about this Stonesinger?"

"Much." Brightstrike bared his teeth. "He is ruthless. He kills without compunction. He carries a pickax that is said to cut through any material."

"Any material?" Gavyn said, lifting his head to look straight at the big Taur-El.

"Any. Stone, metal, flesh, and bone. Of course, it could be a rumor." Brightstrike shrugged. "Or it could be a Giant's weapon."

"A Giant's weapon for a Giant's weapon," Gavyn murmured.

"Don't even think about it," Rowan hissed at him.

Bex's gaze sharpened on them. Was Gavyn still on about destroying Jannik's weapon?

Tera swore again.

"Are you frightened, Captain?" Brightstrike said. Bex didn't like his feral grin.

"*I* am," Lynniki said. "These are all the Taur-Els who don't mind going completely crazy with blood lust right?"

"The frenzy is more nuanced than that—" Suncall started.

Brightstrike snorted.

Suncall sighed. "But yes. Pretty much."

"What is a few Taur-Els compared to your prize," Brightstrike said. He reached behind himself to pull out his hammer.

"Aren't you supposed to be the one who doesn't like violence?" Bex said. "You seem a bit eager for this."

"I am a normal amount of eager." The Taur-El lowered his head, leveling his horns at the manor.

"Sure you are," Bex said.

"Tell them," Suncall said.

Bex glanced at her. "Tell us what?"

Suncall stepped in front of Brightstrike. "If you're going to do this, they deserve to know what's going on inside you."

"You do not know what is going on inside of me," Brightstrike said.

Suncall didn't back down, even though Brightstrike was three times her height.

"What are you going to do?" Bex said, voice rising.

Brightstrike blew out a snort. "You are right. I avoid violence. Just like the others. But this does not make me immune to feeling."

Bex met his eyes. "All right, and what are you feeling?"

Brightstrike raised a hand to point at the manor without looking at it. "Revered Stonesinger is responsible for my partner's death. Guess what I'm feeling."

Rowan winced.

"Oh," Bex said flatly.

Suncall lifted a hand to touch Brightstrike's arm. "I'm not telling you not to be angry. I'm not even telling you not to do the thing I know you're thinking about. I'm telling you, it's still in you to choose. I don't want you to lose everything just because you forgot yourself for a moment."

Brightstrike closed his eyes and breathed deep. "I do not seek violence," he rumbled. Then he opened his eyes to catch Bex's gaze. "I am in control. I can still choose, and I choose to help you because it is the right thing to do. Not because I crave violence."

"Glad we cleared that up," Bex said. She cast a glance at Suncall and then at Rowan. "Well, we're not going in the front door." She extended a hand to Tera. "Unless you think you can storm the place singlehandedly."

Tera rolled her eyes.

"Then we'll do this my way."

"And what's your way?" Tera said.

Bex grinned. "Like a thief."

They left the horses under the cover of trees, and Bex led everyone from the beach up to the back side of the manor.

Tera pointed out likely places where the exiles might have posted guards, and they did their best to go around, but it also looked like the exiles were confident in the knowledge that no Taur-El would risk violence to come after them. There was one bored Taur-El on the roof at the corner of the north wing, but he nodded over his bow and didn't even bother watching the sea.

Bex crept up to what must have been the kitchen yard, past overgrown beds of vegetables. She was pretty sure she spotted a squash as long as her arm buried in the leaves. The door to the kitchens opened with a slight squeak, but Bex slipped her toe under it and lifted, and the squeak died to a sigh as she took the weight off the hinge.

The kitchens stood empty, big cook pots hanging over the fire, crusty with a hundred meals that had never been scrubbed away.

Bex held her nose as she led the others through the room to an empty corridor beyond. As they moved down the hallway, Bex gestured them to stay low and quiet while she crept on ahead, checking each doorway and adjoining passageway to make sure no one was waiting for them.

The whole place had the feel of something that had been abandoned for decades. Debris piled in the corners, and broken furniture stood under swathes of spider webs in rooms long unused. But there were also tracks through the dirt and dust along the floor, showing the paths of the exiles from the kitchen to the parts of the manor they'd taken over.

Despite the tracks, they didn't come across anyone else. The silence made the hair on the back of Bex's neck stand up. If she didn't see or hear anyone, then she didn't know where they were in order to avoid them.

She also had no idea where the exiles would have put the mirror. She needed to find a treasure room of some kind. But all she had to follow were the tracks in the dirt.

She led them down a hall and up a set of stairs. These seemed to have been used recently but not as much as the hall at the bottom. Possibly by Taur-Els checking on their treasure?

At the top, the corridor opened into a wide balcony overlooking a chamber large enough for a ball or three.

Bex glanced over the railing and caught her breath.

At least thirty Taur-Els lounged around the ground floor. Some of them played some sort of game with carved pieces on a board as large as a table. Others ate in the corners, and one or two napped on beds of stained pillows and sheets.

Shit, she'd led them right into the heart of Stonesinger's hideout without meaning to.

"What is it?" Rowan whispered behind her.

Bex made a shushing gesture.

"It's the exiles," Bex said under her breath. "A bunch of them are in that room."

Rowan seemed to take her word for it, but both Brightstrike and Gavyn crowded forward to peek over the balcony while Bex frantically gestured for them to get back down the stairs. Tera finally bodily dragged Gavyn back.

But Brightstrike remained at the railing as if stricken.

"Brightstrike," Suncall whispered. "What is it?"

"Stonesinger." The name dropped like a slab between them, and Bex jerked.

She peered over the edge, down to the ground floor. None of the Taur-Els seemed to sit separate like a stately leader. But there was one who sat at the head of the game table. He wore earrings all along his ears with large, cut gems. A massive pickax with a dark blade lay behind him.

Brightstrike stood frozen. Bex put her hands on his chest and pushed, but the Taur-El remained unmoved.

"Brightstrike," Bex hissed. "This isn't the time or the place."

"I can see him." Brightstrike finally met her eyes. "I have not seen him since he killed Bloomhollow. Am I supposed to just walk away?"

Bex's teeth clenched. She glanced down, but the Taur-Els below didn't seem to notice them. "Yes," she said. "I'm sorry, but yes."

Brightstrike's chest rose and fell beneath her hands. "I do not desire violence," he whispered but not like he was convinced. "I do not. But I want him to hurt the way I hurt."

"And what of us?" Bex said. "What happens to us when you hurt Stonesinger? What happens to you and Suncall and Rowan and Tera and Lynniki?"

Brightstrike's eye latched on hers.

"I don't think it's right that you have to hold the frenzy inside when it's so much a part of who you are," she whispered furiously. "But remember what Tera said. You don't have to lose yourself to violence. You can keep your head while your heart rages. If you lose yourself to it here, you are sacrificing your place with your people, and you'll sacrifice our lives too."

Brightstrike shuddered and closed his eyes. After a long moment he sagged against Bex. She grunted under his weight.

"I apologize," Brightstrike said. "Perhaps there is a place, but this is not it."

He stepped back into the stairwell to lean against the wall. Suncall went with him. She glanced over her shoulder at Bex and mouthed, *"thank you."*

Bex gulped, her pulse racing in her ears as she realized how close they'd been to slaughter.

She tipped her head back, her gaze sliding past the clerestory windows that shed bright light into the ballroom below.

There on the far wall, near the roof, there was another balcony. This one was much farther up the wall and didn't have a staircase leading to it. At least not on this side. The corridor led further down the way, and it was possible the mystery balcony led to a room accessible from that side of the manor.

That wasn't important right now. What was important was the fact that just beyond the balcony was an archway. And through the opening, Bex glimpsed the glint of something metallic.

Her breath caught.

She couldn't quite see from here, but if she backed up to the wall and stood on her tiptoes... there. It had to be a treasure room. She'd seen enough of them to know a chamber lined with chests and sculptures held loot. And at the back, something round reflected the piles. Like a mirror.

It was there. She just had to figure out how to get them up there without alerting all the exiles below.

She turned back to the group and opened her mouth, then paused.

"Where's Gavyn?" she whispered.

Rowan gasped and glanced around, but the brass dog was missing from the group arrayed along the stairs.

"He was mumbling about that weapon," Rowan hissed. "Of course he was. But I got distracted and—"

Bex pushed past them down the stairs, and there in the dust was a rectangular smudge that looked just like Gavyn's odd feet.

She swore. Then gestured for Tera. "Captain. I need you. Everyone else stay here."

"Never thought I'd hear that," Tera muttered.

"I want to come," Rowan started, but Bex frowned at her.

"Keep them here," she snapped. "I can't go chasing everyone around this place."

She whipped around and snuck around the lower level, following Gavyn's footprints. They passed an open door that led to the ballroom, and Bex skipped across, holding her breath. Tera followed, surprisingly silent on her feet.

Ahead of them, Gavyn slipped into the corridor, shaking his head. As if he'd come from the ballroom.

Behind him a Taur-El lumbered around the corner.

Bex didn't have time to call out to him, and every exile in the ballroom would hear her if she did. Instead she sprinted forward, past a startled Gavyn and hit the floor before the Taur-El even had time to turn and see them.

She leaned back and slid into its legs, taking them right out from under him. He went down with a thud.

She struggled to her feet as the Taur-El shook his head, but Tera was there beside her and brought the pommel of her sword down on the creature's head. Bex would never have managed to knock out something that large, but Tera handled it in one blow.

"What—" Gavyn started, but Bex slashed her hand across her throat in a clear threat, and Tera dragged him away down the corridor so they weren't right next to the room full of hostile Taur-Els.

The others waited just inside the corridor, nowhere near the stairwell that Bex had left them in.

"What part of 'stay put' is too hard to understand?" Bex whispered. She divided her glare between Gavyn and Rowan.

Rowan raised her chin. "I wanted to chew him out myself." She turned to the brass dog. "What were you thinking?"

"I wanted to know if it was a Giant's weapon," Gavyn said.

"So you almost got yourself and us killed?"

"I didn't—"

Tera pointed down the hall at the unconscious Taur-El.

Gavyn went quiet.

"What would have happened if you were caught?" Rowan said. "You would have died. We all could have died. All for your selfish quest."

"I wanted—"

"I know what you want, and I'll help you. *After* we get out of this."

Rowan stomped away to breathe hard in the corridor that led to the stairwell.

"I'm sorry," Gavyn said, voice small. "I thought... it doesn't matter what I thought. It was stupid. And it didn't matter anyway. It's not a Giant's weapon. It's normal steel."

"I could have told you that from the balcony," Lynniki said with a raised eyebrow.

Bex struggled against the strange feeling in her chest. Why was she so livid? Gavyn had just done exactly what she would have done. He'd seen an opportunity to get what he wanted, and he'd taken it. What was the big deal? They'd survived.

"Next time you need something stolen, ask me," she said quietly. "You know I would."

"I know. I didn't want to risk you. Only myself."

Bex stood staring at the wall as Gavyn slunk back into the corridor, trying to sort through the conflicting feelings trapped in her chest.

She wasn't just livid that Gavyn had risked their chance at getting the mirror.

He'd scared her. She'd gone charging across that hallway certain he'd been about to get smashed. And if that had started a fight, then Rowan and the others would have been caught in the middle.

Rowan's round face wreathed in smiles rose in her mind's eye.

She raised her chin, trying to hold onto the person she'd been when they'd sailed into the port. That person who would risk everything for Anera. Including her new friends.

But that person was gone. She couldn't even pretend to be her anymore.

Bex realized her hands were shaking.

She turned back to the others.

"I saw where the mirror is being kept," she said quietly.

They stared at her expectantly.

"I need you guys to stay here."

Rowan opened her mouth, but Bex glared her into silence. "I mean it this time. I'm going to have to climb, and I can't bring you guys with me. You have to stay here and not alert any of the Taur-Els."

"You mean that balcony up there, don't you?" Lynniki said.

"We can find another way in," Rowan said. "We're not just going to sit here—"

"There isn't another way in," Bex said and pushed the lie out to cover all of them. They all had to believe her. Otherwise they'd all follow and get themselves killed. "The balcony is the only way in. That's why the treasure room is secure. Stay here and let me get the mirror so we can get out before the guardian finds us."

She stepped past them before anyone could do more than blink.

Chapter 38
Rowan

owan watched as Bex disappeared up the stairs. Something warred in her head, and she couldn't concentrate. Couldn't pin down the feeling because she was too busy being disappointed they couldn't go with Bex.

There was no other door. So of course she had to go alone.

"There is no way that's true," Gavyn said.

And Rowan blinked. The battle crept closer to the forefront of her thoughts. "What?"

"There's no way that's true. Rooms have doors. It's not going to have a balcony and no door." He jerked his chin up to look at Rowan. "She's lying."

That was the war raging in her head. The same as she'd felt in the caves when Bex had deflected her question about the memory. The war between belief and disbelief. Only this time belief had won. Until Gavyn had said something.

The others all wore deep frowns as Gavyn's words penetrated whatever fog kept their thoughts on the impossibility.

Rowan shook her head. "You're... you're right. Why would she say that?"

"Obviously she doesn't want us to follow," Brightstrike rumbled.

"Maybe she wants to take something for herself," Tera said with a growl.

"I thought we were past that," Gavyn said.

Tera shrugged. "Why else would she lie?"

Lynniki heaved a sigh. "Maybe she's angry because she keeps saying 'stay there' and no one 'stays there.' I'll bet that's annoying."

Rowan's teeth clenched. She couldn't decide if she was more angry with Tera for believing the worst or Bex for giving her a reason to.

She paced to the end of the corridor to peer up the stairs where Bex had disappeared. "I can't believe I fell for such a simple lie."

"This proves my theory," Gavyn said quietly.

Tera glanced up. "What theory?"

Rowan didn't say anything, her hand tightening on the corner of the wall. She wasn't sure what exactly it proved.

Yes, Bex had to have some sort of magic that helped her persuade people. But did she even know about it? Was that why she was so angry at mages? Because she *was* one? That didn't feel right.

Rowan shook her head. "I don't know," she told Gavyn. "But I do know we're not letting her go alone."

Chapter 39
Bex

On the second floor of the ballroom, Bex peered over the side of the railing, scanning the floor below and the Taur-Els that congregated there.

This could work as long as no one looked up. And no one ever looked up.

She stepped up onto the railing. The wall at this end of the room was adorned with enough decorative, plaster molding that she could climb easily to the next balcony. It wasn't that far.

She swung out over the Taur-Els crowded below, making no noise.

Her hands twinged, still tender from her panic attack in the cave, and she winced. She could still grip, she just had to ignore the pain.

She found a foothold in a bunch of plaster grapes and transferred her grip to a vine curving across the wall.

The molding cracked under her fingertips and broke. Bits of plaster fell away as she caught her balance. She held her breath as the pieces hit the floor with a patter.

The big Taur-El at the end of the table, Stonesinger, turned his head to look behind him, investigating the sound.

Bex surged up the wall, leaping the last couple of feet to reach the balcony railing. She pulled herself up and over just as Stonesinger looked up.

She pressed herself against the railing, completely still and held her hand over her mouth to keep from gasping aloud.

She turned her head just enough to catch Stonesinger out of the corner of her eye, through the slats in the railing.

The Taur-El stared up at the balcony for a heartbeat that stretched into an eternity. Then he shook his head and sat back down.

Bex blew out her breath and crept a little further into the room so she could stand and the wall would block her from view.

This, Bex thought. *This is a treasure hoard.*

Piles of loot pillaged from traders and villages lined the room. This chamber might have been smaller, sitting under the eaves of the roof, but it wasn't tiny, and it was filled with silver cutlery, plates, statues, paintings, jewelry.

And a mirror nearly two feet long propped against the far wall. It had a handle as if it was supposed to be held by hand, but it was far too big for a Human. Silver surrounded the mirrored surface, and a strip of black metal spiraled up the handle.

Bex's heart pounded.

This was it. The mirror. The Voice of Paralos.

A wave of tingles swept from her head to her feet, almost too fast to identify.

I can't believe it's here, Bex thought. She hadn't actually believed she'd find it. In the back of her head and heart, Bex had believed she'd have to go home and watch Anera die.

But here it was. Anera was saved.

She allowed herself one moment of pure relief, and tears stung the back of her eyes. Then she swallowed down the joy and turned to the practical. How would she get it out of here?

The mirror was big enough she couldn't fit it in her satchel. And she definitely wouldn't be able to tuck it under her arm and climb back down the wall.

There was, in fact, a door to the treasure room. It stood on her right. She could pick the lock to let herself out, but when she knelt beside it, a shadow moved in the crack.

There was at least one guard standing out there, so waltzing out of here wasn't an option.

She stepped to the balcony to look out, allowing a moment of regret for not letting the others come along to help.

But she didn't see the others where she'd left them.

Instead, another figure crept along the upper level of the ballroom. Battered armor caught the light, and bright red hair was a dead giveaway for the knight she'd worried she'd murdered.

Sir Kerrickmore.

A strange mix of relief and exasperation filled her chest.

Thank the Gods I didn't kill him, but that man has the worst timing.

He lifted his gaze, and his eyes caught her where she stood on the balcony of the treasure room.

Oh shit.

She gestured him to silence. It was too late to duck out of sight. But if he did anything stupid, they'd both be killed. Then neither of them would be bringing the mirror to Usara. That should get him to at least think twice.

His brows drew down, then his eyes widened as he recognized her.

Not now, not now. If he alerted the Taur-Els to her presence...

"Thief!" he cried. "There's a thief!"

Bex swore and ducked back into the treasure room as if that was going to help. This was the first place they'd check, even if they hadn't seen her standing there.

Below, Stonesinger roared.

Bex clenched her fists, digging her nails into her palms. Why had he done that? Just to spite her? Well his spite was going to get them all killed.

The door of the treasure room crashed open, and the guard stormed in. The Taur-El carried a war axe nearly as long as she was tall, and red rimmed his golden eyes.

Uh oh.

The Taur-El spotted her and lunged.

She tried to dart past him to the mirror, but his blow caught her across the middle. It was just the haft of the axe, not the blade, but the force of the blow knocked the wind out of her and sent her flying over the railing.

Her stomach clenched as she dropped.

She twisted in midair and reached.

Her fingertips caught the railing of the upper level of the ballroom. She grabbed it, her already damaged fingers screaming. The momentum nearly wrenched her arm out of its socket, but at least she'd broken her fall.

She hung there for a second before her fingers spasmed, and she lost her grip, dropping to the first story.

She rolled when she hit and came to a stop against the wall.

Stars danced before her eyes, and she had to take a few precious moments to clear her head.

Hooves shod in dark metal came into view, walking on the ceiling, and Bex realized she was upside down, legs against the wall and head on the floor.

She scrambled to her feet, back to the wall, and looked up into Stonesinger's face.

He stared down at her, nostrils flaring. His breath came in great heaves, and red crept into the skin around his eyes.

Bex gulped.

Stonesinger jerked his head at a Taur-El behind him. "Go

check for the Human who called out," he said. Then his gaze locked on Bex.

She ducked to the side, hoping to dart past him. She knew it was stupid even as she moved. This was why she tried to never be in this situation.

His hand shot out and closed around her throat.

"Where are you going, little thief?"

Bex choked and gasped as he lifted her off her feet by the throat.

"Stonesinger." Brightstrike's voice rang from above, and Stonesinger turned so they could both see Brightstrike standing in the balcony of the treasure room.

The others crowded behind him. They must have snuck up there and found the door even though Bex had said not to.

Brightstrike kicked aside the body of the Taur-El guard who'd tossed Bex over the edge.

Then he vaulted the railing and jumped down to the ground floor. He landed with a huge thud but managed the fall that had nearly killed Bex with grace.

Brightstrike straightened. "Drop her," he said.

Stonesinger tossed Bex aside, and she slammed into a pillar.

She dropped to the floor and lay there gasping, trying to get her lungs to work again as Stonesinger stalked toward Brightstrike.

"You," Stonesinger said, eyes narrowing. "I remember you."

"You should," Brightstrike said. "You murdered my partner."

"Are you here to avenge him?" Stonesinger snorted. "You know you will not be able to do anything against me without raising a weapon. And if you do, I will kill you unless you use the frenzy."

Brightstrike said nothing.

Stonesinger lowered his head. "And I know you won't. You are too close to Lightway and his beliefs."

Brightstrike pulled his hammer from his back. His breath grew faster, but his eyes remained clear.

"Do not pretend to know me. You made your choices. And because of those, I will make mine."

Stonesinger gestured, and the other exiles gathered, deep rumbles making the floor shake as they surrounded Brightstrike.

"This will not take long, then," Stonesinger said.

Bright afternoon sunlight poured down through the clerestory windows at the top of the walls, and from her place on the floor, Bex saw a beam of light move.

A knife flashed, and Suncall appeared on Stonesinger's back, her blade buried in the thick mane of hair that covered the exile's neck.

The blow would have killed a Human, but the knife was too short to penetrate all the way to a Taur-El's spine.

Stonesinger bellowed, and Suncall flipped off his back as he grabbed for her.

Brightstrike charged.

A tinge of red surrounded his golden eyes, and a shimmery haze rose from his shoulders as he rammed headfirst into Stonesinger.

The room erupted into chaos.

Bex pushed to her feet, using the pillar as a support. Above, Tera leaped from the treasure room to the balcony along the second level, then swung over and down to the ground floor in time to sweep the legs out from under a Taur-El.

Lynniki and Gavyn appeared from another door on the ground floor. They must have found stairs from that side of the manor and sprinted down to join the fray as soon as it was clear that Brightstrike was going to erupt.

Cool hands braced Bex's arm, and Rowan was there, supporting her.

Suncall raced by, shouting to Tera, "You can't fight them. They're built to smash through anyone and anything."

"Well, I'm not just giving up," Tera said, raising her blade to guard and backing up toward the rest of them.

"Then you have to be quick," Suncall said. "Strike fast, then retreat and get the hell out."

"Not without Brightstrike," Bex tried to say, but her voice came out hoarse and small.

Suncall rolled her eyes just before disappearing into another beam of light. "Of course not," the light said.

Most of the Taur-Els were busy with Brightstrike, who fought like a storm, all violent winds and precise lightning strikes with his hammer. But a few peeled off to harry the rest of the group as they backed toward the doors.

Tera took one step back, then lunged forward, hamstringing the nearest exile. "Keep them from walking," she said. "That does the trick."

"Easy for you to say," Lynniki muttered. "Their hammers are a lot bigger than mine." She glanced at the hammer that fit easily into her hand and was clearly meant for beating metal into submission.

Two Taur-Els charged at once, and Tera moved to intercept one.

A flash of light against metal made Bex blink, and Sir Kerrickmore darted between them and the next enemy.

He ducked under the Taur-El's blow and stabbed him through the stomach. Then he wrenched his blade free as the big creature fell.

"Thank-y—" Rowan started.

"You!" Bex slipped out from under Rowan's support and grabbed the knight by the edge of his breastplate, yanking him around to face her.

"They were all safe," she said, fury rising up in chest and

singing down her limbs in intense heat. "Then you started all of this."

"Bex," Rowan cried. "Let's get out of here, before we start anything else."

Blood pulsed in her ears, and she could almost understand what it was like to be a Taur-El, pushing the frenzy down so she could think clearly.

She'd almost had the mirror. She'd almost touched it. Then they could have slipped out of here unseen, and the rest of them wouldn't be fighting for their lives.

But Rowan was right.

Bex let go of the knight's breastplate, and he staggered back a step, his eyes as murderous as hers.

Across the room, another Taur-El staggered into Stonesinger, Suncall's knife sticking out of his leg. They both stumbled.

Brightstrike spun and looped his arm around Stonesinger's neck.

Even from here, Bex could see the red retreat from Brightstrike's eyes as he took a deep breath, and the heat haze rising from his shoulders calmed to a mild simmer.

"Stop," he bellowed. "Leave them." He leveled his hammer at the exiles stalking toward Bex and the others. "Get any closer to them, to any of us, and I kill Stonesinger."

Suncall reappeared next to Brightstrike, breathing hard. Blood coated her bare hands, but she looked ready to finish this fight, weaponless if she needed to.

The exiles, even the ones lost to the frenzy, hesitated, looking between their leader and the little group of Humans.

Bex tried to look menacing, but her ribs hurt every time she took a breath, and her throat ached.

Still the exiles waited, looking for a sign or signal from their leader. But Stonesinger could only wheeze under Brightstrike's grip.

Maybe they'd get out of here after all, if the exiles took Brightstrike's threat seriously.

Bex took a step toward the door.

A violent, cracking sound made her duck as stone and brick rained down from the ceiling.

Claws raked the roof, tearing a giant hole that opened to the sky.

Dark wings blotted out the sun, and a cat-like face stared down at them.

The guardian perched on the side of the manor, taking casual swipes at the roof and tearing off chunks as it went.

It barely even glanced at the exiles, who ran for the stairs, bellowing battle cries.

It tore the roof back far enough to expose the treasure room and reached inside to snatch the mirror.

The huge thing was dwarfed in its paws.

"No!" Bex's cry was lost in Stonesinger's roar.

The Taur-El threw off Brightstrike and leaped for the wall, climbing toward the guardian who had just snatched his treasure.

The guardian sniffed and reached down the wall toward Stonesinger. It swiped a massive paw, and Stonesinger plummeted to the floor, dead.

Then it tucked the mirror under its arm and spread its massive wings.

Bex stumbled forward through the debris of the wrecked roof. If the guardian took off with the mirror, it was all over.

"Imyuran," Bex screamed, taking a chance.

The guardian paused, staring down at her, eyes wide with shock.

Then its face went flat and implacable, and it flapped once, lifting into the air and away.

Chapter 40
Bex

Bex stumbled outside. The others probably followed her, but she couldn't be sure. Everything seemed hazy, and the only way through the blur was to push forward.

This whole time, Bex had been telling herself that it was all worth it. All the lies, the theft, the choices she'd made had been worth it as long as it saved Anera. That was her job. To do all the terrible things so Anera could live.

She wasn't going back empty-handed. She wasn't going to tell Anera she'd failed. Some stupid guardian wasn't going to take everything out from under her.

The horses were still hidden in the forest down the hill from the manor, and she raced toward them, ignoring the way her chest hurt as she ran.

The guardian remained a black blot, in the sky growing smaller and smaller as she chased it north, up the coast.

As the sun lowered over the mountains in the west, she became aware of the others on their horses, keeping pace with her. Even Brightstrike loped beside them, a bloody Suncall clinging to his back.

Bex didn't take her eyes off the sky, pushing the horse as fast as it would go, keeping that distant speck just in sight.

I can make it. It's not a disaster yet. Just an inconvenience. I can catch it. I can...

The black speck grew in the sky, and Bex realized they were gaining on the guardian.

Then she caught sight of the black smear on the horizon and her stomach dropped.

The map of the island sprang to her mind, and she knew exactly what they were racing toward.

No, no, no. Not there.

The northern shore of Taur came into view. The horses' hooves clattered against a ruined road, and a bridge stretched from the coast out into the ocean. Nearly a mile from shore, it plunged through a curtain of darkness.

The noktum spread across the water, its inky blackness stark against the sunset sky.

An impassable barrier and a personal nightmare from Bex's past.

Bex yanked her horse to a stop on the beach.

The guardian hovered, its wings flapping to keep it stable in the air as it floated over the noktum. It waited, as if it wanted to be sure Bex saw it.

Something bright glinted in its paws.

Then it turned and plunged through the curtain of black.

Bex threw herself from the horse and ran a few steps forward. Then she stopped and stood, staring at that black barrier.

It was gone.

There was no other word for it. The mirror was gone. No one went into a noktum and came out again. And Bex knew why, firsthand.

The crawling, slinking sensation of the dark crept over her even now, and she shuddered, shaking off the feeling.

She couldn't get enough air. Her hands shook, and blood beat in her ears.

She'd made these choices. She'd lied. She'd dragged these people the entire way across a continent. She'd placed them in danger. She'd destroyed her chances with a woman like Rowan, all for the mirror.

And now, not only would Anera die, but all of them, every single one of those choices would have been for nothing.

Bile crawled up her throat, and Bex had to swallow to keep from gagging.

She spun and found the others on their horses, staring at the noktum with varying expressions, from horror all the way to resignation. Rowan looked grim, like a warrior strapping on their sword for battle. Suncall and Brightstrike stared, openly shocked.

Sitting on the fifth horse, was Sir Kerrickmore.

Something flared hot and dark in her chest.

She strode to the horse, which tried to shy away from her, but she grabbed the reins and then yanked Sir Kerrickmore from his saddle. He landed on the ground with a clatter of armor.

"Hey, what was that?" Gavyn yelled.

Rowan's mouth dropped open. "Bex?"

Sir Kerrickmore tried to clamor to his feet, and Bex helped him by grabbing his arm.

"You stupid ass. Why did you do that?"

He tried to yank away, but she shook him. "You called out. You alerted them to our presence. You could have let me grab the mirror. You could have just stood there. You could have done anything else, but you didn't."

"I couldn't let you actually have it. You—"

"If you'd let me grab it, you could have stolen it from me any time on the way to Usara. Instead, you ruined everything, and now it's out of reach."

He jerked his chin up, making his ridiculous hair flop into his eyes. He blew it out of his way. "I would never dream of stealing something from another person. I am a knight of Usara. With more honor to my name than you have even in your fingernail."

Bex let him go with a snort, and he stumbled back a step before pointing a finger at her.

"But of course you would think that way. You are the thief."

Tera sighed.

"We've been through this already," Rowan said. "Bex isn't a thief. The mark on her hand is something else. She was sent by the queen."

"Is that what she told you?" Sir Kerrickmore's eyes narrowed on Bex. "A thief and a liar, then. I was the one who was sent with the queen's permission and writ. I am here for Usara's cause. This common treasure hunter usurped my place. Not to mention my resources. The writ she carries was given to *me*."

Bex caught her breath. Nothing was worse than losing the mirror. Nothing could have possibly made her feel lower. But somehow this did.

"Clearly everything she has told you has been a lie. I can only imagine she wants to take the mirror for herself."

Bex glanced at the others. Tera's face had gone stony, like she expected nothing less but was unhappy to be proven right.

Gavyn stared at her. Lynniki's shoulders drooped, and she stared at the grass at Bex's feet.

Rowan... Rowan had gone white.

"Is that true?" she whispered.

Bex hated the way Rowan looked at her. The stricken eyes, the lowered brow that quickly hid the stab of pain. Like Bex had promised her the world and then yanked it away with a laugh.

She wanted nothing more than to soothe away the lines on

Rowan's brow. To take her face in her hands and whisper, *"no it's not true."*

But she had nothing left to lie for.

"Yes," she said, voice still hoarse.

Rowan's face crumpled, the little bit of hope and belief in her eyes snuffed out.

Bex had to turn away. Words had always been her weapon. The only thing she wielded with any kind of strength or cunning. But what else could she say when that one word undermined everything else, and it all came toppling down?

Bex walked away.

Chapter 41
Rowan

Rowan watched Bex's back as she strode into the night.

Gavyn, Tera, and Lynniki's voices floated in and out of her awareness, fragmented like the jagged edges of a broken vase.

"We came all this way..."

"—because of a lie?"

"We knew she was hiding..."

"Not a surprise."

"I don't understand."

Rowan's heart caved, and she struggled to draw in a breath. This wasn't... this wasn't right. She should feel angry. Betrayed. Like the moment she'd realized Jannik didn't care if her sister lived or died. Or the moment her brother had tried to take the lantern. Those had made her furious, and fury had given her strength. She'd ridden into battle for what she'd thought was right. She was not weak or useless.

But Bex's simple admission just made her sad. Tears clogged her throat, and she rubbed her chest, trying to ease the ache in it.

Gavyn sat beside her horse and looked up at her.

"I thought... I thought I knew her," she said quietly. "At least a little."

"She puts magic behind her lies," Gavyn said. "We've never been able to trust her words."

Rowan shook her head even before he finished speaking. That wasn't true. Of course there were moments Bex had tried to get them to believe a lie. But there had also been many more moments when Rowan was sure there had been no coersion between them.

There'd been truth too, and Rowan couldn't let it be buried under the deceptions that had brought her here.

Except Rowan wouldn't have come if it weren't for that first lie. Would she?

Her brow creased as she tried to find her actual feelings and thoughts beneath the web that suffocated them.

She'd been so unhappy, antsy and anxious in the sanctuary. She'd chosen her exile, but that didn't mean she'd enjoyed it.

She'd wanted to believe the lie. She'd wanted to believe someone needed her more than the lantern needed to be hidden.

The truth was Rowan had been easy to persuade. Even when she'd been on her guard against treasure hunters.

Rowan's hands clenched and unclenched on the reins. She thought she knew the type of person who would try to get to her. The selfish, arrogant treasure hunter who would be looking for power or fame or wealth.

Bex was none of those things. Even amid the lies, Bex was still Bex.

So why had she come to the sanctuary in the first place?

The others still argued behind her, Tera's voice the loudest in the fray. They only seemed to care about *what* Bex had done. Not why she'd done it.

Rowan couldn't leave it at that. She'd never been able to

stop asking questions. *Why did the Giants build the way they did? Why does magic work the way it does? Why did someone choose what they chose?*

The why explained the what.

Did Bex know what she was doing when she put magic behind her words?

She wasn't faking the devastation when the mirror had disappeared into the noktum. She hadn't been faking the panic in the dark of the cave when it collapsed.

Rowan swung her leg over her horse and slid to the ground with a wince. The bump jarred her spine, and it had already taken a beating between the cave-in and all the riding.

The others fell quiet as she caught her balance. They'd followed her here. Her, not Bex, if they were honest. They waited, quiet. Even the knight looked to her.

"We still need to find the mirror," she said into the silence.

Tera laughed incredulously. "What?"

"We can't let the guardian take it to its master. It spoke of a war and the return of the Giants. Humanity will need every advantage it can get."

"This is why I was sent," the knight said. "Slayter believes the mirror could be useful to us. And if what you are saying is true, losing it would be that much more devastating."

She met his eyes. "If I can get you into the noktum, are you still willing to go after it?"

He scoffed. "I'm not afraid of a little dark."

Heat rose in her chest and beat in her cheeks. She fought down the wave of irrational anger and opened her mouth.

Before she could respond, Tera pinned him with a glance. "That doesn't make you brave. That makes you stupid."

The knight flushed.

Rowan turned before they could devolve into another argument.

"Where are you going?" Lynniki said.

"Give me a moment," she said, following Bex's footprints in the sandy shore. "I need to learn something first."

Chapter 42
Bex

T he ruined road swept down onto the beach, broad stones set deep enough that they were still steady under the sand.

Where the road met the sea, a bridge continued over the water. It had to be ancient, but its stone pillars stood strong against the waves. It was so straight, she could look out across it and see the entire length.

Before it plunged into the black curtain of the noktum.

Bex stood on the edge of the sand where the bridge started and stared across at that baleful, black cloud.

She hadn't been this close to a noktum in years, and the only way she could stand to be so close now was to hold her flintstriker in a white-knuckled grip against her chest.

Not that it would do her any good in there. She knew that intimately. Even from here, she could imagine the creeping tentacles of the noktum coming for her. She could hear the howls of creatures just beyond the veil, looking for an easy meal.

Her fingers clenched, and the flintstriker dug into her palm, making her blink and remember where she was.

She could at least try to walk in there, feel her way by touch and sound in order to find the guardian and save Anera.

But she couldn't. She bit back a sob. She was a coward.

She'd rather see Anera dead than walk into the noktum, and that made her worse than everything Tera or Sir Kerrickmore had ever called her. It made her a bad sister.

She was everything dark and terrible.

She'd known it since the first time Anera had been too sick to mov, and Bex had snuck out of their room to steal a loaf of bread and some cheese from a stall in the market.

But it had never mattered before. Anera had given her such a sad, disapproving frown, but at least she'd been alive enough to give it to her. Bex had always been able to shrug it off.

This caring about what others thought of her was a new feeling.

Now all she wanted in the world was to go back to the moment after the cave-in when Rowan had smiled at her and the others had included Bex around the fire. In that moment, it had been uncomfortable, but now Bex realized how much she'd liked it. How much she'd needed to feel like she belonged there with them.

She wanted it more than she wanted the mirror for Anera.

There was no way forward from here. The noktum blocked the road. For once, she couldn't put one foot in front of the other. She couldn't ignore everything and take the next step because there were no more steps.

* * *

There was barely any sound in the sand, but Bex could feel Rowan as she stepped up to stand just behind her shoulder.

Bex's grip remained tight on the flintstriker, but her gaze dropped to the water lapping the shore.

"I'm surprised they let you come out here," Bex said quietly.

"The others wouldn't dare stop me, but Gavyn is probably around here somewhere. To keep an eye on me."

"No, I'm not," Gavyn's voice called from a stand of dune grass.

Bex swallowed and turned to face Rowan. She couldn't bring herself to look up yet, but she could at least face her.

"I'd like to explain myself," she said.

"Can you tell me the truth? Are you capable of it?"

The words were quiet, but they cut deep anyway, and Bex winced.

"I guess I deserve that," she said.

Rowan shook her head. "That's not what I... I'm sorry. I'm testing a theory."

Bex was startled enough to raise her gaze. Rowan looked at her with her head cocked. The look of betrayal was gone, but now she stared at Bex like an artifact she was researching. Rowan, who believed the best in everyone, examined her like a strange sort of puzzle. And that was almost worse than the betrayal.

"I've never been good at honesty," she said. "Too many people try to use it against you."

"I won't do that."

Bex swallowed. "I know."

"Why did you come to the sanctuary?"

"I thought you would be the best one to help me get the mirror. I was right."

Rowan shook her head again. "No compliments, please. You're not working for the queen like you said. So why do you want it so much?"

"I need a Giant artifact."

"Why? Fame? Fortune? Power?"

Bex grit her teeth. She'd thought the truth would be hard,

but now it wanted to pour out of her. She couldn't let Rowan think she'd lured them all down here for something as stupid as money.

She pulled her glove off and unwrapped the bandage. Her hand shook, but she held it up so Rowan could see the mark. "My sister has one of these. Hers is here." She laid her palm across her chest. "And it works differently. You said mine drains the mage. Well, hers is draining the life out of her. She's dying, Rowan."

Rowan's lips parted, and Bex took a deep, steadying breath. Talking about Anera made bile rise up in her throat. Especially now that she might never get back to her with the mirror.

"I wanted the mirror because it has enough magic to keep her alive until I can break the mark on her."

"Would any Giant artifact do?" Rowan said, and there was a strange note in her voice. Bex was pretty sure she knew what she was getting at.

"I didn't want whatever you were hiding up in that sanctuary of yours," Bex snapped. "The whole point was to take something no one was using or interested in. I didn't want to fight anyone." She snorted. "Clearly I miscalculated."

"Why didn't you just tell me all this when you came to find me?"

"I didn't think you'd care about a woman you've never met. No one cares about strangers."

"Is that what the world has taught you?"

"It's reality, Rowan. I didn't know I could trust you. You're not like everyone else."

"I said, you can stop with the false compliments. I'm already here, and I'm listening."

Bex flung out her hands. "It's not false. I'm telling you you're special." She ran her fingers through her hair and tried to keep from shouting. "And that... idealism needs to be protected. People like me exist so people like you can keep seeing the best in others. So you can go on thinking everything is nice and pretty. So you can believe no one lies, no one cheats."

"And so you can go on hating me for that?" Rowan's mouth was thin as she gazed at Bex.

"I don't hate you for it." That wasn't what this heat beating in her ears was. "Why would you think that?"

"You're using that belief as a weapon. Whoever it is that you're trying to protect, you're using this against them."

"Because I have to make the tough choices." Bex wanted to pace, but the sand was terrible for stomping. "Just to protect you and let you keep those ideals. You and Anera. You're so much alike."

"Your sister. Her name is Anera?"

Bex scrubbed her hands over her face. "She sees the good in people too."

"It's an illusion, Bex," Rowan said.

Bex frowned. "What's an illusion?"

"You think I don't know there are terrible people? You think I don't know that they lie and steal?" She spread her hands in front of her. "My mentor used me. He tried to take my work. He tried to kill my sister. He ignored and isolated Gavyn. He turned my brother against me and spread lies so everyone believed I'd stolen the Grief Draw."

She breathed hard, and Bex didn't dare interrupt. "I've walked the battlefield of an arrogant lord who cared more about power than truth. I know what people can do, and still I choose to see the good. I choose to surround myself with people I trust. Because I know about the world. I bet your sister does too. More than you give her credit for. The way you view her? That's a mask *you've* put on her."

Bex swallowed. Did she hate Anera for her ideals? Did she coddle her and hide the truth from her? Anera wasn't weak. Like Rowan, she might look like it from the outside but... she'd survived the experiments too. Why would Bex treat her like a glass figurine?

"She's still better than me," Bex murmured. "She doesn't use people. I do, if it will help Anera. I see someone and I think, how can I get the most out of them. I don't care about them the way you do."

Rowan raised her eyebrows. "I think you care a lot more than you realize."

Bex snorted.

Rowan lowered her chin. "You've never once touched me with your right hand."

Bex opened her mouth to protest and paused. That... that was true. She didn't like touching anyone at all.

"Your mark hurts people," Rowan said. "But you're very careful not to touch anyone and use it accidentally."

"So I'm not a complete monster," Bex said with a carefully nonchalant shrug. "I'm still a liar."

"You're not lying now."

Bex met Rowan's eyes, startled. "How can you be sure?"

"Because you're not trying to make me believe you."

Bex's eyes narrowed. "How could I *make* you believe anything?"

Rowan tilted her head. "You really don't know what you're doing, do you?"

"What are you talking—"

"Make me believe," Rowan said. "Right now. Tell me a lie and make me believe it. The way you would normally."

Bex opened her mouth to say, it didn't work like that, but a thought made her stop. There was that feeling, when a lie wasn't quite working or it was too important to mess up. Bex... pushed.

"You have power, Bex," Rowan said quietly, clearly following the thoughts flitting across her face.

"I'm not a mage," Bex whispered. The very thought made bile rise up the back of her throat.

"Neither am I." Rowan held up her hand. "I have one small gift I've learned to use very effectively. I think you do too."

"No." Her voice rose. "No. I don't have magic. I never did. Don't you think the mages would have noticed something when they grabbed me?"

"Maybe you didn't then. Maybe it's something that awakened when they placed their mark on you. Or maybe it's something you were born with and never had the power for until they filled you with energy. I don't know. But when you speak, people believe your words."

Nausea rose, and Bex had to swallow over and over to get the next thought out. "So I magic people."

"By accident, but yes."

"I did that in the sanctuary. I pushed and you said yes."

"Yes, I think so."

Bex choked. "I forced you here." She was no better than the mages who'd kidnapped her and Anera. Out of every choice she'd made, that was the worst. "Oh gods. What am I doing?"

Rowan stepped close to her and raised a hand to touch her cheek. "Nothing. At least not consciously. It was an accident. Now that you know, it can be different."

Bex's lungs seized as she tried to keep from gasping. "That doesn't change what I've done."

"No. It doesn't. But it changes how I feel about it. I am here now because I choose to be."

She stood on tiptoe and pressed her lips to Bex's.

She was warm and soft and everything Bex would have said she wanted. She was right there, and Bex could wrap her arms around her. Keep her there where she made everything better and clearer and brighter.

But there was a startled noise from the dune grass and a rustling, and Bex knew the others had found them.

A shudder rose in her spine and along her arms.

They'd think she'd grabbed Rowan. They'd think she'd coerced her. Again.

She raised her hands and pushed Rowan's shoulders, breaking away from her with a gasp that was barely this side of a sob.

"Sorry," Suncall said from the grass. "We heard shouting."

Bex shook her head and stumbled back from Rowan. "What would you do that for?" she said, arms circling her chest.

"You needed to know my choice," Rowan said.

"I don't understand."

"I trust you, Bex."

Behind her, Tera groaned.

Bex gritted her teeth. "You shouldn't. I made these choices. I knew what I was doing. They weren't all accidents."

"I know." Rowan stared back with that wise look Bex found so annoying.

"And now you're going to say I can do better? Make better choices?"

"No," Rowan said. "You're already better. You're not the horrible person you think you are."

Bex ran her hands over her face to clutch her hair. "You see what you want to see."

"I'm finally seeing you. The real you."

"I'm a shadow. A piece of the dark. You are light, and all I do is blot that out."

"You are Human with a flair for melodrama," Rowan said with a raised eyebrow. "You made these choices because you thought you had to. Because you thought you were the only one who could protect your sister. If all you want is to see how terrible you are, then you can keep lying to yourself. Your power will make you believe it."

Bex gulped. Did it really work that way? Anera had said that Bex always told the best lies to herself.

"Or you can listen," Rowan said. "And tell yourself the truth for the first time in your life. You chose to love Anera when those mages taught you to hate. You chose to protect others from yourself even when it was easier not to. You chose to tell me the truth without trying to force me to believe it. These are not the choices of a shadow."

Bex couldn't breathe. She didn't know what to believe about herself anymore. Or what she'd made herself believe.

"You really think my words have power?" she asked quietly.

"All of them," Rowan said. "Not just the lies. I think you can make people believe whatever you want, including the truth. If that's what you choose."

"And you trust me with that?"

"That depends on what you're going to do with it. What do you want, Bex?"

"I... I don't want to give up on Anera. She deserves to live. But that means I need the mirror, and it's..." She gestured hopelessly to the noktum. "It's gone. I can't follow it in there."

Rowan didn't give her another smile. Not yet. Maybe she'd never see one again. But she did meet Bex's eyes, her gaze clear and strong.

Then she reached to her belt and pulled her lantern from its case.

There was a collective gasp from Tera and Lynniki. Gavyn muttered, "Oh, here we go."

Bex glanced between them and Rowan. Clearly she was missing something.

"You gave me your truth," Rowan said. "Now I'm trusting you with mine." She held up the lantern between them. "This is the Grief Draw."

Chapter 43
Bex

Bex's eyes went wide, and she glanced at the silvery light of the lantern, which never went out, and then to Rowan's face.

The Grief Draw.

"Jannik's weapon," she whispered. The weapon that had caused all the rumors. The weapon that had made Lord Hax attack Lord Karaval. The one that had made Rowan kill Jannik. The one that had been so powerful, Rowan had hidden it away in her sanctuary to protect it from the world.

Bex gulped.

She knew Rowan now. She knew the story had to be much more complicated than everything she'd heard. There had to be a reason she'd brought the thing here.

And there had to be a reason she was waving it around now.

"If I can get you into the noktum and we find the guardian and the mirror, would you keep lying to us to save your sister? Or would you trust us?"

"How could you possibly get us into—"

"Answer the question," Rowan said. "With truth, please, Bex. We're past the need for lies."

Bex deliberately kept her expression open and undisguised. Rowan needed to see everything that went on in her head, even if it made Bex sweat.

"I don't know," Bex whispered. "That's the truth. I don't know. Yesterday I would have said yes. I would lie my ass off if it would save Anera. But today? I don't think so. I thought I had to be the one to make the hard choices. The one to say anything is worth it if it gets me what I want. And I want to save Anera. But not if all of you are dead."

She rubbed her hands down her face. "How do you live with this, wanting the best for more than one person? When the best for one person might be the worst for everyone else?"

Rowan bit her lip, but it was Lynniki who answered first. "You don't make the decision alone."

"You trust your friends to help you." Gavyn pushed through the dune grass, brass glinting, and sat beside them.

"And you respect when they say no." Tera crossed her arms over her chest.

"So maybe let's start with the thing that saves the most people," Rowan said. "If we don't get the mirror back, hundreds, maybe thousands could die if the guardian's master returns. If this war is coming, then we can't let the Giants have the mirror."

Bex swallowed. "I think Anera would agree with that."

Sir Kerrickmore pushed to the front of the group, his armor scuffed and dirty but his expression as righteous as ever. "I thought we were getting it back so I could take it to the queen."

Rowan shook her head. "Let's concentrate on getting it first, and then you two can fight over it all the way to Usara."

Tera rubbed her temples. "I'm confused. You say she has this power. She can make us believe anything she says. And you're trusting her?"

"Not everything," Rowan said, glancing at Bex as she flinched. "She's just more persuasive than the average treasure hunter. If you know it can happen, it's a lot easier to notice when she's doing it." Rowan gestured to the brass dog. "And it doesn't seem to work on Gavyn."

"Love Magic manipulates emotions by manipulating the body. And I don't have a flesh-and-blood body anymore," he said.

"I think it really helps if you want to believe what she says and she really wants you to believe it too."

Gavyn cocked his head. "I started wondering when it was so easy to convince Rowan to leave the sanctuary."

Rowan flushed a bright red, and Bex raised an eyebrow.

"Maybe I really did want to leave."

"Or maybe you really wanted someone charming to come and rescue you," Gavyn muttered.

Rowan kicked sand at him. "Anyway..." She turned to Tera and the others. "I'm not asking you to trust her. But she wants the mirror just as much as we do."

Tera huffed, but she didn't protest again. Rowan smirked like it was decided.

Bex's fists clenched. "You... you don't think we can actually go in there, do you?" She threw her hand out at the noktum.

Rowan just hummed like she was planning a picnic. Not their deaths.

"Rowan!" Bex grabbed her arms. "This isn't like walking into the night." She jerked her chin up at the evening sky. "You can't see in there. It's black, and it creeps in your eyes and mouth, and there are things that howl and want to eat you. But you can't see them, you can only hear them. Please." Bex hated begging, but her voice had risen to a steady cry. "Please don't go in there. It's death."

"Damn," Tera said. "I hate when she starts talking sense."

"Bex," Rowan said, her eyes going wide in her round face. "Have you... have you been in a noktum?"

"They tossed me in," she cried. "They threw me in there and left me to die. Rowan, you don't just walk out again. No one leaves a noktum."

"Not alone," Rowan said.

"Who tossed you in a noktum?" Tera said, eyes narrowed.

"Who do you think?" Bex snapped.

"How did you get out?"

Bex squeezed her eyes shut. Her fingers went to the white streak in her hair. "They tied a rope around my wrist to drag my body out after I was dead. Only they never bothered. They left me there. Anera finally pulled me out before the creatures found me. She saved my life, and I'll spend the rest of my days trying to repay that."

"What was the purpose?" Lynniki said. "To be cruel? What could they possibly want to learn?"

"They wanted to see if my mark would drain the noktum of magic. Make it go away." Bex laughed, high and breathless. "It doesn't, by the way."

"Bex." Rowan slid her hands down Bex's arms until she gripped her hands. Bex felt the shock of it even through her gloves.

Rowan breathed deep, and Bex followed her lead without meaning to, letting the breaths and Rowan's grip steady her.

"You're not alone," Rowan said. "It's not an unscrupulous mage and a rope this time. It's me. I've been in a noktum too. We all have. We went in, and we came out again. Because we have the Grief Draw."

Bex glanced at the lantern where Rowan had dropped it at their feet.

"It was built by the Giants to counteract the noktum. I promise you'll be able to see. You won't be in the dark."

Bex swallowed.

"We asked you to trust us," Rowan said. "Do you?"

"I want to," Bex whispered.

Rowan squeezed her hands, and Bex clung to them for a moment before letting her go. Rowan reached down to take the lantern.

Bex cleared her throat and glanced at Brightstrike and Suncall. The Brightling had waded into the water to wash the blood from her hands.

"You two don't have to come," Bex said. "You should go home."

Suncall shook the water from her hands and looked up at Brightstrike.

"I cannot go home again," Brightstrike said.

"Because of the frenzy?" Because that was exactly what they'd seen in the manor: Brightstrike lost to the battle fury of his people, the haze of it rising around him. "You only did it to help me," Bex said quietly. "And to fight Stonesinger and their exiles. If you hadn't, we would all be dead. Can't Lightway make an exception?"

"There are no exceptions," Brightstrike said. "A Taur-El who has given in to that part of themselves is no longer trustworthy."

Bex chewed her lip wondering if she should even suggest the next thing. "You... don't have to tell them."

Brightstrike smiled sadly. "They would know. I would know." He shook his head. "I made my choice, and I do not regret it. The guardian attacked my people, and the Giants' return would hurt them as well. My people have no way to defend themselves. I will go with you to try to prevent this. If you will have me."

Brightstrike lowered his gaze to meet Bex's.

She gestured over her shoulder toward the manor. "I didn't

see anything in there that would make me not trust you. You didn't seem out of control. And you saved my life."

"I think there is a way to use the frenzy and still maintain who I am," Brightstrike said. "We have not explored the possibility in centuries. But I would like to learn more."

"I think that's fair," Tera said.

"How about you?" Bex asked Suncall. "How do you feel?"

She'd been the voice of reason in Brightstrike's ear this whole time. Of course, it also seemed like she was no stranger to violence.

Suncall stood and slipped her stark white hand through Brightstrike's big one. She looked up at the Taur-El with a rueful smile. "I just wanted to be sure it was his choice. I did not want him to lose his people because of an accident or a hasty decision he'd regret later. I know what it's like to not be able to go home again."

Brightstrike inclined his head to her.

Tera fixed her with a sharp gaze. "And what exactly are you to the Brightlings?" she asked.

Suncall shook her head. "What do you mean?"

"We saw you fight. I don't think you were just a citizen. And you cannot make me believe you were a regular soldier, either."

Suncall's lips twitched in a little smile. "I never said I was." She tilted her head. "I may not be exactly who I once was, but I still know how to keep my mouth shut."

She scampered up Brightstrike's side to perch on his shoulder, and Bex got the impression she was done. They would never have gotten that much out of her if she hadn't wanted to tell them in the first place.

Rowan stood beside the horses, taking the saddlebags off and sorting through them to find anything they'd need. Lynniki gently set the beasts loose. Just in case they didn't come back.

348

Bex swallowed, her throat suddenly dry. They were really doing this. They were heading into a noktum. On purpose.

The others didn't speak, but they divided their tasks without getting in each other's way. They worked as a team, because they had been together for years. They trusted each other.

They'd known about the lantern because they'd all been there when Rowan had found it or fought for it or taken it into the noktum.

It was Bex. And them.

Bex rubbed the mark on her palm, easing the scar tissue just a little.

They were heading into danger because Rowan said it was necessary. Not for Bex.

They didn't quite hate her. At least she didn't think they did. But would she ever get them to trust her again?

While the others prepared, Tera stood beside Bex on the bridge to stare at the noktum. The darkened edge wavered across the stones only twenty feet in front of them.

Tera could have just been standing guard over Bex. She'd never made a secret of her dislike for the other woman. But she wore the same expression she had in Karaval Keep. When Mellrea hadn't been looking.

"Are you thinking about her?" Bex asked. "Your noble?"

Tera glanced at her, incredulous. "How could you possibly know that?"

Bex shrugged and turned to face the noktum with her. "Maybe it's magic, like Rowan says. But I've always been good at reading people. You wore that same expression every time you looked at her."

Tera didn't speak for a long time, and Bex was sure she'd ruined what could have been a tenuous friendship once again.

Finally Tera spoke. "The last time I walked into one of these, it was to save her. Honestly, I thought I'd lost her for good. Turns out, that didn't happen until later. It makes me laugh. I saved her from monsters only to lose her to marriage."

"I'm sorry," Bex said quietly.

Tera glanced at her, eyebrow raised. "Everyone else has been telling me 'it will be all right' and 'she won't go through with it.'"

"I'm trying not to lie anymore."

Tera huffed, clearly surprised.

"You would know her best. Would she marry that man? Whoever it is?"

"If she thought it was the right thing to do? If she thought it would help her people? Yes."

"Even if it hurt you?"

Tera snorted. "I'm the strong one. I'm used to pain. She thinks I can handle it."

"Are we ready?" Rowan asked behind them.

Bex stiffened as Tera blew out her breath.

"As we'll ever be," Tera said.

Lynniki and Gavyn flanked Rowan, and Brightstrike and Suncall waited behind. Sir Kerrickmore stood behind them all, eyes trained on the undulating edge of the noktum.

Rowan raised the lantern.

The darkness before them reacted like a curtain across an open window on a breezy day. It shuddered and stretched, like it was trying to draw away from the light.

"That's funny," Rowan said. "It's never done that before."

"How many times have you done this?" Bex said, voice strangled.

Rowan gave her a rueful smile. "Once."

Bex looked back at the others, who all stared at her. Brightstrike and Suncall just looked expectant. Sir Kerrickmore's jaw jutted out.

Tera and Lynniki looked wary, both with their weapons drawn.

Gavyn stared up at Rowan, waiting.

This was the part where Bex had to earn their trust. There were no words she could say that would undo the harm she'd already caused. They wouldn't believe her even if she could think of any. Only her actions would make a difference.

So she took her courage in both hands and stepped into the noktum first, trusting Rowan to follow her with the light.

Chapter 44
Bex

The black curtain waved, as if trying to avoid Rowan's light, then it split into arms of solid black that reached out to snatch Bex.

She stifled a scream as the noktum enveloped her. It swept over her face, blocking her sight until she floated in a sea of darkness. She couldn't even tell where the ground was except for the feel of it beneath her feet.

Her heart hammered in her throat, and her ears strained for the sound of monsters, the howls she remembered in the distance. But there was nothing. Not even the sound of footsteps behind her.

Where were the others?

She could feel her hands shaking even if she couldn't see them. Nausea rose, threatening to choke her, and a sour taste filled her mouth.

Had Rowan betrayed her after all? Let her walk into the noktum and then left her there? It was no more than she deserved, living the rest of her short days here in the dark, waiting for something to eat her.

She opened her mouth to scream, but nothing came out,

and she flailed, unable to catch her balance without her sight.

She struck something that felt like fabric and a strip of leather, and she clung to it.

The arm twisted in her grasp, guiding her down to the hand which she latched onto, her fingers clammy in their gloves.

"Bex," Rowan's voice said, and Bex turned her head, trying to place the direction. "Bex, you're all right. We're here."

Light grew as a pinprick and then a steady glow, and Bex fixed her gaze on the flame behind the glass of the lantern.

Gradually, her eyes picked out changes in the blackness around her. The ground beneath her feet shifted to a grayscale, stone bridge, and the sky lightened enough that she could make out the difference on the horizon. The water flowing by, under the sides of the bridge, was still deep black, but the light of the lantern flickered across the surface.

Rowan stood in front of Bex, just a few steps away, her free hand stretched out as if reaching to comfort her. But it was Lynniki's hand Bex clung to.

Bex met the Delver's amused gaze.

"I'm flattered, but..." She transferred Bex's grip to Rowan's offered hand.

"All right?" Rowan asked Bex.

Bex swallowed away the panic she'd been dealing with just a second before and nodded. "I'll be fine." Her voice came out hoarse.

Tera was already striding down the bridge, sword in one hand, her eyes scanning the skies. "I guess there's only one way to go," she said.

"And no reason to linger," Gavyn said.

"My people call this the Endless Bridge," Brightstrike said. Suncall rode on his shoulder and peered over the edge to the water below. "Because there is no end in sight. It just disappears into the noktum."

"Do you think it predates the noktum?" Rowan said, stepping along behind and lifting the lantern up as if that helped illuminate more. "Or was it built to go into the noktum?"

The Taur-El shook his shaggy head, making his earrings jingle. "I do not know."

"We should hurry," Tera said from ahead. "The light attracts creatures of the noktum."

"And what are we likely to encounter in here?" Suncall asked.

Rowan kept hold of Bex's hand as they walked. "If the fauna are anything like the ones found in Usara, then we will see giant bats and Sleeths."

"What are Sleeths?" Suncall said.

Lynniki gestured upward. "Flying creatures with fangs and claws. They look a little like otters."

"There will possibly be Kyolars on the bridge," Rowan said. "But I doubt they swim. They're giant cats, like panthers."

Behind them all, Sir Kerrickmore snorted. He brought up the rear of their little group.

Rowan turned to raise an eyebrow at him. "Something to add?"

"In the end that's all just wildlife. Wildlife is dangerous, but it's people who are the real threat."

Bex stared at him over her shoulder. "Right," she said. "The people who want to tear you apart and eat you."

He glared. "People are intelligent. They decide to be evil. The creatures here cannot help it."

"That doesn't mean they can't kill you. People are predictable and a lot easier to defend against."

"Forgive me if I do not agree with a murderer."

With Rowan's hand clutched in hers, some of Bex's confidence returned. "Murderer? The correct insult is 'thief,' thank you. And 'liar,' but that one's not as sexy. I've never killed anyone."

Sir Kerrickmore raised his chin. "You woke the guardian. You're the reason my team is dead."

That was technically true. Gods, how many people was she obliquely responsible for killing, then? The thought made her irrationally angry.

"What was *your* plan?" she snapped. "Sneak in there in a full set of plate armor? Clank your way in and clank your way out? You would have woken it too."

Sir Kerrickmore's lips tightened. "Maybe, but whatever you did made it pick up and leave. We could have found the real hiding place of the mirror if it weren't for whatever you said to it."

Bex opened her mouth, but Rowan squeezed her hand. "That's not true," she said quietly.

Sir Kerrickmore frowned. "What isn't?"

"It wasn't anything Bex said. The guardian mentioned the light of Pyranon." She held up the lantern. "It knew I used a Giant artifact to open the door. It knew we carried one and knew how to use it. That's what spooked it. That's what made it think Humans must be formidable. It's my fault it escaped to find the mirror."

Sir Kerrickmore's mouth worked like he couldn't think of what to say. Finally he met Bex's eyes.

"I'm sorry I maligned you. You might have thrown the guardian at me, but I was wrong about setting it free."

Bex blinked. "Thanks. I think. No one's ever apologized for maligning me before."

"I like to maintain untarnished honesty."

Bex gestured with her free hand. "And I'm sorry I threw the guardian at you." She shrugged uncomfortably. "I thought I was saving my people even if I had to sacrifice you."

"Perhaps subconsciously you knew I was strong enough to face it and survive." He arched an eyebrow.

Bex rolled her eyes.

355

"What is your name?" Rowan asked.

"I am Sir Kerrickmore. Knight of Usara."

Bex snorted. "Well, we can't call you Sir Kerrickmore all the time. What's your first name?"

"Derrick."

Bex bit down hard on her cheek to keep from laughing. "Your name is Derrick Kerrickmore?"

He waved a hand. "No one says it like that. I was Derrick of Kerrickmore before I was knighted, thank you."

"You're welcome, Derry."

From ahead, Tera choked on a laugh, and Bex felt just a little bit more like her old self as Sir Kerrickmore glared at her.

Bex scanned the skies, looking for shapes heading toward them, but there was nothing. The bridge really did seem endless.

Rowan winced and let go of Bex's hand for a moment to transfer the lantern to the other and shake out her fingers.

"Are you all right?" Bex asked.

"Fine," Rowan said. Then she met Bex's gaze with a rueful smile. "My Delver heritage protects me from the sores and the sickness. But it doesn't prevent the pain. It's built up over time, and every time I hold it, it burns."

"Is it actually a weapon?" Bex asked quietly.

"It's more complicated than that. The Giants warred constantly with each other before Humanity fought back. We know very little about that time, but my gift has shown me some of the Grief Draw's history. It was made by the enemies of Noksonon as a way to infiltrate and disrupt the Giants who lived here."

Bex raised an eyebrow. "It's a tool for espionage."

"Exactly."

"So it lights up the noktum. And... and it gave you a map in the caves. What else does it do?"

"This lens is the map." Rowan pointed to the side with the

stylized mountains and trees. "And this one shows the strengths and weaknesses of an enemy. If we get into a fight, I want you to look for the blue highlights and the red. Red indicates an opening or weakness. Blue indicates a strength. Can you remember that?"

"Yes, Professor," Bex said with a smirk. "What's this one?" She pointed at a pane with a repeating wave pattern.

"It's hard to explain. It... multiplies the person holding it. Like an illusion."

Bex tilted her head. "I bet that makes you a lot harder to hit."

"Yes."

Bex's gaze caught on the empty slot on the front side of the lantern. There were four other decorated lenses, but the fifth remained clear. "You're missing one there."

Rowan's face fell. "It broke. When my brother tried to take it. I guess we'll never know what it does."

Bex bit her lip, trying to think of a distraction. "And the last one?" The last pane was decorated with a stylized spiral, lines swirling into the center.

Rowan lifted the lantern to look at it. "I've never had a chance to use it outside of a controlled environment. But it seems to disrupt set spells. Does that make sense? I'm not entirely sure why or how that would be useful."

"Well if these were the tools of a spy, then you have intelligence gathering with the map and the weaknesses. Misdirection with the illusion. That leaves sabotage and assassination."

Rowan looked at the lantern. "Sabotage, then," she said quietly. "The last one is sabotage."

She transferred it back to her other hand and took hold of Bex again.

Bex wished she could take it for a moment to ease the pain Rowan felt, but they'd mentioned it had made Rowan's sister sick. So this was one of those Giant artifacts that was dangerous to touch. Like the well they'd left with Brightstrike's people.

"Is it worth it?" Bex asked. "Even if it hurts you?"

"That's an impossible question to answer," Rowan said quietly.

When she didn't say anything more, Bex squeezed her hand. "At least it seems handy," she said lightly.

Gavyn snorted. "Don't get attached. It trapped me inside it for a hundred years."

Bex blinked, then drew in a noisy breath. "Was that what happened to your body?"

"Yes. Rowan and Lynniki managed to get me out. We might know how to use it, but that doesn't mean it's not still dangerous. Whatever you do, don't touch it." He glared balefully at the lantern. "I'd still like to destroy it."

"Well, that shouldn't be too hard now," Lynniki said. "Just let Bex hold it for a while."

Gavyn, Tera, and Rowan stared at Lynniki and then looked at Bex.

"Would that work?" Gavyn said.

"I don't know," Bex said. "Possibly?"

"If you could drain enough out of it, it would render it inert."

"Or Anera could. Maybe. Would it have to be all at once?" Bex said.

"This is what's keeping us safe in here," Tera said. "How about we don't get rid of it yet?"

Bex snorted, but Gavyn growled low in his voice box, and Rowan glanced down, biting her lip.

"Sounds like an old argument," she told Rowan under her breath.

Rowan glanced up at her. "I went through a lot to protect it. I know why Gavyn feels the way he does, but I can't agree. Too many people have died. And it is still too useful to get rid of entirely."

Bex looked down at their linked hands, thinking about a question Bex had asked her back in the sanctuary and Rowan's peculiar reaction. "Did you have to kill Jannik?" she said. "To protect it?"

Rowan's mouth went tight. "Yes."

She obviously didn't feel guilty about it. The lines marring her forehead and the sides of her mouth spoke of grief, not guilt.

Tera let her breath hiss through her teeth, and Bex's gaze snapped up.

"What is it?" she whispered.

Tera pointed.

Ahead, the bridge finally ended. It stopped abruptly on a small island in the water.

As they approached, Bex could make out the lines of a boat tied up at a little spit of land, like a dock. The oars were still shipped, as if waiting for passengers.

If there was a boat, it had to be a boat to somewhere. This whole bridge had been built as if to get here.

Bex raised her gaze and scanned the horizon.

"There," she said, and pointed. "I'll bet we're going there."

A shape floated out in the middle of the noktum. Bex couldn't tell if it was an island or a large vessel, but it was the only thing out there. If the guardian had come in here, it must have landed somewhere, and that was their only option.

Chapter 45
Bex

"I don't like this," Tera said.

"You're not the only one," Gavyn said, staring at the boat.

"No. I mean, I don't like that we haven't been attacked yet. Light attracts creatures of the noktum. We know that. So where are they?"

"There isn't anywhere for them to land," Bex said. "If there are flying creatures in here, where would they live?"

"Besides the place where we're obviously going?" Suncall said, pointing to the distant island.

Bex winced.

"If there were creatures," Brightstrike rumbled. "They must have fled when an even larger predator moved into their territory."

They all paused, thinking of the guardian plunging into the noktum.

"Good point," Rowan said. "I suppose even monsters have instincts."

They clambered into the boat. It was long enough for five

people to sit on either side, with a high prow on one end and a tiller at the other.

"How is this still here?" Rowan said. "It has to be centuries old. Millenia if it's as old as the guardian."

"Giant magic," Lynniki said.

"That's your answer for everything."

"That's because it *is* the answer for everything. At least everything inside the noktum. Let me know if you see an anchor point for the preservation spell. I'd love to take one home."

"You can take it apart after it gets us where we're going," Tera said. "And back, preferably."

Lynniki rolled her eyes. "You take the fun out of everything."

Bex expected Tera to huff, but the captain suppressed a grin as she settled herself beside one of the oars. Brightstrike arranged himself opposite her and when they pulled together, the boat slipped through the water, away from its resting place. Bex took the tiller.

They set out across the water and made good time. Rowan took the chance to hand out some of the provisions they'd transferred over from their saddle bags. Who knew when they'd have the chance to eat again?

Lynniki ate with her hammer on one knee and her food in her metal hand. She stared over the side, face set in a grim expression.

"What is it?" Bex asked.

"I don't think all the predators in here have been scared off," she said. She stood and drew back her arm to chuck a piece of dried meat into the water almost thirty feet from the boat.

"Good arm," Sir Kerrickmore said.

A huge shape surged out of the water to snap at the bit of food floating on the surface. Enormous jaws thrashed in the water, and a pair of feet tipped with long claws splashed. It looked like a crocodile, longer than the ship they'd sailed here in, with fins sprouting from its elbows and knees.

Bex gulped, her mouth suddenly dry as she realized she could see even more shadows under the surface of the water.

"Row faster," she told Tera and Brightstrike.

Tera swore.

They drew closer to their target, the stationary shape looming larger and larger, but that wouldn't matter if something came at them from underneath.

Lynniki chucked another piece of food as far as she could throw, and some of the shapes swam for it.

"That won't work for long," she called.

Something bumped the bottom of the boat, making Bex's heart leap into her throat. A snapping maw came up out of the water and reached over the side.

Brightstrike surged upright, undercutting the monster's head with his hammer. The creature shrieked and fell back against the water.

Bex's hands clenched on the tiller, completely useless for this.

Tera jerked her chin at Bex, and she abandoned the tiller to take Tera's place at the oar. Lynniki took the other, and they pulled frantically while Rowan steered.

Tera stepped up to the side of the boat and drew her sword. The next sea monster surged toward them, and Brightstrike lined up to bash it. But instead of ramming the boat, it leaped, soaring at them with open jaws. Tera side-stepped and slashed it along its exposed belly.

Rowan braced the tiller, lantern in hand, and she fiddled with the top. Suddenly the light coming from it changed, highlighting the edges of their limbs. Tera's sword gleamed blue, and a red glow rose from her chest, showing the gaps in her leather armor.

Oh, that's what Rowan had meant.

The next creature to approach the boat glowed blue all along it's scaled back, but as it turned to ram them, Bex glimpsed a bit of red under its leg.

Tera timed her strike and stabbed the giant crocodile in the side. Suncall took a running leap from the prow of the boat to land on one of the creatures in the water.

It didn't even seem to notice her weight as it leaped at them. She swung underneath, stabbing her knife into its flank and using it as a handhold as she slid down the creature's side. She dropped back into the boat as the monster shrieked and retreated into the depths with a spray of blood.

Bex's arms burned, and her shoulders cramped, but she didn't dare stop or fall behind Lynniki's rhythm. They were almost there.

Bex craned her neck to peer at their goal. Finally, its shape coalesced into blocky corners with big pillars and towers rising into the air on top of the metal pontoons keeping it all afloat.

"It's a boat," Bex gasped. "A huge boat. How does it stay there?"

"An anchor?" Lynniki said. "And probably more magic. We already know this Giant had tons to throw around."

A head the size of a horse reared out of the water, all long lines with glistening fangs and scales, and it lunged across the boat, but instead of snapping or trying to take a bite out of them, it dove into the water on the other side of them.

"What?" Tera said, spinning to keep it in sight and failing.

"Watch it!" Lynniki called. "Serpent!"

Loops of scaly hide wrapped the boat. The whole thing creaked as the serpent tightened, and bits of wood along the railings snapped under the pressure.

"Dammit," Bex muttered. They were almost there. Bex and Lynniki strained at the oars, but the serpent's weight kept them pinned in the water. Maybe Brightstrike could throw them. But then how would he get across?

Brightstrike was busy, raising his hammer to slam down into the serpent's spine. He and Tera took turns, severing the creature around the middle.

It came apart in a wet splurt, and as it did, the boat surged forward again. Bex turned her head, trying not to gag.

The prow of the boat smashed into an outcropping of the structure they were aiming for. It looked like a dock, complete with rings spaced evenly to tie up boats.

"Go," Tera cried.

Their boat was already taking on water. They leaped to their feet and clambered aboard the Giant vessel that floated out in the middle of the noktum.

As they set foot on the dock, the creatures surging toward them veered off and dove back down into the depths.

Bex stood on the dock, breathing hard. "Why'd they stop?"

"Whatever is here, must be worse than them," Sir Kerrickmore said, gazing up at the vessel.

The structure rose above them, not as big as the central tower of the city in the Shattered Waves. But not small either.

Steps led up from the dock between two small towers and into a central building. Pillars held the roof up and let the night air flow through whatever chamber was beyond.

Rowan held the lantern out and fiddled with the top. "There isn't much of a maze this time," she said. "There's really only one place the guardian can be." She pointed up the steps.

Tera cocked her head. "Are we just charging in there?"

"Yes," Sir Kerrickmore said, drawing his sword.

Bex's hand shot out to hold him back. "No. I want to talk to it."

Sir Kerrickmore looked at her incredulously. "Talk? You want to talk to the killer cat who serves a Giant?"

"Yes." She huffed. "That's what I'm good at, right? Trust me."

Sir Kerrickmore didn't say the obvious, that he didn't trust her, but he did sigh and sheathe his sword.

"I hate to break it to you," Tera said. "But we're going to be fighting, not talking."

She pointed, and Bex saw shadows stand up from their places along the walls. She'd thought they were decorations or crenellations. But as they moved, she realized they were all winged cats. These hadn't been changed as much as the guardian, they still resembled cats, but they stared down at the group with hungry eyes, their feathers ruffling.

"These don't seem to care about the giant predator," Suncall said.

"Maybe they're relatives," Lynniki said, tapping her lips.

Rowan reached across to squeeze Bex's hand as she gulped.

"We'll keep them off of you," she said. "We'll guard you while you talk."

Chapter 46
Bex

Slitted eyes burned on the back of Bex's neck, but the winged cats didn't bother them as they climbed the stairs. She expected them to pounce at any second. But they let the group climb to the top unharrassed.

Here the path led to a pavilion bounded with pillars open to the night air.

At the far end of the pavilion sat a dais with steps too tall and wide to be Human-made. A great, stone seat stood empty, as if waiting for its owner to come home. The guardian sat beside it, still as a statue. Like a docile house cat, so long as you ignored its wings, its size, and the way its eyes glittered in the lantern's light.

One solid wall rose behind the guardian where the mirror hung in an impression that had been carved out specifically to fit it. Its surface reflected the room and the back of the guardian's head and the white light of the lantern as they entered the pavilion.

The guardian's gaze followed them across the tile floor, which was decorated in a dark, swirling pattern that made Bex's stomach lurch.

"I knew you would follow," the guardian said, that deep voice Bex remembered from the chamber below the Shattered Waves rolling across the floor. "Even here, where I should be inaccessible to Humans. But even the noktum cannot keep out the light of Pyranon."

Its voice was full of resignation.

Bex glanced at the lantern and then back at the guardian. "If it makes you feel better, it was pretty difficult to get here."

"It does not. It should have kept you from coming here entirely. I have dealt with many Humans over the years, but none so persistent or as twisty as you."

"I'll take that as a compliment," Bex said with a little bow. "I'm sure we've caused you a lot of trouble. But we can't just leave without the mirror. It's too important."

"Stubborn and persistent," it said with a little hiss. "But you should not be here when my master comes. Despite carrying a Giant's artifact, the experience will not be... pleasant."

An obvious threat, but Bex caught the minute flicker of the guardian's eyes. The way it glanced to the throne and away so quickly she couldn't even be sure she'd seen it.

"I thought you said it was your job to kill anyone who tried to take the mirror," Bex said. "Now you're just going to wait and let your master do it?"

The guardian's eyes narrowed. "No," it said. "I'm going to let them kill you."

A howling growl rose around the pavilion. The same sounds Bex had heard while she'd lain in the dark, her hand aching as she waited for rescue.

Her heart rose in her throat, choking her. Shapes grew in the gaps between the pillars. The winged cats had launched from their perches and now closed in on the pavilion.

Bex's hands shook. She wanted to snatch the mirror and run, but there was nowhere to escape to.

Tera and Rowan and the others spread out, readying their

weapons to meet the threat. Rowan glanced over her shoulder at Bex.

"Keep going," she said. "We've got them."

Bex gulped, forcing herself to trust them to watch her back. They were doing their jobs so she could do hers.

Her friends stepped out to meet the threat, and Bex faced the guardian again. It was turning away, as if to leave its brethren to rend them limb from limb.

No. Whatever happened, she had to keep it here and talking. She couldn't persuade it if it walked away.

"Imyuran!" she cried.

It paused, foot raised and tail lashing.

No, wait. *He* paused. If she was going to see the guardian as a person, she had to treat him as a person, even in her own head.

"Do not call me that," the guardian said without turning back to her. "I do not answer to anyone but my master."

A winged cat slammed into the ground beside her, and Bex winced. A second later, Tera followed, leaping to its back with her sword glinting.

Bex stepped past them, focused on the guardian.

"Your name is yours," she said, raising her voice over the clash of claws on steel. "It doesn't belong to your master. It belongs to you."

The guardian spun, claws gouging lines in the tiles of the dais. "*I* belong to him. Everything that is me is his."

"Does he bind you here?" Bex said, unflinching as the guardian leveled his glare at her. She stepped closer, letting the others clear a path for her to the dais.

"He does not need to. I am faithful," the guardian said, raising his chin. But his eyes flashed to the empty throne again.

"Is he even here?" Bex said, plunging ahead. "Or is this where you're supposed to wait patiently for him? Like you waited all those years in the city? He told you he'd be here when you got back, didn't he?" It was a risky guess.

The guardian's mouth opened, revealing rows of pointed teeth, but he hesitated. He didn't glance at the empty throne again, but he didn't have to for Bex to know she'd guessed right. That surge of heat and satisfaction rose that she always felt went a con was going well. Except this wasn't a con.

"He doesn't even value you enough to come when you need him."

"My value is in my loyalty to him."

"That's not true. Maybe that's what you've been telling yourself, but trust me, I know all about the lies we tell ourselves so we can keep moving forward when we hate ourselves."

"What?"

Rowan had theorized that Bex's words had power. If that was true, she could put power behind any words. Not just lies.

"You aren't just a slave to your master. Your value isn't in how patiently you can wait for him."

The guardian hissed and sprang forward, nose stopping only inches from Bex. Bex heard Rowan cry out from behind her, but Bex didn't flinch.

"What do you think you know about me, little Human?"

Bex met his golden eyes. "You're a collector. You said that place under the city had one purpose. To lure us in to protect the mirror's true location. But that's not true. It had two purposes. It was also your home. You made it that way because you were the one who had to live there for a thousand years. Not your master."

The guardian's claws bit into the tile at Bex's feet. Then they relaxed, and he spun away again, head bowed and wings hanging low.

"What do you want, little Human?" he said, voice quiet. "Why do you argue with me?"

Bex swallowed. Truth was so much harder than lies. "Don't

give the mirror to your master," she said, matching his tone. "Please."

"You ask as if I have the ability to choose."

"You're the one who holds it. In this moment it belongs to you. You can choose whatever you want."

He glared over his shoulder, through the curtain of feathers at the edge of his wing. "Why would I want to betray my master and help you?"

"He's already betrayed you," Bex said, stabbing a finger at the empty throne.

"He is just delayed."

"Maybe. Or he's dead. Either way, he buried you. He gave you an impossible task and then buried you so deep he'd never have to think of you again. He certainly didn't provide any backup plan or instructions in case he couldn't meet you here. Because he didn't care about you."

"And you do?" The guardian snorted.

"About as much as you care about Humans," she said, gambling one more time.

His wings dropped, and the guardian stared back at Bex. "What?"

"You like us. You collect our things. You care about them enough to sort them and preserve them and display them. You're fascinated by us. You watch us, wondering what it would be like to be us."

"Why would I do that?" the guardian said, eyes narrowed.

"We were like you once. Beholden to the Giants. But we chose differently. We fought back. You can choose too."

"I cannot," he cried. He paced from one side of the dais to the other, tail lashing. "I was made to serve them. Humans were not. I was created to guard the mirror. To keep it safe for his return. Do you understand what that is like?" His neck swiveled to pin her with a look. "If you take the mirror, then you are taking my entire purpose."

"Choose a different purpose."

"I was created for this one."

Why did he keep using that word? Did he not remember his own history? Did he not remember what had come before?

"No," Bex said. "You were molded to it."

He stopped pacing, tail still thrashing behind him, but his gaze fixed somewhere over her shoulder.

"That does not... I do not know what that means."

Rowan thought she could do this. Tell the truth with power. She reached back to the memory, the carving on the wall in the Hall of Stories, and pushed with her gut as hard as she could.

"You weren't created by the Giants. At least not for this. You already existed when they came to usurp you. You were your own race. You lived in the forests of Taur. You lived alongside the Taur-Els peacefully."

"I do not believe you."

Bex kept pushing. "Your story is on their walls. Your name was etched there along with their history. They cared enough about you to put it there. As a reminder or maybe a warning of what the Giants could do. You had a life before the Giants took you and made you into their guardian."

She held up her hand. "I know what it's like to be taken and changed into something you didn't want." She pulled her glove off to show him the mark on her palm. "But what they did to me doesn't change who I am—who I choose to be."

There had been fire along those walls and fire in the Taur-El villages.

"You were a Land Mage," Bex said, quietly. "Even before the Giants came and turned you into this. Probably even before Humans figured out the knack for magic. You had a lifetime, a home, maybe a family before. Can you remember it?"

The guardian stood, frozen. Even his tail had fallen still, lying limp along the ground in a thick, furred line.

"You said it yourself. Giants will destroy Humanity if they come back. But if you give us the mirror we can fight back. Don't let them obliterate us like they tried to do to you."

She almost had him. She could feel the belief working through him, and what he did with that would be his own choice. She could only wait and see what came of her words.

"Bex!" Rowan cried. "Bex, look out!"

Bex whirled to see a winged cat blasted back from the top of the stairs. It slid all the way across the tiled floor to Bex's feet and lay still.

Her eyes found the figure at the top of the steps. A pendant hung from her neck, glowing gold and lighting her face.

"Lystra," Bex whispered. "Oh, shit."

Chapter 47
Bex

Lystra strode up the last two steps and drew back her ragged sleeves. Her tattered robes told the story of how she'd survived the cave-in, and her arms streamed blood already.

Bex gasped. "No!" she cried, but it was already too late.

Fire swept across the tiles from Lystra's feet.

Bex's friends and the winged cats all dove out of the way, and whatever hold Bex had had on Imyuran snapped. The guardian glared at Bex and launched himself into the air so the flames wouldn't reach him.

Bex swore and dove behind the Giant throne for shelter.

"Bex!" Rowan called the moment the flames subsided. "Bex!"

"I'm all right," she called back.

"You won't be for long," Lystra cried. "I can't believe how hard you are to kill."

Bex peeked around the edge of the throne only to hear a crack, and a piece of the throne's back broke off and fell.

Bex rolled to the side before it could crush her.

The guardian shrieked. In midair he whipped his head around, looking for a target, then latched on Lynniki wielding a hammer against one of the winged cats. He dove.

Tera lunged to intercept and swept her blade between them.

Bex rolled to her feet and glared down at the mage advancing on the dais. "How did you even get in here?" she said, waving her hands to indicate the noktum. "You'd think this would be the one place I'd be safe from you."

Lystra laughed. "You were not the only experiment during Vamreth's reign," she said. She held up her pendant, and Bex could make out a vial full of some type of liquid that glowed brilliant gold.

"Luminent blood." She smiled, baring her teeth. "It took several dead ones to learn how valuable they were when bled."

Imyuran's head whipped around at the word valuable, and Tera took the opportunity to haul Lynniki back behind a pillar.

Lystra raised her hands, and a wall of water washed across the tiles.

Bex raced for the nearest pillar. It was on the opposite side of the pavilion from the others, but at least it broke the water wall so it splashed on either side of her instead of sweeping her over the edge of the boat and into the sea.

A hand covered in plate mail steadied her, and Bex found herself beside Sir Kerrickmore.

He darted a look around the pillar at Lystra, who screamed with rage. "This is the one who marked you?" he said.

Bex nodded curtly.

His lips went tight, and he squared his shoulders. "Get to the mirror," he said. "If we have that, then we don't have any reason to be here anymore. Maybe we can get out without having to fight the guardian." He cast her a small grin. "Your argument was a good one. I think you almost had it."

He sprang out from behind the pillar, running to the dais

and using the throne as a step to launch himself into the air at the mage.

Lystra didn't even flinch. She raised an arm to block his sword. As his blade connected, light flashed, and he fell away as if he'd struck a shield instead of flesh.

She swept him back with a blow, laying out a fully armored knight with her fist. Sir Kerrickmore fell with a clatter.

But he'd also been hardened on the battlefield, and he lurched to his feet, sword in hand, far faster than Bex would have thought possible in full armor.

Bex ducked out from behind the pillar and sprinted for the back wall where the mirror hung. Water left over from Lystra's spell splashed under her feet as she skidded to a stop.

The mirror hung just past the stretch of her fingertips. How was she going to get it down off the wall?

Sir Kerrickmore stabbed, and Lystra countered. But he danced around as if he'd anticipated her move and swept his blade behind him, catching her unexpectedly.

She twisted and fell with a cry, her leg collapsing under her.

Sir Kerrickmore didn't hesitate. He had her on the ground, and he raised his sword to finish the job.

Lystra snarled and reached forward, blood dripping down her arm.

Lightning crackled around her fist, and she slapped it down into the puddle of water. It snapped all the way to Sir Kerrickmore's feet.

The lightning wound up his legs, limning him in light as it crackled over his armor.

Sir Kerrickmore screamed and went rigid, his blade finally falling from his hand. He fell, seizing violently.

Bex sucked in a breath as the lightning dissipated, leaving Sir Kerrickmore lying in a smoking heap on the tiles.

"Oh no," she whispered, the breath leaving her lungs in a

whoosh. She couldn't get to him, not with Lystra lying nearly on top of him. Not that it would matter if she could. He didn't move or even twitch.

Lystra stared at the body. Or at the tiles. What was she doing?

The mage brushed aside the last of the water, leaving only a streak of damp. Then she swept a hand through the blood on her arm and reached, injured leg folded awkwardly underneath her, as she drew lines across the tiles, connecting two dark swirls with her blood.

"Stop her," Gavyn called from his hiding spot. "That's Line Magic!"

Bex glanced at the pattern set into the floor tiles. Ancient Line Magic the Giants had left here? Nothing good could come of that. Bex turned from the wall where she'd been trying to reach the mirror.

But Brightstrike was already charging, a roar building in his throat, hammer at the ready. The frenzy haze rose from his shoulders, and he raised his weapon.

The guardian sprang into the air, sweeping his wings down in one mighty flap in order to pounce on the mage.

But Lystra's blood had completed the symbol, activating the magic that had lain dormant for who-knew-how-many centuries.

The lines all lit up, glowing through the sheen of water, and air whipped around, forming a cyclone that filled the entire space inside the pavilion. Silvery edges glinted in the tornado, looking like blades.

Lystra knelt in a little section of clear air directly in the center of the funnel.

The wind swept around, smashing Brightstrike back. He howled with pain, and wounds opened up along his raised arms.

"Brightstrike!" Suncall cried as the Taur-El stumbled back and fell heavily to the ground, just inches from the sharpened edges of the spell.

Above, the guardian was caught at the peak of his leap, wings outstretched. The air whirled around him, trapping him there and pinning him so he couldn't move as the sharpened bits of wind sliced through him, leaving wisps of black blood to swirl through the air, mixing with the cyclone.

He yowled in pain.

"Imyuran!" Bex cried.

She darted forward as Suncall bent over Brightstrike.

None of them could get to Lystra in the center of the devastating spell. Even if they had a bow or something to throw, Bex could imagine the wind shredding it before it reached her.

Imyuran hung in the air, mouth wide in agony, but his cries had gone silent.

Bex slid to the edge of the dais and reached down for the line of tiles that swept close to the throne.

Her palm tingled so hard it went numb. She'd never drained something this big before, but she had to try. The look on Imyuran's face made her sick to her stomach, and all she wanted was to make it stop.

Before she could reach the lines of magic, Lystra's eyes narrowed, and the edge of the cyclone pushed out. The sharpened edges sliced Bex's hand, and she cried out and pulled back.

Still it pushed outward, and she scrambled back to avoid the expanding cyclone.

Tera ran to help Suncall get Brightstrike to his feet, and they stumbled out of the way of the deadly wind.

Rowan stood on the far edge, staring at Bex, who crowded against the back wall.

"Bex!"

"I can't reach it!" She couldn't even extend her hand without getting sliced. And she couldn't drain the magic out of it from here.

The edges of the cyclone pressed further out, and Bex flattened herself against the wall, cut off from escaping out the sides.

Across the pavilion, her friends staggered backward, trying to avoid the slicing wind. Soon they would be shoved right off the floating manor. And Bex would be left with Imyuran, endlessly sliced to pieces until she bled out.

Her wide eyes met Rowan's all the way across the pavilion.

Rowan's mouth went hard and thin.

Then she spun the top of the lantern and light sprang out. Through the last pane she had shown Bex.

The one Bex had thought must be sabotage.

The light streamed out like a wave in front of Rowan and swept across the tiles that formed the spell.

The black lines ignited, shining with a silvery light that matched the lantern, and that burning glow crackled across the entire floor, traveling the lines of the spell and setting them aflame.

Bex saw the fire heading for her and pressed her marked hand against her chest, turning her shoulder against the oncoming light.

But it seemed to be trapped following the lines of the spell. The light seared through the tiles, leaving them burnt and stained.

The wind died abruptly, and Imyuran fell to the ground, black blood leaking across the destroyed lines of the spell.

It was unrecognizable now. With the lines broken and pitted and bits of the original tile scattered across the ground, the Line Magic was equally broken.

Hopefully that meant it would never work again.

Rowan darted past the prone Lystra, who screamed and

tried to lunge for her. But the mage still couldn't stand on her injured leg.

Rowan limped up the dais to Bex.

"Are you all right?" She asked. She snatched Bex's hand.

"Don't touch it."

Rowan huffed as if offended Bex thought her stupid enough to touch the mark. She turned Bex's hand to the light to see that it was still intact. It hadn't burned with whatever glow the lantern had sent out.

Rowan's shoulders drooped.

Lystra screamed and rose to her feet, bracing her bad leg. "This is not the end. I will either own you or kill you. I will not leave without one of those."

The guardian twitched, feathers ruffling against the floor.

Lystra raised a hand, but instead of activating one of the spells along her arms, she reached for Bex.

It wasn't like she could actually touch her from the middle of the pavilion, but Bex flinched anyway. And then a wave of weakness washed through her.

She grunted, and her knees buckled.

"What is it?" Rowan said, trying to catch her, and it was all Bex could do to keep her weight from pulling them both to the ground.

Bex shook her head. "I don't know." It wasn't like when a mage took the energy she'd stored up. That felt similar, but the mage had to be touching her. And Lystra was all the way over there.

And then the energy she'd gathered just under her breast-bone collapsed, leaving her gasping.

"Oh," Bex whispered. "Oh, she released it."

"Released what?"

All the magic gathered inside Bex spun out of her, an explosion without sound or fire.

The air gleamed with energy. Free energy. Little glints and glimmers swirled out in a storm of untethered magic.

And Bex couldn't control it or stop it at all.

Chapter 48
Rowan

Rowan's eyes went wide as she realized what was happening.

The energy that powered spells normally came from inside the mage. They channeled it into their magic, and it stayed there. Or it dissipated when the spell was done.

But Bex collected energy like water in a tub. And what happened when the plug was pulled?

The energy swept out, sparkling around them, and tendrils of Rowan's hair lifted like in the moments before a lightning strike. Her skin tingled, and the hair along her arms raised.

And the spark behind her eyes reached out like it did when she called on her gift. Except she couldn't stop it.

Images flashed through her mind, unconnected to a touchpoint.

Bex climbing out of a ruin. Bex speaking with a mage who shook his head about something she'd said. Bex saying goodbye to another young woman who sat wan and drawn at a worn table.

Rowan tried to curb the flow of images, but her gift just reached for more.

She saw the Giant who'd built this place. She saw him commission the guardian and the guardian winging away over the sea. She saw the quarry where the stone was mined. She saw the mirror.

Hundreds of images. Hundreds of memories. Lives flashing before her eyes, fast enough she couldn't make sense of anything.

Her head spun and ached, and she couldn't even tell where she was anymore or if there was ground beneath her feet.

She saw a woman. A Giant with long, black hair stepping toward the noktum. It reached to embrace her like a lover, and she looked back one last time as the darkness enveloped her.

Rowan blinked and realized she was actually seeing with her eyes this time, not her gift. She stared up at the mirror.

And that same woman looked down at her from the glass.

Chapter 49
Bex

Rowan fell to her knees in front of Bex. Bex gripped Rowan's arms, heedless of her mark. But the magic didn't flash or flare or draw anything out of Rowan.

Still Rowan swayed with eyes wide and glassy, and Bex's heart seized. She looked like a corpse standing there.

"Rowan!"

The energy sizzled and crackled around them, a storm of free magic with no spell to anchor it, setting off everyone and anything in its path.

The lantern dropped from Rowan's hand and clattered against the floor. Light sprang out, bathing the side of Rowan's face in that sickly, pale glow. Was it reacting to the free magic? Was that what was happening to Rowan?

Gavyn leaped up the stairs to the dais and flung himself across the lantern. "Don't let the light touch you!" he cried.

Bex raised her arm as if that would shield her, but she didn't think it had touched her. Rowan was standing in the way. And Rowan was immune to it, right?

"Rowan?" Bex tried shaking her, but nothing snapped Rowan out of whatever vision or reaction she was having.

"It's her gift," Gavyn said, using his body to block the rays coming from the lantern. "Something has set off everything. The lantern, Rowan's gift, even the mirror."

Bex glanced up to see the mirror lined in a dark glow that made her stomach roil.

"It's me," she whispered. "I set them off. Lystra released all the energy from my mark."

Her knees still wobbled, but she spun to the mage.

Lystra tried to stay upright in the center of the pavilion, the waves of free energy washing over her.

Bex staggered down the steps, leaving Rowan and Gavyn on the dais. She lunged for Lystra and managed to get her hands on the mage's bloody arms.

Her mark flared, and Bex pulled violently, yanking the magic out of the mage so it poured into her empty chest.

But Lystra twisted in her arms and grabbed her elbows, sucking it back out of her almost as fast as she drained her.

"I can just keep eating the magic you feed me," she hissed. "You can't kill me this way."

Bex screamed in frustration. She had nothing left. No words, no weapons, she couldn't even punch Lystra with their hands locked around each other's elbows.

A black wing pummeled Bex aside, and she slid across the wet floor.

The guardian rose up behind Lystra, wings spread.

The mage went pale as his shadow fell over her. She spun, but Imyuran was already on her. She cried out, but it was far too late.

His lips pulled back, but no sound came out, not even a snarl. So it was far too easy to hear the wet crunch as he landed, and Lystra's scream cut off.

Bex turned her face away and tried to push herself to her feet.

She made it upright just as the mage's life flickered out. Bex had no idea how, but she felt the moment Lystra died.

Something snapped inside her, deep in her chest where she stored the energy. Like a string pulled taut until it broke and the ends sprang back.

Bex staggered under the backlash of that snap. The storm of energy collapsed around her, no longer raging, and with it all of the strength she'd mustered poured out of her.

Her knees buckled, and she fell, but before she hit the floor, wide paws caught her and lifted her away from the broken tiles. As Imyuran rose over her, she expected claws to cut into her back and neck.

Instead, furred arms cradled her as the broken string inside her swayed as if lost or trying to find a new end to attach to.

Bex's thoughts went fuzzy and dim, and she tried to focus. There was something important about how her mark worked. If she could just remember.

Her mark had used energy constantly. And it found that energy by draining Lystra. With Lystra gone... what would happen to Bex? Would her mark try to drain her? Like Anera. Had she gone through all of this only to end up in the same situation as her sister?

Stars burst in her eyes, blocking her vision of Imyuran staring down at her with concern.

She could feel the noktum pressing around her, its oily presence seeping into everything. Black claws teased a strip of darkness out of the noktum. The string that had tied her to Lystra flailed, and the end burned just like Bex's mark until it snapped and latched onto the strip of darkness.

The burn eased, and the dark around them changed, going from that slick feeling to something softer and oddly welcoming.

The paws laid her down against the cool tiles, and Bex

flexed her fingers against them, trying to blink the stars from her eyes.

"Do not fret, little Human."

The floor of the pavilion spun under her, and she clung to it, hoping she wouldn't get flung off.

Shouts reached her ears, and she tried to look up, though the world still tilted wildly.

The others raced toward her, Rowan ahead of all of them. The antiquarian fell to her knees beside Bex as Tera and Brightstrike pounded past and planted themselves between Bex and the guardian. Lynniki, Gavyn, and Suncall surrounded them.

They... they were fighting for her. They thought the guardian had hurt her. Was she hurt?

She'd been about to die, her life drained out through the spell on her hand. But the dark end of the string was anchoring the mark now, keeping it from draining her life.

They cared about her. That was a funny feeling. All warm and shivery and nice.

But if she didn't say anything, they were going to fling themselves at the guardian, and all of it would have been for nothing.

Tera raised her sword.

"No," Bex said, pushing to her elbows.

They all hesitated just long enough.

"Don't."

* * *

Rowan reached out as Bex tried to stagger to her feet and helped brace her. The others fell back, staring at Bex as she looked up at the guardian.

He sat on his haunches, wings dragging behind him as he returned her gaze.

"You..." she gasped out. "You did this. You fixed me."

"What?" Rowan said. She looked down at Lystra's mangled body and winced. "Your mark?"

"It was going to eat me, like it eats Anera. He... fixed it."

"I saved your life," Imyuran said. "You might not thank me for it."

Bex's brows drew down. Every second she spent after the flailing end of the string was anchored made her feel just a little bit better. "Why?"

"Your magic needs something to draw from. Some power source. Either it would drain from you or from the mage who cast it. Since the one was no longer an option and the other would eventually kill you, I found a third option. I linked you to the noktum."

Bex gulped.

"It is a vast source of magic. It will never run dry, and I kept the connection small. Small enough for a Human so it will not overwhelm you."

Yes, but now she was irreparably connected with the thing that had haunted her nightmares since she and Anera had escaped the experiment.

Bex rubbed her chest. "Why did you do this?" she asked quietly.

Imyuran glanced at the grisly remains of Lystra. "You told me the truth. About myself. But also about you. She sought to bind you. Or kill you if you did not bend to her wishes. I could not sit by and watch another bound against their will."

The others all looked at Bex.

"She was right?" Tera said. "You were a slave?"

"I had forgotten. My people died while I was forced to serve the Giant who changed me. These are but scraps of their memory." He gestured to the winged cats that lined the pavilion, waiting with glittering eyes.

"When my family was gone, it was easier to not remember

them anymore. Or to remember something different. My servitude was less painful if I believed I had chosen it."

Bex's lips thinned. "I'm sorry I made you remember."

"I am not. You were not wrong. My master... no, he is my master no more. He left me in that chamber for hundreds of years. He disappeared and made no provision to release me when I finally delivered the mirror here. And he left dangerous spells that could swallow me as easily as a trespasser." He touched the tiles that held the broken spell.

Then he stood and padded to the throne on the dais. He reached out and pushed the throne, toppling it down the steps.

Bex watched, breath held as he reached up to the mirror and drew it down off the wall. The glass reflected a dizzying view of the pavilion as he swung around.

"I do not wish for you to watch as your race dwindles in the face of the Giants and the only way forward is to bury your own memory."

Imyuran held out the mirror.

"Take it. And may you fare better than I did."

"Thank you," Bex said quietly.

"What will happen to you?" Rowan said.

"It would be better if I was not here when the Giants return." Imyuran tipped his head back. The roof was in the way, but Bex got the impression that he was staring toward the night sky and the stars that would be visible beyond the noktum. "I will find somewhere to recover. Somewhere I can fly." He lowered his gaze back to Bex, and his inhuman lips twitched in a little smile. "Perhaps somewhere I can continue my collection."

Chapter 50
Rowan

T wo days later, Rowan watched Bex's profile as they waited on the docks in Palmolivar.

Imyuran had ferried them out of the noktum two at a time until they all stood together on the shore. Bex had seemed especially reluctant to say goodbye to the guardian. They'd probably never see him again. But he hadn't lingered.

From there, they had made their way back to Brightstrike's home town. Most of them had needed medical care after the fight with the winged cats and the slicing whirlwind. Brightstrike included. But Lightway had met them at the gate, face stony.

Brightstrike had faced the elder with a straight spine, despite his wounds. The rest of them would have stayed, but Lightway made it clear their conversation was to be private.

So they had gone on, leaving Brightstrike to whatever fate his elders decided for him. At least Suncall had stayed with him.

Rowan hoped whatever had happened, the two of them would come say goodbye before the rest of them left for Usara.

But that was looking unlikely.

Bex shifted from foot to foot on the dock, glancing between the ship and the wharf. Not only were they waiting for Bright-strike and Suncall, Tera had yet to appear this morning.

Rowan placed her hand on Bex's shoulder, and the treasure hunter instantly stilled and gave her a sheepish grin.

Lynniki stepped past them, rolling a large crate up the gangplank.

"All secured?" Bex asked.

Lynniki gave her a jaunty salute. "I built a tank for it. The salt water should keep it from killing anyone just traveling next to it. And it looks like the Mavric iron is confined to that strip on the handle. So, it's easily avoided, as long as no one puts their hands all over it."

The carving on the back of the mirror matched the carvings on the doors of the chamber beneath the Shattered Waves. A woman with long hair and a dress flowing in the wind raising a horn to her lips.

Rowan watched the crate as Lynniki maneuvered it aboard. After she'd had that glimpse of a face while Bex's magic had been raging and Rowan's gift had triggered, the woman had retreated and Rowan hadn't seen her again.

"Are you all right?" Bex asked quietly.

"I don't know yet," Rowan answered truthfully. After what she'd seen, she wasn't sure she would ever be all right again. The Giants had a long and bloody history. Their cruelty knew no bounds, and she'd seen it firsthand. Not just the memories of the lantern. But now the memories of... someone else. Someone connected to the mirror.

Rowan reached for Bex's hand. The one with the mark. She twined their fingers together, pressing her palm to the scar.

Bex stared down at their linked hands. "I never thought I'd be able to do that."

"Your mark still works. This is just the advantage to being with a Delver."

Bex swallowed, and Rowan watched the movement travel all the way down her long throat.

"Have you decided what to do with it when we get back?" Rowan jerked her chin at the crate Lynniki was directing the sailors to store below decks.

"No." Bex watched as well. "I can't... I can't leave Anera to die but..."

"You wouldn't have to," Rowan said quietly. "You said the mirror would just be a stop gap. Something she could use to keep herself alive until you found a way to break her mark." Rowan turned to face her. "What if you could break her mark first?"

Bex opened her mouth, brow furrowing, then she glanced down at the case on Rowan's hip, and her eyes went wide.

"Would it work?" she whispered.

"We saw it destroy the Line Magic left by the Giants," Rowan said. "It might be dangerous, but so would being exposed to the mirror for long periods of time."

Rowan watched the thoughts cross Bex's face. It seemed the safer option to Rowan. And it meant that they would be able to use the mirror in the upcoming fight with the Giants. But Bex had been on this mission for so long, would she be able to see this as the solution she needed? Would she be able to give up control over Anera's fate to Rowan?

Bex swallowed. "I'll think about it," she said as Tera finally came into view, Brightstrike and Suncall trailing behind her.

"Are you ready?" Lynniki called from the ship, poking her head over the railing. "What took you so long? You'd think you'd be eager to get home."

Tera rubbed the back of her neck and wouldn't meet their eyes. "I'm not coming," she said.

Rowan's eyes widened. "What?"

"I'm not going back to Usara," Tera said. "At least not yet."

Hunaa, the leader of the Demaijos traders walked along the

dock toward them. The rest of the traders waited back on dry land.

Tera gestured to Hunaa. "I'm going to visit Demaijos. I want to learn about my people. Figure out who I am and... and what I have to offer before I go back."

"But what about Mellrea?" Rowan blurted.

It was the wrong thing to say. Tera's mouth hardened. "She has her duties, and she won't hesitate to do them. Whether I'm there or not."

"Tera, you can't just leave her to make this decision by herself."

"She made it without me, and I was standing right there." She stopped, breathing heavily staring out to sea. "Maybe she's right, and I shouldn't be there to watch."

She gestured behind her. "But she'll still need a guard captain. Someone to watch her back. So I'm sending one."

Brightstrike inclined his head to her.

"Tera..." Rowan began.

"Please don't argue about this," Tera said, voice more plaintive than Rowan had ever heard her. "I'm doing the best I can for her, but I don't have to put myself in a position to be hurt more."

Rowan's face crumpled, and she fought to hide it. She could only nod as Lynniki came down the gangplank to say goodbye one last time.

"Are you coming home with us too?" Bex asked Suncall as Gavyn and Lynniki each said goodbye to Tera in their own ways.

"I go where Brightstrike goes," Suncall said with a sad, little smile up at the Taur-El. "I'm used to my exile while his has only just started."

"They kicked you out, then?" Bex asked.

Brightstrike jerked his chin up. "It is tradition."

"That doesn't necessarily mean it's right," Rowan said.

"No," Brightstrike said. "I believe we must learn ways to live with the frenzy. But with exiles like Stonesinger making life difficult for my people, I am the only one who sees things this way."

"We will be glad to have you, Brightstrike," Rowan said.

"Even if your people are morons," Bex added.

Rowan cast a glare at her, but Brightstrike huffed a surprised laugh.

"And we just won't tell anyone you're accompanied by a Brightling assassin." Bex winked at Suncall.

Suncall returned with a mild look. "Pure conjecture," she said.

It wasn't until the ship was underway and Taur dwindled in the distance that Rowan let herself feel the grief that had threatened to wash over her as Tera clasped her shoulder and said goodbye.

"Are you all right?" Bex asked beside her.

The wind stung her eyes. "No. I'm... I'm angry. And sad and all sorts of things right now."

"I think she's hurting," Bex said. "And she's allowed to choose something that makes the pain less."

"Yes," Rowan said. "But she's left me with the hardest part."

Bex glanced at her.

"Explaining to Mellrea."

Chapter 51
Bex

Bex probably didn't have to bring every single member of her little band to the palace to meet Slayter. But she wanted as much of a buffer between herself and the mage as possible. And more importantly, between herself and Khyven the Unkillable. He seemed like the type to kill first and interrogate the corpse.

They hadn't made port until late afternoon, but Bex couldn't stand putting this off another hour, let alone the whole night. So they'd all traipsed up to the palace as darkness fell.

This time, she told the guard at the door she had a delivery for the queen's mage, and it wasn't even a lie.

Now they waited in a parlor where Bex didn't feel comfortable sitting on any of the furniture.

Lynniki looked bored, cleaning out the joints of her metal hand. Gavyn sat beside her, watching. Brightstrike had taken up a position in the corner, and when he stood still, he looked like a rare statue imported from Taur. Especially with Suncall sitting on his shoulder.

And Rowan perched on the edge of an armchair, watching Bex pace.

The door opened, and Slayter came in, looking just as Bex remembered him. Khyven loomed over his shoulder.

Slayter stopped short and blinked at the array of people in the room.

Khyven's gaze locked on Bex, though she did notice he kept Brightstrike within his line of sight as well. The man moved like he was walking into the Night Ring for a bout.

He pointed. "You. What do you want now?"

Bex raised her chin. "Don't start yelling at me. I've brought you what you wanted."

She raised her boot and kicked the crate that rested in the center of the room.

She'd thought long and hard about this the whole way back from Taur. She'd thought she would be fighting Sir Kerrickmore for it. She hadn't realized she would be fighting herself.

If she kept the mirror, she could ensure Anera's survival. But Usara would lose a valuable artifact they would need if the guardian was right and the Giants came back.

If she gave Slayter the mirror, she would have to trust Rowan to save Anera.

She already trusted the antiquarian with her life. Why was it so much harder to trust her with Anera's?

Slayter cocked his head. "The mirror. You found it."

Bex took a deep breath and nodded at Lynniki.

The Delver quit tinkering with her arm and hopped down to throw back the lid of the crate.

They'd already cleared away most of the sawdust so Slayter and Khyven could stare down at the mirror gleaming back at them from a glass case full of seawater.

"Bex said you've been looking for Giant artifacts," Rowan said quietly.

Khyven glanced between Bex and the mirror. Slayter made a happy, little noise in the back of his throat. "The Noktum Mirror."

"It's called the Voice of Paralos," Rowan said.

"Voice?" Khyven said.

"I believe it connects whoever can wield it with a voice in the noktum. A Giant named Paralos. She resides there."

"How do you know this?" Slayter said.

Rowan glanced at Bex. "When we retrieved it there was... an explosion of energy. I have a gift that allows me to see memories. And I saw a woman succumbing to the noktum. I believe it was Paralos. She's still there. Still connected." She raised her hand as if to touch the mirror, but her fingers hovered inches away. "I can't see her anymore, but for that one moment, I caught a glimpse of her in the reflection. The carving on the back... it's her."

"We have reason to believe something is coming," Bex said. "The Giants are returning. You'll need this if you want us to survive."

"Who told you this?" Slayter asked.

"Someone who worked for one," Rowan said.

Bex's mouth twisted in a rueful grin. "He doesn't work for him anymore."

"That's not... something everyone needs to know," Khyven said, lowering his voice.

"*My* gift is talking to people," Bex said, jerking her chin up. "And getting them to believe me. But I know when to keep my mouth shut." She waved a hand at the mirror. "And when I'm out of my depth. I figured you would be better equipped to use this when it becomes necessary. And it's going to be necessary. Soon."

"So you retrieved it," Khyven said.

"I had a team," Bex said, indicating the others. "And Sir Kerrickmore. He died so I could bring this back."

"The mirror, a Taur-El, and a Brightling," Slayter said, hands raised as if he wanted to run his fingers along all three. "You have a habit of finding the rare and valuable."

Brightstrike gave him a nonplussed look, and he dropped his hands.

"As long as you don't try to sell us," Suncall quipped.

"Wait here," Khyven said, then slipped out of the room.

Slayter stayed, glancing between the mirror and Brightstrike in the corner. Finally he chose to step closer to the mirror. "What is this box?"

Lynniki leaned over to point at the brass joints along the glass which kept the water in. "Salt water. Certain salts keep the Mavric iron from killing ordinary Humans."

"Genius," Slayter said. "We've been experimenting with different types of materials to isolate the effects..."

The door opened again, and this time a servant came in, snuffing out the majority of the lights along the walls, leaving only one lit candle.

Bex glanced at Rowan, who rested her elbow against the Grief Draw's case. None of its light leaked through, but Bex knew Rowan would be ready to draw it out if anything threatened them.

Khyven stepped into the room again, a woman accompanying him. A jeweled net held her dark hair back from her face, and she wore a gown of deep red velvet. The faint candlelight glittered in her eyes.

It took Bex a moment in the dark. She hadn't seen the Queen in Exile much in her life. Only that once on the balcony as she'd addressed the crowd, right after she'd taken the throne back from Vamreth.

But as soon as Bex realized who stood before her, she knelt. Rowan followed suit with a wince.

"Your Majesty," Bex murmured.

"You're the one who retrieved the mirror?"

"With help, Your Majesty."

The queen glanced at the rest. "I can't imagine it was easy."

Bex extended a hand as if to agree. "No, it wasn't."

"There was a sunken city," Lynniki said, ticking things off on her fingers. "A bunch of Taur-El exiles, a floating noktum, and a guardian monster who tried to kill us. Don't worry, he's Bex's friend now."

"It was indeed difficult," Brightstrike rumbled, and all eyes in the room latched on the big Taur-El.

"But we had an experienced antiquarian," Suncall said, indicating Rowan. "And the best treasure hunter in Usara." She grinned at Bex.

"Maybe not the best..." Bex said under her breath.

"Definitely the most persistent," Lynniki said, and Rowan hid a smile.

"You have experience with Giant artifacts," the queen said, as if it wasn't a question.

"Yes, ma'am," Rowan said quietly. "We all do."

"And you mentioned a noktum?"

Rowan met Bex's eyes. "Yes," she said simply, but she did not pull out the lantern.

The queen held her eyes for a moment, waiting for an explanation. Bex bit her lip. If Rowan didn't want to mention the Grief Draw's particular power, especially to a queen, Bex wasn't going to force her. She knew what it was to keep secrets. And which ones were worth it.

Finally the queen nodded, a barely perceptible sign of approval.

"I assume you're looking for payment," the queen said, gesturing to the mirror.

"I believe she wanted a job," Khyven said. "Originally."

The queen raised her eyebrows at him. "That's convenient. I find I need employees. Those willing to assist the kingdom. Having someone around who can find things would be handy."

Bex's gaze flicked to Khyven, who smirked.

"You mentioned you wanted something dangerous," he said.

"It will definitely be dangerous," the queen added. "You're right that the Giants are coming. They won't remain dormant for much longer. I need people who are used to Giant magic and have experience with Giant-made creatures. I need people who have traveled the noktum and lived to tell about it."

That was a lot more than Bex had bargained for. She hadn't even seen Anera yet.

But if Anera lived... then what? What came after? Especially now that she'd dragged Rowan out of her exile and gathered people who felt suspiciously like friends—friends who had very peculiar skills.

"I have a sister. Any responsibilities I take on would come after making sure she's safe," Bex said.

"That's fair," the queen said. "And after that?"

"I would consider it," Bex said. If only to keep her options open. She didn't have to sell her soul to a queen, but it wouldn't hurt to have one looking out for her.

Rowan started laughing, hard enough to stumble backwards.

"What?" Bex said.

"This is how we met," she gasped out. "You told me you worked for the queen. Now it's true. You made it come true."

Bex grumbled, "I didn't do anything. It just happened."

* * *

Bex pounded up the stairs to the rented room that Anera shared with her and Conell. Rowan and Gavyn followed, a little slower. The others waited at the Unlocked Door where they had rooms. Bex wanted them to meet Anera, obviously, but maybe not all at once. And she needed to see how her sister was doing first.

Bex burst through the door, and Conell shot to his feet from where he'd been sitting beside the bed. From the look of it, he'd been sleeping in the rickety chair, holding Anera's hand.

He stared at her, wild-eyed. "Bex..."

Bex strode forward and clasped his shoulder. It wasn't a hug, but it was more than he was used to from her.

She knelt beside the bed. Anera lay there, her face pale against her lank, dark hair. She could barely raise her hand to greet Bex, but at least she seemed well cared for, her hair clean, and the sheets had been changed recently.

Her mouth formed Bex's name, but no sound came out, her glassy eyes fixed on Bex's face.

"Anera," Bex breathed. "I'm sorry I was gone so long."

Anera didn't seem to care; she grasped for Bex's hand and Bex let her.

"Did you..." Conell started but trailed off as Rowan stepped into the room with Gavyn on her heels. Conell gaped.

"I brought someone." Bex glanced back to find Rowan already had already drawn out the lantern.

"This is Rowan." Bex nodded to the brass dog at her feet. "And Gavyn. Guys, this is Anera and Conell."

Rowan gave them both a wide smile, and Gavyn ducked his head.

Bex swallowed. "They can help."

Anera raised her hand and Conell knelt to take it in his. He smoothed back her hair as she closed her eyes.

"We'll take all the help we can get," he said.

Rowan wasted no time. She adjusted the top of the lantern, which Bex now knew was the way she made the light shine through the different panes.

Rowan met Bex's eyes. "You should probably wait outside. I don't know what this will do to your mark."

"I was there the first time, when it broke the magic in the tiles."

"That was an emergency. I haven't experimented enough

with this lens to know its limits. It would be better if there was nothing else magical around." She nodded at Gavyn. "Including you."

Conell snorted. "You must not know her very well. There's no way she'll—"

Bex had already stood and was squeezing Anera's hand. "I'll be back as soon as it's done. Don't be frightened. Rowan is..." She glanced at the antiquarian with a smile. "She's very good at what she does. And I trust her."

She drew herself away from Anera, leaving her hand limp on the bed covers. She slipped out the door, heart in her throat.

Gavyn followed, and they closed the door behind them. "Be honest," he said. "How hard was that?"

Bex rested her head back against the wall. To her surprise she smiled. "Not as hard as I thought it was going to be."

Chapter 52
Rowan

The light of the lantern fell across them all in silvery waves. The brand on Anera's chest hissed, and the dark lines writhed as if trying to escape.

It had to be as painful as the original brand had been. But the girl held her breath and gritted her teeth. She was obviously as used to pain as Rowan was.

She'd explained the process of the lantern as best she could beforehand and made sure Anera knew what was coming and agreed to it, but it was made that much harder by the fact that Rowan could only guess what the sabotage lens would do after seeing it in action once.

Rowan bit her lip.

Just a little bit longer. Almost there.

The lines of Anera's brand shattered like the tiles in the pavilion, and Anera fell back against her blankets.

Rowan slid the lantern back into its case, holding her breath. Then she drew the edge of Anera's nightgown back to examine the burned out brand. It looked like so many broken pieces of pottery floating just under Anera's skin. Rowan cautiously touched the edge, but she felt nothing. And she wasn't sure if she would as a Delver. But Bex would know if the magic of the mark was broken for good.

As would Anera.

She blinked and sat up, color coming back into her cheeks.

"What did you do?" she said, rubbing her chest.

"The light burned through the lines so they don't form a symbol anymore. The magic is broken. It can't drain you."

Anera laughed, high and breathless. It would take her a while to rebuild her strength after being so sick for so long, but Rowan was sure she'd be just fine now.

Conell dropped to his knees at the edge of the bed, and Anera threw her arms around him, laughing and sobbing at once.

Rowan quietly let Bex and Gavyn back into the room.

"It's done," she murmured, and Bex raced for the bed.

She collapsed beside them, and Anera and Conell threw their arms around her, drawing her into their joy.

Through their arms, Bex looked back at Rowan. She didn't smile, but the look in her eyes was unmistakable, and a wave of warmth flooded through Rowan.

Rowan bit her lip and looked down.

Gavyn sat at her feet, watching the reunited family with his head cocked.

"Are you going to ask Bex to drain the lantern?" Rowan said. "To try and destroy it? I'll bet she could."

Gavyn hesitated, then looked up at her. "No."

"Why not?" Rowan said.

"You were right. We can't discount the good along with the bad. The lantern can save lives."

He nodded to Anera.

"And... something tells me that like the mirror, Humanity is going to need the Grief Draw as well."

Chapter 53
Bex

Bex watched Mellrea's face as Rowan told her where Tera had gone. It went colder and colder, the corners of her mouth pulling down and her eyes going tight.

Bex didn't have to know her well to see and feel the hurt that radiated under her skin.

Mellrea waited till Rowan was done and then she stood, her eyes on her feet. She looked up at the Taur-El and gave him a pained but polite smile.

"Brightstrike was it?" she said. "It's very nice to meet you. I'm sure we'll work well together."

Then Mellrea strode to the door.

"Mell?" Rowan said.

Mellrea raised a hand but didn't turn. "I'm all right," she said, a little breathlessly. "I'll... I'll be all right. I just need some time."

They sat there in a room in Karaval Keep, Rowan and Bex on the sofa, Lynniki in the corner fiddling with something that made clinking sounds, Gavyn resting with his head on his front legs, and Brightstrike and Suncall standing at the window looking out over the town.

They were subdued and quiet, but Bex still felt comfortable. Safe even. She didn't have the anxious knot in her gut reminding her this was a noble's home. Tera had trusted this noble and that meant... well, it meant a lot, but she'd never say it to Tera's face. If they ever saw her again.

"Has the queen sent word?" Lynniki said. "Are we going after something else yet?"

She was asking Bex and Rowan. Like they were some sort of leaders.

Rowan glanced at Bex, and Bex said, "Not yet. But I'd rather we didn't scatter. If she needs us, it will be soon."

"And fast," Rowan added. "If something happens, it will be quick."

They didn't know the Giants were coming back. Not for sure. But Imyuran had been sure there would be repercussions for Humans. And Bex was inclined to trust him, considering how many years he'd spent serving a Giant.

"We'll be ready," Bex said.

Rowan smiled at her and reached across to squeeze her hand. Bex squeezed back.

More Eldros...

Gavyn was once a Land Mage before he was kidnapped and forced to work on the Grief Draw. His sacrifice saved Keinwen's life.

Sign up here to read his story in Light Woven, an exclusive prequel to The Pain Bearer.

If you enjoyed this novel and the world it's set in, then the creators of the Eldros Legacy would like to encourage you to don thy traveling pack and journey deeper into the mysteries of the world Eldros and all the myriad adventures set therein.

The mortal world of Eldros is coming apart. The Giants, who once ruled its five continents with draconian malice have set their mighty designs on a return to power. Mortals across the globe must be victorious against insurmountable odds or die.

Come join us as the Eldros Legacy unfolds in a growing library of novels and short stories.

Books by Series

Relics of Noksonon
By Kendra Merritt
The Pain Bearer
The Truth Stealer

Legacy of Shadows
by Todd Fahnestock
Khyven the Unkillable
Lorelle of the Dark
Rhenn the Traveler

Legacy of Deceit
by Quincy J. Allen
Seeds of Dominion
Demons of Veynkal

Legacy of Dragons
By Mark Stallings
The Forgotten King
Knights of Drakanon (Forthcoming)
Sword of Binding (Forthcoming)
Return of the Lightbringer (Forthcoming)

Legacy of Queens
By Marie Whittaker

Embers & Ash

Cinder & Stone (Forthcoming)

The Dog Soldier's War

by Jamie Ibson

A Murder of Wolves

Valleys of Death (Forthcoming)

Warrior Mages of Pyranon

By C.A. Farrell

Dark & Secret Paths

The Areyat Islands

by Aaron Rosenberg

Deadly Fortune

Stealing the Storm

Crimson Fang

By H.Y. Gregor

Stonewhisper

Short Stories

Here There Be Giants by The Founders (FREE!)

Dawn of the Lightbringer by Mark Stallings

The Darkest Door by Todd Fahnestock

Electrum by Marie Whittaker

Trust Not the Trickster by Jamie Ibson

Fistful of Silver by Quincy J. Allen

What the Eye Sees by Quincy J. Allen

A Rhakha for the Tokonn by Quincy J. Allen

About the Author

Books have been Kendra's escape for as long as she can remember. She used to hide fantasy novels behind her government textbook in high school, and she wrote most of her first novel during a semester of college algebra.

Kendra writes science fiction and fantasy featuring main characters with disabilities.

When she's not writing she's reading, and when she's not reading she's playing video games.

She lives in Denver with her very tall wife, their book loving progeny, and a lazy black monster masquerading as a service dog.

Visit Kendra at
www.kendramerritt.com

facebook.com/kendramerrittauthor

instagram.com/kendramerrittauthor

goodreads.com/kendramerritt

tiktok.com/@kendramerrittauthor

Also by Kendra Merritt

Mishap's Heroes Series

Magic and Misrule

Death and Devotion

Trust and Treason

Illusions and Infamy

Sparks and Scales

Wastelands and War

Creation and Calamity

Mark of the Least Series

By Wingéd Chair

Skin Deep

Catching Cinders

Shroud for a Bride

A Matter of Blood

After the Darkness

The King in the Tower Collection

Daybreak Colony Duology

Surviving Daybreak

Daybreak Sentinel

Eldros Legacy

The Pain Bearer

The Truth Stealer